ILLUMINATING NYX

PALDIMORI GODS RISING

T.L. CALLAHAN

DRAGON MOUNTAIN
PRESS

First published in United States of America by Dragon Mountain Press
LLC 2021

1

Callahan, T.L. Illuminating Nyx: Paldimori Gods Rising 4

Library of Congress Control Number: 2021900292

PB ISBN: 978-1-7332562-2-3
EB ISBN: 978-1-7332562–1-6

Edited by: Book Nanny Writing and Editing Services
Cover design by: Covers by Juan
Artwork by: Eva Jhonson

Publisher: Dragon Mountain Press LLC, 1250 W. Ohio Pike # 199 Amelia, OH
45102

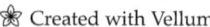 Created with Vellum

For my sister, Tonya: You left this world far too young but will live on in my heart always. 🤍

PROLOGUE

September

TORCHES LINED the massive marble columns of the Order Hall stretching out towards the tall double doors of the great entrance at the far end of the room. Their flickering light threw dark shadows over a statue of the long-dead dragon protector of the Paldimori ancestors perched on a ledge above the doors. The guides—the elite guards from each of the six Paldimori Houses—stood at the two other entranceways as if statues themselves, each with their hands on the hilt of their swords. High above us, the paintings that covered the cathedral ceiling seemed to dance in the wavering light and the air crackled with anticipation.

This hallowed hall had seen centuries of decisions made by our Kyrion predecessors—leaders of the ancient Paldimori Houses—but today marked a new chapter in our history. One I was forcing us toward, however much I regretted the difficulty it was causing the man I had admired since I was a child —Bennett Young, Kyrion Chaos. Even we Kyrion who made up the ruling council of the Order of Chaos must abide by the rules of our society.

"It is time, Bennett," I said to the supreme leader of the Paldimori world. My voice echoed through the Hall breaking the tense silence that had been mounting since the six of us had taken our seats around the table this morning.

Out of the corner of my eye, I watched Bennett straighten in the seat to my right. His black robe hung more loosely on his muscular frame than it had months ago. Dark smudges underscored his brown eyes and his caramel-colored hair was a mess that told of the toll this situation had taken on him. The shadows from the torchlight played over his handsome face creating a duality that mimicked the inner turmoil that rolled off of him like a palpable force in the room: the leader who must enforce the rules of our society versus the man who wanted to protect his bond-mate.

"Bring the accused forward," Bennett demanded as he used his telekinesis powers to open the grand entrance doors.

I shifted uneasily in my high-backed chair and gathered my strength for the battle I knew was to come. The hum of immense power spilled into the room and brushed enticingly against my skin. The lure to break every rule I prided myself on and stop fighting against my powers was nearly over-whelming. My fellow Kyrion sat placidly, unaffected by Lia Davies' power, while my knees began to shake. I wasn't like the other Kyrion who had been marked at birth as one of the most powerful descendants of the Primordial Gods destined to lead their House. I was an imposter. My brother's inade-quate substitute—as my father liked to remind me. Even so, I held the title of Kyrion Gaia—leader of the House of Seasons —and I had a responsibility to protect my people from any threat. Even one that caused my palms to sweat with fear whenever she was near.

The silence was shattered by a woman's angry curses coming from the hallway beyond the main entrance doors. Lia's lack of respect for our Hall grated on my already fraying nerves as I steeled myself to face the embodiment of everything I had been fighting against my whole life.

Two guides prodded her through the door. "Touch me again, and I'll relocate your balls," Lia Davies snarled as she jerked her arm out of the grip of the male guide escorting her.

Beside me, I sensed Bennett struggling to control his powers. His fists clenched upon the table as he glared at the man who had touched his bond-mate. A tendril of his power caused the torches to suddenly flare higher. I swallowed down my sympathy and reminded myself this was necessary. Those who broke our rules and laws had to be punished, even the Chosen who were prophesied to either doom or save our race. I was a firm believer in the prophesy and that the Chosen *would* be our saviors. But Lia challenged my faith with her wild and reckless behavior. She needed to be tamed to work within our society.

Guide Zeno Reece from the House of Truth smirked and motioned for Lia to lead the way. Lia's second escort, Guide Emory Sullivan from the House of Shadows, pushed her black and smoky purple-streaked braids over her shoulders as she assessed the room for danger.

And there was danger here. It permeated the room, prickling along the skin of every person present as if waiting for a spark to ignite it into an inferno. Lia's powers only added fuel to this combustible situation. They pulsed through the air too vast for even the kóvo—the cuff of silver leaves upon her bicep that should lock them away—to fully contain. The hum of power doubled as she approached, calling to me like the most tempting seductress. My throat went dry, and my hands trembled as I fought to ignore the need clawing at me to take those powers as my own. To fill this craving inside me that no food or drink could quench.

Green light unfurled from my fingertips, and I quickly hid them under the table. I shut out everything else as I imagined the parched tree at my center, the partially withered roots reaching for sustenance in a dry and desolate landscape. My powers wrapped around a tendril of Lia's. Her powers shivered like a frightened rabbit caught in the cage of my roots. The sip of power cooled the burning thirst for a second, only making me want to take more and more.

I repeated the rules I'd created for myself as I imagined wrapping my hands around those deadly roots to contain them:

Rule number one: never show weakness unless I want others to use it against me.

Rule number two: no one will ever fully own me as long as my mind, body, and soul are my own.

Rule number three: I rule over my powers; they do not rule me.

I didn't live by rules because I wanted to but because they kept people safe—from me.

"*I rule my powers,*" I repeated to myself, wresting them back under my control until the green lights vanished.

Lia frowned and rubbed her chest, clueless about what had just happened. Bennett half rose from his chair as if he could sense something wrong through the Desmòs—the bond that linked them. It was a connection I could never share with another and didn't want to. I pressed my fists against my thighs as guilt hit me for taking that stolen sip of Lia's powers and for what this trial today was doing to Bennett. I wished I could change so many things, but altering the past was not a gift the gods provided.

Bennett watched Lia raptly. His fascination with her from the moment they met is why we were here now. The way she distracted our previously infallible leader was part of the reason why I disliked her. Her opinionated and unpredictable nature contributed to my judgment of her as well. But the worst of it was that her powers were like a lodestone that everyone wanted a piece of— especially me. My personal problems with Bennett's bond-mate aside, she was his weakness, and we needed him to be strong. He had already proved once that her influence weakened his rule when he defied our traditions and abandoned his duties for her.

Bennett had whisked Lia off to the House of Chaos base a few days ago right in the middle of training for the second competition of the Paldimori Games. I had called a meeting of the Order, and Bennett had teleported back to attend. He was irritated with me, but it was within our rights to question his unorthodox behavior. The other Kyrion had sided with me in demanding an explanation from him for his actions. Bennett had stated that he returned home due to the attacks on his House and was completing his Bonding Ceremony with Lia while there. We had accepted his reasons but were forced to question him once again when allegations were brought to us. The second time he had been called before us he had brought along his Archai—his advisor—to give testimony that he had the best interests of his people in mind and Lia was not a threat to our society.

But Lia *was* a threat.

Finally satisfied that Lia was fine, Bennett dropped back into his chair. His agonized gaze never left his bond-mate as she stared at the back wall refusing to acknowledge any of us. "Lia Davies of the House of Chaos," Bennett stated with an irritated growl. "You stand accused of disobeying a direct order from your Kyrion when you were told not to interfere in Dia King's claiming by the Goddess Gaia. Not only did you disobey my order, but you attacked me—" Bennett cut off abruptly as flames ignited from his wrists to his elbows giving away how angry he still was over being trapped by his bond-mate in a circle of trees and burning boulders.

He gathered his composure and extinguished the flames. "You attacked your Kyrion. None of which would have happened had you not disobeyed my first order which was to stay at Prometheus until I returned. In your escape from my home one of my most trusted guides, Christos Athan, was killed. Your own sword pulled from his chest."

Bennett motioned to the black sword that lay on the table in front of him. Lia flinched as her eyes landed on the sword. Her lips parted on a shaky breath and a glimmer of tears filled her eyes. Then she squared her shoulders and glued her eyes on the wall once more. Bennett's anger melted away, and he looked ready to rush to her rescue. *Goddess Gaia give me strength! If I could still touch someone without the fear that I would rip their powers from them, I would gladly choke that stubborn woman. We had lost a valuable member of our society, and she had broken too many laws to count by attacking Bennett. Yet, all she had said about it for the last three days was that it was an accident.*

"What have you to say for the list of crimes that you stand accused of?" Bennett asked in a strained voice, likely hoping his bond-mate would give him anything that could be used in her favor.

"Not fucking guilty," Lia gritted out. "Save your breath and don't ask me to explain myself again. I'll tell you the same thing I've said at least a dozen times: I was attacked at Prometheus, and in the confusion, accidentally stabbed Christos. I was upset from Grayson nearly dying and Dia being trapped inside that rock." She sighed tiredly and glanced briefly at Bennett. "You were keeping me from going near Dia when I'd just heard that she may be dead … I may have acted rashly but I was trying to help my friend."

Silence descended on the room for a few moments, and I knew Bennett was struggling with asking for the vote. *I could spare him this much, at least.* "We have heard the accused. Testimonies have been heard from any who bore witness. What is your ruling, Order of Chaos?"

"Reprieve," Bennett said almost desperately.

"Reprieve," Kyrion Eros, Jaxon Baines, seconded.

"Recompense," Kyrion Nyx demanded, pushing aside her white robe in irritation. "Let her serve her betters until she understands her place. Since Guide Athan had no family, she owes a life debt to Kafàli Devon Harris, leader of the guides."

I agreed that making Lia a servant would indeed be a punishment for the girl who loved to break our rules, but a life debt was extreme. A life debt meant that her life was literally in the Kafàli's hands. He would have full say over everything Lia could do for the rest of her life. It was only used to punish the most severe crimes against another Paldimori. Yes, a man had died, but I wasn't entirely sure that his death had been anything other than the accident Lia claimed. After all, she was hot-headed, brand-new to her powers, and people had been trying to kill her from the moment she set foot in our world. Honestly, it could have been much worse.

"Recompense," I agreed. "Servitude in each House to learn about our world and train in each of her powers as they wake. Surely your brothers will make her life difficult enough that she would beg for mercy, Kyrion Nyx."

The only other female Kyrion smiled like the cat that had gotten the cream. "Oh, it would be their honor. I agree to your terms."

My terms received a third and fourth approval. The majority had decided Lia's fate.

Before the verdict could be announced, Lia stumbled forward. The two guides grabbed her arms. Lia cried out in pain as she pressed her hands to her temples and a shockwave of power swept across the room. A gasp escaped my lips from the unexpected surge of need that hit me as my own powers clawed to suck in as much of the wave as possible.

Lia dropped to her knees as pulses of different colored lights ran over her skin. Guide Zeno Reece, who still held Lia's arm, hissed as the lights also traveled up his hand. He jerked his hands away to clutch at his bare, tattoo-covered chest as golden light blazed from the double-sided hammer symbol of his House at its center. Guide Emory Sullivan stag-

gered back as well, her braids floating around her. For a
moment, the edges of her body blurred into smoke.

Then, just as suddenly, it all stopped.

Lia remained on her knees gripping her head, her face
contorted with pain. Emory hesitantly placed her hand over
Lia's forehead, and the guide's amethyst eyes began to glow.
"She's having a vision … How is that possible?" Emory asked
in awe.

Wind whipped through the room bringing the scent of
smoke and the distant sound of a roar. Lia slumped to the
ground unconscious. Two index-card-sized pieces of paper
fluttered to the ground in front of the two guides. Emory
picked up the card at her feet. Her no-longer-glowing
amethyst eyes scanned over the card in confusion. "It's an
invitation to the Games."

Zeno scooped up his own card and said, "What the hell is
this? Guides can't compete in the Games."

"Lia, what have you done?" I whispered as all hell broke
loose.

KADE

Two Days Later

THE HOT TEXAS sun beat down on me where I sat on the grassy hill on the south side of the land overlooking my home, the clear blue sky stretching on for what seemed like forever over the 283 acres of Aces Ranch. The modest tan house with its wraparound porch, the big, gray barn, and the fenced pastures of cattle seemed so small in comparison to that wide open sky. It was a beautiful sight, sitting there between the red-tinted canyons to the west and the green rolling hills of scrub brush to the east.

The wind kicked up, bringing the smell of hay, farm animals, and manure to me even acres away. They weren't smells most would call appealing, but to me, they meant safety. Those scents had chased away the choking stench of stale whiskey and cigars that clung to our home no matter how much Mama cleaned. Like the memories of my daddy, they lived on inside that house and could never be truly erased.

The breeze rustled the leaves of the old oak tree off to my

left where I'd carved my initials when I was younger. The tree's branches spread over the older section of headstones toward the back of our family cemetery. My horse, Juniper, snorted as she swatted flies with her tail and nipped at the grass growing taller around the plain gray markers. I stretched out my legs, feeling every ache from getting the cattle relocated this morning, and opened the top few buttons on my jean shirt, welcoming in the breeze to cool my sweaty chest. I scooped a handful of water from my canteen to scrub the grit from my short ginger hair and beard, leaving them for the wind to dry as I rinsed my mouth and spat before taking a drink. The cool water was refreshing after so many hours in the saddle herding stubborn cows. I set the canteen aside next to the wrapped sandwich I'd packed for lunch and my brown cowboy hat.

"Howdy, Mama," I greeted the headstone next to me in a strained whisper. Pain hit me square in the chest like it did each and every time I visited here. Seventeen years later, the pain of her loss had dulled to something less crippling, but it never truly went away. Mama had been my whole world, the only other person I'd known that was different like me. The only other person I knew that was descended from the Goddess Demeter.

Memories of Mama's sweet smile and her gentle voice filled my head. I remembered the days laying in the cool shade of the trees when Daddy wasn't around, and how she'd tell me stories about our people—demi-gods with powers over the harvests and fertility. My favorite stories, though, were the ones about the warring descendants of the six Primordial Gods. The story went that the Primordials Gods were put on earth to bring balance. The first was Chaos, son of the God of Chaos himself. The strongest of the primor-dials with all powers, he was their leader. Chaos took part of himself to make Gaia and Eros, with powers of light. Then came the dark god of the underworld, Tartarus. The neutral god, Erebus. And last the dark goddess, Nyx.

When humans came along the gods became involved in guiding the rise and fall civilizations. Then they began having kids with the humans. The Primordials lost sight of their purpose and set up their own kingdom on an island in the Aegean Ocean called Atlantaiònia. They called themselves Chaonians. The first twelve children of the Primordials were called Titans, and they were the strongest of all descendants. The Titans eventually separated from their cruel parents and formed their own kingdom on Mount Olympus where they changed their name to the Olympians.

Mama had all kinds of theories about why the Chaonian War started, but the family journal that had been passed to her through many generations was the one I believed. That the Olympians wanted to take over ruling the descendants to save them from the cruelty of the gods. Instead, the war split the descendants into two sides who were destined to always be fighting: the Paldimori, direct descendants of the Primordial Gods, and the Olympian Omàda, descendants of the Olympians. As a kid I'd thought those stories of our ancestors made us like the superheroes I watched on TV. I'd wanted to join them in the fight against the Paldimori. It wasn't until later that I'd understood that there were no winners in a war: everybody lost something.

"I know it's been a while since I visited, and I'm sorry for that." I ran my fingers through the grass feeling the hum of the earth reaching for me even though my powers were locked up.

"Daddy's made a real mess of things again." I tiredly rubbed the back of my neck. Daddy had claimed that me and Mama had cursed him with our strange powers. He couldn't admit that he was a shitty rancher or that he was scared of what he didn't understand. It was easier to join the long line of Downing men who were drunks and gamblers. Why break with a tradition starting all the way back with his great-grandaddy who had won this ranch in 1867 in a poker game? Back then, Aces Ranch had been one of the biggest spreads in Palo Duro Canyon and a thriving cattle business. Each generation of Downing men had only been successful at two things: gambling away pieces of the ranch and ruining the Downing name in west Texas. "Daddy didn't just gamble away a few acres or a horse this time, though, Mama. He bet the whole damn ranch. Lost it all lock, stock, and barrel to a man from El Paso who has the paperwork to prove it."

I spat in the grass again, as if I could erase the bitter taste of defeat. It was a taste I knew all too well thanks to my daddy. "You and me, Mama; we have a lotta bad memories tied to that house. Doesn't matter that Daddy's been in prison now for six months for beatin' another woman. He'll always live here ..."

I'd been five when I'd first figured out that something darker lurked behind the picture of the happy family I thought I knew. Money was tight, and Daddy had started drinking in the evenings. He'd loudly complain about the stuck-up townspeople who didn't want his business and the worthless ranch his daddy had left him with. Mama would quickly send me off to bed. Then one night I had gotten up because Beans, the floppy stuffed pony my mama had made me, had wanted a drink of water. My parents' bedroom door was open, and Daddy's angry voice had scared me when he yelled, "Demon!"

Glass shattered, and Mama pleaded with him to stop. I crept closer to the door as he continued to shout. "Been usin' your devil ways to grow that garden out back. I know it. That idiot in town that you sell to knows it. Talkin' 'bout your secret to growin' such prize-fuckin' peppers." He stumbled forward and ripped her shirt down the middle as she cried, trying to back away. "Devil's whore! Wearin' his mark. Thought you could lie to me and tell me it was a tattoo, but I read enough of that journal of yours."

Daddy punched Mama in the stomach right over the symbol of Demeter that she'd been born with. She grunted and fell to her knees. She spotted me standing in the doorway clutching my pony to my chest.

"*Baby boy*," she'd whispered through our mental connection. "*It's fine. Go back to bed.*"

Daddy had kicked the bedroom door closed but the sounds of thumps and pain-filled moans had continued through the night. The next morning Mama had been sick and stayed in bed late. Later that day she cried out when I hugged her, and that's when I'd seen what he'd done. Daddy had branded her with the ranch initials right over top of her symbol. She had made excuses for him that day and every day since. I'd believed her because I loved her more than anything. And Daddy had always been good to me. He'd taught me how to catch a ball. How to ride a horse and plant the fields. It wasn't until he found out I was just like Mama that things had gotten worse for all of us.

I'd wished a million times that Mama and I would leave. The cancer would still have gotten her, but maybe by then she wouldn't have been too tired to fight it. Then again, maybe it was always gonna end this way. Mama was too kind and gentle for this world. She'd never raised her voice or a hand against anyone. That was part of the reason she'd left the House of Harvests and the war with the Paldimori behind. The other reason was to protect me, but I hadn't learned about that until the day she died.

I'd been a scared sixteen-year-old clinging to Mama's frail hand as if I could make her live just by begging. My heart had felt like it was being crushed as she'd dried my tears and told me how proud she was of me. She'd asked me to take care of my sister Hope. Then with her last breaths she'd dropped a bomb on me—Bruce Downing wasn't my real father. My father had been from the opposite side of the war and Mama had planned to run away with him. Until he left my pregnant mother to complete the Desmòs with his true bond-mate. Mama had fled to the human world, heartbroken and desperate. Where she'd met Bruce at the local diner and gotten married within a week. I'd understood then that all those times she'd told me about how the Desmòs ripped apart families that she'd been talking about us.

Pain and anger gripped my chest, ripping at the scabs on my heart. My world had turned upside down that day. I'd lost my best friend and the one person who had loved me unconditionally. I'd also lost who I thought I was, and for a while, I'd lost myself in the bottle too, as if I wanted to prove how much of Bruce Downing was in me despite not being his biological son. But Hope had changed all of that—she'd changed me.

My powers spilled out, tingling across my skin and sinking into the ground where my hand rested. "Damn it!" I pulled my hand away from the now-taller section of grass that my powers had affected and drove my fist into the patch as if I could erase the evidence that I was something *other.* My powers had always been strongest at growing grasses and grains. It had been a while since they had gotten the better of me, though, and slipped past their containment. But thinking about Mama got to me every time.

I reined in my powers with a grunt of annoyance at myself. I pictured a silo inside me where I stored those tan grains of light. Then stuffed the escaping tan lights back through the opening at the top and slammed the lid closed. Mama had suffered so much because of who she was and what she could do. I wouldn't let my powers destroy my life —or Hope's—like they had Mama's.

"The thing is, Mama, I can't keep Hope in that college she just started at *or* save the ranch." I pulled up one of the long blades of grass that I'd accidentally grown and practiced tying knots. "All I've ever done is ranchin'. I don't have a degree, and no one around here would hire a Downing man."

I tossed the knotted blade of grass aside and picked up another. "It would be like losin' you all over again not bein' able to visit you like this. And there's Hope's future to think of. She loves it here, and one day, I wanna pass this place on to her. Once she's got her veterinary medicine degree, she's plannin' on making all kinds of changes to our operations." Pride filled me at the strong woman Hope had become. Followed by a sense of longing as I wished again that Mama was here to see her. "I've screwed up plenty in raisin' her, but I think you'd be proud of our girl. You and me, Mama; all we ever wanted was to not live in fear. But our Hope has big dreams, and I'm tryin' hard not to crush 'em."

Mama had been surprised to find out she was pregnant so long after having me. She'd named the baby after what we both needed in our lives: Hope. And my little sister had lived up to her name. The day I'd stumbled home smelling of cheap booze and cheap women to find Hope locked in a closet sitting in her own waste and a bruise swelling her cheek had been the last straw. Maybe in some ways, Daddy had been right: maybe there was something evil living deep inside me. Whatever it was had come alive that day, demanding justice for what had been done to my baby sister. And it had gotten its wish. I'd been consumed by a white light that burned as hot as my rage. If Hope hadn't slipped her little hand into mine at one point, Daddy would have been dead. Seeing him lying on the ground, his face a bloody mess and burn marks in the shape of my hands on his arms had scared me. I'd nearly become the man I hated that night, and I'd made myself a promise that I'd never let that storm inside me loose again.

I shook off the memories and scanned the land that was as familiar to me as the back of my hand. The open fields I'd galloped across at breakneck speeds, feeling as untamed as the wind. The winding canyons hemmed in by tall, red-rock cliffs where you never knew if the next bend would bring you face-to-face with a rattlesnake or a beautiful cluster of prickly pear cactuses with their bright yellow blooms. I both loved and hated this place at the same time. But I'd fight to keep it for Hope, even if that meant going back to the Paldimori Games.

2

KADE

"You pig-headed, mutton-brained fool," Hope accused, as she thumped a book against my chest the minute I climbed our old porch steps. The sun was heading toward the horizon, and it was almost time to leave for the Games. I'd only stopped by the house to shower and say my goodbyes. But the little spitfire in a peach-colored sundress and worn cowgirl boots glaring up at me wasn't going to make it that easy.

"Stop avoidin' me. You can't go back there. You told me yourself that Mikhail guy drowned in the last competition. It's too dangerous."

"Why hello to you too, sis." I drawled, slapping my hat against my jean leg to knock off the dust which had gathered from riding along the fence line one last time checking for any needed repairs.

"Don't you try that charm on me, Kade Downing." She waved away the dust as I brushed off my shirt. "You've been avoidin' me all day, but we're gonna talk about this."

"Avoidin' you? It's called work, college girl," I said, just to see that angry flush creep across her cheeks. Hope worked just as hard as anyone on this ranch, but she didn't have much time for that now with her classes and assignments. I wanted her fully focused on college, but that didn't mean I wouldn't take the chance to poke at her. She hit me with the book again, and I grabbed it.

"This doesn't look like a textbook. Have you been readin' those historical romance novels again?" I teased, trying to erase her worried frown. "*The Taming of the Duke* by Eloisa James," I read.

She grabbed the book back and turned to angrily stuff it into her brown backpack sitting by the front door. Then she stomped back over to me, her sundress swishing around her knees with every step.

"Stop tryin' to distract me," she demanded, poking a finger into my chest. When I grinned, she hissed at me like a pressure cooker about ready to blow its lid. "I'm not a kid anymore. I'm eighteen, and soon as I graduate college, I'll get a job," she declared passionately, jabbing me in the chest again. "That'll help with payments and bills. I'll do your vet work for free. Let me help. You know I'm better than old Yancy already," she huffed, and I tried not to smile. The local veterinarian was nearly eighty and set in his ways. Hope had learned as much as she could from him, but he wanted nothing to do with technology. My sister had big plans to change the future of large animal veterinarian work in our county, if not the world. "The ranchers in this area would be fools not to use me instead."

"I'm sure they'll be linin' up when they hear you callin' 'em fools." I grinned as she tossed her long strawberry-blonde curls over her shoulder and propped her hands on her hips. "I know you're gonna be a great vet, but whatever money you make is yours." She started to protest, but I just shook my head. "Hope, the El Paso man ain't a bank. He's not gonna let us make payments. We pay the market value of the ranch to him by November or we lose it."

Her shoulders slumped, and I hated seeing that worried

look on her face. My little sister always thought there was a solution for everything, and I loved that about her. She had Mama's kind heart, but her tenacity was all her own. She would make her own path in life no matter what happened. Just like any parent, I wanted to help make that path a little easier.

The old boards of the porch groaned as I pulled Hope into a hug. The scent of her honeysuckle shampoo filled my nostrils, reminding me of when she was little, and how I would brush her hair before bed each night. The little girl I'd raised was all grown up now, and she deserved as much of the truth as I could give her.

I sobered as the fear I'd been trying to dismiss hit me. Thankfully, Hope hadn't gotten any of Mama's powers and hiding mine from her had been good practice for the Games. I had figured out pretty quickly once I set foot on the island of Sotirìa that the Games weren't for a reality show like the entrance form had claimed. The name Paldimori Games should have tipped me off, but I hadn't believed they would be that bold. Mama had told me we were supposed to stay hidden from the humans. The power within the island of Sotirìa had tugged at me, begging me to let my own powers free. Then during the ceremony to pledge ourselves to the Kyrion there had been no doubts that I was surrounded by the Paldimori people from Mama's stories. But it had been too late to back out. I'd been scared shitless of being discovered that first day since part of my DNA came from their mortal enemies. Mama's warnings had haunted me: "Never tell anyone who you really are, baby boy. One side of the war wants to use us, and the other side will kill you because that's what they were ordered to do." I'd turned on the Southern charm, acting like the clueless Texas boy they would expect and kept my powers on lockdown. And it had worked.

After the fear of being discovered had faded a bit, I had been awed by the island and the people. They used their powers so subtly sometimes that it was easy to rationalize it all, and I wondered if I could do that too. Excitement had filled me with the possibility of finding other members from the House of Harvests. After all, if I had been invited to join the Games, maybe more Olympians had too. Maybe I could learn to use my powers instead of just hiding them away.

I couldn't tell what the other contestants were, but it was the attacks on Lia that had put the fear of god into me. Lia had been shot with an arrow during the chariot race of the first competition and we all thought she had died. I'd stood there in shock as my guide—sweet, motherly Grace—had confessed she had only been trying to scare Lia away and not kill her. Grace had become like a second mother to me and her confession had floored me. My heart ached even now with a tangled sense of grief and anger. My reluctance to trust anyone in the Games had doubled.

Before Grace had been able to point the finger at the others involved with the attacks on Lia, she had been lifted into the air by some invisible force and had her neck broken. A chill chased down my spine as I remembered that sound and the sight of her hanging there in the air like a limp doll. Bennett had lost control of his powers, and I'd realized I was in way over my head. The powers I'd seen him use that day were beyond anything I could have imagined. My powers seemed like parlor tricks in comparison. The sky had darkened above him as the wind began to howl and batter against us. The ground shook, sending me stumbling. Trees ripped up from the ground and were sucked into a funnel cloud. Fire surrounded Bennett, moving along the grass in ways I'd never seen it behave before.

That was the moment it truly sank in that we were descended from *gods* and our powers could destroy this world. In some ways, I'd been relieved to know there were others out there like me, but that day had woken a healthy dose of fear in me. If the war between the Paldimori and the

Olympians ever spilled over into the human side, I had no chance of protecting Hope unless I learned to use my powers. I owed it to Hope, to Mama, and to myself to go back there. Hope was right about the danger, but all of my options were leading me right back to the place neither of us wanted me to go. The Games were the first and biggest gamble of my life.

I let go of Hope, and she looked up at me expectantly. There was a vulnerability in those big blue eyes that reminded me of Mama, and it took everything I had not to cave.

"Hope, you're right; it is dangerous. But there ain't a bank out there that will give me a loan. I can't sell off the animals or equipment since they belong to someone else now. Three-million dollars could change everythin' for us."

"Not if you're dead! You can ask to stay on as a ranch hand or somethin'. We'll figure it out."

"They're gonna turn this place into some kinda tourist attraction," I confessed, and Hope winced. "I already talked to the El Paso man, and he has no use for me. No one around here is gonna hire me. I already tried that too. This is my last shot. I need you in my corner on this."

Hope squared her shoulders and gave me a determined look. "I'm always in your corner, big brother." She grabbed me in a tight hug and laid her head on my chest for just a moment before pushing me toward the door. "I love you. Now go shower; you stink."

"I love you too," I said. Then ruffled her hair and darted through the door before she could punch me.

"You better kick their asses at that competition!" she yelled after me.

I took a quick shower and dressed. Then I grabbed my duffle bag off the bed and the white index-sized card lying beside it. For such an innocent-looking piece of paper it sure had stirred up a lot of trouble.

An image of the coldest blue eyes I'd ever seen filled my

head as if I'd called her up just by thinking about trouble.
When I'd won one of the training races during the first
competition in July, the servants had explained that they
could offer themselves up as my prize. I'd been pissed as hell
—not just that servants were still being used, but that they
were being handed out like towels for the contestants to use.
The four young ladies that were assigned as my personal
servants had quickly corrected me. They'd explained that, in
their culture, it was an honor to be a servant and that they
competed to be part of the Games because it was the most
freedom they had from the strict traditions back home. Basi-
cally, it was their time to sow some wild oats before settling
down.

I'd just turned down one of my servant's offer to be my
prize when the beautiful petite blonde owner of those cold
eyes had walked up and planted a kiss right on my lips. I
hadn't had much time for relationships while raising a kid
and running a ranch, but the lust that had hit me with that
kiss had melted my every inhibition. We'd made out in the
training area like teenagers and spent the night heating up the
sheets. She'd been gone the next morning, and I'd never even
gotten her name. There was something about our time
together though that left me feeling unsettled. I vaguely
remembered Kyrion Gaia—the beautiful but cold woman I'd
pledged to be champion for in the Games—trying to tell me
something when the blonde had her tongue in my mouth, but
I'd been oblivious to everything except the lust burning
me up.

I winced in shame at my behavior. That hadn't been like
me, but it had happened. All I could do was chalk it up to a
moment of weakness.

I shivered as something cold and dark seemed to move
inside me for a moment. I shook off the feeling and read the
invitation card again:

YOU ARE CHOSEN
CHILD OF BOUNTY
WHAT YOU SEEK YOU MAY FIND
TRUTH. LOVE. FREEDOM.
ALL COULD BE YOURS IN THE PALDIMORI GAMES
BOUNTY OF THE HEART
ANERRHIPHTHO KYBOS

It still didn't make a damn bit of sense to me.

There were two things that I did know for sure, though. The first was that the Paldimori were messing with the contestants' memories. I'd asked a few pointed questions during the second competition after things didn't seem to add up. It had been pretty clear that the other contestants didn't have a clue about Lia being shot and had bought that story about her being too injured in the chariot race to return to the second competition. Maybe my powers protected me, but I had seemed to be the only one unaffected.

Second was that Lia was something different. She'd come back from the dead, for god's sake, but I'd noticed it before then. I'd first started spending time around her because she'd made the Paldimori uncomfortable, and I'd thought she might have been like me. It hadn't hurt at all to be around a beautiful woman who could make me laugh either. There was something about her that called to me like I'd found a long-lost friend. I'd felt the same about Dia King when she had taken Lia's place in the second competition.

I knew exactly what I was up against going back there. I'd been cautious and no one had suspected anything so far. I planned on finding out as much as I could about my powers these next few weeks.

I tucked the card into the back pocket of my jeans, grabbed my bag, and headed toward the front door. I stepped onto the porch to find Hope sitting astride her mare and holding Juniper's reins. She handed me the reins, and I swung up into the saddle with my bag across my lap. We pointed the horses toward the open fields to the north where an airplane waited to take me to Sotirìa. We made the ride together in companionable silence. I glanced off toward the cemetery on the hill and sent up a silent plea: *Watch over me, Mama. I could use your help to win that prize money and figure out how to protect Hope from our world.*

3

ARIANA

FATHER'S nine allies and their bond-mates exited the large wooden door at the front entrance to the palace in Kardia— the home base for the House of Seasons. I stood several feet from the door underneath the braided archway of trees that rose up to touch the roof of the palace two stories above. My powers flowed out, lighting up the phosphorescent minerals embedded in the trees' bark and the pathway that led toward the front half of the valley. The couples bowed perfunctorily as they passed by me and walked down the pathway to their homes. Finally, the night grew silent as they passed beyond my hearing, and I breathed a sigh of relief. These dinners were a painful but familiar exercise in concealing my disgust with the fawning adoration laid at Father's feet.

I looked longingly at the cliffs rising up around our valley, wishing I could have spent this evening in the jungle instead. The faint glimmer of the barrier that concealed our lands rose above the tall cliffs and into the night sky. The barrier around Kardia prevented anyone who wasn't from our House from seeing or entering our home. Our ancestors had sought out the most remote, uninhabited location deep in the Congo jungle and built our home here around 1200 BCE. Few, if any, of the human forest tribes ventured close to us. Those who did acknowledged our connection to the goddess; they left us in peace and protected our secret. Several of the families in our House—like my advisor, Fayel's—bore the dark skin and short stature of our human neighbors. I, on the other hand, looked like Mother and her ancestors with my lighter, peach-toned skin and curly, dark blonde hair. My brother, Aegeus, had gotten Father's darker features. I also knew that many of the outcast villages—descendants who had decided to live outside a House's rule and protection—had co-existed with the human forest tribes for centuries. But the times had changed, and the peace of the rainforest had long been shattered by unspeakable acts of conflict, atrocity and cruelty against both the humans and the outcast villages who lived beyond our barriers. I would put an end to it all if I could but I was struggling to save my own people.

I reluctantly turned away from the temptation of the jungle and walked back into the palace. I closed the door behind me and turned right down the hall leading to the parlor. The grating sound of our last remaining dinner guest's laugh filtered out of the open door, and I slowed my pace. Ekert Nazary was the eldest son of Father's greatest supporter, and as of my thirty-first birthday last month, my betrothed. To say I was displeased with our arranged bonding was an understatement, but it was tradition among our most powerful families. These arrangements typically happened at birth, but until I'd become Kyrion four years ago, I had been too much of a liability with my "special" powers to risk endangering Father's allies. As Kyrion Gaia my worth had gone up significantly and successors were needed. Father had even written a provision into the contract that I was to wear the kóvo to suppress my powers once bonded. The docu-mented excuse was so that my strong powers would not interfere in the creating of children but it was another way for him to control me.

Since our House was traditionally matriarchal, my mother would have been the one to negotiate my bonding contract, but everything had changed when she gave up the throne to my father. Syris Dupree had worked to bring select men into equal power and our way of life had drastically changed. Our once simple and humble lives had been disrupted with the luxuries Father had brought in from the human world as evidenced by everything in this palace. I grimaced as I walked past a painting on the wall that looked like a child had accidentally spilled something. It was hideous but no doubt expensive. Father had sold off nearly all of the emeralds given to us by the goddess by the time I took the throne. I had managed to save a few and kept them well hidden.

I stopped several feet from the parlor door. Under cover of the dim hallway, I tugged at the cap sleeves of my moss-green dress. I allowed myself that one outward display of the anxious energy churning inside me before making sure the stoic mask I wore for all the world to see was in place. My father was up to something this evening, which never boded well for me. He was like a spider who patiently lured prey into his shiny web making them believe with each step that the choices that took them further into his trap were their own. With all of my years of practice I had gotten better at sidestepping those traps to minimize the damage, but I hadn't escaped unscathed.

Not when Father was constantly looking for even the tiniest crack in my armor and would use that one point of weakness to become my undoing. What Syris wanted most was complete control over me to ensure that I became the Archigós—supreme leader of all Paldimori. The position that was currently held by Bennett. The Archigós was both a position and a mark. The position was most common and went to the most powerful Kyrion—who was almost always from the House of Chaos. Being marked as the Archigós by the God of Chaos was something so rare it had only happened a few times throughout our history and never from birth like Bennett's was. The only other way to become Archigós was to invoke a law to call on the God of Chaos to grant the position. Although we had recently heard that Archigós marks were appearing in various Houses amongst the Omàda. Yet another change occurring in our world since Lia had come along.

I had stalled in fulfilling Father's demand to pursue the Archigós position, and I was being punished for it. My brother, Aegeus, had been captured and tortured by the Olympian Omàda four years ago. He had slipped into a coma, and my father had tried everything to bring him back to us, including seeking help from human doctors and their equipment. Nothing had changed. Except that Father had seen my weakness in my love for my brother and used it against me. Syris had hidden Aegeus away in a secret location that he would only teleport me to when I behaved. Father typically left the daily Kyrion work to me, as long as I did not interfere in his pursuit of his luxuries. Taking over as Archigós, though ... Becoming the supreme ruler over all Paldimori was not the same as conceding to his request to have a set schedule for the hunters and the areas they would target each month.

My visits with my brother had been cut off for two months now because I refused to take Bennett's position. Every day not being able to see if Aegeus was still alive and being cared for ate at me. It was tearing my heart apart to choose between my brother and what I believed was right. Bennett was a good leader. I had followed him when we trained together as Kyrion. I would follow him in all things, except where Lia was concerned. But it no longer mattered what I wanted; my time had run out. Father had given his ultimatum at the same time he announced our dinner plans this evening: either I took the Archigós seat or I would never see Aegeus again. I had agreed and negotiated to have my brother released into my custody if I succeeded. But I had my own plans, and they included getting myself out from under Syris's thumb.

My hands shook and my heart beat madly in my chest with dread as I approached the door to the parlor. Servants poured the men drinks as I walked through Father's favorite room, its starkness perfectly reflecting the man himself. The pristine pale tile floor and the custom shelves that lined three walls were like the public image that he'd carefully crafted. The glass fronts of the shelves displayed his collection of the finest of everything from liquor to artwork. The ugly metal-framed armchairs that sat in a grouping near the back of the room were as lifeless as his rotten soul and a jarring contrast to all of the light in the room. The ten chairs—one for my father and each of his allies from the most powerful families in our House—were positioned in front of the wall of windows that looked down over the homes of our people.

I took a seat opposite my father and braced myself for whatever he was plotting.

"I hear that you set the terms for the sentencing of the Chaos Chosen, daughter." Syris's pale green eyes assessed me as he sipped gin from a crystal tumbler. Faint lines creased his chestnut skin, daring to show evidence of his sixty-five years upon this earth. The neck and cuffs of his beige tunic top and matching pants were embroidered with the House of Seasons symbol of a green leafy tree. A gold circlet that looked like interlocking branches with emerald leaves circled his bald head. His wrists were adorned with matching wide gold and emerald cuffs.

The garish display of wealth made my stomach turn. I knew how much my people had suffered to elevate him to this level of status. I thanked the goddess once more that my eye color was the only thing I'd inherited from this man. "While I applaud you for finally acting as the true leader of the Order as our Kyrion should be, you were too easy on the girl," Syris admonished me. "Servitude in each House won't teach that willful child her place. Only by making an example of her will you show them all that the House of Seasons is to be feared."

"As always, you are both wise and well-informed, Father," I replied in an even tone that belied the frustration roiling inside me. The verdict of Lia's trial had been hastily recorded but would not be carried out until this competition was over. I had only informed Archai Fayel of those details tonight, and my advisor wouldn't have said a thing to my father. She had more than once compared Syris to the militant group who had kidnapped her as a child when she had accidentally crossed beyond the barrier surrounding our lands. She hated my father nearly as much as I did.

Father snapped at the servant for rattling the glassware, and I pressed my hands into my lap. Every person in our House deserved to be protected and respected no matter their position or power. Yet Syris didn't see it that way. Soon it wouldn't matter. Once I removed Father's hold over me, he and his supporters would be dealt with.

"Your father is right," Ekert said, smoothing out a wrinkle in his dark blue tunic. The man looked like a shorter replica of my father. Even his clothes matched in all but the color. "Disobedience must be pulled out by the roots to prevent it from ever growing again."

Syris raised his glass in agreement and Ekert's drab olive-colored eyes gleamed with satisfaction.

I nearly rolled my eyes. Ekert's constant need for my father's approval was annoying and made him seem younger than his thirty-seven years. He often repeated whatever Syris said too making me wonder if my betrothed had any original thoughts of his own.

I made a non-committal noise in response to Ekert's views on disobedience and declined the drink the servant offered.

"Don't worry, Kyrion Ariana," Ekert said lifting his

tumbler to swirl his gin around as he gave me a conde-scending smile. I hated how both of these men thought women were weak and beneath them. I wanted to sentence them both to work with the women in the hamlet and see how long they would last. "When we become bond-mates, I will make sure you no longer have to deal with the stresses of leading this House."

Syris smirked at me with all of the smug glee of a man whose plans were coming together nicely. He quickly affected an air of sadness when Ekert looked his way. "Your mother was too soft for the throne as well."

Pity and guilt mixed with my irritation. Mother's fate had been sealed the day she was born bearing the large tree symbol that marked her as the next Kyrion. Although she'd been a daydreamer ill-suited for the role, the God of Chaos had selected her, and there was no escaping her duty. Her arranged bonding to Syris—the most powerful boy born in several generations—was expected to bring great power back to our House. Instead, their bonding had been a disaster.

The story known to everyone outside of our family was that Aegeus's birth had weakened Mother too much for her to continue her duties. Then when I was born, she had fallen ill with a debilitating disease that had also affected me. It was all lies. The truth was that Mother had happily handed over the throne to Syris. I'd often wondered if I was created the way I was to punish my mother for not fulfilling her destiny. What-ever the reason, the childlike shadow of a woman locked in the west tower would never be the same again. And as my father often reminded me, it was all my fault.

My powers had triggered at birth and fed off of Mother's to the point that she nearly died. Power-draining typically left a Paldimori unconscious, but after a few days they were able to recharge. But when my parched tree fed deeply enough, the powers were absorbed into me and their original owner was unable to recover what they had lost. All Mother was left with was a tiny spark of her powers that kept her alive. Father had cleverly disguised the truth by banishing both Mother and I to our separate tower rooms. There we had remained largely ignored, except for the servants who tended to us. Syris had played upon the sympathies of our people for a man grieving his "ill" bond-mate and newborn daughter to shut down any rumors. Anyone who questioned him was made an example of by public trials with witness testimony usually from Father's allies. Those found guilty became outcasts.

Syris glanced out of the night-darkened windows with a troubled frown. "The rigorous training to become a Kyrion broke your mother's spirit long before she took the throne. As her co-ruler, I helped as much as I could but there was only so much I could do. Then Aegeus was born …"

I bit my bottom lip to hold in the accusations I wanted to hurl at my father for the lies he carefully planted to draw Ekert into his trap.

"My poor boy. If only he had listened to me." Father cleared his throat as if overwhelmed with grief for his son. "But he was brave to try to defend that outcast village from the Omàda. One day they will pay for what they did to him."

Aegeus had followed Father's lead in most things, but the one time he had defied Syris led to where he was now. As far as anyone beyond a few people knew, my brother had died along with the Talosi—soldiers who typically guarded the home base of a House—that he had taken into battle with him. With one miscalculated move and no successors brought forward to claim the position, I had become Kyrion.

It shouldn't have been possible, but no one had answers as to why no successors had been born after Aegeus fell into the coma. There had been times throughout my life when I had been at death's door, and I could swear that I could feel a connection inside me like a string between two points. It was a warm, comforting feeling that urged me to find whoever was at the other end. Those times I had been too weak from beatings to hold back my powers, and they had traveled along the connection only to have it cut off abruptly. Father had taunted me that my powers were seeking out people's energy and killing them without even having to touch them. I'd locked myself down tighter behind my walls until I felt nothing, and eventually, those connections had stopped.

Ekert tapped his glass. "If only you could become Kyrion again."

I nearly snorted and silently thanked Gaia for our laws that forbid a prior Kyrion from re-taking the position once their time had passed. I like to think Syris had selected me as Kyrion because I was the second most powerful person in our House after my brother and had already gone through Kyrion training. But I suspected it had more to do with me being the only child he had left. I'm sure Syris would have found a way around the laws to prevent me from taking the throne if he hadn't been consumed at the time with seeking revenge for what happened to Aegeus. He'd spent weeks pleading with the Order to gather an army and take revenge on the Omàda for what they had done. The Order had denied him repeatedly. Syris had since funneled all of his anger and grief into plans to get me into the position of Archigós. I think he still planned to get his revenge through me, but I had no intention of starting a war with the Omàda.

Father refilled his tumbler and took a long drink as if to gather his courage to continue his sad tale. "My bond-mate gave me a lovely son and daughter at great cost to her health."

Ekert leaned forward, lapping up every detail. I'd heard some version of this pity story too many times, and I wanted to leave. But I wouldn't. Syris hadn't yet gotten to his grand finale and that is where the trap usually lay. I could recite the different versions of this story he used almost as many times as my father had coldly made me recite all the ways in which my birth had ruined our perfect family.

"I had no choice but to take over as Kyrion until my son could come of age," Syris stated and Ekert nodded, agreeing wholeheartedly. "Then Aegeus was taken from us, and Ariana fell sick as well. I've only ever wanted what was best for my family. You'll be my family soon, Ekert. I need to know that my daughter is in good hands."

My fingers dug into the armrests of my chair as I worked to keep myself calm. Father was speaking about me like some trinket he was passing down to the next generation. Fury burned within my chest and green light flickered under my palms. I could end my father's manipulations and control over my life right now. All I had to do was let my powers free. There would be no more being confined to the east tower or any other room. There would be no more cutting words or thinly veiled threats. No more having to plan every word or action to not show any weaknesses for him to target. For a moment I relished the sweet taste of freedom that his death could bring.

Then an image of my mother pressed against the windows of the west tower looking lost and alone hit me. I'd seen her do that thousands of times since the windows of our towers faced each other across the courtyard. If I killed my father, I really would become the monster that I fought hard not to be. How could I face myself or my fellow Kyrion after that? I already couldn't bring myself to tell the other Kyrion the truth of my horrible past. I would have to spend the rest of my life lying about what I'd done.

No, I couldn't do it. My life was already built on lies, and I hated every one of them.

I PULLED my powers back and breathed a sigh of relief that the men had been distracted with opening a new bottle of gin.

"You did what was necessary, Syris." Ekert toasted my father. "Look at all you've done for us. We have nice houses with running water, plenty of food, and trade with the human world to get us anything we want. Lesser men in your position would have crumbled under the obligations of being Kyrion, raising two children, and dealing with your bond-mate's and daughter's illness." Surprisingly, Ekert raised his glass to me as well, and I suspected that he was slightly drunk. "Thank the goddess, Kyrion Ariana recovered!"

"Yes, we must be thankful for that," Syris agreed sarcastically, but Ekert was oblivious.

I swallowed down my objection that the niceties he mentioned were only true for the powerful. Until my father became Kyrion our House had always lived a simpler lifestyle than the other descendants due to our need to be close to nature. It made us strong, but it was also a hard way of life that claimed my people far too young. Our House had been and still was to some extent suspicious of any technology. Introducing our people—especially the larger population of the less powerful that lived in the ramshackle hamlet near the main entrance to our valley—to change had to be done at a snail's pace. I still struggled to convince some of those in the hamlet of the benefits of indoor plumbing over a latrine.

Syris had used the excuse of an ailing bond-mate and daughter to demand a healthier environment for everyone. What he had really meant was a more comfortable life for him and his allies. The palace and nine stone homes had been built through the back-breaking labor of our people. That had started the segregation of our people into the privileged powerful and the poor less powerful. Under Syris's ambitions, change had come rapidly and dozens of lives had been lost to make his vision a reality. Some of the less powerful had worked tirelessly to clear the dense forest. Others had used their powers sometimes to the point of depletion to create the material needed. Still others had braved the journey into the human world to barter or purchase the things Syris requested. The less powerful had done all of the work yet had never enjoyed the fruits of their labor for themselves. Every chance I got I tried to give back to them, whether it was food for their table or care for the families torn apart when loved ones had become outcasts.

This inequality would be stopped once I exposed Father's lies and got his allies on my side. I just needed to find my brother first to remove the leverage that Syris had over me.

Syris motioned toward Ekert. "Thankfully, I had great men like your father to support me. Just as I will be here to support you when you become co-ruler of this House. It's a good thing you've begun your training already. Although, I found I learned best by doing."

"Archai Fayel has been most helpful," Ekert stated but couldn't quite hide his grimace. I nearly laughed out loud because I knew Fayel had used her knives to make a point more than once during his training as my co-ruler. "I learn best by doing as well. Maybe we shouldn't wait to complete the bonding. I could learn quicker if I was already performing my duties."

My breath stuttered in my chest, and I knew from my father's grin that he relished my reaction. I composed myself and said calmly, "Ekert we could not possibly move the date of our Bonding Ceremony forward any sooner than next summer. These types of events, especially for a Kyrion, require many preparations. My dress has barely begun to be made."

"Oh, well, yes, that's true—" Ekert looked uncomfortably between me and my father. This felt like that human game of what I think the humans called "turkey," where they tried to make the other person move out of the way.

"Perhaps you could order a dress from Paris like other Kyrion have done." Syris sipped his gin waiting to see what I would do. He referred to an incident where Lia had sent a runner—a servant who goes into the human world to procure items for a House—from the House of Chaos last month into Paris and nearly gotten the servant killed. France had been taken over almost entirely by the Olympian Omàda, and it was extremely dangerous to attempt to enter the country. He was both making fun of Lia's ignorance of our world and trying to rile me by comparing us. Little did he know that I'd side with the exasperating and naive Lia over him any day.

"What an excellent idea, Father. We will show our support of Kyrion Lia. After all she has made such a big impact on our society already by abolishing the law against allowing outcasts back into our Houses. Surely this will be a fresh new change as well." I silently applauded myself when Father nearly choked on his drink. "Ekert, perhaps you have a runner that you could send to Paris for my dress?" I asked innocently.

Ekert's eyes widened in panic. "I would do anything my Kyrion asked of me. B-but that's Omàda territory. I'd be sending someone to their death for a dr—"

Syris cut him off. "No need to waste what work is already underway. We aren't in competition with the House of Chaos." His tone said that we were far superior. "Bonding Ceremonies shouldn't be rushed."

My relief was short lived.

"Surely Ekert will be accompanying you to Sotirìa tomorrow then to continue his training?" Syris said, tapping his finger against his empty glass.

Ah, so this is what Father's goal was for tonight. He wanted another spy during the Games, one that would be by my side at all times in the guise of learning the Kyrion role. The Games had been delayed as we'd scrambled to find replacements for those contestants who, like Lia, would no longer return to competing. This had dragged out what should have only taken four weeks into a little over two months. The Games had taken more of my time and attention than ever, pulling me away from my search for Aegeus and my plans to rid myself of my father. That had all worked in Father's favor and now he had gained the upper hand again. I contemplated all of the angles and couldn't find a safe way to decline bringing Ekert with me. What Father seemed to be forgetting, however, was that once I was in Sotirìa I would be free to do as I pleased. If I decided to leave Ekert knitting clothes for our people the entire time I could.

"Of course, there is plenty to be learned at the Games," I agreed.

"Ekert, you will want to be there when Ariana invokes the Law of Metis. After all, there has only been one other time in our history that the supreme leader position has been challenged, and then only because the Archigós died." Syris stood from his chair, his shadow falling over me. It took every ounce of my restraint to remain seated and not give any sign that his looming shadow intimidated me. "We will have a celebration soon enough when our House has re-claimed our place as ruler over all Paldimori just as our Goddess Gaia did after the Chaonian War. I'm sure you will be happy to see *everyone* on your return, daughter."

He meant I would finally get to see Aegeus once he had proof that I'd taken the Archigós role from Bennett. And he planned to use Ekert to notify him as soon as it was done. "Yes, I look forward to that."

"Then I bid you both goodnight," Syris said and strolled from the room.

Ekert quickly scrambled to his feet, swaying slightly, and said he would see himself out.

The sooner I rid myself of both of these men, the better my life would be. As if my parched tree seconded that notion, the roots lurched toward Ekert's retreating back. Green light spilled down my arms and across the floor. I pulled at the roots of my thirsty tree, absorbing those green lights back into myself until they lay deceptively dormant.

I had my plans for ridding myself of my father. Unfortunately, the only way to free myself from my betrothal contract was to find my true bond-mate, but that was unlikely and unwelcome. Rule number two was there for a reason: *no one fully owns me as long as my mind, body, and soul are still my own.* The last thing I needed was a man in my life who would try to conquer those parts of me as well.

5

ARIANA

"KILL HER, KILL HER, KILL HER!" Mother's anguished screams echoed through my bedroom. They were so loud here at the back of the palace near the west tower where she lived, that there was no escaping them.

After Ekert and Father had left, I had retired to my rooms. But as soon as I lay down Mother's moans had started and soon escalated into the screams that I knew from experience would only stop when her strength ran out.

It was on nights like these that I actually missed the east tower room on the opposite side of the palace that used to be mine. There, at least, the screams were muffled somewhat by the distance of the courtyard between us. I'd moved into the Kyrion suite of rooms immediately after my coronation ceremony as per our tradition. I had worked weeks on making this suite a place that I could relax in by bringing the jungle indoors. Gone were all of the gold and sleek modern trimmings that my father loved. Fayel had taken it all to one of our runners who could convert anything into human cash, and we had bought boats, tools, and clothes for the less powerful. Now this room was my refuge—except from the screams that seemed to funnel down the stairs of the tower and the hallway between us directly into my room.

I sighed loudly, conceding to the fact that the much-needed rest for the Games tomorrow wasn't going to happen. I slipped from my large, round bed in the center of the room. It was braced between the trunks of four broad Moabi trees. Their parasol-like crown of branches stretched wide overhead to create the roof of my bedroom. The branches were woven so tightly together by my powers that not a drop of the rain typical for this time of year could get through.

I walked into the alcove off to the left where heliconia flowers with their bright red ladder of blooms had been coaxed to grow eight feet tall and two feet wide. Dresses and cloaks in every shade of green hung from their sturdy lobster-claw-like petals. Woven ilala palm shelves were spaced between the large flowers and held clothes from the human world that I'd never had a chance to visit. The east tower had been my prison from the time I was born until the age of six when Aegeus had talked Father into sending me to Tantalus —the fortress that floats somewhere in the clouds over the Arctic Circle, making it neutral territory since it didn't touch any land claimed by the Houses. Representatives from each House lived on the island year-round devoting their lives to perfecting their powers and training Kyrion from the age of seven until they took their thrones, typically at sixteen.

Kyrion-in-training usually returned home frequently or, at least, for a long break to celebrate the winter solstice. But Father had wanted Aegeus to remain at Tantalus until he had reached his first major goal of growing his own staff from a seedling. My brother had come home four years later to find me nearly starved to death, covered in filth, and scared of my own shadow. I shouldn't have been permitted to go to Tantalus since I hadn't been marked as a Kyrion successor, but Father made it happen so that I might "learn something to make me useful." Aegeus had saved me from a slow death by neglect but sentenced me a brutal hell that was my home for fifteen long years—longer than any other Kyrion. It was there that the rules I lived by had been born. They had offered me a way to cope with the harsh discipline and endless training.

I stripped off my thin nightgown and quickly dressed in a pair of soft black pants and a black shirt. I exited the alcove and stopped to use the bathroom. Then I headed toward the balcony doors across the room. I glanced longingly at the bathing pool as I walked past, but another harrowing scream had me picking up the pace. I hurried over to the rock ledges that made up the right side of the room. Several red cushions with bright yellow flowers lined two sections of rock that jutted out to form a sitting area near the balcony doors. A table made from a large column of rock with a wide, flat top sat between the seats. I plucked an orange from the bowl of fruit on the table and stuffed it into my pocket. Bramble—the red fox that I had found beaten and starved inside the barrier to our lands several years ago, likely kept as a pet by one of the militant groups—poked her head out of a wide crevice in the rocks near the back wall that she'd claimed as her den.

"Hello, Bramble. Are you up for a walk tonight?" I asked through the mental connection I could share with animals.

"Night. Jungle. Search. Man," she sent back to me. They were more impressions than real words, but I knew what she meant.

"Yes, we will search the jungle for Aegeus again tonight," I confirmed.

Since my father always teleported me to see my brother on our short visits, I had no idea where to look. We had always been able to locate each other, though, when we were in close proximity. I just had to find the right area and that extra sense would do the rest. His room could have been any one of the dozen bedrooms in this palace, but this had been the first place I'd checked. My best guess was that Father had created Aegeus's room in one of the cave systems nearby. I'd already searched the valley, the land to the north, and the land to the east. Time was running out to find Aegeus before I was forced to bond with Ekert and whatever freedoms I had now would be harder to maintain.

Bramble stepped from her den and stretched. Her orange, cream, and black fur rippling with the movement. We headed toward the balcony doors at the back of the room. The moon was a full round ball in the dark sky illuminating the man-made clearing behind the palace when we stepped onto the balcony. Humid air wrapped me in its embrace, and monkeys chittered their greetings from the trees as I approached the stone railing. Another scream pierced the night; the pain evident in that sound tore into me like the whip I'd endured at Tantalus. Logically, I knew that my mother's condition wasn't my fault, but the guilt was a suffocating burden that plagued me all the same. Guilt, anger, and helplessness built inside me. Any moment my own screams would join hers if I didn't get out of here.

I scooped Bramble up into my arms and used my powers to pull ropes from the tree to wrap around my waist. I'd put the ropes there for the monkeys to play on. I loved to watch them in the evenings, especially after a hard day. They never failed to coax a smile from me.

We were lifted over the railing by the ropes and slowly began to lower toward the ground. The monkeys ran across the limbs of the tree making a game of who could steal the orange. Their mischievous fingers tugged at my clothes and hair. One of the smallest dropped onto Bramble's back and swung around my arm to retrieve the fruit from my pocket. My fox friend let out a warning grumble. The little monkey flashed us a smile and then raced away with its reward. I smiled and patted Bramble's head. Some of that pressure inside me lessened.

I loved animals. They had simple needs and their loyalty

could not be bought. They didn't know how to deceive or manipulate. Unlike people.

Once we reached the ground, the ropes returned to the tree branches, and I set Bramble down. She preferred not to teleport, and I only did it when she came to Sotirìa with me. *"I will go over the south cliff wall. Meet me on the other side,"* I requested, sending her a mental image of the location.

Bramble darted across the clearing and into the dark woods.

Sometimes the protections that prevented teleporting in and out of the valley were irritating, but I would never endanger my people by removing it. I teleported across the valley to the only section of the cliffs surrounding our home that wasn't a sheer vertical wall. It was one of the few ways into and out of the valley aside from the main entrance. But it took a lot of physical strength and strong powers to navigate them. I'd never seen anyone else use these ways.

I found a foothold in the rock face and began to climb. Here, Mother's screams couldn't reach me and the burn of my muscles straining as I pulled myself up the cliff soon cleared away the last of the pressure inside me. Sweat clung to me by the time I pulled myself up onto the ridge at the top. I took a moment to stretch my aching limbs. Then I turned toward the direction I needed to go to meet up with Bramble and reached out with my powers asking for assistance from the jungle. The layers of the rainforest were very dense and the quickest way to travel was by canopy. The warm acceptance of the jungle washed over me, and I took a running step. The vegetation came alive around me; saplings bowed out of the way, liana vines parted, larger trees shifted their branches providing steps for me to rise high into their tops. I jumped from tree to tree seeking aid from the forest as needed.

Finally, I dropped down to the bank of the Lomami River several miles to the south of Kardia, close to the barrier that separated us from the human world. Bramble slipped from the trees to trot along beside me as I followed the bank. We searched for hours using my powers and Bramble's nose but found nothing. I dropped to my knees in the soft silt of the riverbank and hung my head. My shoulders slumped at another failure. I sank my hands into the dirt as if it could take away the ache inside me. Mentally I called out to my brother even though I knew he couldn't answer. "*Aegeus, please …*"

There was too much I wanted to say but the words wouldn't come. Years of repressed fears, heartache, and guilt swamped me. I fell onto the ground and curled into a ball as tears slipped down my cheeks. Bramble whined and curled against my back, offering comfort that I didn't deserve. All I'd known was pain from the people who were supposed to love me. I'd long ago isolated myself from everyone—including my brother—to keep that pain from destroying me. I knew Aegeus hadn't had a choice about leaving me behind when he was sent to Tantalus and that he'd been trying to help by getting me sent there too. Some part of me though hadn't been able to fully trust him. Now I would give anything to have him back and the chance to prove I could open up to him.

My dirty fingers traced over the ground and a small plant grew. Why couldn't my powers be this simple always? Gaia was life and her descendants were life-bringers not life-takers. Why was I different?

I'd learned over the years that my parched tree was roused by really powerful people and by any perceived threat. Lia was both of those things and my ultimate challenge. The fact that I'd been able to be within ten feet of her without losing command of my powers proved how far I had come since my childhood. I'd had so much trouble controlling that part of me when I was young and too many other people had suffered for it. I hadn't touched another person since I was six years old because my touch meant death. The memory of that day drew me in and added to the heartache breaking me apart.

My bare feet scuffed the cold stone floor anxious to get this over with so I could see my brother. My long-sleeved green dress rustled in the wind that whistled through the open window slots high above. The instructor droned on about what I needed to do. I hated every minute of the training, but at least, I wasn't in Kardia with Father. Here in Tantalus, I could spend time with Aegeus when our lessons were done for the day.

My instructor snapped at me to focus, and I looked back down at the small brown seed in my hand. I was to grow my own staff from the seedling as every Kyrion Gaia had since the beginning. The staff was to be a marker of my progress as I learned all there was to know about becoming a Kyrion—not that I was fit to take the throne, as Father liked to remind me. Aegeus had showed me his own twisted oak staff the day before with its achievement markings, and I wanted mine to be just like his. Minutes turned into hours as I forced my powers into the seed, but nothing happened. My instructor berated me, calling me the tainted heir and a useless spare. The sun set and still I hadn't made the seed grow. The instructor demanded that I remain in the training room until I learned what should have been a simple task. He left me there sobbing while I clutched the tiny seed to my chest.

I stayed in that cold room alone for three days with only the daily visit from my instructor to check on my progress and the food delivered by a servant. At some point my little body had grown numb to the cold and the pain of sleeping on that hard floor with only a few rags I'd manage to scrounge up. Every day the instructor threatened me with never letting me see Aegeus again, but I just couldn't make my powers work.

On the third day, the door opened at mealtime, but I didn't stir from my spot curled up on the floor. The servant entered, but instead of sitting my plate by the door, she came over to kneel beside me. Her kind green eyes welled with tears as she set a steaming bowl of soup beside me. Carefully she pulled my cold and stiff body onto her lap. She wrapped her coat around me and nudged the bowl to my lips. Eventually I unthawed enough to sip the hot soup that hit my empty belly like fire.

Finally, when the warmth had returned to my skin, the tears came, and I wrapped my arms around the woman's neck. I sobbed into her shoulder until I felt hollowed out inside. She wiped my face and told me she would help me with my lesson. She scooped the tiny seed from the floor and dropped it into my hand. Then coaxed her earth powers out, trying to show me how to make a connection. My powers gradually come out to brush against the seed before they retreated once more. I tried over and over.

What if Father and the instructor were right? What if the Goddess Gaia hated me because I wasn't built right? What if I was a monster filled with darkness instead of the goddess's light? Fear pressed in on me until I couldn't breathe. I grabbed the servant's hand needing to feel the comfort of someone who believed in me, but instead, my powers latched onto hers. Then the screaming started.

When I came to a short brownish-black staff half the length of my arm lay beside me, along with the body of the kind servant. Her unseeing green eyes stared back at me from a face as gray as the stone floor. I whimpered and scrambled away. Father grabbed me by the arm and shoved me back down next to the servant. "Your instructors have informed me of your failures. You're an abomination brought into this world to test my strength. Make no mistake you'll be the one who breaks." Father grabbed the back of my neck forcing me to look at the dead servant. "You nearly killed your own mother and now this. Look at what your weakness has done, Ariana."

I cried great wracking sobs as I looked at the woman whose name I had never known — at the woman that I had killed. My whole body trembled with regret and sadness. The soup I had eaten sloshed in my belly. I fell forward throwing up on my dress and the floor. Father turned away in disgust.

The instructor pulled me to my feet and handed me my staff. "Your powers are formidable, Ariana. Yet, you are weak. Your body and your mind must be stronger than your powers if you are to make them heed your will." He gripped the sleeve of my dress, careful to avoid the mess I'd made and brought me over to the dead servant. "All powers can be used to bring life or to destroy it. This is a decision that we each make when we wield our powers. Look hard at this pitiful woman. This will be the fate of everyone you touch if you let your power free." His rough fingers pinched my chin and raised my face up to meet his sinister smile. "We will teach you discipline."

Father jerked me from the instructor's grasp and shoved me to my knees beside the dead servant. "Discipline can be found through many methods, but there's only one way I have found that leaves a lasting impression. Let us begin your new lessons." My staff clattered to the floor as the first of the lashes landed across my back, and I fell forward onto the servant's body screaming in agony.

I shook my head to dispel the memory, my body trembling with cold as if I had been transported back to that room. My legs felt weak as I pushed myself onto my knees. Bramble climbed into my lap, and I stroked her soft fur. Here under the cover of darkness with only Bramble to see, I had finally been able to let go of some of the worry, grief, and frustration that had amassed over these last few months. The jungle was the only place I had ever been able to be myself. The animals here offered me comfort and acceptance. They were my family more than anyone left back in Kardia. But I wouldn't give up on Aegeus. I would bring my brother home and protect him no matter what.

6

KADE

I SHUFFLED to the right and ducked under the punch aimed for my head. But I didn't move quick enough to miss the foot that landed in my side. The blow wasn't full force, or I'd probably have cracked ribs. My opponent backed away, letting me regain my balance. I moved forward with my fists up to protect my face. Cold sweat dotted my skin and my fists trembled as I threw a punch that she easily dodged. Rapid fire punches nailed me in the chest, knocking me back several steps.

My father's voice filled my head: *Gonna beat the evil outta you, boy.*

I fought reflexes from my childhood to curl into a ball on the floor. Every punch weighed on me like bricks piling up to bury me under all those memories. But my daddy wasn't here, and I wasn't a kid anymore. The training area wavered around me as I tried to get my arms up to block the blows, but my muscles were too tight with remembered fear to work right. Lightning flashed deep inside me and sizzled along my nerves, raising the hairs on my arms. How had my storm slipped its chains this easily? Fear gripped my chest in a vice, and I backpedaled, landing on my butt on the gym mats.

My own haunted baby blue eyes looked back at me from the wall of mirrors along the rear of the gym in the underground training area of Titan Tower—the building inside Mount Titan where we stayed while competing in the Games. Blood trickled from a cut on my lip. My black gym shorts and green T-shirt clung to my tense muscles. Cool air brushed against my damp skin. The musty scents of the cavern were replaced by the metallic sent of blood. I swiped at my stinging lip, smearing blood onto the back of my green sparring gloves. Static electricity sparked along my fingers. Whatever demon was chained way down deep inside me, it fed on anger, hate, and cravings for justice. It was my dumb luck that these sparring sessions were triggering all kinds of memories and feelings.

I clung tight to my happy-go-lucky cowboy image. Then propped my arms on my bent knees and chuckled at myself. The lightning fizzled out before it could be released.

"Great Mother, forgive me! I don't know my own strength," my sparring partner, Dia King, exclaimed, her azure eyes wide with remorse as she stared down at me. "Are you ok, Kade?"

Sweat glistened on her golden skin and dampened the long locks of multi-colored brown hair that had escaped the messy bun on her head. She'd gained a couple of inches in height since I'd last seen her. Her neon orange tank top and pink yoga pants showed off a lot more toned muscle too. Maybe those changes were what the Kyrion had meant when they'd said Dia had been "reborn" as Gaia's Chosen during the last competition?

Mama had never mentioned anything about the Chosen. But I'd never forget stumbling out of the doorway of Stone Shadow Castle disappointed that I'd lost the second competition and having a large egg-shaped rock appear right in front of me. I'd made up some excuse that I'd seen Dia inside the rock before it had closed up all the way. But the truth was I had felt Dia inside and been able to see her through the rock. I'd never been able to do anything like that before. Every time I came here to Sotirìa, my powers seemed to get a boost.

Dia offered me her hand and pulled me to my feet with little effort.

Green lights swirled around her hand as we touched, and my own powers stirred. I released her quickly, pretending to rub my sore ass. I flashed Dia a disarming smile, aiming to distract us both. "Aww sucks, ma'am, ya sure showed my backside the what-for today, but I reckon I'll survive," I said, exaggerating my Texas twang and making her laugh. "Thanks for helpin' me up, ma'am."

"Stop ma'aming me or I'll be calling you Cowboy Cutie for the rest of the Games," Dia threatened with a laugh as she brought up the nickname her best friend Lia had given me during the first competition. With Lia gone, it felt like we were missing part of the team. That feeling that tugged me toward the two best friends was strong, but I was reluctant to trust it. What if they were using their powers to influence me like the Kyrion were tampering with people's minds?

Dia's guide, Molly West, yelled from the edge of the mat for her to stop babying me and take me out next time I went down. The feisty guide had been rooting for my blood since we'd been assigned sparring partners this morning. Molly might well get her wish too if I couldn't get my head on straight. My thoughts were a mess of bad memories, worries over Hope, and trying to sort out some kinda plan to get the answers I needed around here.

"Sorry, ma—" Dia squeezed me in a bear hug cutting me off, then bounced away to get lectured by her bossy guide.

Chris Erickson grinned at me in amusement from the sidelines where the other contestants waited their turns. I shrugged in a 'what can you do' way and stepped off the mats to sit on the weight bench near my guide. Chris was the youngest of us, barely out of college. He was gangly and shy with big black glasses and shaggy dirty-blonde hair. He was a nice kid who had latched onto me as a sort of big brother ever since we met. Chris wanted to win the Games to pay back the money his grandfather had loaned him to go to college. His sparring partner, Maya Li, stood beside him with her arms crossed. The tall Asian woman had a calculator for a heart and was probably deducting points from my chances of winning. If this third competition was going to be a fight of some kind, Maya might be right about my odds. I preferred to charm my way out of a situation. There'd been enough violence in my house growing up that I tried to avoid it whenever possible, but I would do what I needed to win.

The Games required six contestants each year to compete in six competitions before the grand prize winner could be picked. Each winner of a training race was given minor prizes, but the grand prize went to the person who won the majority of the competitions. I had won the first and Dia the second. Last week we'd been sent home to wait while a new contestant was picked to replace Mikhail Lorenzo—the man who'd accidentally drowned last time. I sent up a silent prayer for his family as I made my way over to sit on a weight bench. I didn't miss the man—he'd been disrespectful to women for a start—but his death was still a tragedy. That was the one memory we all still retained from the prior times here, but it made us all a little more on edge too.

I was starting to think we might have good reason to be even more cautious. Lia had been attacked in the first competition and never returned to the Games. I wasn't too sure Mikhail hadn't also been attacked. Now another of the original contestants, Nikki Starr, had been replaced. We'd been told that Nikki—the curvy chatterbox who had spent more time trying to seduce all the men than trying to win the competitions—had dropped out. But I'd overhead the servants saying something about her being an Olympian spy.

How many more of us were here and how could I separate them out from the Paldimori?

Dia gave me a thumbs-up from across the mat as I dabbed the last of the blood from my lip. Her guide swatted her hand down like she was consorting with the enemy. I nodded back that I was all good. I stretched my legs out in front of me and grabbed the towel to wipe the sweat from my neck. We'd started off the day with a four-mile run and moved on to sparring this afternoon. I was ready for a cold shower and a beer, and it was only day one.

My guide, Cadence Paxton, handed me a bottle of water, and I thanked her before gulping down half of it. I smiled at the short, auburn haired girl hovering beside me nervously. Cadence told me that she'd been in training for a while, but this was her first time as a guide in the Games. She had taken her grandmother's place after Grace died. A pang of longing hit me to hear one of Grace's pep talks or see her knitting some padding for my ass like she would have threatened to do if she was here. Why had Grace attacked Lia and tried to force her off the island?

The sensation of cool flower petals brushed across my skin and the scent of vanilla in an exotic forest teased my nose. That seemed to happen every time my Kyrion was focused on me. I would have written it off as a Paldimori thing, but it never happened with anyone else. I raised my eyes to meet Kyrion Gaia's pale green gaze on the other side of the gym. It wasn't a hardship looking at her. She was like a fairy-tale princess all decked out in her long green dress and green robe. Star-shaped white flowers dotted the curly dark blonde hair piled loosely on top of her head. Her straight-edged nose and high cheek bones gave her a severe look that was only slightly softened by pouty pink lips—lips that never appeared to smile. She was barefoot as were the other Kyrion. She stood ramrod straight with this regal "don't touch me" air and a stillness that could make me forget sometimes that she was real. Until she opened her mouth and cut me off at the knees with a few well-placed words that reminded me too much of the cutting way my daddy had talked to me.

I doffed an invisible hat to Kyrion Gaia and watched as that frosty stare cooled a few more degrees. Sometimes I wanted to muss her up just to see if she had any real emotions under all that frost. Other times, I swear I caught a glimpse of hopeless despair in her eyes that reminded me a lot of Mama. Those times I was tempted to try to extend the olive branch. But I'd gotten frostbite once already, and I didn't enjoy the cold. Kyrion Gaia had warned me the day after I slept with the cold-eyed blonde: "That girl you slept with was not a servant to be claimed as a prize. She should never have interfered. You would do well to stay away from her before she ruins your life as she has done to others. I expected better judgment from you. Then again, you are friends with Lia, so perhaps I overestimated you to begin with. I need a Potential who is focused on winning. Do not get distracted with these dalliances again."

Apparently, I was of no use unless I was winning. For some strange reason that bothered me.

I looked away as embarrassment heated the back of my neck. My behavior that day wasn't like me. I hadn't been with many women over the years since I wanted to be there for Hope, but I usually treated them with more respect than I'd shown the blonde or my Kyrion. I had no idea what Kyrion Gaia had against the blonde but there was a deep-seated hatred there.

The two newest contestants were sparring now. The woman who had replaced Nikki was a guide by the name of Emory. She wore gray and dark eyeliner a lot. Her long black braids were streaked with a smoky purple color. She never said much when a well-placed glare or smirk would do. Another guide named Zeno had taken Mikhail's place. His chest was covered in tattoos from his neck down; he never wore a shirt and had a quick temper.

Emory ducked and sidestepped every move Zeno made. Her amethyst eyes were alight with humor as her partner's frustration at not landing a blow increased. They danced across the mat putting the rest of us to shame with their skill. Competing against these guides would have been pointless, but the Kyrion had assured us that they weren't eligible for the prize money. Instead, the two guides would be competing for a favor from their Kyrion. To make things a little fairer, they also wouldn't get their own guides and had to give the rest of us a head start in all of the competitions. Emory landed a blow, taking Zeno to his knees. She smirked as he cussed and punched the mat. He got to his feet, and they bowed to each other. Then stepped aside for the next team.

Chris caught my eye giving me a look that said "help me." His glasses were taped together over his nose after Maya had punched him in the face in the last round. Unfortunately, there was nothing I could do to help him. I gave him an encouraging thumbs-up, and he nervously stepped out onto the mat. Maya walked in measured steps toward him, likely estimating the time it would take to knock him out. They bowed to each other and the fight started. Maya came at him with a series of punches that Chris backed away from until he reached the edge of the mat. Before he could shift direction, Maya landed a punch to his gut and a kick to the back of his knee that took him down.

I winced in sympathy. Chris and I were good when it came to the running and warm-up exercises that we started off with each morning. But between the two guides and the two women kicking our asses, the shot at that prize was looking slim for us. I could only afford to lose one other time and still have the majority win. There were three more chances left after this, but I had no idea how difficult the

future competitions would be. And Hope was counting
on me.

We all had our own reasons for wanting that prize and
desperation made people do crazy things. If I was also right
about the possibility of more attacks, then this could get ugly
quick.

I watched the other contestants, making a list of what I
knew. Maya's weakness was that she overanalyzed everything and that made her hesitate to take risks. Chris was
smart but lacked physical strength and confidence. Dia was
sweet as pie and wanted to be friends with everyone but she
also had a competitive streak. Emory and Zeno were clearly
trained to take on anything. Deep down inside there was a
rumble like thunder followed by a flash of lightning as if my
power was saying "you can defeat them all if you'll use me."
The question was, how far was I willing to go to win?

7

ARIANA

I BUNCHED up the long hem of my chiffon dress as I stepped off the elevator onto the three-thousand-square-foot area that made up my floor near the top of Titan Tower. Like the Kyrion suite back home, I'd remodeled this floor to be my sanctuary while on the island. Over the years it had also become the sanctuary for the various animals the Houses had rescued from hunters and poachers. Their sounds filled the air as I crossed the tiled floor with the mosaic House of Seasons tree symbol, the hem of my robe trailing behind me. Directly ahead, a wall of glass in the sunken living room looked out over the valley below. I turned away from the portion of my floor that held all the modern trappings of a home and headed right toward the forest. My connection to the earth and creatures was a soothing balm that I sorely needed right now. The tiles ended, and my toes sank into lush green grass. The smell of greenery filled the air. The trill of birdsong welcomed me home as I navigated through the trees by rote, letting the power that lived within Sotirìa soak up through my bare feet. The power cocooned me in its familiar embrace and strengthened my connection to the Goddess Gaia.

I pulled seed from my right dress-pocket as I continued to walk and tossed it into the air. The pieces hung suspended overhead as dozens of different species of birds dived from the trees to grab their meal. I stopped as a doe and her spotted fawn came over to nibble the other pocket of my dress. I smiled and pulled out a drawstring bag of blueberries. The deer's warm presence filled my head, conveying their joy as they nibbled the sweet treat from my palm. A bit of the tension from the day eased away.

The trees and other plants swayed toward me in greeting as I continued through the forest. I stopped at a short raffia tree, that offered me a hammock made from its huge palm fronds to lie on. I settled into the makeshift bed sending my thanks to the tree through my touch. There were a thousand things that needed my attention, but for just a moment, I wanted to forget it all. A ring-tailed lemur climbed onto the branch beside me and offered me a banana that he knew I favored. I'd grown an assortment of nut and fruit trees here to keep the animals fed while I was away. I thanked him for the thoughtful gift, and he scampered off to eat his own snack of tamarind seeds. I peeled the banana and ate it slowly, my thoughts churning no matter how much I wanted to shut them out.

Lia's trial had tested me nearly to my limits. Thankfully, she was being held on the contestant floor that had been hers during the first competition, well out of the way until this competition was over. The Order had immediately gone from the trial into discussions about how to adjust to having a Chosen and two guides compete in the Games. All three were stronger and faster than those Potentials without powers. And after seeing Potential Kade Downing's performance today, he needed every advantage in this competition to secure the win for my House.

It should have been against the rules for guides and

Chosen to participate but these were unprecedented times. The invitation cards created by our ancestors to only activate for those descendants with the potential to become something more had selected Emory and Zeno. There was a saying that we Paldimori lived by: *Anerrhiphtho kybos*—let the die be cast. As much as I wanted our traditions preserved, we had no choice but to honor the will of the God of Chaos.

As was the way with all Houses, Aegeus had passed down the oral knowledge of the Kyrion while we had been at Tantalus. He had told me that the Games were designed to find the strongest descendants lost to the human world after the Chaonian War had splintered our society. And that the competitions were crafted to awaken a Potential's powers. But now I wasn't so sure. Lia and Dia had unlocked a new dimension of the Games that had led them each to waken a Primordial God: Chaos and Gaia. Bennett and I had both noticed an increase in the powers of our Houses. That had given our people a small reprieve from the continued loss of powers that grew worse with each generation of descendants, but all of our powers would continue to decline until we found a permanent solution. The answer to our salvation that I believed only the Chosen could attain.

Why had the gods not emerged when they were woken? Would their re-emergence bring back all the power we had lost?

"Aegeus, I wish you were here." I smoothed the empty banana peel between my hands. That familiar ache to have my brother back with me tightened my chest, and for a moment, I struggled to breathe past the pain. I wanted to be home searching for him more than anything, but I couldn't condemn Bennett for abandoning his duties here on Sotirìa and then do the same. Duty had to come first. "I wish you would hold me, brother, and tell me it will all be all right. I cried the day you stopped trying to touch me; but even then, I could not open up to you. If you were here now, I would share everything with you, even if you rejected me and called me the monster that I am."

Regret crushed me under its unforgiving pressure. Like gravity, it kept me grounded in my past: stuck in a cycle and never able to move forward. One day it would totally consume me. But not today. Not before I accomplished all that I needed to do to secure my brother, evict my father from my life, and help the Chosen save our people.

"Aegeus, I suspect that the Games were meant to unlock the powers of the Chosen. Centuries of contestants and never has a god been woken until now. That must mean that only the Chosen can wake the gods and somehow the Games provide them the access to do so."

I worked through all of the pieces but came back to the same conclusion. We had four more Chosen to find but very little time. Dia was our best chance. "Dia and Jaxon are working to translate the writing on the walls of the Lotus Temple. The answers must be there somewhere." My nails pierced the skin of the banana peel as uncertainty filled me. Dia had found the temple in the Emerald Rainforest here within Titan Tower, and as one of the Kòri—Gaia's warrior handmaidens—had been able to unlock its doors. "What if the writings do not give us the answers we need? What should I do, brother?"

I don't know when I'd begun talking to Aegeus like this. But it helped me to feel like he was still with me. Like there was someone who would always be there for me.

"Goddess Gaia, please guide Dia to uncover the answers we need," I pleaded. As usual, there was no response. Dia was the only person who had talked to the goddess in thousands of years, and that hurt more than I would ever admit. "If we can stay the course for a while longer, there is still a chance for our salvation. But time is a luxury that cannot be bought, and I fear ours is running out."

Yesterday a human airplane had breached the outermost barrier around Sotirìa, setting off the alarms. Protocols had been followed, and thankfully, the plane was directed away from our shores. How much longer would the protections that kept us invisible to the humans and our enemies last? The Olympian Omàda were no longer just attacking outcast villages. The House of Chaos's guard towers had been attacked recently. What would happen when our powers weakened to the point we could no longer hide?

The Kyrions' traditional renewal of our bonds with the Primordial God that we descended from were no longer enough. Even here on the island—created to be a sanctuary for our people after the Chaonian War—the powers were fading. The measures our ancestors had taken to spread the six Houses across the world and only come to Sotirìa during the Games was no longer slowing the decline. We had all tried so hard to keep our people and our ties to the gods alive, but we were failing. If the barriers crumbled completely, we would be left vulnerable.

Bitter resentment gripped me in its tight fist. "I should be home searching for you, brother. Instead, I am here catering to these Potentials just as our ancestors have done for centuries." My nails ripped into the flesh of the banana peel. I stood from my makeshift hammock and tossed the peel into the forest where it would fertilize the soil. Restless energy prickled along my body as I paced back and forth. "The Potentials come with the stench of the cities clinging to them, taking our hospitality as their due and making demands. They tout their false loyalty while greedily demanding more from us. Then have the audacity to cry foul when the competitions do not go to their liking. All the while, we Kyrion watch and wait for a sign that our people will be saved. But they all fail."

There were plenty of contestants who crossed the finish line, but few had succeeded in unlocking their powers to join our world. Those that never awakened their powers were sent home with altered memories of a nice vacation, and we would start all over again. Year after year, the competitions would end with disappointment. Then we would go back to our respective bases around the world and wait for new Potentials to be selected. This year, finally, the cycle had been broken, and we dared to believe that after generations of upholding the traditions we would be blessed with the solution to our diminishing powers. But we had been fools.

We had been betrayed by Grace when she attacked Lia and still had not found her accomplices. Our sanctuary had been endangered by Nikki when she attacked Dia with water powers that only a descendant of Poseidon would have. Then she escaped.

Our protections that kept our enemies from invading our society had failed. First the invitation card that brought Nikki to our island. Then the torque necklace that was given to each Potential to wear that should have rejected her as unworthy of the god's powers. The gems set into the necklaces were imbued with powers that offered the contestants protection and allowed them to call on their Kyrion in a time of need. But the necklaces were also designed to keep our people safe by assessing the Potential for worthiness to possess the powers of the gods. Lia had been the only one to show any reaction when the torque had been placed around her neck— another reason I doubted her—but she had ultimately passed the test. As had Nikki.

How could that be? The Olympians had turned their backs on our gods. How could one of their descendants be worthy of the god's powers?

For every step we had taken forward recently there was another setback—like the traitors among us and Lia's treasonous actions. No good came from breaking the rules, and Lia wasn't the only one to have done so. The rules protecting the

Potentials who entered the Games had also been violated with the attacks on Lia and Dia, and the death of Mikhail.

My heart said to search for Aegeus and find a way to avoid taking Bennett's position from him. My head said to take the Archigós position as Father insisted, in order to see my brother and use the position to demand our people put more efforts into helping Dia fulfill the prophecy. My rules said to not show weakness or be ruled by others. My heart, mind, and rules were at war with each other. I felt like I was being tugged in too many directions and was in danger of being ripped apart. There would be consequences for me no matter what I chose to do; just as there would be consequences for our world. Our society was unraveling quicker than any of us was prepared for.

I pressed the heel of my hand against the tree symbol between my breasts, its position at the top of my torso a testament to how powerful I was. All of this power and I still felt helpless to divert our people from this well-trodden path toward our demise. Would my decision be the catalyst to disrupt that course or the fuel to speed us toward it?

"This all seems wrong, Aegeus. Somehow Lia has disrupted the natural order of our world and the ripples of her actions are still spreading." Dread filled me just thinking about the repercussions to come. Were we seeing some of those consequences already with the increased attacks from the Omàda recently?

"Kyrion Gaia, have you returned?" Ekert called out.

I prayed to the goddess to give me strength to deal with the man occupying one of my guest rooms. I took a deep breath and wiped away all traces of the turmoil inside me. Then exited the forest to meet him by the elevator. "Good evening, Ekert. I trust your day has been productive?"

"Yeees?" he replied uncertainly. "Not that I'm questioning you, Kyrion Gaia, but is this the best way for me to learn to be co-ruler? Testing my powers by having me create the baskets and nets makes sense. But what will I learn from cataloging the animals and plants?"

All of Ekert's bravado had disappeared now that my father was no longer around to encourage him. I worked hard not to sigh in exasperation at my gullible betrothed.

"A Kyrion is always aware of their surroundings down to the smallest detail. I was testing your skills at observation," I stated. He glanced at the clipboard in his hand and then to the forest behind me with a determined look. It wasn't a lie, but there were other methods I could have used. This was just the most time-consuming. "As a descendant of Gaia, we more than any other House must care for the animals and land. How else can we help to nurture the goddess's gifts if we do not first learn about them?"

"But I know all of Kardia. Why would I need to learn about these animals and plants that come from other places?" He gestured toward Bramble who lay near the wall of windows soaking up the last rays of sun.

"We are not in Kardia now, are we?" I challenged him to think beyond the obvious. "There may be times in a Kyrion's life when we need to travel to other locations. To other Houses or even the human world."

"When would we ever need to go into the human world?"

"You will learn about the human's leadership structure and weapons in your Kyrion training," I informed him. Some Kyrion, like Jaxon, mixed with the humans regularly. He had even gotten one of their paper documents that said he could be a lawyer and helped us to settle issues that sometimes came up. My knowledge of the humans was limited to what I had overheard, but one day, I foresaw all of my people embracing those human-made tools that would make our lives easier while still staying true to our connection with nature. "Most of what we know beyond that comes from the runners' interactions with the humans. If our shields fail, we will no longer be able to remain hidden. The humans may well become necessary allies."

Ekert nodded, but he still looked confused.

I tried not to lose my patience. "Your meal will be served in the dining room here on my floor. Ask the servants for anything you need. Goodnight, Ekert." I turned to go down the hall to my own bedroom. Normally, I would sleep in the forest, but I preferred to have walls around me to keep out any prying eyes.

"Your father has asked for an update," Ekert called after me. I stopped but didn't turn around. I needed more time; however, it appeared that I wouldn't get it.

I believed in the Order of Chaos. For all of our differences, the Kyrion worked well together when faced with a common problem. At least, we had until recently. Everything was breaking apart: our traditions, our rules, our protections, our safeguards, and the Order. Jaxon and I still pushed for us to uncover more information about the prophesy and how to fulfill it. Nyx and Tartarus wanted us to embrace the weapons our new allies in the House of Light created with their blending of powers and technology. They wanted us to fight back against our enemies. Erebus, as usual, was neutral, but I could tell there was something he was waiting for. Bennett had refused to pick a side. He was like a wounded shadow, tearing himself apart over the role he had played in destroying his relationship with Lia and putting her through the trial. Guilt pricked at me, but I wouldn't change what had happened. The Order was sworn to enforce our laws and rules even when it came to those that we loved.

This was a precarious time; one wrong move could lead to our destruction. I could tell myself that our people needed a strong leader, one not distracted by personal conflicts. I could tell myself that Bennett and the other Kyrion would understand if they only knew of my predicament. Regardless, I had made my decision. I couldn't abandon Aegeus again. My father may have forced this on me, but I was determined to be the Archigós our people needed.

"Tell my father that he will have word of my success soon enough," I replied and retreated to my bedroom.

IT WAS day two of training and I had gotten my concentration mostly under control. At least enough not to get bloodied. Like the first competition, we stopped to have lunch midday in a clearing in the wooded area of the training floor. The four servant ladies assigned to me gathered around the chaise lounge I was directed to, encouraging me to put my feet up and relax. I knew things were different in the Paldimori world from my previous time here, but having servants still felt uncomfortable. I stretched my legs out on the weird couch. One of the ladies offered me a plate filled with grilled meats, cheeses, and fruit. I declined another's offer to wipe the sweat from my face with a cool cloth. The other two fanned me with large palm leaves. When I was finished eating, I moved my feet off the couch. I reached out without thought and brushed loose grass off the seat before the curly-headed servant could do it.

The lady's eyes welled with tears. "Ma'am, are you ok?" I asked in confusion.

The servant's bottom lip trembled, but she didn't say anything. I jumped to my feet worried that something was wrong with her. Cadence rushed over and patted the girl on the back. "Potential Downing didn't mean to dishonor you. He just doesn't understand our ways." Cadence looked up at me like I'd kicked a puppy. "You're happy with her work, right?"

Shit! I'd forgotten how seriously the servants took their jobs. I still didn't understand the Paldimori world. To me it seemed demeaning to make these people do things for us that we could do for ourselves. But it clearly meant a lot to these ladies to help me. Besides I didn't need to draw attention to myself. "You did amazin' handlin' that plate. And I swear I won't wipe off any more furniture."

Cadence chuckled, breaking the tension, and the servant ladies all joined in. I let out a silent sigh of relief.

I excused myself to take a walk through the woods. I needed a minute to get my racing heart back under control and just breathe without so many people around. There were whole days back home when I didn't say a word to anyone but the cows. Hope liked to tease me about being a loner sometimes and had been hinting lately that I needed to start dating. I had no plans to complicate my life even more with a relationship. I wasn't opposed to a friendly conversation, but sometimes I preferred when it was only me and the endless clear blue sky. There was a kind of peace to it that allowed me to appreciate that there was a big ole world out there beyond my problems.

I picked up a couple of rocks lying strewn along the ground and rolled them between my fingers. What was Hope doing right now? Was she still mad at me for choosing to come back here? Did she think I was no better than Daddy for taking this gamble on our future? I missed her sassing me and getting all excited about the plans she was making. It had been just me and Hope for so long, I hadn't realized how much I'd come to rely on her company. Soon enough she'd be graduating college and have her own career. Where would that leave me? Stuck with the ranch while she went off to make a name for herself and one day have a family of her own?

I hadn't thought much beyond the next bill to pay or mess to clean up in a long time. Frustration over saving the ranch, worry over Hope, and uncertainty about my own future mixed together forming a storm of emotions. Lightning flashed inside me, and the rocks I'd meant to gently toss went flying off into the woods like bullets. Damnit! I bent over and put my hands on my knees, struggling to find my calm. When that didn't work, I sat down and dug my fingers into the loose soil of a bare patch of ground. Tan grains of light trailed down my arms and down into the ground. Roots slithered between my fingers and dug into the dirt.

Memories of the first time I'd discovered I was different filled my mind. I'd been eleven. My clothes didn't fit right cuz I'd shot up three inches over the summer. Ginger fuzz had dotted my face in random patches that looked like I had the mange. My voice squeaked, and I'd started spending a lot of time in the barn with a *Playboy* that one of our ranch hands left behind when he quit. I'd been settling back on a hay bale to get down to business when grass suddenly sprouted up around me and wouldn't stop growing. Luckily, Daddy had been passed out. Mama had shown me how to clean up the mess I'd made and how to hide my powers. Some nights we would sneak out to the fields and Mama would read to me from her family journal. Then she would show me how to listen to what the land needed and give it a nudge with our powers. For a while, I'd enjoyed being special and sharing those gifts with Mama. Until Daddy found out, then everything had changed.

I forced my thoughts on to better times and slowly the storm settled. I ran my hand over the newly formed grass, feeling as if I'd planted some of my worries here so that I didn't have to carry them with me.

I returned to the clearing just as additional servants came

to clean up. Our personal servants passed out bags to each of us. The guides directed us to the grandstand area nearby where we were to change into the clothes inside the bag we'd been given. About twenty minutes later I was suited up and exited the restroom to find Cadence waiting for me. "Follow me," she said, leading me down the wide dirt path that we ran each morning as part of our warm-up. We passed by the gym area and kept going.

I tugged uncomfortably at the mock-neck collar of my new clothes, and Cadence fought a smile at my fidgeting. Her matching outfit looked a whole lot better on her petite but curvy body. I looked like a damn idiot in the one-piece green and black jumpsuit. It covered everything south of my chin and the lightweight material clung to me like a burr. The green sections on the chest, back, and sides were made of a mesh material. A series of loops rounded the waist starting at the sides and around the back like a toolbelt. Supple knee-high boots and gloves completed the strange outfit. I was just thankful that they'd put zippers in all the important places.

We stopped to wait for the other contestants to join us. I shifted my weight from one foot to the other feeling skittish as a rodeo rider sitting on the back of a bucking bronco for the first time. Once everyone had arrived, Kafàli Devon Harris—the tall black leader of the guides—commanded me to step forward. The first of the contestants to be called, I walked toward him hesitantly. Cadence trailed alongside me, her auburn ponytail swinging as she clapped like my personal cheerleader. I stopped in front of Devon, and Cadence tumbled into my side. I grabbed her arm to pull her in front of me where it was safer for everyone.

"I meant to do that," she stated with a cheery smile over her shoulder. Those words seemed to be Cadence's personal slogan. She said it every time she ran into something—which was pretty often. I tipped an invisible cowboy hat at her. She wrinkled her pale freckled nose at me, but her emerald eyes were shining with laughter.

Devon gritted his teeth as if we were a huge pain in his ass and then pointed to a rack beside him. "Get your pole and step up to the line," he snapped in his deep voice.

I grabbed the pole with the green House of Seasons symbol at the top between two vertical lines of dots. The pole was a little taller than me and heavier than expected. Cadence stayed by my side as we stepped up to the black starting line marked across the rock floor. One more step and my feet would be planted on blackened folds of lava rock. Steam seeped through cracks in the floor on the other side of that line to create hot clouds that wove through the peaks of tall red columns of rocks. The columns were of varying sizes and stood like abandoned soldiers across an area a bit smaller than a football field. A few narrow ridges with lava flowing down their sides like waterfalls cut through the sections of columns. The air smelled of smoke, and the heat radiating from the area was so intense that it made the exposed skin on my face sting.

The other contestants were called forward to grab their poles and get in line.

"This afternoon you will each train with your guide on this course. You may only move forward by using the columns or ridges." Devon gestured to the area in front of us. "There will be a practice race tomorrow with assistance from your guides. Day four, you will race on your own, with a small reward of your choice for the winner. Finally, the competition will be on day five. Get started."

Cadence tucked her arm through mine. "Ready?"

"After you, ma'am," I said only half teasing.

"Oh, I forgot to ask." She nodded toward the tallest columns at the center of the course. "You're not afraid of heights, are you?"

"I'd prefer having my feet firmly planted on the ground, but I'm up for the challenge."

She squeezed my arm and said, "You wouldn't wanna run across that ground anyway. It's been known to collapse in places."

I scratched at my short beard, trying to hide my grimace.

"I pinky promise I won't let you fall," Cadence said and wrapped her pinky around mine. Then she gave me a sunny smile and tugged me forward still holding onto my finger.

I had no idea how someone almost a foot shorter than me and weighing a heck of a lot less was going to live up to that promise, but I followed her anyway. I just kept telling myself I was one step closer to that prize money.

The black rock crumbled and slid beneath my boots as we walked toward the first short columns. Heat radiated off of the red-hot rocks as I stepped up onto a column about three feet by three feet. Sweat rolled down the back of my neck. Luckily, the jumpsuit seemed to be keeping me from frying like an egg on the hood of my truck in July. The column was just wide enough to fit both of us if we stuck close to each other. Cadence gave me an encouraging nod and shot her right hand up into the air. I looked up just as a long cord anchored to a sliding track in the rock ceiling above lowered toward us. Cadence grabbed the cord and squeezed past me to attach it to my jumpsuit. She tested it with a tug and stepped back around me.

"See," she said as she grabbed a second cord. "I never break a pinky promise."

"I never doubted you," I replied in relief.

She laughed as if she knew better and walked me through how to hook up her safety line.

"What now?" I asked.

"Now you jump," she said, giving my forearm a quick squeeze, then sliding behind me. "Oh, and don't let go of your pole. You're going to do great!"

"That's it?" I asked skeptically. "Just jump and hold on to the pole?"

"What am I forgetting?" She ticked off the list on her fingers. "Safety suit. Safety line. Hold on to the pole. Oh, make sure the ground is solid and gauge your jump; not too hard or too soft. That's about it."

"All right, here goes," I said dubiously.

I took stock of the next column about eight feet away. It was slightly wider than the one we stood on but about the same height. I stabbed the ground with the pole, testing different spots. Then my gloved hands gripped the top of the pole where the House of Seasons symbol was and I pushed off. I shouted in alarm as the pole lengthened to twice its original size, shooting me way up into the air. I dangled there for a moment with my heart galloping in my chest, drowning out whatever Cadence was yelling at me. My hands slipped several inches, and I wrapped my legs around the pole. It started to tilt to the left into another contestant's area. My gaze met Dia's wide eyes as she frantically pointed to the flying arrow symbol on her pole. What was she trying to tell me?

The pole tilted further, and I knew if I didn't do something, I was going to slam right into Dia. She pointed again and pressed one of the dots to the left of her House symbol. The pole in her hands shortened to the size of a baton. With one hand firmly gripping the pole I reached up with the other toward the line of dots beside the House symbol on mine. My finger depressed the left bottom dot, and the pole collapsed into the baton-sized version. Oh shit!

One minute I was falling and the next I was brought to a jarring halt by my safety harness. I dangled several feet above the ground, silently thanking every deity I could think of that Cadence hadn't forgotten the safety line. Cadence raised her hand, and I could see swirls of green power directed to the

track above me as she slowly lowered me back onto the
column she was still standing on.

"Now I know what I forgot." Cadence fretfully tugged at
her ponytail, her cheeks hot with embarrassment. Those big
emerald eyes glittered with tears. "The pole length is
controlled by the buttons on either side of the House symbol.
I'm so sorry, Kade. I was so excited to be here, I didn't do my
job."

I ran my hand over my short hair and took a deep breath
to calm my racing heart—and my irritation. Grace would
have given me all the information last night and told me what
to expect. I tried hard to remember that Cadence wasn't her
grandmother. I looked at her and my irritation melted. I
wasn't into kicking kittens, especially sad ones with big green
eyes.

"I'm still safe and in one piece. You kept your promise." I
patted her hand, and she gave me a wobbly smile. "Let's
agree to have a team meeting *before* we're in the middle of a
trainin' exercise, ok?"

"Deal," she agreed, holding out her pinky finger.

I laughed and gripped her pinky with mine to seal the
deal.

9

ARIANA

THE TORCHES MOUNTED on the columns lining both sides of the Order Hall flickered as if they too were as exasperated with the room's other inhabitants as I was. I had requested a meeting of the Order to determine how to bring the Games back under our control. We needed new rules to account for the challenges of our time. The Kyrion had been here for over an hour and we seemed to be talking in circles. Ordinarily, we would be downstairs watching the contestants train to assess their skills and weaknesses. But after Ekert mentioned my father wanting an update last night, I knew I couldn't delay any longer. Today would be the day I would be judged by the God of Chaos to determine if I was worthy to become the Archigós. I hadn't been able to eat all day and my nerves were fraying. I had grown used to being around the Kyrion's strong powers, but with my emotions raging, my parched tree was agitated today. It hungered and ached to be given just the smallest sip of another's power.

My palm pressed up against the underside of the massive hexagon table that took up the middle of the room. The symbols of our Houses were burned into the tabletop in front of each of us and surrounded the black sun symbol of the

Order of Chaos at the center. My fingers trembled as I fought my parched tree and the emotions threatening to overwhelm me. The wood of the table held residual traces of its former life as a living tree, and the wood rubbed against my palm as if offering comfort. That brief touch helped me to fight back the parched roots of my tree that kept trying to reach for the powers of my fellow Kyrion.

"It is for the best," I stated once again.

Bennett sat rigidly on my left, the muscle in his jaw ticking steadily. He had been in a deadly mood since the trial, likely fueled by Lia's continued refusal to see him. I feared if he spoke, he might loosen that tight grip on his control and unleash his significant powers on all of us. Even more, I feared I would relish his loss of control and feast on his powers until there was nothing left. Jaxon lounged in his seat on the other side of Bennett, one leg thrown over the arm of his chair. His foot swung harder and nearer to the table as this meeting dragged on. I was sure at any moment he was going to kick the table across the room in frustration.

Kyrion Nyx, Theia Lambros, was seated beside Jaxon and glared daggers at me as she added to my annoyance by drumming her fingers on the tabletop. Kyrion Tartarus, Remy Bronzen, sat beside her twirling a karambit knife around his left hand in a complicated series of moves like a deadly stress ball. Kyrion Erebus, Maddox Petralia, sat as silent as a ghost in his gray robe.

"I don't see why it matters if I have dinner with you boring bunch or with my bond-mate," Jaxon stated, running his fingers through his shoulder-length blonde hair.

I nearly rolled my eyes. "You only need to remain in your formal role as Kyrion during training and any other events that we attend together with the contestants. Is it too much to ask that you do what should be obvious already? To maintain the composure of a Kyrion during those times and not that of a love-besotted fool?"

Jaxon turned those midnight blue eyes on me, his normally playful smirk made a brief reappearance when he said, "There have been plenty of 'love-besotted fools' in these Games. Why change things now? The rules for the Games haven't been added to in a thousand years or more."

"You know as well as I do, Jaxon, that this is different. You did not care about the harem that followed you around looking for a turn in your bed." As a descendant of Eros, Jaxon was an attractive man that most women might find hard to resist and the contestants who came here were no exception. Now that he had completed the Desmòs with Dia, he had eyes only for her. It was keeping his hands and other body parts away from her that was the problem.

More than once she had been late to practice or mysteriously vanished along with her amorous bond-mate. I was glad that he had found his other half, but they were both distracted. It was dangerous to let your heart rule your actions. My mother had followed her heart instead of the rules by giving up the throne to my father. That one selfish act had destroyed her children's lives and our House matriarchy. We needed these new rules to keep everyone safe. "Your energetic libido aside, Potential King cannot realize her full powers with you distracting her from her training. These rules will help to alleviate any unsavory interference in training the Potentials. They cannot be distracted from their purpose."

Jaxon turned a smug look my way. "One day, Ariana, you're going to find yourself bonded to a man who will show you that life is more than your precious rules."

Theia chuckled and lifted a goblet in toast. "Thank the gods one of you said it. This is the most excitement we've had since that one Potential of Maddox's thought he was a demon and tried to barter her soul for a smoothie shop in Cabo San Lucas. Remember that, Maddox?" Theia pushed her long black hair behind her ear as she smirked at Kyrion Erebus. He sat beside me in his gray robes, his tanned face, framed by his black hair and beard, expressionless. He remained silent, although his silver eyes gleamed with amusement.

"See, even Maddox agrees with me," Theia insisted. "You seriously want to make more rules to cut out what little fun we might have? That stick up your ass is starting to chafe the rest of us, Ariana."

"Grow up, Theia," I said, leveling her with a stern look. The roots of my parched tree lurched toward her and my fingers dug into the table until one of my nails broke. The pain in my finger helped me regain command as dread, desperation, and anxiousness ate at me. *Is now the time? Would the God of Chaos find me a worthy Archigós? Will I be able to lead our people to a better future than what we face now?*

My tangled emotions had me lashing out at Theia as I said coldly, "This is not one of your father's businesses that you can dabble in until you get bored. You are a Kyrion until the God of Chaos marks your replacement. The title demands great respect and responsibility. It should not be abused to entertain you. Our people are dying while we sit here pandering to these Potentials and hoping they will show the slightest ounce of promise. We need to support Gaia's Chosen, Dia, in solving the prophecy."

Little arcs of electricity danced around Theia's fingers as her drumming on the table became louder. Static electricity lifted strands of her hair as her anger rose. My powers flexed beneath my skin like a hungry snake, scenting the air for more. Always more. I feared my parched tree could consume the powers from the whole of our world and still be hungry. I took a drink of my wine as I recited my rules until my powers calmed.

Theia slammed her goblet down on the table, her ample breasts nearly spilling out of the top of her low-cut white dress as she leaned forward. "You think I don't know that? The sooner we're done with the Games, the sooner we can return home. Unlike the rest of you stuffy blowhards, I actually have a life waiting for me back in Nemeseia."

Spoiled. Selfish. Entitled brat.

Of course, Theia wanted to return to the home base for the House of Night. She was more concerned with parties and luring men to her bed with her scandalous fashion sense than saving our people. At only twenty-six, Theia and Jaxon were the youngest amongst the Kyrion and hadn't been shaped by the same experiences as the rest of us. Tantalus hadn't systematically stripped away their individuality and reshaped them into the mold of a traditional Kyrion. Theia's parents had refused to send their precious little girl to such a place. And Jaxon had been spared the worst of it because of Bennett's fierce protection of his adopted stepbrother. I don't think either of them realized how fortunate they were.

My palm pressed harder underneath the table until the wood quivered beneath my touch. *I am sorry, my friend.* I sent the message into the wood as I gentled my touch. The wood wrapped around my hand in a brief hug that smoothed the frayed edges of my nerves. Even though Theia and I exchanged volleys quite frequently, I didn't usually let her antics rankle me. Today I was on edge and knew I would not find peace until I did what must be done.

"Do not be so eager to rush the Games. After all we have seen this year, I fear the ending will not be what we expect," I cautioned.

"Some of us would welcome change and the chance to get our society caught up to the twenty-first century." Theia shot me a fake smile as her finger traced her House symbol on the table pointedly. "Look, all I'm saying is that maybe if you could accept that the rules are fine as they are and traditions are sometimes meant to be broken, we could get back to the Games." She sat back in her chair, her plump lips set in a pout. "You should be happy; I don't have a chance of winning with the spineless college boy that got picked for my House.

How is it even fair that these two"—she hitched her thumb toward Remy and Maddox—"get to let their guides compete? Let's all put our guides in the Games and finish this."

As the only two matriarchal Houses, Theia and I should have been a united force to be reckoned with. Yet, every Kyrion of the House of Night had resented the fact that they weren't as powerful as those descended from Chaos, Gaia, and Eros. Our Houses were strongest because our gods were the first made and were created directly from Chaos' essence. But our historical records suggest the methods used in that creation weakened Chaos enough that it was nearly a century before he created the other three gods. Whatever methods were used to create Tartarus, Erebus, and Nyx had slightly dampened their powers. There was even more tension between my House and Theia's because our powers were nearly polar opposites: Gaia was pure light, while Nyx leaned more toward the darker side. Since the Houses of Nyx, Tartarus, and Erebus were weaker in power, they tended to band together. I fully expected Remy and Maddox to jump in with their agreement, but they remained silent.

"There is no conspiracy against your House, Theia," I assured her again. "Maddox and Remy's guides were *selected by invitation* to participate in the Games. You saw this happen the same as we did. The gods are responsible for this, not us. Let it go."

"Enough," Bennett barked. "Ariana has good reason to want these new rules added." No one dared mention what had happened with Lia, but with the way everyone suddenly avoided eye contact, we were all thinking it. "I agree to the proposed rule changes. I, Bennett Theo Young, Archigós of the Paldimori and Kyrion of the House of Chaos, issue these additional rules into effect immediately for the Paldimori Games: Rule Four—Kyrion will maintain the comportment expected of their station when interacting with all contestants. Rule Five—Kyrion who suspect that a contestant might be a viable bond-mate must report this, and it will be the decision of the Order as to what actions need to be taken."

The binding power of the new rules rushed over us. Then Bennett pushed away from the table and strode out of the room. Relief filled me, but that was quickly followed by unease. Bennett had implemented those rules without setting it to a vote for the Order to decide. I looked around the table and saw the same worried looks on the other Kyrion faces. Bennett had done the same thing a couple of weeks ago when Lia asked him to abolish the law that prevented communication with or providing protection to outcasts. Was Father right? Was Bennett too consumed by his relationship with Lia to be the leader we needed now more than ever?

Jaxon rose from his chair and gave me a mocking salute. "If you'll excuse me, I'm going to spend the rest of what's left of this day with my bond-mate. My 'energetic libido' has needs, you know."

Theia got to her feet and smoothed her short dress down over her shapely hips. "At least my father taught me to bend before I break. What did yours teach you, Ariana?"

You do not want to know the answer to that, I thought as she sauntered away, oblivious to the burning thorn that she had pricked me with.

Remy nodded to me. "We will bring in other guides to assist where needed, since Emory and Zeno will now be contestants." He hesitated for a moment, his whiskey-colored eyes appearing to glow softly in the dim room. "You give Theia too little credit, Ariana. She may not have been through what we did, but she is not the weak child that you believe her to be. Do not let your black-and-white rules blind you to the truth." Then he walked away.

Maddox cocked his head to the side as if he was waiting for something from me. Then he nodded and left as well.

What would my father do if he found out I had missed my chance today? Would Aegeus suffer because I still hesitated to remove Bennett from his rightful seat? The urge to rush back to Kardia and find my brother before Father found out about this was nearly too much to resist.

I sat there in my chair, alone. Always alone. My chest tightened with the weight of every decision laid out before me, and I knew my reprieve today was only prolonging this torture. It was as if I was slowly sinking into quicksand with no escape possible. Even if I were to reach out for a helping hand—seeking the comforting touch of others that I both craved and feared—I knew no one would be there to save me from my burdens.

Darkness surrounded me. I blinked my eyes just to make sure they were open, but it was the same endless black. My ears strained to pick up any noise but there was nothing. Cold pricked my skin like knives making me shiver so hard my body jerked awkwardly, my hand hitting what felt like rough stone. Sapphire eyes blinked awake several feet in front of me. I shielded my eyes as the bright blue lit up the dark like the sun. The eyes dimmed to a soft glow, and I dropped my hand. A naked man stared back at me from his place sitting on the stone floor. His long black hair covered most of his body and the floor around him. It was matted with dirt, rocks, and bones. A bowl of water, a half-eaten moldy piece of bread, and the bones from hundreds of rats were scattered around him indicating he'd been here for a long time. Thick cuffs with strange writing on them circled his thin wrists and ankles. Scars, dried blood, and dirt covered his pale body. The air smelled like mold, decay, and a ripe sewer.

I crouched down to his level like I had done many times when Hope was scared as a child. I kept my voice low and friendly as I said, "I'm Kade. Can you tell me your name?"

His eyes widened, and he looked around anxiously.

"I'm not gonna hurt you," I promised him. I moved forward a

*step and pointed to the cuffs. "I wanna help you. Can you tell me
where the key is?"*

*His thin arm lifted, the muscles wiry but still showing strength.
The chain that attached the cuff to the wall clanked as he started to
point to something. The scuff of feet sounded behind me. The man's
eyes widened, and he grabbed the chain keeping it still as he lowered
his arm. His lips struggled to form words, but no sound came. It
took me a minute to read his lips as they slowly formed the word
"Go!" I looked over my shoulder as more sounds came but there was
only darkness. I turned back to him determined to help, but he shook
his head. Those sapphire eyes brightened until again they lit up the
room. Suddenly a gust of wind hit me, and I was falling down into
darkness.*

I jerked awake, sitting up in bed with my heart galloping
in my chest. I scrubbed my hand over my face and paused at
the tingling of my fingertips as they began to heat back up.
My whole body shivered with cold, and I bunched the blankets around me. I had dreamed of those sapphire eyes every
time I came back to Sotirìa, but this was the first time I'd ever
seen more than that. What did it mean? Who was the man
and why was he a prisoner?

Once I was warm, I kicked the covers aside and put on my
jeans and a black T-shirt. There was no going back to sleep
after that disturbing dream. It was still dark outside the wall
of glass that made up one side of my bedroom. I finally had
my chance to get some answers around here. I made my way
to the elevator and pushed the Up button remembering that
we'd been told the Kyrion lived toward the top of Titan
Tower. If any information about my powers or a secret
weapon to keep Hope safe was stored here, I was guessing
the Kyrion kept it close to them. I just had to avoid getting
caught snooping on their floors. The doors opened, and I
stepped inside the oval-shaped interior with its mahogany
panels. A projection of the starry night sky moved across the
elevator ceiling. Dozens of buttons with symbols on them

lined the wall beside the elevator doors. I pushed one at random and pressed myself against the side wall to avoid being seen immediately when the doors opened.

The elevator slid to a smooth stop and the smell of the ocean drifted through the open door. I listened for any sounds but only heard falling water. I cautiously exited the elevator, stepping out onto a stone walkway lined with tall columns that ran along three walls of this floor. My breath seemed loud in my ears as I quickly hid behind one of the wide columns. I peeked around the right side of the column taking in the area. A soft breeze came through the open fourth side of the room across from me. The moon hung low in the sky beyond, lighting up the mountain ridges far below and spilling into the room. A rocky cliff jutted out from this room over the valley below. The water from the huge pool that took up the center of the room spilled over the edge of that cliff and down the mountainside. Six large stone statues of the Primordial Gods—three on each side—stood beside the square pool with water pouring from their raised hands. The only color on the statues was the robes they wore similar to the Kyrions' in black, green, red, gold, gray, and white. On the domed ceiling above, a painting of twin galaxies looked down from a starry sky like a pair of eyes.

Vanilla mixed with some exotic forest scent reached me, and my hands gripped the column in panic. I knew that scent and the woman who wore it wouldn't be happy to find me outside my rooms. When the crack of harsh words didn't come, I peered around the other side of the column I was hiding behind. Off to the left of the room, Kyrion Gaia moved down a set of underwater steps into a rectangular section of the pool that was separated by a low wall. She looked like the fairy-tale princesses from the books Hope had loved for me to read to her when she was little. Dark blonde curls hung loose down to the middle of her back. Her peach-toned skin seemed to glow in the moonlight. The knee-length thin nightdress she wore showed off her natural curves making my jeans uncomfortably tight in the groin. Steam rose up around her from the heated water that lapped at her stomach when she stopped in the center of the pool. Her head dropped to her chest and her shoulders stooped as if the weight of the world sat there.

An oily sensation moved inside me making me think of that cold-eyed blonde I'd spent the night with. I could practically feel her hands on me again, and I thought I heard a female voice whisper, "*Ah, there you are, cowboy.*" My arousal quickly died away as a sick feeling swept over me and grew with every touch of that oily blackness inside me. I took a step back toward the elevator with no thought but to escape that sensation.

Kyrion Gaia's pale green eyes snapped up to meet mine. The woman who I'd come to recognize as a predator who picked off weak prey with a few cutting words or damning looks was gone. The woman who looked at me right now with pain spilling out from her eyes was a wounded soul silently screaming for help. My heartbeat stuttered like she had reached into my chest and given it a squeeze. Images flashed through my head of Mama looking at me like that every time she cleaned the blood from my skin when Daddy had gone at me with his belt. The skin along my back itched. Thunder rumbled and lightning flashed deep inside me.

Justice.

The rumble of thunder seemed to repeat that word over and over again inside me. My fists clenched and arcs of white light flashed brighter inside me, begging to be let loose. Another image came to me of Daddy lying in the mud at my feet with blood coating his face. I stopped in my tracks. No, I wouldn't become my father. I wrestled the lightning back down and shook out my hands, forcing myself to relax. I hadn't realized that I'd moved to the edge of the pool, but I stood there right out in the open. There was no possibility I could hide now. All I could do was wait to see what my Kyrion would do.

That female voice whispered, *"Interesting. We're going to have so much fun together."* Then the oily darkness inside me disappeared. I shook my head thinking maybe I was going crazy.

Kyrion Gaia's brow furrowed in confusion. She pressed a hand between her breasts where the tree symbol of her House showed through the thin material of her nightgown. Then it was like shutters slammed down, and all that I'd seen in her eyes disappeared behind that frosty exterior. That glacial gaze warned me to keep my distance. "Potential Downing," she said in that condescending voice that I hated. "How did you get here?"

"The elevator," I answered, hooking my thumbs in the belt loops of my jeans and slouching a bit to look like the laid-back cowboy who just got confused about where I should be.

She gave me a look that said my bullshit wouldn't be tolerated, but with a weary-looking wave of her hand she dismissed me. "This floor is off-limits to contestants. I am not sure how you were able to enter without the room … without security alerting me, but you need to leave."

I nodded, letting out a silent sigh of relief. "Yes, ma'am."

I turned to leave but then hesitated. *What are you doin', Kade? Just go before she decides to ask more questions.* Then I remembered the pain in her eyes and turned back around. "Leavin' would be the easy thing to do but maybe not the right thing." I had the feeling that I'd surprised her, but it was hard to tell with how tightly she kept herself locked down. "You can tell me it's none of my business, and I'll respect that. But it seems like you might be havin' trouble sleepin' too. I can be a pretty good listener if you wanna talk about it."

She looked up at me with a confused expression as if no one had ever offered to listen to her problems. Even with the cold barrier she'd pulled around herself that warned me off, she still looked lost. She reminded me of the painting hanging on my sister's bedroom wall. Rapunzel had been one of Hope's favorite princess books when was she was little. I'd bought the painting based on the Brothers Grimm version of Rapunzel for Hope from an artist's tent at the county fair. Kyrion Gaia looked just like that sad and lonely girl looking out at the world from her tower balcony. The only difference was my Kyrion seemed to be trapped inside herself. Her fingers clenched tight around the ends of her wet hair before she pushed it back over her shoulder. It was a telling gesture of the stress she was trying to hide.

She opened her mouth to say something but all that came out of was a soft hiss as I began to undress. Her thin dress was nearly transparent and clung wetly to her skin. It was hard to keep my eyes from straying down that tempting body, but I managed it. I kept my eyes locked on hers as I started down the steps in my boxers. Her mouth dropped open and a pretty blush spread across her cheeks. I may have flexed my muscles a bit more than needed as I walked into the pool. Kyrion Gaia blushed even harder and hastily turned her back to me. I couldn't help the smile that spread across my face. Kyrion Gaia wasn't the cold, regal robot she pretended to be.

She controlled herself way too quickly and turned to me with that cold mask back in place. "Potential Downing, I thought I made myself clear that you were to leave."

"You did, ma'am," I agreed as I leaned back against the low wall separating this heated portion of the pool from the rest. I stretched my arms out on top of the wall, getting comfortable. I'd spent weeks taming my horse, Juniper, after I saved her from a neighbor who was going to put her down. She'd been prone to biting anyone who got too close, not much different from my Kyrion. Patience went a long way in dealing with fractious animals, and I'd guess, sharp-tongued women too. "This water looked like it might help with the aches left behind from our sparrin' today. Seems to me this pool is big enough for the both of us."

I closed my eyes and let my body slide down into the water before she could say anything. Kyrion Gaia may have been several inches shorter than me, but I didn't doubt she could force me outta this room if she wanted. I wasn't gonna give her the opportunity. I hadn't realized how tense I was until each muscle began to relax with the warmth from the water surrounding me. It was peaceful and calm under the water, something my life had never been. I wondered about Kyrion Gaia's life, but I wouldn't ask. Someone that guarded wasn't about to open up easily.

Why was I here trying to help a woman who only saw me as a game piece to be moved around for the best chance at winning the competitions?

I knew why, but I felt stupid admitting it. That glimpse of vulnerability she'd shown tonight had caught me and reeled me in. Not just because that pain I'd seen reminded me of Mama but because seeing that crack in my Kyrion's tough exterior had reminded me of myself as well. I'd had Hope to pull me outta my downward spiral; who did Kyrion Gaia have? But there had been something about her even before tonight that kept pulling at me, like she was someone I should get to know even though that sharp tongue reminded me every time that getting close was a mistake.

My breath ran out long before I was ready to resurface. I stood up and wiped the water from my face. My eyes meet my Kyrion's across the width of the heated pool. Her eyes dipped down to my chest, and for a minute, something flashed across her face that looked very close to longing. But it was gone so quickly I must have imagined it. I leaned back against the short wall once more and let the silence stretch out between us.

"Why are you here, Potential Downing? Why enter the Games?" she asked in a breathless voice a while later.

Fear that she suspected something knotted my muscles up once again.

"To win the money just like everyone else," I replied with a sheepish smile.

"Your words say one thing, but your actions say another," she stated with a calculating look. "It is my job as your Kyrion to watch and assess you. You have good instincts, but you hold yourself back. In the first competition you attempted to circle back around to help Potential Lia Davies when her chariot ran off the road, nearly costing you the win." She tapped a slender finger with a broken nail against her chin. "In the second, you gave up your lead position to make sure Potential Dia King was unharmed and then you let her go up the trail to the ridge first. That time you *did* lose. When your guide is near, you are more concerned with her safety than your training. And your sparring with Potential King was deplorable." She listed what she saw as my faults like we were simply discussing the weather over afternoon tea. What had made her go from semi-relaxed to attack mode? "Do you think those women or anyone else here needs to be rescued? Let me assure you they do not."

I hadn't been able to save Mama. My chances of saving our ranch and protecting Hope were looking slim as well. "I'm no hero," I replied.

"Yet, you still want to be," Kyrion Gaia taunted me. "Or is it that you are too afraid of letting yourself off of the leash? Do you imagine that you will win these Games by continuing to play the gentleman? You will lose. And fail at achieving whatever your real reasons are for needing that money."

Her harsh declarations landed like a series of knock-out punches that left me reeling. I struggled not to show how her words had hit their mark. "How can I go wrong with you and Cadence to train me?"

"By continuing to hold yourself back," she replied, refusing to let this go. She crossed her arms, her eyes blazing

with conviction. "The world needs more gentleman like you
—everywhere but on the battlefield. And that is exactly what
the Games are—a fight to see who the best is. Winner takes
all. If you cannot focus and fight as if your life depends on it,
then you are of no use to me. Will you be the champion my
House deserves or not, Potential Downing?"

Her words reminded me how like my daddy she really
was. Why had I wanted to help this shrew? Anger scalded my
chest: at her for calling me out and at myself for being gullible
enough to think this woman needed anyone. I hadn't had a
choice but to take the verbal and physical abuse Daddy
dished out when I was a child. But I wasn't a helpless boy
anymore, and I refused to just take her words lying down.

"Wantin' to help others isn't a weakness. Everyone needs
a helpin' hand at some point, even you." My curled fists
pressed into the wall behind me. "My mama worked herself
to the bone every day of her life under the thumb of an angry
drunk with a gamblin' addiction. All she got in return was
black eyes and broken bones for tryin' to keep him from
runnin' our ranch into the ground. I couldn't protect Mama,
but I made a promise to her on the day she died that I would
be the kind of man she would be proud of. I've worked hard
at being a better man than my daddy, and I think she'd be
pleased with how I turned out. What would your mama say
about you, Kyrion Gaia? What would you say about
yourself?"

The blood drained from her face, and she braced her hand
against the side of the pool looking like she was going to be
sick. My anger cooled immediately. There was no victory here
when we both were left hurting. Never again would I let
myself be drawn into this verbal sparring match.

"I'm sorry, ma'am. That was uncalled for." She stared at
me with that haunted look making me want to go back these
last few minutes and erase my words. I cleared my throat. "I
told you about my mama so you might understand that I'll

never agree that protectin' anyone else is a weakness ... but I can see where it could hurt my chances of winnin' these Games." I scrubbed my hand over my short hair, trying to find the words to get us back on steady ground. "I might not be the Potential you want, but it looks like I'm all you've got. Just like you and Cadence are all I've got to help get me ready for these competitions." I offered her a sheepish smile. "You and me don't have to like each other to do what needs doin' to win the Games. I'll agree to stop holdin' back and tryin' to save everyone around me unless they ask for my help. If you agree to a do-over between us." I walked to the middle of the pool and held my hand out toward her. "We might find we actually make a good team if we can put our differences aside. What'll it be, ma'am?"

She had regained her composure again and walked regally toward me. She didn't take my hand but said firmly, "Agreed. On one condition," she continued defiantly, and I almost grinned, "you call me Kyrion Gaia or my lady. Not ma'am."

"You have yourself a deal, ma—uh, my lady."

"Good," she said and headed for the steps. "Then you will train with me."

11

"I couldn't protect Mama ... I think she'd be pleased with how I turned out. What would your mama say, Kyrion Gaia? What would you say about yourself?" Kade's words played on repeat through my shower. They followed me as I dressed in a green jumpsuit similar to those the contestants wore. He'd meant to wound me the way my words had wounded him, but he'd done something much worse—he had made me question those things I considered absolute.

I knew next to nothing about my mother, yet I had blamed her for the misery of my life. Her choice to give up the throne had seemed selfish and immature. Without that one act Syris would never have been able to corrupt our House the way he had. Never once had I asked myself what her life had been like to lead her to the choices she made. But I was asking those questions now. Had Tantalus broken something in her like Father said? Goddess knows, there were days while I was there that I begged for the constant cycle of training and torture to be over with.

I braced my hands against the bathroom sink and studied myself in the mirror. Since my release from Tantalus ten years ago, when I had finally gained command over my powers, I'd pursued my goals with a single-minded intensity that allowed room for nothing else in my life. Operating in the shadows, I'd helped the less powerful by making and sometimes taking things they needed from the palace. My brother never mentioned my activities, likely because I overheard a lot and was able to help him in small ways by passing along information. Removing my father's blight upon our House had proved more difficult. In fact, working toward any of my previous goals had gotten considerably harder with the added duties of being the Kyrion and dealing with my father.

I had become too wrapped up in outsmarting Father and lost sight of who I wanted to be. Maybe I had become more like my father than I realized.

I had been restless tonight, my mind unable to rest from all of my worries and the need to be searching for Aegeus. Kade had walked onto the wading pool floor and offered something no one else ever had: someone to listen. My defenses had kicked in, and I'd pushed him away. But he'd shocked me by refusing to leave, and I admired him for it. Lounging back against the low wall, he'd looked far too handsome, and I'd started to notice things about him that I hadn't before. He wasn't just my Potential but a person. A confident person who wasn't afraid of doing what he believed was right no matter what. A kind person who genuinely wanted to help people without expecting something in return. I'd judged Kade as foolish and incompetent. Someone who would never survive in my world of power struggles and hidden agendas. But maybe I was wrong. Maybe his strength came from an inherent goodness that couldn't be tainted by me or anyone else.

I didn't know, but I wanted to learn more. It was as if once my eyes had been opened, I could no longer look away. My skin had tingled like it was charged with static electricity as he watched me tonight. The silence had built between us, and I'd nearly given in to the need to walk across that pool to touch the hard planes of his chest. I wanted to know if there were truly people like him in the world or if he was pretending. That's why I'd demanded that he train with me.

I used my powers to bring my staff to me as I boarded the elevator. The door opened on the training floor, and I was torn between wanting to go back and daring to move forward. Baby blue eyes assessed me from head to toe and everywhere they touched my skin tingled.

"Maybe we should get Cadence," Kade suggested in a husky sounding voice.

A vision of Kade's lean muscled body in nothing but a pair of black underwear made my pulse race. My throat went dry as I imagined his touch on my skin. I suppressed the shiver of excitement and—if I wasn't mistaken—arousal that wanted to take over my body. *Rule number two: no one will ever fully own me as long as my mind, body, and soul are my own.* "We are the only ones awake, and there is no time to waste if you truly want to win. The other contestants will be here in a few hours."

I used my powers to pin the long locks of my hair up with purple and white *Mondia whitei* flowers that grew in the arbor that surrounded my throne back in Kardia. Kade moved close enough that I could feel his body heat all along my back. I held myself perfectly still, unused to trusting anyone this close. My parched tree took advantage of my moment of inattention and struck.

Horror filled me. I turned with a warning on my lips but green lights already surrounded Kade. They twisted around his body as if looking for a way in. I stared in shock. The thirsty roots of my powers had never hesitated to sink immediately into someone and begin to drink. But it was almost as if a shield surrounded Kade. What were his powers? How strong was he? Could his powers not be taken because they hadn't awakened yet?

I snapped out of my shock and pulled my powers back.

Kade watched me curiously but didn't say anything. I stepped back, putting plenty of distance between us. The possibility that my powers couldn't hurt Kade made me tempted to reach out and touch him. For just a moment I imagined feeling his hand in mine, and I ached to take back the distance I'd put between us. But I wouldn't risk his life on a guess. I turned to the rack to grab the pole for the House of Seasons and tossed it to Kade. He caught it easily, but I didn't stick around to watch his muscles strain that tight jumpsuit.

"Now the real training begins," I called over my shoulder as I walked onto the course.

I led Kade over to a pair of columns about waist high and planted my staff against the black lava rock. Using the staff to assist me, I jumped onto the column and gestured for Kade to climb onto the other. "For this competition, that will be your greatest asset," I motioned to the pole in Kade's hands. "Think of it as an extension of yourself. With the pole you can jump higher, reach further, grip tighter, and so on." I tapped the tree symbol near the top of my staff. "You have already seen what the buttons on either side of the House symbol will do. The pole can do much more if you can master it."

The writing on my staff began to glow with a green light as I fed my powers into it. This would be one of the ways in which Kade's powers would be tested. If he could make a connection with the pole, he would be able to make it obey his every command. If he wanted the pole to form into a sword, a ladder, or a climbing rope it would do that and much more. "Any tool can become a weapon in the right hands." I twirled my staff in my hands. The wind blew strands of my hair around my face as I twirled it faster and faster until it was nothing but a blur. Then I sent it spinning toward a rock nearby. The force of the impact shattered the rock and pieces scattered across the ground. "Your task today is to learn to rely on the pole and form a connection with it as if you were one."

I jumped from the rock and retrieved my staff. I walked Kade through a series of exercises. First, he practiced using the buttons on the pole in a variety of situations and drawing it quickly from the various loops on his jumpsuit. Then we moved on to attack and defense motions. The heat was intense in this simulated version of Tartarus's punishing fields, and we took frequent breaks to rehydrate. I made Kade climb the side of one of the tall columns of rocks and guided him on how to use the pole to assist him. Then we practiced vaulting and then combined defense moves with everything he had learned well into the morning.

Kade missed the early warm-up exercises with the other contestants, but I notified the other Kyrion telepathically. Still, we received a couple of questioning looks when the other contestants finally joined us on the training course. Kyrion weren't usually very hands-on with training, plus Kade was dripping with sweat and his face was smudged with black from the rocks. They likely thought he was being punished.

"Guide Paxton," I called to the girl standing on the starting line and looking like she had no idea what to do with herself. "Join us."

Cadence walked over with her shoulders slumped and gave me a stiff bow. Kade watched the exchange silently, but he'd angled himself to step in front of Cadence to protect her if need be. That he thought he had to protect my own people from me was irritating, but I shrugged it off.

"I meant no offense, Guide Paxton, in taking on your duties. You needed your rest, and I was already awake," I explained gently. "You have performed your duties well in the Games. Your grandmother would be proud."

The young girl smiled at me and stepped forward as if she would hug me before she caught herself. She dipped into a deep bow. "Thank you, Kyrion Gaia, for your kind words."

I could feel Kade's gaze on me like static electricity tingling over my skin, but I ignored him. "Our Potential is in need of your service now," I advised Cadence. "You will attack, and Potential Downing will use all that I have taught him to defend himself as he moves along the rock columns. Let us begin."

About midday I called a halt to our training and we all walked toward the lagoon where the servants had set up lunch. Once out of sight of the contestants, I teleported back to my room to shower and change. I grabbed an apple from the kitchen and finished it off before walking to the elevator. Ekert came out of the forest as I started to push the button. Red splotches of smashed strawberries stuck to his light blue tunic. His matching pants were covered in grass stains. The pages on the clipboard he held were ripped and covered in dirt.

"Ekert, are you all right?"

"These animals have no respect for their rulers," Ekert jabbed his finger toward the forest. "Look what they've done to me!"

"What ..." I cleared my throat to keep from laughing. "What happened?"

"I saw those lemurs take food from the kitchen," Ekert explained while he picked a chunk of strawberry off his shirt. "I chased them down and demanded that they give back the Kyrion's food. Instead, they threw it at me! Then a marmot stole my clipboard. That fox of yours ran between my legs when I tried to get it back, causing me to fall. The birds ripped my notes and tucked the paper into their nests. This whole forest is out of control!"

The forest was suspiciously silent behind him. I suddenly wished I had one of those human contraptions that made copies of real life onto paper—picture takers, I think they were called. A paper of Ekert in this condition would look better on the walls of the palace than Father's choice of paintings. "Animals are Gaia's gifts, untamed by her hand nor ours. They are not servants, Ekert. I am sure that having an unfamiliar person in their territory upset them."

"I'm the one upset!" he screeched. "Kyrion Gaia, I respectfully insist that I accompany you as you perform your duties. Your father agrees with me. He has asked that I tell that you he wishes to speak with you this evening about your approach to my training and the progress on your promotion."

Since neither Syris nor I trusted each other with telepathy that could leave a person open to mental manipulation, we mostly communicated through other methods. Apparently, Father had appointed Ekert as his communicator rather than going through Fayel. Gaia give me strength; my time had run out. The apple I'd just eaten soured in my stomach at the thought of having to talk to Father directly. I would ensure my mental shields were fortified. What would he do when he learned I'd missed my chance to take the Archigós position once already? "Of course, I will speak with my father tonight as he has requested. Go and clean up quickly. I must return to the training soon."

While Ekert retreated to his room to shower and change, I walked into the forest. Bramble poked her head out of some bushes, and I chuckled. "Good girl." I praised her and rubbed her head when she came forward to brush against me. The other animals came out of hiding as well. "Thank you all for that entertaining gift."

Ekert returned moments later and we silently took the elevator to the training floor. I sent a mental message to the Kyrion and others who would need to make adjustments for my guest. *"My future co-ruler will accompany me today to observe my duties."*

We walked into the lagoon area, with Ekert slightly behind me as was tradition. I moved toward my seat, the only empty tall-backed chair that sat near the rocky edge of the lagoon. A smaller chair was placed behind mine for Ekert. I

declined the servant's offerings, my stomach tied in knots
about my upcoming conversation with my father. Ekert
ordered servant after servant to bring him things, adding to
my irritation. He, like Father, treated our servants as if they
were inferior instead of valued members of our House that
deserved our respect for their loyal service.

To distract myself from Ekert and Father, I watched the
group sitting in the grass across from the lagoon. The contestants and guides sat in small clusters, talking and finishing
their lunch. Servants roamed the area beginning to gather up
finished dishes. My eyes wandered over to Kade of their own
accord. He sat with Cadence, Dia, and Chris. They all seemed
to be laughing at something as Kade twirled his hand in the
air over his head and then flung his hand out. It was something I'd seen kids in the hamlet back home do when they
were roping pigs. As if he felt my gaze, Kade looked right at
me. He doffed an invisible cowboy hat my way. Instead of
irritating me as it usually did, I found myself somewhat
charmed and nodded back. There was an infectious vitality
around him that drew people in, and I was no exception.

Kade's gaze slid to Ekert behind me. His lips moved but I
couldn't make out the words. I assumed he was asking about
Ekert since Cadence glanced our way. I wondered what she
would tell him and surprised myself by hoping she didn't
mention our betrothal.

I tapped into my connection with nature and used the
trees closest to the group to listen to their conversation.
"That's Ekert Nazary," Cadence said. "He's the son of one of
the most powerful families in the House of Seasons. He's here
to, uh, learn about House duties at the Games."

"Why's he sittin' with the Kyrion?" Kade asked with an
edge to his voice that wasn't there before. "Seems like he'd
learn more from the servants."

Cadence fumbled to give him an explanation without
sharing all my personal details and my estimation of her went

up. She was going to do great things once she found her place amongst the guides. "Oh well, uh, I mean he's not a servant. Uhm, he's actually ... he's going to be Kyrion G—"

"Lunch is over," I declared, teleporting in right behind Kade.

The servant collecting dishes from Dia bobbled his tray in surprise. His tray tipped toward the contestants and the dishes started to fall. The servant's mouth gaped open in silent terror, his eyes not on the coming mess, but on me. I reached out with my telekinesis, stopping the dishes before they fell and sliding the tray underneath them. I held the tray out to the servant who bowed to me deeply, apologizing for his clumsiness.

"Rise and take the dishes to the kitchen," I stated gently to the terrified servant. "The fault is mine for startling you."

The servant stared with wide eyes and gingerly took the tray from my hands. He bowed repeatedly as he backed away. Cadence smiled up at me like I was her idol, and I straightened uncomfortably. I wasn't the kind of person anyone should want to imitate. Kade stood and helped the women up. I turned to walk toward the training course, and Kade fell into step beside me. Only my bond-mate should ever take position beside me, but I didn't say that. I suddenly felt awkward and didn't know what to say to the man.

"I think your mama would be proud," Kade whispered to me. "We're gonna make a fine team, partner."

Warmth and joy filled my heart. I dared not look at my Potential for fear everyone would see that there was a crack in my armor that he was slowly whittling away at. Ekert rushed over to us and started to lecture Kade about knowing his place. Kade just doffed that invisible hat again and jogged ahead of us leaving my future co-ruler to sputter in disbelief. I covered my mouth to hide my smile. How many times had I smiled today? I'd spent hours in the jungle playing and laughing with the animals. But all I'd really noticed about people was whether they were an ally or an enemy. Until Kade Downing offered me kindness and made me think about the kind of person I wanted to be. I felt myself changing around him and it terrified me. I needed to cover that crack in my armor well before I faced my father.

12

ARIANA

THE EVENING DINNER DRAGGED ON, and I struggled not to have my betrothed escorted from the small table behind me as he made non-stop demands of the servants. All of the Kyrion had all quickly tired of his attempts to brag about himself and my father. Remy had thrown one of his knives and it landed right between Ekert's fingers. Ekert had quickly excused himself to his room after that, and I was finally able to breathe a little easier. We dined outside of Titan Tower this evening, in the valley where my ancestors had once lived. The rich bouquet of floral scents from the field of flowers surrounding us mingled with the smell of the platters of food the servants were dispensing. The Forest of Epochès where Kade had won the chariot race in the first competition made a beautiful back-drop as the sun began to descend over Mount Titan. After the heat of the training course today, the cool breeze and open air was a welcome relief.

Quail, duck, yams, yeast rolls, and various other dishes were scattered across the long table that the servants had tele-ported to this meadow for the Kyrion. I sipped wine from my goblet and watched the contestants and guides sitting on their blankets amongst the flowers. I tried to let the murmur of conversation and beauty of Gaia's gifts ease the tension knotting my muscles, but as the time to meet with my father drew closer the tension only worsened.

I set the wine aside, not able to appreciate its taste for the dread that soured everything at the moment. My attentions strayed to Kade. Just looking at him caused a confusing mix of emotions to swirl inside me. I could name the one I knew well—fear. The rest were foreign invaders that urged me to act irrationally, like going over to sit closer to him. Kade clapped the boy beside him on the shoulder like a proud older brother as Chris finally tied his piece of grass into a lasso. Kade draped an arm over his bent knee as he took another drink of beer from his mug. Then plucked a blade of grass and placed it between his two hands before blowing on it. Chris pushed his glasses back up his nose, concentrating intently on whatever Kade was telling him.

I'd spent all afternoon consumed with examining my time with Kade more than watching the training. I'd come to the conclusion that getting close to my Potential had been a mistake. I was destined to be alone even when surrounded by people; my powers made it so. I'd allowed myself to believe today that there could be something more for me. The possibility of feeling the touch of another person; the freedom of talking with someone without having to weigh the consequences; and a thousand other things most people took for granted. The truth was, and would always be, that I was toxic. My mind was full of dark memories, and my heart was a stunted thing that no one should be burdened with. As if that weren't enough, my touch could bring death to anyone with powers. Whatever was between us, I needed to keep my distance from Kade. The world needed good people like him, and I refused to be the one who snuffed out his bright light.

I picked the napkin up from the lap of my green chiffon dress and dabbed my lips before setting it aside. A servant took my plate away, and I thanked her before settling back in my chair. I forced my mind away from Kade and on to my duties. The Kyrion had received notice this afternoon of attacks against two villages. Both villages were filled with outcasts from the House of Shadows—Maddox's House. The villages had been burned to the ground and there had been no survivors. I could feel the quiet rage that radiated from Maddox even sitting two chairs down from him. The villages were located in France, in heavily populated Omàda areas. All of the Kyrion had ordered the guides that remained back at our House bases to double their efforts to establish communications with any outcast villages.

After Bennett abolished the old outcast laws at Lia's request—a reckless proposition that was not fully thought out or agreed upon by the other Kyrion—a few of the villages had agreed to submit to the House rules in exchange for our protection but many hadn't. The villages were often simple, with nothing more than the basic necessities and no real defenses. They were easy targets for the Olympian Omàda, and because House members had previously been banned from communicating with outcasts, we had no warning systems in place to help them. That was something that Jaxon was working on, but the outcasts were resistant. After all, they had abandoned their House affiliations for a reason. In my House alone nearly three hundred people had walked away from their home during the thirty-five years of my father's tyrannical reign.

Our world balanced on the brink of chaos, and it wouldn't take much more to push us over the edge. As if my thoughts had conjured up the physical manifestation of chaos, a wave of power burst to life beside me. My parched tree reacted before I had a chance to process what had happened. Bennett's hands and arms erupted in red flames with a black center. The green light of my powers collided with the flames making a sizzling sound. I watched in horror as my powers began to drink from Bennett. Suddenly the black flames lurched forward overtaking the typical red of Bennett's powers and pain seared into my chest where my symbol was located. The black flames sucked my powers into its dark embrace with a hunger greater even than my own. It felt like my insides were being scraped out as those flames continued to take. Bennett's arm jerked in a hard spasm that severed our interlocked powers and bourbon sloshed from the goblet still clutched in his hand. I stumbled to my feet as Bennett slumped forward and his head hit the table with a *thump*. My power felt weaker than before, but I couldn't worry about that now.

"Bennett!" I shouted through our mental connection. The shout bounced back to me as if it had hit a wall. I quickly formed a protection bubble around our table to hide our conversation and felt Theia's powers join mine to create an illusion that wouldn't alarm the contestants. Jaxon leaned over his stepbrother from his other side but dared not touch him. The black powers twined around Bennett's own red fire-based powers were unlike any energy signature I had seen before. They certainly were not from any of our six Houses.

"Is this some kind of attack?" I asked Jaxon as the other Kyrion gathered around.

"I don't know," Jaxon replied, holding his hand over Bennett's. The black flames lashed out like a snake nearly catching Jaxon before he pulled away. They climbed the side of the goblet Bennett still held loosely, and everywhere they touched dissolved into black ash.

"Holy gods," Jaxon exclaimed as he jumped back. "What the hell is that?"

"The Talosi guarding Lia say that she has collapsed as well," Remy stated grimly. "Who could incapacitate two of the strongest descendants in our history?"

"I don't know, but Dia is going to help get everyone back to their rooms just in case this is the Omàda." Jaxon glanced over the table at Maddox. "Can you get a read on what's happening?"

Maddox's eyes gleamed with swirling silver as he reached his hand out to hover over Bennett's head. Then he dropped his hand and said in his quiet voice, "No. His shields remain strong."

"If his mental shields are still intact, how could someone get to him?" I asked.

No one answered. Kyrion mental shields were among the strongest. Shielding was one of the first things we learned. If our enemies had learned how to bypass our shields, then we were doomed.

Bennett's eyes fluttered rapidly behind his closed lids. His skin grew more ashen as the minutes passed. A bolt of white light speared into Bennett's arm and Theia yelped. The hand she had thrown her power with was covered in blisters. If it had been anyone less powerful, they probably would be dead. She clutched her hand to her chest and scowled at me like it was my fault. "What? It isn't like the rest of you were doing anything. I at least tried to help him."

"How is zapping him with lightning supposed to help?" I asked, exasperated with her impulsive behavior.

She shrugged. "It was worth a shot."

Bennett groaned and the flames died away. He gripped his head in both hands and slumped back in his seat. When his eyes opened, the brown was dotted with smudges of black that slowly faded away. Bennett croaked out, "Attack ..." I handed him a goblet of wine and he gulped it down. "Vision." He cleared his throat and tried again. "Lia had a vision. Gods, the things she saw ..." His eyes gleamed with pain and unshed tears. He suddenly looked up at me and grabbed the sleeve of my dress, being careful not to touch my skin. The Kyrion all knew I didn't like to be touched but not the reason why. "Kardia—"

"*Kyrion Gaia!*" I jumped at the urgent shout of Fayel's

voice in my head. *"The Omàda have broken through the barrier around Kardia."*

"Fayel," I replied, my hands shaking. *"Where are they?"*

"A hunting party is surrounded on the north side of the Lomami River." She sent me a mental image of their location. *"The Omàda have not yet found the entrance to the valley. I have ordered all Talosi but those with me to guard our home. We go to rescue the hunters."*

"Fayel, no," I commanded, but she had severed our connection. Terror gripped me, and my powers surged looking for the threat.

"Ariana," Bennett cautioned me in a rough voice. "I am not your enemy, but the true threat is coming."

I looked down at where he was carefully keeping my hand from touching him with the pressure on my sleeve. My hand that was enveloped in a green swirl of power stretching out toward his chest. *Goddess save me, I had nearly unleashed my powers without even realizing it. I could have killed everyone around me.* I quickly withdrew my powers and stepped away, putting distance between myself and everyone else. I gathered my fractured composure around me and mentally reached out to Cadence to make preparations to leave.

"The enemy has already come. My House is under attack," I stated calmly, while inside a massive wave of emotions battered at my defenses. "Fayel is leading a group of Talosi to rescue a hunting party trapped outside of the valley. The Omàda have not found the entrance to the valley yet but it is only a matter of time. I must go."

"Not alone," Bennett stated, his eyes ablaze with the fury he had been suppressing since he was forced to put Lia on trial. "Send us the location. Devon will gather the guides. I have alerted Archai Selene Roussos—"

"Bennett, no!" I gasped. This was not the way we handled attacks upon a House. Jaxon and I shared a concerned look. The Houses handled their own issues. The only exception had been when a village called Chaméni Elpída—full of outcasts from the House of Seasons—had been attacked last month. Jaxon and Dia had accidentally been teleported through a portal right into the middle of the fighting and all of the Kyrion had worked together to rescue them. The Omàda typically only sent a squadron to attack at one time. If all of the Paldimori Houses sent forces in droves to eliminate this threat, it would be seen as an act of war. I thought that once I became Archigós I could prevent this, but it was happening, and I was out of time to stop it. "We cannot do this."

"Ariana, a darkness is coming for us. For all of this world. I have seen it," Bennett said in a raspy voice filled with fear and pain. "It does not care what House you belong to or which god you worship. It will kill indiscriminately until this world is covered in ash and the blood of descendants and humans alike." The haggard lines and the ashen color of his face said more than words could how bad the vision had been that he had shared with Lia. Bennett's father had never broken his reserved control no matter how much he berated and belittled his son. Bennett had been a child the same as us at Tantalus, but because he was our leader, he took on our punishments as well as his own. Never once had the instructors broken his composure. But it has been broken now, and everything he was feeling was laid bare before us. Bennett was scared.

"This is *our* fight," he continued, his voice growing louder as he shook off the effects of the vision. "My people died when the watch towers at the House of Chaos were attacked a couple of weeks ago. Your people will die today." Bennett's dark brown eyes met mine. "These attacks are no longer targeting outcasts or our people who journey outside of our House fortifications. They are going after our home bases. I will not wait for them to crawl into my bed to slit my throat." His voice softened when he looked around at all of us, and I could tell from the way he had to swallow several times that he had seen our deaths in that vision. "The Omàda have been pushing us toward war all this time. I do not know if they are the darkness I saw, but they feed it with their actions. Today we begin to eliminate those that feed the darkness, and maybe we will have a chance at saving this world for all of us."

Theia rubbed her hands together in anticipation. Remy's golden hammer appeared in his hand and he swung it to rest over his shoulder. The edges of Maddox's body faded as he partially stepped into Thanatos to confer with the dead.

"Selene will teleport a unit of Talosi from the House of Chaos. I suggest the rest of you do the same."

"If you send soldiers from every House to fight, the Omàda might see this as a declaration of war," I stated out loud, wanting to make sure Bennett knew what he was doing. "I must go to help my people now. I ask once more, Archigós, is this the right choice for our people?"

"Protecting the world just became our responsibility," Bennett stated glumly. "There is no other choice."

13

I slipped from the elevator back out onto the training floor.
The guides had rushed us back to our rooms straight from
supper in the field of flowers and then disappeared. The
contestants—other than me, Dia, Emory, and Zeno—protested
leaving the outdoors so early in the evening after training
underground for two days. They hadn't seen what I—and
apparently the others—had seen: Kyrion Chaos collapsed face
down on the table while the other Kyrion surrounded him
looking worried.

The other contestants had waved goodnight to their
Kyrion and didn't seem to find anything strange as we passed
by on the way back inside. The faint outline of a bubble
layered with another misty shroud surrounded the Kyrion
table. The layers must have blocked what the other contestants saw. Somehow, I wasn't affected.

The guides had been distracted with worry and in a hurry
to get back to the Kyrion when they saw us to our floors. And
that gave me another chance at getting my answers.

I ducked behind a shelf of hand weights in the gym area
just in time. A group of people appeared out of thin air near
the elevator. There were at least twenty of them, wearing

scaly black armor with the symbol of the House of Chaos across their chests. A tall woman with a long braid of golden-brown hair snapped out orders as they jogged away toward the tunnel that led out to the field of flowers. A second group appeared; this time dressed in wispy gray jumpsuits with hoods covering their heads. All but one of this group jogged away. The last man turned, searching the area.

"*This will work,*" that familiar female voice from earlier stated.

That oily sensation I'd felt earlier today slithered throughout my body taking control of my limbs. One minute I was behind the shelf of weights worried I was about to get caught, the next I teleported in behind the man. My arms wrapped his neck in a chokehold. He tried to flip me over his back, but I held on until he slumped in my arms. I stared down at him in shock. What was happening? Why couldn't I stop this?

I could only watch as I dragged him into the forest and took his clothes. I fought to find a way to take my body back, but my efforts were only met with a familiar female chuckle. Then I was teleported again to the wide opening of the cave that exited out into the field of flowers. Groups of twenty guides from each of the Houses gathered around the Kyrion. I slipped in with those wearing the gray jumpsuit of the House of Shadows like the one I was now wearing.

"Tonight, we protect the House of Seasons and show the Omàda that we will no longer cower away from this fight," Kyrion Chaos's voice filled the cave and seemed to be coming from every direction all at once. "Your Kyrion has shared the location with you. May the gods guide you and watch over each of you."

"*I'm only supposed to observe and report,*" that female voice stated with a pout. "*I've been locked away from all my toys for too long. I think it's time I had some fun.*"

The next thing I knew humid air pressed against my skin

soaking the gray jumpsuit and making it hard to breathe. A dark jungle surrounded me, the only light coming from the moonlight that made its way through small openings in the thick canopy above. Palm leaves brushed against my arms and legs as I followed the others in my group. My boots sank into the soft forest floor as I stepped over and around vines. One by one the guides disappeared into the thick jungle.

Why was this happening? And where the hell was I?

The woman's voice answered. *"You're in the House of Seasons' territory in the Congo rainforest. Led by the very boring object of your desires, Ariana Dupree—or as you know her, Kyrion Gaia."*

I tried to speak to ask who she was and how she could control me. But she shushed me and said, *"Quiet, cowboy. The natives are restless."*

"You can hear my thoughts?" I mentally asked, but she didn't answer. *"What's your name, ma'am? Why am I here?"*

"So polite, cowboy," she chuckled. *"Call me Peithō. Now stop distracting me; we have a show to catch, and I'd hate to miss the action scenes."*

We approached a tall tree with wide branches that extended above the canopy. Wind swirled around my legs lifting me up into the air and setting me down on a large branch near the top of the tree. The moon hung low overhead, lighting up the tops of the trees below me for miles in every direction. A few yards from where I sat, the trees thinned, and a small hill led down to a riverbank. A group of seven dark-skinned men and women in homespun clothing stood back-to-back at the top of the hill. Green rays of light flowed from their hands and launched into the woods around them.

"Those are hunters from the House of Seasons," my unwanted companion pointed out. *"Not very powerful, but they're just the appetizers."*

I gripped the branch beneath me tightly. Inside, I pulled and pushed at that oily darkness, but it only seemed to coat me more. I fought harder trying to take back my own body and prayed this was all a dream.

Wicked laughter filled my head. "*Yes, cowboy, this is all a dream. It makes things so much easier when my toys are in denial.*"

Below a ball of fire launched from the darkness hurtling toward the hunters. Several of those green ropes of light reached out to the river to scoop up water and bring it toward the hunters. The water formed a shield in front of them. The fire ball collided with the water shield and exploded into a cloud of steam. The steam reformed into icicles that rained down over the hunters as they shouted and ducked for cover. The night went silent for a moment as they re-grouped. Then a dozen axes hurtled through the air from another direction. Green ropes of light pushed into the ground around the hunters to build a mound of dirt. Most of the axes embedded into the mound and vanished. A couple made it through, and screams filled the night as two hunters fell to the ground.

Another hunter's light around his hands dimmed and then went out completely. He dropped to the ground unconscious. The hunters closed ranks around their fallen friends. Then another man stumbled and fell as a dagger pierced his chest. One of the women hunters launched a green ball of light in the direction the weapon had come from. A bolt of lightning slammed into her back, and she crumpled to the ground. My thigh muscles tensed, and if my body hadn't been locked into place, I would've joined the fight. Those hunters needed help.

"*Tsk-tsk, cowboy, this isn't your rodeo,*" Peithō admonished me. The sensation of fingers brushed over my biceps and my heart jumped in surprise. "*Brave but stupid,*" Peithō laughed. "*The way I like them. What would you do? Rush into the middle of the battle to protect the poor hunters?*"

"Yes," I replied, my fists curling against my knees. "I don't know what's happenin' here, but those people need help."

"*In our world, it's survival of the strongest. And the strongest decide who lives and who dies. You don't believe might makes right?"* she asked in a curious tone.

"No, just because you can do something doesn't mean that you should," I replied. "The strong exist to protect the weak."

"Brave but stupid, like I said. Not really surprising since you were raised with the humans," Peithō said with distaste.

A white-haired woman dropped from one of the trees into the middle of the group of hunters. A half dozen others joined her, all of them in dark green leather-looking armor. They surrounded the hunters, their long spears held at the ready to attack. My grip clenched hard around the tree branch with dread as I waited for them to finish off the helpless hunters.

"Ah, the Talosi have arrived. It's about to get interesting," Peithō's voice quivered with excitement.

To my surprise the Talosi placed themselves in front of the hunters, shielding them from the attackers. Thankfully, they had help. Now I needed to help myself.

There was something about Peithō … I knew that voice; but from where? A memory teased my mind, but I couldn't bring it into focus.

I'd worry about that after I got my body back.

My muscles coiled in anticipation. Tan grains of my power from Demeter spilled from the silo where I kept it stored. Lightning flashed, begging me to release everything I had on Peithō, but I ignored that part of me.

"You come from a gambling family, right, cowboy?" Peithō asked disrupting my concentration. My power sputtered out, aided by those oily black tentacles that smothered the tan grains of light. *"Wanna make a bet? Talosi from the House of Seasons versus the Omàda. Personally, my money is on the Omàda."*

"How'd you know about my family?" I asked. How much of my thoughts and memories could she see? Did she know what I was planning?

"Oh, I know lots about you, cowboy," she laughed, and the

feeling of fingers trailing down the scars on my back made me shudder. The memory of Daddy pressing my face into the dirt with his boot as his belt lashed my back swept over me. I'd never wanted to feel that helpless again, but here I was trapped inside my own body. *"Ah, Kade, your daddy issues are showing. Such a pain, aren't they? Mine put me in time-out recently, but I got tired of listening to him. Now I make my own choices."* An invisible hand gripped my chin forcing me to watch what was happening down below while I fought to free myself. *"I would love to remind you how well I know you, but we might miss the best part of the show. Watch."*

This time I paid attention when her command swept over me. That oily darkness moved inside my mind and through every bit of my body like tentacles. I pulled at one and managed to dislodge it, but another took its place.

"You're being very naughty fighting against me, Kade." Peithō sighed. Then my right hand grabbed the pinky on my left hand and snapped it sideways. Pain curled me forward, but the only sound I could make was wheezing. *"Such breakable toys. Be a good cowboy, or I'll have to punish you again."*

I cradled my injured hand in my lap, helpless to do anything but watch as I'd been ordered. Green light spread from one Talosi to another until a green-tinted dome formed over the hunters. Fire, weapons, lightning, and water launched from the forest toward the dome. The lightning caught my attention, and I traced its path back to a patch of thick palm leaves. Was that savage storm inside me just another power of Demeter?

The white-haired woman who seemed to be leading the Talosi twirled her spear and shouted orders to her people. A couple of hunters helped them create a net of vines that caught the weapons mid-air, while others swept water from the river to stop the fire. Boulders were launched to meet the lightning. The few things that made it through hit the dome and bounced harmlessly away.

I had never seen anything like this. My fears tripled for Hope's safety in a world where these kinds of powers existed. No one would be safe if this fighting spilled over into the human world.

Suddenly, screams filled the forest from all directions. Followed by the sound of weapons meeting in battle. Lights of various colors arced through the forest and collided in explosions. Kyrion Chaos appeared at the riverbank; his body was covered in black armor and tendrils of red power radiated out around his body.

"*Bennett*," Peithō whispered in a breathless voice. A strange giddy sort of anticipation filled my body, but it wasn't mine. Was I feeling what Peithō felt?

Kyrion Chaos—er, Bennett—unleashed his power and a thunderstorm gathered above him. Thunder boomed and lightning flashed across the sky, giving me a better view of the full-on battle taking place in the trees. Wind whipped by, forcing me to hold onto the tree branch for dear life. Fire surrounded Bennett's hands and turned into whips that lashed out into the forest. They pulled people from the forest and held them in the air as the fire burrowed into their mouths, eyes, and ears. More screams filled the night until they cut off abruptly when the bodies turned to ash. Three men rushed Bennett, lashing out with powers and weapons. He blocked each attack with fire, and then teleported to the nearest man to drive his fist into his opponent's face. Another person teleported in behind Bennett.

I tried to shout a warning, but my mouth refused to work.

Ariana's staff met the sword aimed at Bennett's back. She shoved the attacker away and spun to deliver a kick to his chest, knocking the man to the ground. Her staff formed into a set of katanas, and she quickly severed his head. My Kyrion was a bad-ass. Like a beautiful avenging angel, she spun to meet another attacker. A man lifted his hand, drawing water from everything around him, including Ariana. She stumbled and fell to one knee. My heart galloped in my chest and light-ning flared from my hands to burn handprints into the tree limb.

No, don't hurt her!

I stood up, my desperation to help Ariana somehow over-riding Peithō's commands. Before I could make my move, Ariana's fingers burrowed into the ground as a green pulse of light sent a ripple of power out around her. The trees rustled and limbs grabbed her attacker around the waist. They hefted the man into the air, breaking his hold on her. Then the tree slammed the man into the ground with a sickening thud. Other trees joined in picking off the enemy until silence finally fell.

Ariana glanced in my direction as if she could sense me watching her. Whatever control I had gained disappeared, and I was forced to sit down on the branch once more. "*If your crush wasn't watching, I would make you pay for that right now!*" Peithō shouted with rage. The oily darkness inside me squeezed my lungs until I was gasping for breath. Then suddenly it loosened its grip, and Peithō's mood shifted so quickly she nearly gave me whiplash. "*Naughty toys always get punished,*" she promised in a haunting little-girl voice that scared me more than anything she'd done so far.

Down below, the white-haired woman shouted for Ariana and my Kyrion rushed over to help the group of hunters. Cheers rang out as people stepped from the trees to join Bennett near the riverbank. The Paldimori had won.

A tangled mix of jealousy and smug satisfaction came from Peithō. "*A great show, thanks to your star. Bennett always was the best of them. But now it's our move.*"

REMY POUNDED his massive double-sided golden hammer on the table in the Order Hall, halting the arguments that had been growing steadily louder. His gold robe fluttered with the sharp movement. His bare forearms flexed with agitation; each taut muscle displayed to full effect by the rolled-up sleeves of his gold shirt. Amber flames danced in his oval, whiskey-colored eyes as he glared at each one of us. With his long black hair worn in a topknot, it was not hard to believe that his ancestors had ruled as warrior kings in the Indonesian Majapahit empire before the Games had re-claimed them for our people. A hint of their native Javanese accent flavored his words as he said in his gritty voice, "Calm the fuck down, or I will feed the lot of you to my lava pits."

I didn't doubt that Remy would follow through on his threat: the ruler of the underworld took his punishments very seriously. Theia huffed as she fell back in her chair, but she didn't say anything else. Jaxon smirked and arrogantly waved his hand to indicate Remy had the floor. The fight last night had been too close to Kardia's valley for me to relax until the barrier was repaired and strengthened. Luckily, that was being worked on right now and should be done in a couple of days.

For a moment, I thought I'd seen a dark figure watching the fight from the trees. When I checked later, I'd found a set of handprints burned into the tree branch. More Talosi had been stationed throughout the jungle to keep watch. I'd returned to the valley along with the hunters to see to the injured and assist with preparing the dead for burial. Then I'd met with Father.

My blood ran cold at the pleasure he had taken in declaring that Aegeus had not received his meals for the last two days due to my failure to secure the Archigós position. My brother was being starved while I had to endure these senseless arguments amongst the Kyrion. All of our years as a cohesive council working to help our people had unraveled. My throat convulsed as I choked down the words I wanted to shout. The truths about the torture my brother was enduring, my contempt for this petty squabbling, and the need to protect our world in the way the gods had intended—through the Chosen.

I grew a vine between my hands and anxiously twisted it around my fingers. I was being careful not to expend large amounts of power since they had not recovered from that brush with the black flame surrounding Bennett yesterday. With the fight last night my powers were running low and I was exhausted. Jaxon had added research into the black powers we'd seen to his growing list. For now, there was nothing more that could be done until we knew more about what had happened during the shared vision. Tension filled every corner of my body. It was just as well that my powers were not at their fullest for what I must do today.

There would be no pleasure in taking the Archigós posi-tion, but I questioned now if Bennett's own actions hadn't been leading us toward this. His decision last night may well have put my House in greater danger and would certainly have untold consequences for all of our people. Now Bennett, Remy, and Theia wanted us to strike immediately against the Omàda. But our people were not prepared for a large-scale war. Other than the Kyrion, Talosi, and guides our people were not trained to fight. Most were servants, farmers, weavers, blacksmiths, and similar skilled laborers who trusted their Kyrion to keep them safe behind the walls of our House bases. Jaxon and I seemed to be the only ones who grasped that to attack now would cost us a heavy price.

My House was the smallest at nearly seven-hundred people. Of those, there were one-hundred and three Talosi and guides after the deaths last night. Jaxon's House of Arrows was the largest but were as ill-prepared as my people. Neither of us had the number of skilled fighters needed to win a war against thousands of Omàda. Even if my House had the numbers, how could I tell my people to pick up their handmade tools and charge into war against an enemy who used weapons like the gun we had found at Chaméni Elpída? The clear glass barrel of the gun held the glowing golden serum the House of Light—former members of the Omàda and now our new allies—had created to use against us. That serum knocked a person unconscious and allowed others to view their memories. Lia had convinced Bennett to travel to the House of Light's base in Sicily to meet with her father's people a couple of weeks ago and gotten them both put under that mind-stealing serum. Another reckless move on the steadily growing list for Lia that just proved how dangerous she was.

Bennett, Remy, and Theia believed that our new ally's technology would be the surprise that we needed to win against the Omàda. But I didn't trust the House of Light or their serum.

"You two"—Remy punctuated his words by jabbing a

finger at Theia and then me—"speak your truth and be done.
I am sorely in need of a drink and entertainment. Seeing the
anjing," he snarled, calling the contestants dogs in Javanese,
"race through the replica of my punishing fields this afternoon will not be as satisfying as the real thing, but it is better
than listening to the lot of you bicker any longer."

"If we were not bound by our traditions to carry out these
Games, we could be preparing for war right now," Theia
huffed.

"We are bound by more than tradition or did you forget
the oaths you swore as a Kyrion, Theia?" I asked through
gritted teeth. "We are bound to our duties, including these
Games. I hope to never learn the consequences to breaking
our oaths to the God of Chaos."

Theia ignored me and patted Remy's forearm as if he was
a favored pet. He raised his lip in a snarl so savage I was sure
he would rip her arm off. Instead, he tugged his arm away
from her and sat down in his chair, caressing his hammer.

"You're right, Rem," Theia said without a care that the
savage man sitting next to her was giving her death glares.
"The race will be starting soon. I couldn't possibly miss my
little college boy tripping over his own feet and losing this
race like he has all the others." She turned to me and her
pouty lips stretched into a placating smile. "I have a thousand
Talosi and guides trained and eager to shed the blood of the
Omàda. With the other men and women of fighting age, we
easily have another five hundred to fill our ranks from the
House of Night alone." She grabbed the papers lying in front
of her and held them up for me to see. A hand-drawn map of
Mount Olympus where the Omàda lived—excluding the
House of Light who had abandoned their original home base
—filled the front page. Descendants of Hades lived elsewhere
too. They had never been considered part of the Omàda but
as Dia's father had proved they were still a threat. If we didn't

eliminate our enemies all at once they would only re-group. It wasn't enough to cut off the head of the snake like Theia was suggesting. "The strategy my father has outlined is the best option. He has been gathering information about our enemies for years. All seven of my older brothers are seasoned guides just waiting for me to give the command. With the weapons from the House of Light, we can bring down every one of those khuy."

I gripped the vine hard and it snapped in half. Is this how far we had fallen? That we resulted to calling our enemies dicks in Russian and putting all of our faith in a tentative alliance that had yet to be tested. "We are not ready for this," I stated. "We should fortify our bases in preparation for retalia-tion after the events of last night and recruit volunteers to join the ranks of our Talosi. In a month's time when the Games are completed, we will have trained soldiers and our people can be prepared if war comes to us."

Theia scoffed, "Don't be a fool, Ariana. The Omàda will strike back hard and fast. We can't afford to play by your rules of 'fairness' or wait for the war to come to us."

Jaxon jumped to his feet, his red robe fanning out behind him on an invisible breeze as his wind powers stirred. He listed all of the ways again in which his House would be wiped out without the proper training. Remy jumped in to state his thoughts, and we were back to arguing again. Maddox's silver eyes assessed me as if he was waiting for something, but I had no idea what he was thinking. He typi-cally followed along with Theia and Remy, but when he chose to voice an opinion it was usually neutral. We were getting nowhere. Was now the right time to do what I needed to?

Bennett shifted in his seat on my left, and I turned to see what he would do. In the past he had been quick to shut down any arguments amongst us, and I waited now to see if he would intervene. That he would prove to be the leader I had respected since childhood. A person I could trust to work with me to save my brother and our people. Dark circles underlined Bennett's eyes as he ran his fingers through his spiky hair, still looking shaken by the vision from yesterday. He had spent most of this meeting with that faraway look in his eyes that said he was speaking telepathically to someone. My fists clenched around the halves of the vine; Lia—it always came back to her.

When Bennett's walls had crashed down last evening, I'd felt the guilt, anger, and heartbreak that was eating away at him. I ached for him, but we were at a pivotal moment for our world and we needed our leader. The fact that he was distracted even now, combined with how extremely affected he had been by Lia's growing powers so that her vision had completely incapacitated him, was alarming. My hands tightened further around the halves of the vine and it disintegrated. The small taste of power pulled from the vine whetted my parched tree's appetite and green ropes of light slithered under the table. For a moment I was tempted to let them seek out Lia and eliminate the true problem. But her soul was tied to Bennett's through the Desmòs and to kill one would mean death for the other.

Please, Bennett, give me a sign that you are still the leader I should follow.

But Bennett remained silent.

Any hope that I had held onto died, and I turned away from him in anger. The green ropes of my power stalked beneath the table and this time I didn't draw them back. I stood from my chair, letting them all see my powers writhing around me. My words cracked through the room drowning out all other conversations. "What you propose would be no better than throwing bodies at the feet of the Omàda! Most of the able-bodied members of our Houses are untrained in combat. Other than the highest-ranking positions, their powers are weak. My hunters depleted their powers in only a few hours and collapsed, leaving themselves defenseless."

"Then what is the solution, Ariana?" Remy growled. "We cannot go on sitting like clueless zebu as the white tiger stalks us."

"The Chosen are the answer, just as the gods promised in the prophecy. We should train our people but also seek to help the Chosen rise to their full power. We have never been closer to fulfilling our destiny than now," I declared.

"You mean those vague stories passed down from one Kyrion to the next? How do we even know that the prophecy is real? What if it's all lies made up by our ancestors to keep us bound by these stupid rules?" Theia stood and slammed her palms down on the table. "Centuries of our ancestors devoted their lives to these Games and keeping the Houses hidden, for what? We *think* we've found a couple of Chosen, but are they really? Dia is too soft, and Lia is a traitor." She waved her hands around the room. "The gods aren't here. They're still trapped or asleep or whatever. *We're* the ones who are suffering! I'd rather my end came fighting the Omàda then fading away with our powers."

Jaxon sat up in his seat and propped his arms on the table. "The letter from Lia's mother said there would be six Chosen. When my Dia was claimed as a Chosen by Gaia, Lia received the same powers. Ariana's right. I think Lia is the key," he stated, his midnight blue eyes blazing with fierce determination. "We need to find the other Chosen, and once they're claimed, Lia will have all of the powers of the gods. That's how we'll win."

Maddox's quiet voice broke the tense silence when he asked, "What do the translations say from the writing on the walls of the Lotus Temple?"

Jaxon glanced at Bennett, his chin set at a defiant angle. Jaxon usually went along with whatever his older stepbrother said, but it appeared that Lia had come between them. "From what Dia and I have translated so far, they confirm Lia's story: Titan Theophanes was the human name used by the Primordial God Chaos. The first passage referred to him as 'King Titan Theophanes of the Chaonians, earth-bound son of the God of Chaos.' How would Lia know that unless Titan really has been appearing to her? His human name is not found in any of our texts."

Jaxon tilted his head as if turning something over in that intelligent brain of his before he continued. "I think Titan's name was removed from our history books because he was the one who used Voice—the outlawed power that compels others to do your bidding regardless of their will—during the Chaonian War to declare the Omàda our enemies. That compulsion has weakened over the centuries, but we still feel it." He sat back in his seat. "We're going back tonight to start on the next section of the wall. Dia thinks that if we find a way to break the Voice command, it will help stop the fighting between the two sides."

Jaxon's gaze shifted back to Bennett and a look of pain tightened his face. "I've followed in your footsteps my whole life, brother. I've always admired you for your control, but now I see what it's cost you." Jaxon swallowed thickly. "You and Lia have both made mistakes and hurt each other. You're both afraid to trust, but you're stronger together." He glanced at me and shrugged. "Sorry, Ariana, but I don't think your rules apply in this case. I was overruled about putting Lia on trial, but I can't condemn her. Not for what I believe was Christos's accidental death and not for attacking Bennett when she was only trying to protect her best friend—my bond-mate. I say we give her a reprieve and get her help tracking down the other Chosen."

I was so surprised by Jaxon's recommendation that my powers shut down without me having to fight to bring them back under my command. I didn't trust Lia to be anywhere near our efforts to locate the other Chosen—or near me.

"If you will recall," Bennett stated with a growl. "I requested that Lia only be assigned Talosi escorts until Christos's death could be investigated further. I too was overruled by the majority vote of this Order. Just as you all voted—in my absence, might I add—to call me back here to answer for my abrupt departure from the Games to go to Prometheus. Then when my father"—he snarled the word as if it was repugnant to him, and I completely understood the sentiment—"brought accusations against me. I came here on the day of my Bonding Ceremony to yet again defend myself. I will not be questioned any longer. If one of you think you would be better suited as Archigós, then take the position from me."

"No, of course we don—" Jaxon started to say, but I held up my hand.

Maddox stared at me from across the table with a small smile and said, "Two paths diverged, but what lies at the end makes all the difference."

I tightened my shields just to make sure he wasn't listening to my thoughts.

Jaxon looked at me with wide eyes. "Ariana, don't. We can—"

"No way." Theia suddenly leaned forward in her seat like I had finally done something to impress her.

I stood from my chair. "I, Ariana Gian Dupree, Kyrion of the House of Seasons, invoke the Law of Metis." I raised my hands up to the sky and my powers danced along my arms. "If the God of Chaos sanctions that I be Archigós over all Paldimori, let your will be known."

My powers flared high enough that green light touched the tall ceiling. The feeling of being assessed both inside and out slid over me. A coldness slipped into my skin and eternity flashed behind my eyes as my body was taken over. A voice that sounded like a thousand mixed together issued from my lips as the God of Chaos spoke through me. "Possibilities.

Potential. Hope. Destruction. The path is yours to forge, Archigós."

I slumped forward bracing my hands on the table. My body felt both hollowed out and full at the same time. A connection to all of the gods snapped into place. Connections to thousands more of our people formed to let me speak mentally with each of the Paldimori. Silence stretched out as I pushed myself away from the table on shaky legs. Shocked faces of the other Kyrion surrounded me. But there was only one I needed to see at the moment.

Bennett still sat in his chair, his fists pressed upon the table and his jaw clenched tight. He slowly stood and then bowed stiffly to me. "Congratulations, Archigós."

My throat was tight as I whispered, "I had to—"

Bennett held up his hand, "An Archigós never explains herself unless she is called to do so."

Like we had done to him.

Maddox's silver eyes gleamed with something close to relief as he said, "What is your first order, Archigós?"

I faced the other Kyrion. "As Archigós I declare that we will finish the Games and continue to search for the Chosen as our first priorities. The Houses will begin preparations for war, and we will reassess our readiness in a month's time."

My gaze met Ekert's where he sat against the wall watching everything. His hands gripped the arms of his chair tightly as if to keep himself from bolting for the door to escape all of the tension in the room. Hopefully today's events convinced him he was better off with the forest animals.

"Inform my father I have completed my task."

Ekert grinned triumphantly, *"Your father says a job well done is well rewarded."*

Thank the goddess!

Power blasted into the room, knocking me back into my chair. Bennett bellowed in pain. His eyes turned pure black.

Red and black flames ignited along his arms. He pressed his hands against his temples as if he could squeeze the vision out of his head. He lost control of his powers and the ground shook beneath our feet. The torches along the columns burst into huge fire balls that shattered their housing. Wax and pieces of metal rained down around the room. I cried out in surprise, and we all ducked for cover.

Pain ripped through me as a piece of metal several inches long lodged itself into my right arm. Suddenly everything stopped, and Bennett dropped into his chair looking exhausted. His troubled gaze settled on my injury as he wiped the sweat from his forehead with a trembling hand. "The vision … I am sorry, Ariana."

Jaxon ripped the bottom section off of his shirt and rounded the chairs separating us. "I won't touch you, but let me help." He didn't wait for me to respond but used his telekinesis to wrap the cloth around the base of the metal piece sticking out of my arm. Blood dripped onto the floor and saturated the makeshift bandage. Everything seemed to move in slow motion as Maddox extended his hand and the doors flew open on the other side of the room.

A doctor and several servants poured in; no doubt called telepathically by one of the other Kyrion. They took in the damage around the room in shock. The columns were scorched, and some had chunks missing. Debris littered the area. Several cracks split the stone floor. The doctor approached me, and it took all of my willpower to let him get close enough to examine my arm. My powers thrashed inside me, wanting to drink everyone around me dry in retaliation for my injury. Sweat saturated the hair at the base of my neck. My body trembled from having the doctor so near and holding my powers back. The doctor worked quickly using his telekinesis to remove the metal, clean the wound, and bandage it. I silently repeated my rules like a prayer until it was done. I thanked the doctor and he moved on to help with any other injuries. I approached Bennett who stood apart from the others staring up at the dragon statue over the main entrance doors. Regret and guilt etched weary lines across his face.

"This was not your fault, Bennett," I assured him.

"It is," he replied quietly, "I thought I could control every aspect of my life and our world. Now I have control of nothing." Then he walked away.

15

THE STENCH of trouble filled the air of the training area like someone had stepped in a pile of manure. Cadence's smile had disappeared, and she had been unusually quiet all morning. Devon had pushed us twice as hard as normal in warm-ups and was biting everyone's head off. Zeno had a black eye and busted knuckles. Molly's shoulder was bandaged. They had shrugged it off as some accident, but I knew better. They'd won the fight last night but not without their own losses. I'd seen bodies being carried out just before Peithō had teleported me from the rainforest back to my room at Titan Tower.

Peithō had threatened more punishment if I told anyone about her being in my head or spying on the fight last night. I'd countered with an offer to "behave" if she didn't take control of me again. It pissed me off that I had to bargain with her at all, but it had been horrible being unable to make my own body obey me. My skin crawled every time I thought of that voice in my head. A cold sweat broke out across my skin at the possibility she could take control of me at any time, and I couldn't do a damn thing about it.

I'd spent a nauseating half hour cussing up a storm while

I splinted my pinky finger with a toothbrush. I'd made up some excuse about a barbell falling on my hand when Cadence asked me about it this morning. She'd laughed at my attempt at self-treatment and called a real doctor who had splinted my finger properly. It made training with the pole harder and, just my luck, today was the first race.

If I could win this practice race, then I'd have a good shot at winning the competition. *Mama, I'm gonna need your helping hand to show me the right path to win this today.*

I waited anxiously at the end of the line of contestants, my boots planted on the black starting line of the training course. Dia gave me a thumbs-up from her spot to my left. On the other side of her, Maya was focused on the course. Chris leaned around them with a hesitant wave, sweat dripping down his temples. I holstered my pole in the loop of my jumpsuit and gave him an encouraging nod.

My thoughts drifted toward Ariana. I remembered how lost and alone she'd looked standing in that pool in her night-gown. The harsh way she'd told me I was no use to her if I didn't fight harder to win the Games. The kind way she'd praised Cadence when she joined us in training yesterday. And her apology to the servant who dropped the tray of dishes. Then seeing her last night kicking ass in the jungle. I'd thought I had Ariana figured out and had written her off as a prettier imitation of my father. But she wasn't. Yes, she could cut a person apart with her words, but it was like she used them as a way to keep people from getting too close. She was a mystery that I was starting to want to solve. Maybe my luck in figuring her out would be better than it had been in finding out anything else around here.

A ripple of power swept into the room, amped up to a level that screamed danger. My own power stirred inside me and grains of tan light drifted out from the silo I stored it in. The six Kyrion strode toward us with grim faces. I could see their powers as they crackled and popped around them like fireworks on the Fourth of July. That was new. The guides shifted nervously, and I got the feeling that something else had happened. My attention settled on Ariana. I stilled, my muscles locked up tight as stone. Her normally peach-toned skin was pale. Her eyes dark with misery. I'd seen enough injured animals to recognize the protective way she favored her right arm. All I could hear was my heart pounding as anger crackled through my veins.

I'd crossed the distance separating us before I'd even thought about it. When I was a couple of feet away, Cadence pressed her hand against my chest stopping me in my tracks. I wanted to push past her, but Cadence was only doing her job to protect her Kyrion. If I looked as crazy as I felt I would stop me too. My back itched and stung like I'd rolled around in nettles. My fingers clenched around the pole at my side to keep from reaching for the arm Ariana was trying to hide behind her green robe. I wanted to demand to know what had happened. Both were actions that would get me punched by my fiercely independent Kyrion.

How had I gone from not liking this woman to wanting … I had no idea what I wanted, but I didn't like seeing her hurt.

Power pulsed around Ariana pulling me forward and pushing me away at the same time. "Guide Paxton, please give my apologies to Kafàli Harris for the delay, we will begin in just a moment." Ariana pinned me with a look that said this better be important. "My Potential apparently has something he needs to say to me."

Cadence shot a worried look at each of us but then bowed and left to do as she was told.

I angled myself with my back to the others and stepped closer to my Kyrion to give us privacy. I treaded on shaky ground here, but there was this nagging need that drove me to make sure she was ok. Ariana didn't back away, but her tense posture said she definitely didn't like me being this close.

"What are you doing, Potential?"

I reached for her arm and Ariana flinched away as if she expected me to hurt her. Green lights flickered over her hands where they gripped the edges of her robe tightly. I recognized the signs of someone else who'd experienced trauma and anger scorched my insides. Lightning streaked along my limbs as that thunder chant started: "*Justice! Justice! Justice!*" Now I knew why she always seemed to stand apart from everyone else, even the other Kyrion. There were no physical signs, but I knew from experience that the damage to your heart and your head didn't heal as easily as skin.

"I do not know what has given you the impression that I would welcome your touch, Potential Downing, but I do not." Ariana's biting tone warned me away, but it was her eyes that told me the truth. In them I saw that sad and lonely woman trapped inside, not knowing how to break free. "I am not interested in being one of your dalliances nor in becoming friends. You are here to do one thing and that is to win the Games."

Damn my dick for doing my thinking that day I'd slept with the cold-eyed blonde. That wasn't one of my best moments, but it really seemed to bother Ariana. Why?

"I was worried 'bout your injury and wanted to make sure you were all right," I explained. Then held up my hand to stop her when she would have protested. "I know you don't need anybody protectin' you. But we're partners now, workin' together to win the Games. Lookin' out for each other comes with the job." She relaxed a bit. I silently did a fist pump in celebration that she hadn't launched more icy word darts at me. "Who I share my bed with is my business. But as my *partner*, I'll tell you that I haven't been with anyone but that one woman in years. I didn't go looking for her ei—"

What little color she had drained from Ariana's face and her lips parted but no sound came out. She cleared her throat and asked in a strained voice, "Did she force you?"

"No," I replied quickly, but there was a burning in my gut that said there was something not quite right about my actions that day. "I mean, I wasn't exactly thinkin' straight. I was flying' high with my win of the trainin' race, and I got caught up in the moment when she kissed me."

Ariana nodded like she wasn't exactly convinced. "She has been detained elsewhere and will thankfully not return to the Games." She hesitated. Then looked up at me with a vulnerability that made my heart pound all over again. That look right there is why I would risk any number of harsh words to help her. "She …" Ariana swallowed thickly as if choking down whatever emotions were riding her. "She has a habit of persuading men into her bed and making them think it was their idea. For a time, she was with someone I care about. He was not himself when she was near."

"I'm sorry you and your friend had to go through that."

"My brother," Ariana said hesitantly, "It was my brother."

"Thank you for sharin' that, partner," I said softly as I stepped closer, stupidly relieved that the man hadn't been someone Ariana was involved with. I grabbed the pole from the loop at my side and used it to carefully raise her injured arm. "Now will you tell me if you're ok, my lady?"

What I really wanted to ask was "can I please touch you?" I could almost feel that soft skin under my hands I wanted to touch her so bad.

Ariana blushed and her lips parted on a soft exhale. This was the closest I'd ever gotten to my Kyrion. The scent of her and the heat from her body brushed against mine making me ache for her. She didn't flinch away from me or flay me with her sharp tongue. I watched that tongue peek out to moisten her pink lips, and it took all my restraint not to kiss her.

"I-I am fine," Ariana replied in a breathy voice that did nothing to calm down my desire for her. "It was an accident. The doctor gave me something for the pain."

"Then I should probably get back in line," I said, my eyes glued to Ariana's lips as I leaned closer.

Peithō chuckled in my head. "*Go ahead, cowboy. Kiss her. Fuck her. I'll even offer pointers. The gods know she's in need of someone to show her how to have fun. She's been mopey and boring her whole life.*"

I backed away sharply. Any arousal I'd felt replaced with disgust at Peithō's cruel words. I marched back toward the training course, cussing myself and this creature inside me. Maybe Daddy had been right about there being a demon in me. Whatever she was, I needed to get rid of her. But I didn't know how. I needed answers worse than ever, but every time I set out to get them, I ended up running into my Kyrion.

Could Ariana have the answers I needed? I couldn't just ask her about demon possessions or how to defend myself with powers, not without giving away that I was an Olympian descendant. Could I trust Ariana with my secrets?

16

KADE

I took my place back at the starting line. Devon gave me a warning look to stop messing with his schedule and then called out for us to get ready. An image of Hope flashed through my mind and strengthened my resolve to win this. Even winners of a training race received prizes. I already knew I'd be asking for money to be sent back home to my little sister.

"Go!" Devon shouted, and we sprinted forward.

My feet slid on a fine-grained section of black lava rock and I used the pole to keep me from falling. The first small column of rocks came up quickly and I boosted myself with the pole as I jumped on top of it. I vaulted from one column to the next, never losing my rhythm as I passed the first section. Then came the hard part: the tallest section of columns and ridges. There were no safety harnesses today. Should I risk taking the harder but shorter path?

To the right, a cluster of columns rose to various heights from the ground like needles in a pincushion. To the left was a taller narrow ridge about twenty feet long. Lava poured down each side of it bringing intense heat and smoke. Those ridges sat like a nearly perfect dashed line cutting through the columns of rocks to the end of the course. The ridges were the quickest way to the other side but also the most dangerous. From the last two days of training on this course I knew which columns were more stable, which ones took the most amount of skill to jump, and how difficult it was to cross those ridges. My finger pressed the button on the pole to lengthen it to twice its original size. My hands gripped the pole about shoulder width apart just below the House symbol, and I took a calming breath.

I pushed off while jabbing the pole toward a safe spot on the ground. Then arched my body the way I had been taught and soared through the air. The ridge came closer, the heat from the lava stealing my breath for a moment as I passed over it. Then my feet pounded down on the ridge top, and I bent my knees to keep my balance. The ridge top was a couple of feet wide, narrower in certain places. I held the pole in both hands and used it to help me balance as I walked across the ridge. Sweat poured from my brow to drip down into my eyes, making them sting. I blinked to clear my vision not wanting to chance losing my balance by wiping my eyes.

I made it to the end of the ridge and gauged the jump to the next one. The next ridge was the highest point in the course and the hardest to reach. It had a curved end that angled away from me which meant I had to go right over the wall of lava or attempt to jump past that curved section. I rolled my shoulders and pushed the top button on the pole. It lengthened again, and I took aim. I vaulted through the air, my eyes on the target. I sailed over the curved end of the ridge aiming for the center, but I had miscalculated. The center of the ridge passed by below me. My pole thumped into the side of the ridge and a hissing sounded as it met the lava. For a moment I hung over the opposite side as lava flowed only a few feet below me, then my hands slipped.

Lightning flashed inside me brighter than ever before and an electric shock traveled over my body. The world around me went white, and I closed my eyes to block out that blinding light. Lightning exploded from my chest leaving me breathless. I lost my grip on the pole and fell straight toward the lava.

"Descendant of mine, how have you summoned me?" A husky, heavily accented female voice asked. This wasn't Peithō—she had been suspiciously absent all day. This new woman filled me with wild energy making the hair stand up on my body like that minute right before lightning struck nearby.

"Who are you?" I asked.

"How easily my children forget me," the woman sneered. *"I am Nyx, goddess of the night, dreams, illusions, and prophecies. Why do you call to me if you know not who I am?"*

"I didn't—"

I slammed into rough rock, and my hands scrambled to find something to cling to. The smell of ozone filled my nose. My arms strained with the full weight of my body as I hung from the lip of the ridge. My feet burned from the heat of the flowing lava right below me. I grunted as I pulled myself up to sit on the ridge. A sigh of relief escaped me. *Thank you, Mama, for watchin' over me!* I got up on my knees and looked down over the side of the ridge where I had landed. A section of lava roughly in the shape of my body had solidified into black rock. I ran my hand over the top part of that rock in disbelief. Had that lightning inside me just saved my life?

I got to my feet shrugging off the aches from slamming into the rock. I wondered about the lady calling herself a goddess, but I'd have to sort that out later. Thankfully, the pole still leaned against the side of the ridge. I collapsed it down to see the damage and was surprised to find it was still in perfect shape. I searched the course looking to see where the other contestants were. Dia was at the midway point with me. Chris and Maya were a little further behind. Emory sat crossed leg on top of a column watching me. Zeno's bare torso gleamed with sweat as he hopped along ridges as if it was nothing. A shimmer appeared behind him and for a moment I could swear I saw a pair of hands push him. Then he fell over the side and out of sight. Was this some kinda Paldimori hazing? I looked back at Emory, and she gave me a salute as if to say "you're welcome." Then she hitched her thumb toward the end of the course motioning for me to get going.

The descent back down from that highest ridge wasn't easy, but I was able to navigate the others without any more accidents. My arms strained as I vaulted from the last ridge onto the shorter columns. I vaulted from one to the other until I landed on the open section of black rock at the end of the course. My thigh muscles burned with the impact, and I wiped the sweat from my brow as I struggled to get my breathing under control. Rocks tumbled next to me and Dia landed about twenty feet to my left. She gave me a smile, then bolted toward her flag hanging on the cave wall.

I dropped my pole and sprinted toward my own flag. My chest heaved as hot air filled my lungs, and I pushed even harder to reach my goal. I leaped across the last several feet grasping for the flag. My legs gave out and I thumped face first into the ground. The sharp rock sliced into my forehead, but I didn't care. I looked up at my fist and there in my grip was the flag with the House of Seasons symbol.

I rolled onto my back grinning like an idiot. Dia kneeled by my side, her own flag gripped in her hand as she shook her head at me. "Congrats, superman. Your flying stunt won you the race."

I grinned up at Dia, excitement swelling in my chest. Hope was going to get some of the money she needed for the next semester of college. My smile faltered as that oily shadow swelled inside my mind and for a moment everything went out of focus. A feeling of frustration swept through me, followed by a spike of mischievous delight. A warm pressure met my lips and then my vision cleared. My hands were wrapped around Dia's biceps while I held her against me and claimed her mouth with mine. I pushed her away and got to my feet in confusion. "Dia, I'm sorry. I didn't mean to do th—"

All I saw was a flash of his red shirt, then Kyrion Eros's fist crashed into my face. I stumbled back against the cave wall gripping my aching jaw. But it was the look of disappointment on Ariana's face before she turned and walked away that left me feeling bruised.

Peithō's familiar laughter filled my head. *"I told you naughty toys always get punished. Don't test me again, cowboy."*

17

ARIANA

I PACED before the wall of windows in the sunken living room on my floor. The sun glistened off the water of the winding stream in the green valley far below. Bramble issued a low whine as if she could feel the emotions running rampant through me. I walked over to sit on the step beside her and ran my hand along her soft fur, attempting to soothe us both. I should be down on the training floor discussing the race with my Potential, but I had needed to get away. I had asked Ekert to handle awarding Kade his prize and my annoying future co-ruler had eagerly agreed. Guilt and shame at not fulfilling my duties myself tried to weigh me down, but I had no capacity for them. My mind was full of worry over Aegeus. I'd even braved telepathically contacting Father, but he wasn't answering.

My heart, on the other hand, was full of this strange ache, and I feared my Potential was to blame. *"Now will you tell me if you're ok, my lady?"* Kade's husky question had sounded like he was asking for much more. He'd been so close to me, closer than anyone had been in a long time. He smelled of wheatgrass after a storm, a smell I knew from the attempts Father made to grow different imported crops in the valley.

Kade's body heat had wrapped around me, making me want to burrow into him like a security blanket. My lips had ached to feel his kiss. In that moment I'd lost sight of my duties and everyone around us. I'd trusted him alone to be the gentle and patient man to give me my first kiss. Then he'd jumped away in disgust and kissed Dia instead. I felt used. Like I was some inexperienced, pathetic girl he was laughing at.

Anger and hurt filled me. I had been drawn in by Kade's charming smile and his innocent offers to be "partners" in the Games. For the first time I was personally invested in seeing my Potential win. Instead, he had showed me exactly how he felt and risked all that we had been working toward by kissing a Kyrion's bond-mate. Had Kade been a member of any Paldimori House, that offense could have gotten him executed. Bonds were sacred to our people, especially the Desmòs like Jaxon and Dia shared. Kade was fortunate Jaxon only punched him.

I wanted to punch Kade too. There was something about him that had slipped past my defenses. It was as if he had looked into the depths of me, seen exactly who I was, and wanted to help me anyway. I knew my fears held me prisoner every bit as much as my tower had when I was a child, but I refused to risk anyone's life to see if I could overcome my powers. Kade saw me all too clearly but still had gotten closer.

Kade confused and surprised me. I would have known what to do with a calculated ploy to win me over for his own benefit. I could have handled spite or ridicule. But Kade had sincerely meant everything he said to me. It was there in his handsome blue eyes that promised me I could trust him. It was there in the honesty that radiated from his kind soul like a beacon calling me from my isolation. Until today. His eyes had been cold and triumphant as he glanced at me after that kiss with Dia. Then he had looked shocked and upset when he noticed me watching him. But he had been too late, I'd seen enough.

I should thank him really. He had saved me from making a mistake that probably would have killed him. I had already been on edge due to taking over as Archigós, and Kade's attempt to touch me had startled me. A lifetime of bad memories had crashed over me. Being locked in the freezing tower room at Tantalus for days at a time whenever I struggled in my studies. The whips that sliced into my tender skin for every perceived infraction, leaving splatters of blood upon the floor. The doctors that I begged to kill me when the pain of healing was nearly as bad as receiving the injuries. Every touch I'd known except for Aegeus's had brought pain. If Kade had touched me in that moment I would have drained every drop of his powers and kept on feeding on his life energy until it was gone.

I shook off the memories and suppressed every emotion until I was numb. Then I reached out to my advisor. *"Fayel, have you seen Syris?"*

"No, ma fille," Fayel replied sounding tired. *"Not since this morning after I checked on the injured hunters. He was speaking with Ekert's father when I entered the palace, but they stopped talking when they spotted me. They're up to something."*

"Syris is always plotting." I patted Bramble's head one last time and used my telekinesis to bring my staff to me. I quickly practiced a few moves and was glad to find my arm only hurt a little from where the metal had pierced me. *"He has not responded to my requests to speak with him. I am coming back. I cannot trust that he has taken care of Aegeus as agreed to."*

I was prepared to fight for my brother if need be.

"What about the Games? Won't you leaving them give Syris a reason to question your judgment?" Fayel asked.

"The race is finished. I am taking a few hours to ensure my brother is still alive and well," I stated flatly. I had done as my

father demanded; now he needed to hold up his end of the bargain. *"I will meet you at the main entrance to the valley."*

"Yes, Kyrion," Fayel replied unhappily.

I teleported to Kardia. The heat and humidity welcomed me back like an old friend. Overhead, the transparent barrier only visible to my people glimmered in the afternoon sun, except to the south where the hole was still being mended. I breathed in the scent of damp earth and green things, and a part of me welcomed the feeling of being home. The other part of me dreaded the dark memories that always tugged at me when I was at the palace. The soft forest floor pulsed beneath my bare feet sending out the message of my return to Fayel and the Talosi guarding the broken barrier. I waited until I felt the returning message that the forest was safe before I began to move. My senses came alive as the forest and animals called to me. Their familiar presence like the encouraging touch I needed to face my father.

I pushed through the thick foliage and stepped out into a small clearing. Even this high up the side of the mountain the sun struggled to reach the forest floor through the thick canopy. A raspy female voice called out, "Mieux vaut être seul que mal accompagné."

Fayel's French was as flawless as if she had learned it in Tantalus like I had, instead of from the militant group that had kidnapped her as a child.

"It is better to be alone than accompanied badly," I translated back to Fayel, letting her know I was alone. This was one of several phrases we had adopted over the years to communicate without my father knowing.

I scanned the trees looking for the white hair that would give away her location but my Archai was the leader of the Talosi for a reason. When I failed to find her, a raspy laugh sounded from up above. A tiny, dark-skinned woman swung down from a large tree branch to the ground in front of me. Her dark green eyes gleamed with delight that I had not been able to locate her. Her moss-green fighting leathers were splattered with mud. A bandolier of throwing knives crossed her chest. Her long white hair hung in a braid over her shoulder. She walked toward me on bare feet and thumped the end of her long spear onto the ground. Then bowed deeply.

"Archai Fayel, good afternoon and good health to you." I made a swooping hand gesture similar to a triangle with a curved tail acknowledging the loyalty and commitment that she had communicated with that bow.

She rose from her bow and fell into step behind me as I made my way toward the valley's main entrance. "How are the repairs to the barrier going?"

"Nearly finished," Fayel responded.

"Thank the goddess our people will be safe again soon," I said with a relieved smile. "We will toast our House in celebration for all that we have accomplished once the barrier is complete."

"Our people would welcome a celebration. This year has been hard on us all," Fayel said, gripping her spear until her knuckles turned white.

"Yes, these are difficult times. Perhaps a winter solstice celebration for all of the Houses like our ancestors once held?" I asked.

My advisor smiled her first true smile in days. "A great idea, ma fille. You will make an excellent Archigós."

Elephants trumpeted in the distance and chimpanzees chittered in the trees above as we made our way over to a giant lombi tree. The buttress roots spread out like tentacles in every direction anchoring the tree to the forest floor. I followed one of the largest roots, trailing my fingers along the top of the rough bark and feeling the vibrant life of the tree. The roots became taller as we neared the base of the tree, rising up around us to block out the sunlight. We passed through the heart of the tree and entered a dark tunnel through the mountain. Lizards and frogs glowed softly from the walls of the tunnel; the frog's sweet song was one I had always enjoyed as a child.

Sunlight blinded me for a moment as we exited the tunnel onto a wide ledge. When my eyes adjusted, the valley of my home stretched out before us surrounded by protective mountain ridges on all sides. About fifty yards to my right a waterfall fell from a rocky outcrop into a lagoon where kids splashed and women washed clothes. The water flowed into the Lomami River that twisted through the valley and across most of the area within the perimeters of Kardia. Men in small boats cast their nets and shouted to each other. Directly below us a dirt path ran between small mud-brick houses with banana leaf roofs. Cows, sheep, pigs, and other animals roamed freely in the cleared area off to the left of the village.

On a hill overlooking the river, sat nine stone houses with slate roofs and well-maintained yards—the homes of Father's allies. Near the center of the valley sat the palace, towering over it all. Even looking at that building had my ire rising, knowing what my people had gone through to bring such opulence here. Massive pink ivory trees gripped the stone foundation like hands and twisted up to form four tall towers at each corner. Servants had traveled all the way across the Congo and Zambia to Zimbabwe to steal saplings and spent months growing them into the tower formations. The inner walls of each tower showed off the tree's unique pinkish-red color that had fascinated me as a child. An open courtyard lined with date and fig trees took up the center of the palace. In the courtyard was the arbor covered in purple and white *Mondia whitei* flowers where the Kyrion and co-ruler thrones sat.

I scanned the valley again but there was no sign of my father. I tried to reach him telepathically but still nothing. "Syris is not here," I gritted out in frustration.

"What will you do, ma fille?" Fayel asked, sounding concerned.

"I will search as much of the western lands as I can for Aegeus. If Father has not returned two hours from now, I will have no choice but to go back to Sotirìa." Father's disappearance just when I was about to get everything I needed to banish him was too convenient. I didn't trust that he wasn't doing this to keep from fulfilling his part of our bargain. I was back where I started with needing to find my brother myself.

Fayel's sad look nearly made my emotions break through the icy shell I'd wrapped myself in. "May the goddess guide you on your search, ma fille."

"Thank you, Fayel," I refused to look at her for fear I'd give in to the tears burning behind my eyes. "You should return to your duties before Syris's spies notice your absence. I will contact you once my search is done."

She bowed deeply once more and then walked back the way we had come to continue her work on the barrier. I teleported to my bedroom in the palace and changed. This time I traded my dress for a green T-shirt and green leggings that would help me blend in with the jungle since the sun was still up. I teleported to the west cliff face and used my powers to move the large boulder that covered an access point to the underground river. I plucked a large palm leaf from a nearby tree and thanked it for its gift. Green light swarmed over my skin and across the palm leaf as it grew to my height. Then I grabbed each end, holding it over my head as I jumped feet first into the hole in the ground that the boulder had concealed. I fell straight down into darkness. The sound of rushing water and the slightly fishy smell of the river became more pronounced as I descended.

When the light surrounding me reflected off of the surface of the water, I bent to place the palm under my feet. Then used my powers to bring the water up to meet me. Descendants of Gaia weren't as talented with water manipulation as the descendants of Poseidon, but the most powerful of us could at least control the water in certain ways. I landed on

the waterspout with a splash, but the giant palm leaf kept
most of the water off of me. I lay down on the palm leaf,
keeping my arms and legs tucked tightly against my body.
The water rushed forward, carrying me through the underground system. A short while later I emerged out onto the
Lomami River, shielding my eyes as they adjusted to going
from pitch black into the bright sunlight. I sat up on the palm
leaf, letting the jungle relax my tense muscles as I floated
along at a slower pace.

I steered my leaf toward the bank and started walking. I
searched every rock and tree in the area for any indication
that my brother was nearby. But I didn't find anything. All
too soon my time ran out. I settled onto a sun-warmed rock
next to the river, my shoulders slumped in defeat. "I have
failed you, Aegeus." I whispered, the words scraping
painfully against my tight throat. My fingers dug into my
thighs, the pain helping me fight back the tears of frustration.

"Fayel, any news of my father?" I asked through our
connection.

"No, ma fille, Syris has not returned to the valley."

"Thank you, Fayel."

I closed my eyes. "Goddess Gaia, please hear me. I need
your guidance more than ever. Tell me the right path to take."

Butterfly wings brushed against my cheek and I opened
my eyes. A yellow butterfly—Gaia's preferred messenger—
flapped its small wings as it hovered only inches from my
nose. Then it landed on my chest in the V of my T-shirt where
the House of Seasons symbol peeked out. The goddess had
given me a sign, I just had to determine what it meant.

18

KADE

I HAD SPENT the last hour looking for Ariana but hadn't been able to find her. The other contestants had retired to their rooms already. Frustrated, I returned to mine too and jumped in the shower. When I was done, I tossed the towel onto the bathroom sink and pulled on a black T-shirt and boxers. I padded barefoot out into my bedroom and stared at the bed wishing I could sleep. But I was too on edge for that. I turned my back on the bed and stalked toward the closet. The door banged into the wall from the force I'd used to open it and a breath hissed through my teeth. I grabbed a pair of jeans and scooped up the black backpack sitting on the floor. Then dropped the backpack onto the suspended bed that was connected to the ceiling with thick brown vines. I pulled on my jeans and sat on the edge of the bed. It swayed gently as I pulled my backpack to me and unzipped the front compartment. Moonlight spilled across the bed from the wall of glass along the back wall of my bedroom and over the journal I pulled out.

The journal's leather-bound cover was scratched and stained. The cord that held it closed was frayed and in need of replacing. Pages in various shades of color marked the decades of my ancestors who had added their notes and stories to this book. I flipped to the newest section toward the back. The scents of old leather and Mama's favorite sweet pea flowers filled my nose. I thumbed through the pages cramped with Mama's writing and drawings until I found the symbol for the House of Harvests. My finger traced over the bundles of cut wheat with a sickle blade between them. Mama had been proud to bear Demeter's mark. What she hadn't been proud of was how her current House leader supported the war the House of Storms—Zeus's descendants—wanted. Mama said that her House had been neutral in the past, but under the new leader they were forced into the war. She hadn't liked to talk about it much, but after seeing that fight in the jungle, it seemed like the war was coming no matter what anyone wanted.

"I miss you, Mama," I whispered. "If there're answers about my powers here, I haven't found 'em. I'd sure welcome your advice right now."

I closed my eyes and waited for her soft voice to guide me. Instead, a memory I hated surfaced. Mama had practiced my powers with me in secret for a year, but I had gotten cocky. And that had been the worst mistake of my life. I'd been twelve the day I learned to regret my powers. I was on the edge of becoming a man but not quite there. The perfect mixture of clueless and fearless, I'd been testing my limits in every way including my powers. It was winter, and we'd gotten a rare dusting of snow in Texas. Daddy had gone to town to pick up the meat from a couple of cows we'd had butchered. Standing in the middle of a snow-dotted field with no one around and too full of myself to think I would get caught, I'd been excited to let my power loose. I'd started off small enough, just to see if I could grow wheat in December. When I proved that I could, I'd pushed to grow more and more. It wasn't until a fist slammed into my face that I noticed I wasn't alone.

"Here I thought you mighta taken after me," Daddy had growled down at me with the stench of whiskey on his breath as I lay bleeding on the ground. "But you got that demon blood in you just like your mama, boy." He stomped down on my arm. The crack of bones breaking sounded loud in my ears. My scream echoed across the field as snowflakes peppered my face. My blood mixed with the snow and trampled wheat stalks as Daddy beat me until I couldn't even whimper. From then on, he used my powers when it suited him to make money. Then he would beat me for using my powers and being a devil spawn. Then he would beat my mama for ruining his life and giving him a demon son. It was a cycle that hadn't stopped until Hope had given me the courage to stand up to him.

I closed the journal and placed it in my backpack. The truth was I'd never accepted my powers because I blamed them for turning the only man I'd known as my daddy against me. It was ironic that the powers I had denied most of my life, might be the only way to protect Hope from the war I was afraid was going to spill over into the human world. I prayed that day would never come, but I wasn't one to stick my head in the sand.

Surprisingly it wasn't Mama's voice but Ariana's that helped me understand what to do. *"You have good instincts, but you hold yourself back."*

I pulled on my boots and grabbed the pole I had been using in training. Then headed to the elevator. I stepped out onto the training floor a few minutes later and rounded the gym area. I was passing by the lagoon when a flash of red caught my eye. The rock wall of the cave jutted out in a ledge to the left of the lagoon. A red door I'd never noticed before sat under the shadowed ledge. Curious, I strode toward the door. Lights turned on overhead as soon as I opened it. The floor of the large room was covered in red mats. Practice dummies lined the left wall. The back wall on that half of the room displayed weapons from throwing stars to swords. Archery targets lined the right wall. The back wall on that side of the room held dozens of bows, arrows, and other accessories.

My skin tingled with anticipation as I walked toward one of the dummies. Beating the crap out of a practice dummy sounded like a good way to work off this energy and test my powers. I pressed a button to lengthen the pole, took up a defense stance and attacked.

"Ya," I shouted as the pole hit the man-shaped torso of the practice dummy with a satisfying thud.

The anger and frustration poured out of me. This time I didn't try to keep my powers contained. Tan grains of light spilled to the floor as I attacked again and again. Arcs of lightning flashed across my knuckles. My next strike landed harder making the dummy's head wobble. Strike. That was for Peithō taking control of me. Strike. That was for Peithō making me kiss Dia as my punishment for fighting for control of my own body. Strike. That was for damaging the fragile trust I had started to build with Ariana. On it went as I worked through my long list of grievances.

Ariana had disappeared right after the race. Kyrion Eros had glared at me all through supper not letting Dia leave his side. Dia had watched me like there was something she was trying to figure out. I hadn't been able to apologize to anyone. And I definitely couldn't tell them that it hadn't been me but the demon inside me that had stolen that kiss. I was as trapped by my bargain with Peithō as I had been when she took over my body. My pole slammed into the dummy hard enough to make my hands sting.

Peithō had all the power in this situation, leaving me feeling helpless. A feeling I knew all too well from my childhood and hated. The steady *thwap* of my pole hitting the dummy filled the room as my thoughts kept circling. I needed help but who could I trust?

Ariana's flushed face popped into my head from that almost kiss this morning. I'd gotten a brief look inside that icy tower she kept herself locked inside, and I'd been drawn to the woman I saw. For all her strength there was something soft and vulnerable there that tugged at a part of me. For a moment it was almost as if we were connected by something bigger than the both of us. But Peithō had ruined the moment, like she had everything else lately. I struck the dummy harder, pissed off all over again. When I swung at the dummy this time, lightning flowed down my arm and over the pole. The pole shifted into a long sword and my mouth dropped open in shock. White light filled the room as the sword made contact with the dummy. Seconds later the singed head of the dummy rolled across the floor to land at my feet.

"What the hell was that?" I said into the empty room.

Had that been what Ariana meant about the pole being able to do much more if I mastered it?

"*Impressive, cowboy,*" Peithō whistled. "*You may be even more useful than I thought.*"

I ignored her and dropped down onto the mat, panting. Several long minutes later I pushed to my feet feeling pleasantly exhausted. I picked up the dummy's head and sat it awkwardly back on the neck, trying to hide the damage. I pushed the door to the room open to leave but stopped in my tracks as soon as her scent hit me. I looked up and met Ariana's wide eyes. She stood beside the lagoon in her training jumpsuit. Her staff twirled around her hands in a blur. The water in the lagoon sloshed wildly as emotions warred across her face. Then her walls came up blocking me from seeing what she was feeling, and the water settled down. The staff came to rest at her side.

"Potential, why are you not resting for the competition tomorrow?" Ariana asked.

"I had a lot on my mind," I said, letting the red door shut behind me. "Ariana, I'm—"

"You will address me as Kyrion Gaia or my lady." She bit off each word with a brittle finality that made my chest ache. There was my proof that we were right back to where we started.

"My lady, I wanted to apologize for earlier," I started, but she held up her hand.

"Do you intend to give the competition all of your focus and efforts?"

"Yes, I'm in this to win. I just wanted you to know that it wasn't me today …" I struggled to find a way to explain. Peithō's oily darkness slithered inside me as if she were just waiting for me to break our bargain. "I mean, it was, but I don't usually go around kissin' just any woman. Dia is like a sister to me. I—"

"Potential, your dalliances are ill-advised but your own to choose," Ariana said indifferently; her gaze was focused somewhere over my shoulder. "Though, I will warn you that Potential King is Kyrion Eros' bond-mate, and you risk your life by pursuing her. She is similar to what I believe you call his 'ball-and-chain' where you are from."

I coughed to cover my laugh. "Uh, we usually just call them *wife* if we don't wanna have to sleep with one eye open." She cocked her head as if filing that away for later, then nodded. I closed the distance between us, watching for any sign that her walls were thawing at all. "I don't wanna have a 'dalliance' with Dia. I'm not interested in *her*." I collapsed the pole down and used the tip to push her loose hair back over her shoulder. The pulse in her elegant neck fluttered like crazy and a wave of relief made my legs feel shaky. If she was still affected by me then she could still be reached. "That won't ever happen again."

She swallowed thickly and stepped back. I wanted to close the space between us, but she was still skittish. I didn't want our time together to end though. "I was practicin' with the pole, but I'm still having' some trouble with the attack moves. Could you show me again?"

Ariana confidently strolled toward the open section of the floor and turned to face me. "Show me what you remember."

I smiled. My Kyrion was a sucker for someone who needed her help. I was going to use that to spend more time with her even if I got my ass handed to me in the process.

19

KADE

I EXTENDED the pole and walked through a series of wrist, knee, and rib strikes. Ariana called out corrections, but when I was finished, she seemed pleased. "You are improving; but in the midst of the competition, it will be more important to act rather than replicate the perfect positioning. We will fight and you will learn what I mean."

"Are you sure?" I asked, glancing down at the bandage on her arm.

She ignored my question and twirled her staff around. Then brought it to a stop in front of her and tapped the end against the floor. She walked a circle around me dragging the tip of the staff along the rock floor as she went. I stood still, my hands tensing and releasing their grip on the pole as I waited to see what she would do. The sound of her staff continuously dragging along the ground lulled me into a false sense of security. "The Games are about what is not seen as much as about what is," Ariana advised as she circled behind me once more.

Then I was shoved from the front and stumbled backward. I lifted my pole to defend myself but didn't know what from. Ariana's staff still dragged along the ground behind me and no one was in front of me. She circled me again. Her pale green eyes danced with challenge, and there was a look on her face that made me think my Kyrion was actually having fun. "The mind is a powerful tool that few remember is part of their arsenal," she said as she moved behind me again.

I gripped the pole tightly, on alert now for any tricks. The dragging of her staff stopped abruptly, and I turned, bringing up my pole to block her strike. Her staff knocked against my solar plexus hard enough to make me grunt. "Strike one," she said pulling back. "Your opponent will never play fair if they want to win. Use all of your senses in any fight."

I tried to bring my pole around to sweep Ariana's legs, but she had already moved. She tapped her staff against my kidney. "Strike two. Anticipate where your opponent is going, not where they are."

I grabbed her staff to pull her toward me and swung my pole at her knees attempting to drop her to the ground. She used my hold on her staff and launched herself into a side flip over as I swept at her legs. She landed on my other side, leaving my arms in an awkward crisscross. Before I could let go of her staff, she used my grip to tug me into to a spin. I stumbled, releasing her staff, but managed to keep my feet. Ariana lunged forward using the basic strikes she'd taught me, and I patted myself on the back for blocking most of them. Just when I was beginning to feel confident, she crashed her staff into my pole with rapid fire strikes, knocking it from my hands. I gulped down air and felt the tip of her staff press tight to my throat. "Strike three. Victory is never assured until the battle is over."

My arm muscles stung from the hard-hitting strikes, but mostly I was filled with the thrill of pitting myself against Ariana. She was the most amazing woman I'd ever met. She was a mixture of contradictions that kept me wanting to know more about the confident but vulnerable warrior princess. She looked fierce and beautiful in that tight jumpsuit that showed off every curve. Her cheeks were flushed with our mock battle, and her eyes were glowing with the closest thing I'd ever seen to happiness. Every inch of me itched to pull her into my arms and kiss her right now. But I wouldn't. Not so soon after kissing Dia. I wanted Ariana to know that when I did kiss her that there was no one else in my head but her.

I knocked her staff away from my throat and bent down to pick up my pole. *"Your crush on her is cute but don't waste your time. Ariana doesn't have a passionate bone in her body."* Peithō taunted me.

I shook my head as if I could knock her loose from my brain. *"My thoughts and feelings aren't any of your concern,"* I replied to Peithō.

"Are you ok, Kade?" Ariana asked.

"Fine," I gritted out, picking up the pole in a tight grip.

"Everything about you is my concern," Peithō said, and that oily darkness spread inside me. What would she do to Ariana if she took over my body now? *"It's amusing how much you care about Ariana. But if she knew about our connection, she would kill you in a heartbeat."*

My heart pumped faster in my chest and cold sweat dotted my forehead. Was she right? Would Ariana kill me if she found out?

"Let's play a little game, cowboy," Peithō crooned to me. *"You beat Ariana in your little training exercise, and I'll leave her alone. I'm such a good sport, I'll even give you a boost."*

The oily blackness spread throughout my body. I moved quicker than ever before with an uppercut strike at Ariana. She cried out in surprise but blocked my pole in the nick of time. The force of the blow was so great it rattled through my chest. Ariana looked worriedly at me. "Kade, are y—"

Before I could say anything, my body was already in motion.

"Stop!" I shouted at Peithō. Ariana's staff blocked the

strike aimed for her ribs, our weapons crashing together again with a loud crack. I thought quickly and came up with a reason that might work to give me back control. *"I want to win this on my own."*

"Fine," Peithō huffed. *"But make it good or our deal is off."*

Ariana's staff landed with a painful thwack against my thigh.

I moved aside quickly and repositioned myself to attack. Ariana's face was set in determination as she waited for my next move. I lunged, throwing out strike after strike. Ariana had been right: this was all about action not about getting it perfect. She countered every strike. We moved across the floor attacking and blocking like we'd been training together for years. There was a mutual respect and admiration between us as we gave it our all. I laughed as I did a quick combo move that nearly made it past her guard. She smiled in return, and it was like the sun came out from behind the clouds. I wanted to see that beautiful smile on her lips every day. Need rushed through my body, sizzling along my tired muscles.

Our weapons clashed once more with a loud crack, but we didn't pull away this time. Breathing heavily, we watched each other across the two feet that separated us. My need had to be stamped across my face: it was too great to hide anymore. Ariana bit her lower lip; her cheeks were flushed with the exercise and something that looked like longing. Our eyes connected and held. It was like my soul reached out to hers and latched on.

Tan grains of light sifted to the floor and grass sprang up around our feet. Lightning struck out from my chest and traveled up the pole. Peithō shrieked inside my head making me wince, but her oily presence was gone. Green light snaked up the staff in Ariana's hands and our powers collided at the point where our weapons crossed. They twisted and circled around each other just like we had been doing the last couple of hours.

A glowing blue circle formed around the iris of Ariana's eyes. The air crackled with anticipation, and I felt something shifting inside me like I'd finally found a piece of me that I didn't know was missing. That soft feel of flower petals brushed against my mind.

A hesitant little smile curled Ariana's pink lips but then quickly disappeared.

"Your eyes ..." we said at the same time.

"No," Ariana whispered, backing away. She grasped for the green light tangling with my powers and yanked them away. For a moment I'd felt as free and peaceful as when I rode through the fields back home under the clear blue sky. Then it had been ripped away as if only a dream. Ariana stumbled back a few more steps, fighting against the pull of our powers. "No," she said louder, "this is not what I want. I am too close to earning my freedom from one man to give it up to another."

My powers still searched around me looking for that connection but the fear on Ariana's face had me shutting them down. "What happened? What are you talkin' about?"

"Our powers sought to make a connection between us. They recognized what I did not," she stated. Her hands gripped the staff tightly as if still expecting me to attack. "The change in our eyes confirmed the god's intentions ... we are destined to form the Desmòs—"

A chill raced up my spine. The very thing that had destroyed the possibility of a future with my biological father and sent Mama running straight into Bruce Downing's arms. Fate had just come full circle and stabbed me in the back. "It's a bond and shared mark that ties two people's souls together even in death."

"Yes," Ariana said slowly and lifted her staff in a defensive stance. "How do you know that?"

I studied her for a moment. Would Ariana turn against me because I was from the wrong side of their war? *I'm sorry,*

Mama, but I can't hide anymore. The odds were stacked against me being able to protect Hope by myself. I was about to make the second biggest gamble of my life. "My mama taught me. She was a descendant of Demeter and once a member of the House of Harvests."

"Goddess save me," Ariana gasped. "The God of Chaos cannot be heartless enough to force the Desmòs between me and a son of our enemies."

"I'm not your enemy." I lowered the pole and placed it on the ground to prove my point. "I grew up in the human world. I didn't even know the human my mama married wasn't my real daddy until I was nearly grown. I've never used my powers much. Surely, we can work somethin' out? I don't wanna disappear like Nikki did or end up dead like Mikhail. I just wanna learn how to protect my sister."

"You should have thought of that before you came here," Ariana snapped. Then rubbed her right temple. "Nikki was an Olympian spy who got away, and Mikhail really did drown by accident. We are not monsters. If only it were as easy as trusting your word and making you swear an oath to one of our Houses," she replied tiredly. "Lia and Dia's powers were blocked. They had no knowledge of our world before coming here. You, however, freely admitted that you knew of your powers already and were even trained. You hid who you were all this time. That you are half Olympian; part descendant of Demeter and part … The lightning—do you know the House of your real father?"

"No," I said, then hesitated when I remembered that other female voice in my head this morning. "Mama said he was from the other side of the war. I … this sounds crazy, but I think the goddess Nyx talked to me. Could that mean …?"

"It is possible that your father is one of Nyx's descendants? Yes. That would mean you could very well be one of the people we have searched for, but I have seen the dangers that have come from trusting too easily in the Chosen until they learn our ways. We cannot afford another like Lia bringing havoc to our world." Ariana's lips pressed into a hard, thin line. "I cannot risk my people's lives. You will be placed under guard until the Kyrion decide what to do with you. Do not worry, as a contestant you are protected from any harm.

"As for the other ..." Her eyes were sad when she looked at me. "I am not what you are looking for, Potential. The Desmòs ... it is a mistake."

Even though I didn't want the bond either, I still felt gutted by her words. Quietly I replied, "You're right. It's a mistake."

20

ARIANA

THE TALOSI HAD ESCORTED Kade to his room with instructions to stay close by him. I stared down at the water in the lagoon still in shock from finding my true bond-mate. Of the select few people who received the Desmòs, I never thought I would be one of them. For a brief moment I had looked into Kade's eyes and imagined our life together. Days filled with love and laughter to replace all of the darkness of my past. But then I'd seen my powers feeding from him and killing us both. I couldn't take that chance.

I teleported to the top of the wall that rose a few inches above the water of the lagoon. I had come to the training floor tonight to work myself into exhaustion in hopes of being able to sleep after another failed attempt at finding Aegeus. The hours I'd spent in the jungle at Kardia should have helped to quiet all of the emotions fighting for space inside me, but they hadn't. My trip had only added worry over what my father was up to and what the message from the goddess meant. Instead, I had run into Kade and my worries had doubled. Was he a Chosen or a spy for the Omàda? Would the other Kyrion vote to remove him from the Games and keep him prisoner like Lia?

I crouched down on top of the wall that divided the practice area portion of the lagoon, still trying to work off my restless energy. The narrow ledge was all that kept me from plunging into the deep blue water only inches away on either side of me. Below the surface of the water, horizontal rows of holes were cut out of the wall at various depths that the contestants had raced through during the training for the last competition. I extended my right leg and the staff out to the side, keeping my movements fluid like the water. Then stood up and lifted my left knee high with my toes pointed as I pulled my staff back and lunged forward in a strike.

I hadn't been prepared to see Kade just yet. Not after seeing him kiss Dia. That longing ache had filled my chest again seeing him tonight, but this time it was accompanied by disappointment and anger. Why had he kissed her?

I shouldn't have cared, but I did. I cared too much about many things where Kade was concerned. I knew all about his troubles with the ranch due to the research Jaxon undertook on each contestant. I wanted Kade to win the Games, not for me but for him. I wanted him to be a Chosen we could rely on. I wanted him to be … mine.

His words echoed through my head. *"You're right. It's a mistake."*

My heart hurt and I wanted to yell at it to stop being stupid. Kade could never be mine. But then why did the gods bring us together?

"The gods do not make mistakes." I mockingly snarled the phrase we had been forced to repeat during lessons at Tantalus as I struck out with my staff again.

Yet, clearly, they had. I could not be bonded to Kade. For his sake, as well as mine. If Kade became a Chosen, then being around him could be like being near Lia. I was barely able to contain my powers being around Lia short periods of time. How could I spend my life tied to someone that constantly tempted me to drain their powers away? All it would take was one tiny mistake and Kade would be dead. And what about me? I had spent my whole life imprisoned in one way or another. I wanted to experience real freedom for once. Freedom to make my own choices. Freedom to speak without first having to weigh every word and constantly be on guard. Freedom to be me, not just existing in someone else's shadow.

We had walked away from the Desmòs, and that had been the right thing to do. Then why did it feel wrong? And why was I breaking my own rule by not telling the other Kyrion I had found my bond-mate amongst the contestants? I had argued to implement that rule to prevent another Kyrion from being distracted from their duties like had happened with Lia. The rules were there to keep us all safe; but I had denied my bond and would not let myself be distracted from my goals. Besides, Theia would surely demand that Kade be kicked out of the Games, likely saying everyone had an advantage over her contestant. I couldn't do that to Kade.

I launched into a cartwheel over top of my staff and struck out with the weapon as I landed on my feet. I worked through a complicated series of strikes with the full force of my muscles as if I could defeat every worry weighing me down.

"Archigós for a day and already I am overwhelmed," I said, disgusted with myself. "Perhaps I should not have announced my new position to all of our people this morning."

Surprisingly, it had been Maddox that recommended I make the announcement right away. The telepathic announcement this morning had been the second act of my new position and that had been followed by many more as the day wore on.

The other Kyrion had updated me on their House preparations for war. Jaxon had informed me that he had found nothing in his research about the black flames that had appeared twice when Bennett shared a vision with Lia. The powers the black flames had taken from me had not returned, and I was beginning to think they never would. I was still tired, but I no longer knew if it was from my weakened powers or the stress of my new position. Jaxon had also informed me that new translations of the writing on the Lotus Temple had only provided more historical information: the Primordial God who called himself Titan had a son who was predicted to be nearly as powerful as his father. At this rate I worried that we would never find information on the Chosen in time to locate them all before we were forced into war with the Omàda.

I had been in telepathic discussions with Fayel on and off throughout the day as well. The Kyrion all knew the duties of the Archigós, but Bennett had made this position look easy. Then again, he had been the only descendant in history to be born with the Archigós mark and had trained since birth. I made a mental note to set aside time to ask for his advice. Though Bennett would be well within his rights if he refused me, since I had taken the position he was born to from him. I winced as I remembered the last words he had spoken to me: *"Now I have control of nothing."*

How many times in my life had I felt the same?

I had never wanted to hurt him, but I didn't know how to fix things between us.

"Goddess guide me," I pleaded in a hoarse voice choked with regret. "Right and wrong. Light and darkness. They were once very clear. But everything is starting to blur."

I crouched once more and freed my powers. Green lights spilled from me and across the surface of the water. My powers pulled up spouts of water on each side of the wall and they twirled in the air. I used the twirling water as targets, shattering them into droplets as I landed each blow. Kade's sad face as he was escorted away by the Talosi tonight broke my concentration. I missed my target and nearly fell into the water.

My thoughts and emotions were all over the place, and I didn't know how to gain back my numb defenses. For once in my life, I had bent the rules, and now I feared my convictions were not as strong as they once were.

I desperately needed to regain my previous composure before I faced my father. For years I had worked on the wording of his sentence to be outcast from our House when I was ready. After all these years, he had finally made a mistake. I hated dragging Aegeus into this, but it was Father's treatment of him that had given me what I needed to declare Syris a traitor to our House. Father had been too impatient this time to weave his web with carefully worded traps to lure me where he wanted me. Instead, he had threatened harm against Aegeus to coerce me into doing what he wanted. And coercion of a Kyrion was against our laws. His days in the House of Seasons were numbered. Even if I had to use that memory serum on Father to find Aegeus and obtain the evidence needed to convince his allies of his traitorous actions.

Except, I had to find Syris first.

I spun my staff around my body, then thrust it out in front of me. I twirled the staff again and added a front kick. Cool water splashed me as I destroyed the last couple of water targets. I bowed to the water and teleported to my bedroom. I used my telekinesis to send my staff over to rest near my bed. Bramble trotted over to nudge against my leg, and I dropped down to my knees to pet her.

"I am confused, Bramble," I said as I stroked her soft fur. "I met my intended bond-mate tonight. He is all I would have wished for in a bond-mate if I had ever let myself dream of that kind of connection. Yet, the blood in his veins and his powers are half Olympian." I sat back onto the floor and crossed my legs. Bramble climbed into my lap and found a comfortable position to lay down. "If Kade is Chosen, then three of those we have found have one parent who is Olympian and one parent who is Paldimori. Does combining our bloodlines make a Chosen? Is that how the gods intend to save our people? By reuniting our bloodlines like they were in the beginning?"

Bramble whined in her throat, and I resumed petting her. "Why would the gods welcome back the children of the very people who betrayed them? The prophecy says that the Chosen would be our saviors or our doom. Have I been focusing too much on the savior part?"

Dia and Kade were good people that I doubted could ever hurt someone unless it was to defend those they loved. Lia was more unpredictable and reckless. Still, I didn't think even she would deliberately cause the destruction of an entire race of people. Maybe accidentally, but not intentionally.

"If I formed the Desmòs with Kade I would be able to see his thoughts and emotions," I mused. Then shook my head. I wouldn't give up my freedom or risk killing Kade to prove he could be trusted. "Bennett and Jaxon formed the Desmòs with the other two Chosen before we knew of their mixed heritage. They were able to prove beyond a shadow of doubt that the women told the truth. If Kade is descended from Nyx, then illusion would not work on him. Maddox's mind manipulations clearly did not work on him. We cannot let him go free knowing all that he does about us."

What was I to do with a half Olympian bond-mate that I could neither claim nor release?"

CADENCE SHIFTED NERVOUSLY against the side wall of the elevator as we rode down to the training floor the next morning. I leaned against the back wall, feeling like suspect meat in a sandwich, with the guards crowding either side of me. The Talosi had escorted me back to the bedroom on my floor and stayed just outside my door all night. The minute I'd stepped out they had been glued to my heels like silent shadows. I tipped my head back against the mahogany wall. The projection on the ceiling above showed a blue sky dotted with puffy white clouds that made me long for home. Had Hope gotten the money from the race I'd won yet?

Cadence slapped the gloves in her hand against her thigh.

"Are you nervous?" I asked, ignoring the guards.

She startled, dropping the gloves, and thumping her hand against the dark wood wall. Cadence forced a smile as she rubbed at her sore knuckles. "I meant to do that," she claimed, but it lacked her usual playful tone.

I carefully scooped up the gloves and handed them to her slowly, trying not to alarm my guards. "What has you all jumpy today, ma'am?"

"Kaaaade," she groaned out my name. "I'm too young to

be a 'ma'am.' I bet my grandmother loved that, though." She shot me a genuine smile this time, but it quickly faded. "I'm not worried ..." I gave her a disbelieving look. "Fine, ok, maybe I am. I mean, you're descended from the Omàda. That's seriously crazy because you shouldn't have been able to come here. But I don't think you want to hurt us."

She gave me a wobbly little smile that didn't cover up her fear. My heart broke a little that she viewed me as the enemy now just because of my family tree. At least they hadn't killed me. "Look there's stuff going on that I can't tell you. Although, I really should be able to tell you because you're clearly one of the Chosen. But you have to be clai—uh, I mean you have to win first."

The elevator doors opened and the guard motioned me forward, cutting off our conversation. We exited the elevator and joined the other contestants gathered near the lagoon. The guides seemed to be discussing details for the day in their own little group off to the side. The only Kyrion present was Ariana. She and Dia stood in the meadow across from the lagoon, well away from the others. Dia motioned agitatedly with her hands as she talked. Whatever she was saying had Ariana's brows furrowing in concern. When they both glanced my way, I knew they had to be talking about me. From the tension between them it couldn't be good.

I stepped forward ready to apologize to them both for my behavior yesterday, but a body crashed into me. I huffed out a breath as Cadence's arms squeezed tightly around my waist, her head nestled against my chest as she giggled out her trademark phrase. Her unbridled spirit reminded me of Hope back before the trouble this past year. God, I missed the sound of Hope's laughter. She should never have had to worry about losing our home.

I hugged Cadence back as she whispered, "I'm sorry. I know you aren't like them. It was ... we fought the Omàda a couple of days ago. It was my first real combat, and I was scared. And when I found out you were one of them, I just …"

"It's ok, Cadence," I said gently. "You're smart to be cautious. This war between our people is scary for all of us. I don't believe good or bad is limited to a certain House or people. Maybe someday we'll settle our differences and no one will have to be scared of lettin' people know who they are."

"Good luck, Kade," Cadence said with a little hitch in her voice as she pulled away. "Now go win this competition. Remember if you get into trouble, call out for Gaia."

"Guide Paxton, I need to see you," Devon growled. Cadence jogged off to where the other guides were trying to hide their amusement at the sweet girl. Devon motioned for her to follow him, no doubt for another tongue lashing. She had been in trouble almost constantly since she got here. I wondered what made her want to be a guide; she didn't seem like the trained soldier type. I hoped Devon wouldn't be too hard on her.

I walked over to join the other contestants. Chris came over, nervously adjusting his glasses, and rattling off guesses about what we'd face in this competition.

Cadence returned to the other guides with flushed cheeks, her eyes trained on the ground. I scowled at Devon, but he strode past without noticing. Our guides motioned for us to pair up with them, and then we were on our way. We turned right away from the lagoon and deeper into this massive cave until we came to a wall with several dark entrances. We took the second tunnel from the left. The darkness of the tunnel was broken by motion-activated strips of lights overhead about every thirty paces. After several twists and turns, light appeared at the end of the tunnel, and the smell of the ocean filled the air.

We trailed out onto a white sandy beach, squinting in the bright sunlight. The beach spread out about fifty yards in either direction. Six wooden row boats lined the sand near the water's edge, each bearing a House symbol. Out past the shallows huge rock formations rose up out of the ocean. I followed Cadence over to our boat and helped her push it into the water. The cool ocean waves lapped at my boots as I held the boat for her to get in first. Then I hopped in after her and looked around for the oars. Before I could ask where they were, the boat moved forward on its own, and I fell onto the seat with a grunt. Cadence giggled behind me, and I was relieved to know that she hadn't been cowed by Devon.

The boat rocked with the tide as we headed toward the rock formations. We passed under arches and navigated around tall slabs of rock that formed amazing shapes. Once we were out on the open waters, the boats formed a line with plenty of space between each boat. I watched from our position at the back as the boats turned left to follow along the tall rocky cliffs of the island. Several minutes later the boats angled toward the cliffs. I sat forward in my seat as the first boat disappeared—seemingly into the rock face.

"Wha—?" My voice cut off into a surprised yelp as our boat passed into a hidden break in the rock wall and darkness surrounded us. Screams echoed, mixing with the sound of rushing water from what could only be a waterfall, as the boat suddenly started to fall. I gripped the sides hard enough to splinter the wood and pressed my feet against the bow to brace myself. We splashed down moments later. Cold water drenched my face, but my jumpsuit kept the rest of me dry. The boat picked up speed as rushing water carried us through the darkness.

Finally, we exited onto a wide lake. The six boats clustered together as we all took in the sights around us. Steam drifted up from the surface of the water, and I could feel the heat on my face. Bright sunlight penetrated through the clear water to reveal formations along the rocky bottom that looked like old volcanos. Several deadly geothermal pools in vivid aqua, green, and gold colors dotted the shoreline. Charred black cliffs surrounded the roughly oblong area. The gentle breeze carried the smells of ashes and sea salt.

A geyser sprayed into the air and the silence was broken by Chris's shriek. Maya snorted and crossed her arms. Chris's face was red with embarrassment as he looked over at me; as though I would be disappointed that he had broken some man-code. "I didn't know Disney World rides had gotten this excitin'," I said scratching my beard in feigned confusion. "But I'm gonna have to ask the age-old question: Are we there yet? And when do I get my mouse ears?"

Devon grumbled about people talking too much. Cadence giggled at my attempt to shift attention off the boy. My eyes met Dia's amused ones, and we shared a smile. Then what I'd done yesterday hit me, and it was my turn for my cheeks to burn in embarrassment. I mouthed: "I'm sorry."

She tilted her head, looking me over. I wasn't sure what she was looking for, but she seemed happy with whatever she found. She waved her hand in a "forget it" gesture. Well, she'd been a lot easier to apologize to than I'm sure her husband would be. I was lucky Kyrion Eros had settled for giving me death stares, instead of punching me or using his powers on me every time he saw me.

Our boats scraped against a low stone wall with six short stone columns as the docking area. Our guides stood to grab the chains attached to the sides of the columns and clipped them to the ring at the bow of each boat. We climbed from the boats and followed our guides along a cobblestone walkway. To either side of the wide walkway was the same charred black rock the made up the cliff faces. About a quarter of a football field away the rock stopped at the edge of a large cluster of trees.

Ahead of us an entranceway was set into the face of the cliff. Steps the width of the walkway led up to a set of giant red doors. Eye shapes were carved from the rock on either side of the door and six more in a circle above it. The eye at the top of the circle was twice as large as the others and had a gold throne filling the pupil. We were maybe half a football field away from the steps when our guides directed us to stand on a hexagon-shaped stone in the walkway that bore our House symbols. The stones were probably about five feet wide, and I could see several more just like them every couple of feet along the walkway in front of us. Cadence gave me a thumbs-up and then patted her hip as if to remind me to trust the pole. Then she jogged off to join the rest of the guides on the steps.

Movement from the rock eyes over the doorway caught my attention. The Kyrion had teleported to their seats inside the hollowed-out pupils. Ariana sat ramrod straight on a small wooden bench on the left side of the circle with her hands folded in her lap. She wore a strapless corset top that looked like poured concrete and made my pulse jump with the way it molded to her every curve. The symbol on the front looked like a real tree whose roots formed the skirt of her dress. Standing behind her was Ekert Nazary, the man who had given me my prize money for winning the training race. He'd introduced himself as future co-ruler to the House of Seasons and then gone on to read me his long list of things I'd done wrong in the race.

Below them, Kyrion Erebus in a gray shirt and black leather pants looked like he was meditating. At the bottom of the circle, Kyrion Nyx lay on her side with her head propped up on her hand. Her other hand trailed along the crescent moon-shaped cutout that split her white leather top all the way down to the chainmail skirt sitting low on her hips. Up the right side of the circle, Kyrion Eros's feet dangled over the edge of the eye, and his fingers gripped the ledge. His intense focus was solely on Dia. His bare chest was covered in chain-mail with a red flying arrow symbol and paired with black jeans. Above him, Kyrion Chaos stood with his arms crossed.

The look on his face as black as the armored vest and leather pants he wore.

At the top of the circle, Kyrion Tartarus sat in that golden throne. His bare chest was covered in a metal-plated vest with buckles that strapped over his shoulders. At its center was the golden hammer symbol of his House. He wore black leather pants and just like the others, he was barefoot. Lying across his lap was the biggest golden hammer I'd ever seen. He picked up the hammer and stood.

"This is Minos, the first location of the House of Truth. To pass through these doors requires strength of character and knowing your own inner truth. But it also requires agility and good judgment. Choose your path wisely. Truth will show you the way."

He banged his hammer on the arm of the throne and the ground shook. The eyes on either side of the entranceway doors opened and lava poured out. The cobblestone path around us began to break apart. The stones collapsed with a deafening rumble. Dust shot into the air. I dropped into a crouch and covered my head. Debris bounced harmlessly off of my jumpsuit. Finally, it was silent. I stood up to find we were surrounded by a deep pit. The lava ran down channels to either side of the entranceway and flowed into the pit. The sulfuric smell of hot stones melting filled the air as the lava formed a lake below us.

I swiped the dust from my sweaty face and checked on the other contestants. Dia stood up from the pillar beside mine and nodded that she was fine. I could see the rest of the contestants getting to their feet as well and turned my attention back to our challenge. The holes in the wall closed, cutting off the flow of lava. The only part of the walkway that still remained were the hexagon stones that had the House symbols on them. They were all now tall pillars standing in rows in the middle of the lava lake.

Now how're we gonna cross this? I wondered.

As if in answer to my question, the pillar beneath me trembled. Then suddenly it began to turn. I stumbled, trying to keep my balance. I pulled the pole from the loop at my side and hit the button to extend it to its normal size. Then jammed one end into the rock beneath me to help steady myself. My feet were braced wide apart, as a hissing sounded from below and steam rose into the air. Streams of water poured out of the pillars from multiple sections. Then everything stopped, and we were once more facing the entrance to Minos. The other pillars were no longer in a neat row ahead but scattered across the pit in every direction.

The House symbol beneath my feet lit up with green light. I took that as my sign to begin and hesitantly stepped toward the edge of the pillar. The water had hardened the lava below. *Guess that's how we're gettin' across.* I gripped the pole and looked for a pillar with my House symbol. There were two directions to choose from. I decided to take the right route.

I pressed the top button of the pole, and it lengthened into its longest form. I prodded the lava rock below until I found a safe spot and then leaped. My body soared over the pit, and then my feet landed on the next House of Seasons pillar. The same thing happened again, and I had to pick a new path. The third time I landed on a pillar, that oily darkness slithered into me.

"Cowboy, I don't know how you pushed me out of your head last night but that was very naughty. Now I'll have punish you again. But not just yet. It's finally time you became more useful than stirring up the Kyrion," Peithō declared with excitement. *"Although, seeing Jaxon—the one you know as Kyrion Eros— nearly explode with rage was hilarious. Kissing Dia had to be the highlight of your boring day, right? It certainly was mine."* Her grating laughter filled my head, and I got the feeling once again that I knew her. *"It's fun being naughty, isn't it? C'mon, you can tell me; I promise I won't tell a soul. Scout's honor."*

I ignored her taunting and frantically looked around for help. Whatever Peithō was planning, I wanted no part of. Ariana hadn't killed me for being part Olympian. She'd actually said something about me being protected as a contestant. I was done being anyone's puppet.

I spotted Cadence watching me and waved my hand to signal I was in trouble. I pointed to my head trying to warn her where the problem was. Cadence just smiled and gave me two thumbs-up. How could I get her to see I needed help? I tried to signal her again, but my body locked down.

"No one can help you, Kade," Peithō said, as her oily darkness covered my insides. *"They have no clue that I'm inside your head. Be a good little toy and don't try to spoil my fun."*

My body jerked awkwardly into motion under Peithō's control. I spun around taking note of the other contestants. *"Eeny, meeny, miny, joy! Find a Chosen to destroy. Don't let them go even if they beg. Oopsy! I think I broke their leg."*

I tried to speak but my lips were sealed shut. *"What're you doing?"* I mentally shouted in alarm as my pole swung out to hit the contestant closest to me.

Luckily, Dia ducked and the pole sailed over her head. She jumped to her feet; her face red as she yelled at me. Whatever she was saying was drowned out by the sound of the maniacal laughter in my head. *"She's small but scrappy! Those toys are the most fun to break. But let's try someone a little easier for now. It's your first time, after all."*

"First time?" I asked still fighting to push her out of my body. How had I pushed her out last night?

"Oh no, cowboy, it's not what you're thinking." The sensation of her hands squeezing my butt made me want to scrub down for hours. Thankfully, her touch disappeared quickly. *"I know it's not your first time for that. As lovers go, you should be happy to know you rank in my top ten. I like it a bit rougher than you were willing to go, but don't worry, I'll teach you. If you survive."*

"I don—" I damn near hyperventilated when it dawned on me exactly who I was talking to. She'd whispered similar words to me the night we'd had sex. I hadn't known her name then but I'd heard the servants talking about her and put the pieces together. *"Natalie!"* I growled with hatred, knowing now that this wasn't some evil part of me but a real-life person. *"Or should I call you Peithō?"*

"Bravo, you figured it out," she said condescendingly. *"Too many people know my real name, and I couldn't have them ruin my fun, now could I? I think you deserve a prize, cowboy. I'll even let you collect if you do this one thing for me,"* she wheedled. What did she take me for? There was no way on god's green earth I'd ever help her with anything after what she'd done to me. *"Pretty please, Kade?"*

"Natalie, you used me to try to come between Jaxon and Dia. You damaged the trust I'd built with Ariana." My grip tightened around the pole as my anger mounted. *"You forced me to spy on the Kyrion in the jungle that night when they were fightin' the Olympians. You used me against my will, and you still are. I'll never help you of my own free will."*

The fact that I'd slept with this evil creature made my skin crawl. Then I remembered my strange behavior that night. *"The night we spent together, what did you do? I never would have* disrespected any woman by making out in a hallway or by ignoring Ariana when she needed me."

"I do what I want now that I've left Daddy Dearest behind," she replied in a coy tone. "*Since you're going to liven up my day with some fun in a minute, I'll play along. I seduced you, and you let me. My power is to bring out a person's deepest desires. Then I give them what they want. Most see me as whoever it is that they fantasize about, but not you.*" She sounded impressed as her oily darkness tightened around me almost as if she were caressing her prize possession. "*You must have some ability to see through mind-altering. It's been hard work keeping my connection to you and controlling you. But I would say you were worth the effort.*"

"Why me?" I asked.

"*Honestly? At first, I thought that Lia wanted you, and I will take everything from her, just like she did to me. I wanted her to see us together, but just like all the other men of hers I slept with, she didn't care. She's only ever cared about Bennett. My Bennett!*" The oily blackness squeezed me tight as her anger rose. "*Of course, I tried to kill her,*" she scoffed, like that was the normal thing to do when another woman caught the eye of the man she wanted. "*My bastard 'brothers' shipped me home to Daddy. My friends abandoned me because they worried I would tip off the Paldimori to our plans. I was told to stay behind this time, but I've never been good at doing what I'm told unless it benefits me. Once I was able to re-connect with you, I had the perfect spy to watch the action unfold. It was brilliant; everyone fell right into line like we knew they would.*

"*As for that annoying little prick that thinks he's my brother.*" She spat the word out like it left a bad taste in her mouth. "*Jaxon needed to be reminded of his place. We don't need the playboy to grow a pair of balls now that he's bonded. Pity both of my brothers will have to die now,*" she said, as though it was nothing. "*I had such plans for Bennett. I think he's the only man I could ever really love.*" Then her mood shifted again when she said happily, "*Oh, well.*"

"*What're you plannin'?*" I asked, trying to get any information I could.

"*Nah-ah, that's all you get. Now back to our goal of the day,*" she reprimanded me like a child. "*I need you to kill all of the Paldimori Chosen ... especially Lia.*"

"Never!" I shouted out loud and struggled to shove her from my mind.

"*Freewill is so overrated,*" she huffed. "*Honestly, though, I do have more important things to do than kiss every person I meet so that they'll fall under my persuasion,*" she sighed and traced a finger along my jaw. "*Now that I have you, my friends want me back. They can be really demanding sometimes. If the rewards weren't so yummy, I might think about switching sides.*"

She hummed as if considering it for a moment, while my anger built within a body I had no control over. "*Nah, too many rules.*" Her lips ghosted over mine. "*I don't like to break my toys until I've gotten a few more miles out of them but you haven't left me much choice. Bye, Kade. If you see the Primordial Gods after you die, give them a message from me: You lose, assholes.*"

KADE

NATALIE'S oily black presence infested every part of me. My body vaulted from one pillar to the next, no longer sticking to my House symbols. Chris was the contestant furthest behind. He stood at the edge of one of his House pillars as he tapped his pole on the lava rock below. Natalie forced me onto his pillar and stored my pole into the loop of my jumpsuit. I watched as my finger tapped his shoulder, and he turned with a relieved grin. My voice came out a cruel growl, "You are pathetic."

Chris's smile disappeared as Natalie's words—the painful words she'd used me to whisper to him—sank in. The defeated look that cut off the light of innocent trust in his eyes gutted me. I shouted and thrashed against her hold trying to fight my way clear. "*Don't do this, Natalie,*" I pleaded. "*I'll do anythin' you want; just don't hurt anyone.*" My voice cracked as I begged, "*Please ... Chris is just a kid. Please don't hurt him.*"

"*Aww, aren't you just the sweetest? You should have thought about your punishment before you tried to tell that idiot guide of yours about me. Now, normally, I would take my time, but I have people to see about a new mission.*" She sighed regretfully, and for a moment, I thought she might change her mind. "*I wish I could keep you, but my friends would never have let you live. Only one side can win this, cowboy. And I plan to be with the winners."*

Then she shoved Chris off the pillar. His screams echoed around the pit until they were cut off abruptly when he hit the black rock below. Lava began to ooze up through the breaks in the rock around his still body. Shock at what she'd done—at what she'd used me to do—hit me like a Mack Truck.

Everything seemed to be happening as if from a distance. Natalie vaulted us over pillars with ease as we closed in on another contestant who was further away from the others. Zeno glared at us as we landed in his path. Our middle finger raised and he laughed. It was all the distraction Natalie needed to jam our pole into his gut. He grunted and gripped his stomach, staring at us in annoyance. "Cut that shit out. You wanna fight? Save it f—"

Before he could finish, our pole slammed into the side of his head. He managed to partially block with his arm, but not enough to completely avoid injury. Blood dripped from a cut over his temple and ran down his cheek. He snarled and swung his pole at us. We ducked the blow and a gust of wind that had to be Natalie's power poured from my hands.

Zeno fell from the pillar with a shouted, "Fuck you!"

A bellow of rage sliced through the air coming from the direction of the Kyrion.

"Uh-oh, you're gonna beeee-ee in troouble," Natalie sang. *"Remember what Bennett did in the jungle? He's going to burn you from the inside out after he tortures you for a very long time. My sexy stepbrother is pow-er-ful."* She hummed appreciatively, and I nearly lost my lunch. How could anyone be this evil? How could she do that to Chris? Or her family?

"Don't judge," she huffed. *"I've loved Bennett since I was four years old. He would've been mine too if it wasn't for that bitch, Lia. If only I could find a way to break their bond,"* she mused. *"Then again, I have a better offer on the table now. Who wants to be co-*

ruler of the Paldimori Houses, when you can be queen of the fucking world?"

The girl was a few sandwiches shy of a picnic. I tried to shake off the shock and form a plan for kicking her out of my body. What the hell had I done the last time? I hesitated to think more deeply about what had happened with Ariana that night. Natalie didn't seem to be aware of what we had discovered about the connection between us, and I wanted to keep it that way. We jumped to another pillar as the Kyrion gathered on the steps in front of Minos's red doors, watching us with deadly looks.

"Don't worry," Natalie reassured me. *"The Kyrion can't interfere in the Games unless they're called by their Potential or there's a unanimous vote. It's rule number two of these stupid Games."* I could practically hear her rolling her eyes. *"Besides, this is Tartarus's turf, and he isn't going to let anyone interfere. He, at least, believes in survival of the strongest."*

Maya tried to sneak past on our right, but Natalie was quicker. Our pole lashed out, but it missed the other contestant by a mile. Maya shot a scowl our way, and then vaulted to another pillar. Natalie laughed and turned us toward the other two contestants. Dia stood on her pillar as we got closer, not bothering to run. She gazed at us with a devastated look as tears streamed down her cheeks. Everyone had seen me kill Chris and Zeno. There was no coming back from that.

Our lips pulled back into a feral smile as we landed on a pillar about twenty yards away from Dia. "I guess this is hello and goodbye, *sister*," Natalie said in a voice that sounded like my evil twin. Dia swiped the tears from her cheeks but didn't try to run from the demon in front of her.

Dia cocked her head to the side, studying us. Green light twined with whitish-blue and red flowed down the pole in her hands as she pointed it at us. The powers brushed against our body but quickly pulled away. Dia's eyes widened. "Natalie! I should have known after you did something

similar to Bennett and that poor cop. You love to turn men
into your little puppets, don't you? I told Ariana that something had been off with Kade when he kissed me. You played
Kade all wrong. He doesn't have a cruel or scheming bone in
his body." Dia tightened her grip on her pole and stepped
forward. "When did you get control of him?"

"Oh, Kade and I have *history*. I just lost my grip on him for
a little bit when I was forced to go home to my stepfather and
get therapy for my wild ways," Natalie replied, sounding
bored. Then she shifted gears. "Did your BFF, Lia, tell you
how I nearly took Bennett and everything else from her.
That's what I'm going to do to you too."

We lunged forward, our pole slamming into Dia's. She
blocked us but fell to one knee as our wind power tangled
around her legs. Dia rolled across the pillar and grew a vine
from her free hand to wrap around our ankle. She rose to her
feet and tugged the vine. With her other hand, she swung the
pole at our head. We teleported away and appeared behind
Dia. I tried to yell for her to watch out, but my mouth wasn't
working again. I couldn't be the cause of one more death.

Something inside me broke and blinding white light
seared my chest. Every part of me felt like an exposed wire,
raw and dangerous. Anger built inside me, but this time I
didn't try to stop it. If anyone deserved wrath to be unleashed
on them it was Natalie. I burrowed deeper into that place
inside of me where the storm lived. The smell of ozone and
tears surrounded me. I visualized wrapping my hands in the
white flashes of lightning and yanked it free.

*This is for the good men who died today. And for the pain you've
caused too many people.* For the first time since my mama's
death, I welcomed the burn of anger. Years of pain fueled me:
All of the beatings, Mama's death, the responsibilities that I
had to carry, the helplessness of not being able to protect
Hope. I attacked that oily darkness like a beast, burning it
away with the lightning that flashed in and around me.

Natalie cried out in shock. *"Look at all that power!"* she hissed as I forced her to retreat one oily black tentacle at a time. *"Join me, Kade. My friends won't hold you back with all these rules and bowing down to the Kyrion."*

"Go to hell where you belong," I replied as I continued to fight her.

Natalie shrieked and grabbed for control of my body. At her command, my pole whipped out blindly, trying to finish taking out Dia. I threw another lightning bolt and regained control enough to toss my pole into the lava pit. My body dropped onto the stone pillar, convulsing as the internal battle continued. I chased after Natalie as she fought dirty, attacking my body instead of facing me. She squeezed my lungs until spots danced before my eyes and bashed my ribs one by one. She slowed down with every strike I landed, but at this rate, I'd be dead before I could stop her.

Cool hands brushed my temples and a familiar voice whispered in my ear, *"Let me in, Kade. I can help you."*

Natalie screamed, *"No! Don't listen to her."*

"It's Emory, Kade," the other voice said soothingly. *"Open your shields, and I can break Natalie's hold on you. I'll force my way in if I have to but I'd rather not. That might cause permanent damage to your mind. Think of a door in your mind and open it for me."*

Natalie gripped my heart in her fist and started to squeeze. My lightning slipped from my hands as I lost my concentration. The *thump-thump* of my heartbeat sounded slower and slower as Natalie tightened her grip. My fingers clawed at my chest trying to free her invisible grip. I clung to images of Hope and Ariana. There was too much I still needed to say and do. I refused to leave them like this. I used my fading strength to imagine that door in my mind and kicked it open.

Natalie's suffocating oily darkness wrapped tighter around my heart, doubling her efforts to kill me. Emory's

presence drifted into my body like a weightless cloud
blocking out the burning of the sun on a blazing hot afternoon. Emory wrapped herself around the darkness trying to
crush my heart and Natalie screamed. The oily trails that
hung like spiderwebs inside my body turned to smoke and
disappeared. Natalie cried out in pain, and then she was
gone.

"*I don't think there's any permanent damage, at least, to your
mind,*" Emory said inside my head. "*But the rest of you is in
rough shape.*"

"*Thanks,*" I replied, my body feeling like one big ball of
pain. "*I'm not sure I coulda fought her off much longer.*"

"*You're welcome. I never liked that bitch anyway. Hopefully, I
did enough damage to keep her from vamping on anyone else for a
while.*" Emory hesitated a moment before continuing. "*You
know Chris's death wasn't your fault, right?*"

"*I may not have been in control, but it was my hands that ended
two men's lives today,*" I said with a hollow ache in my chest.

"*You didn't kill Zeno,*" Emory informed me. "*I doubt that
bastard knows how to die. But even if he were dead, that would be
on Natalie's hands not yours. Don't borrow burdens, Kade, there're
enough in life to keep us all in therapy for a few lifetimes.*"

I snorted a laugh and regretted it when sharp pain crashed
over me. Emory exited my mind. I blinked up at her as she
kneeled over me, my battered body lying on the cool stone of
the pillar. She awkwardly patted my shoulder.

"I've called for our doctor. He'll come check you over and
give you something for the pain," Emory said. Silence
stretched between us for a few minutes. "I, uh, I'm sorry
about Chris. We retrieved his body to send home to his
family."

"I didn't know him. Not really." I grunted as I tried to sit
up and pain took my breath away. Emory cussed at me and
told me to stop being a stupid macho man. I settled back on
the ground. "Chris … deserved my time and attention, but I

was too wrapped up in my own head to bother." My fists clenched, and I welcomed the painful scrape of stone against my knuckles. "Chris was here doing somethin' selfless to help his grandpa. The rest of us are just tryin' to get ahead. No one deserved what happened, especially him."

Emory nodded. Then turned her head quickly as if the subject made her uncomfortable. Her fingers fiddled with the end of her purple-and-black-streaked braid as her strange amethyst eyes remained trained on the Kyrion. "They granted my request for a rest break, but the competition won't be stopped for much longer. Are you going to drop out?"

"No," I replied immediately. Chris's death would not be in vain. "I'll keep on for my sister—and for Chris."

I was going to win this and get his grandfather the money Chris wanted him to have.

Emory smiled. "I knew I liked you. Now we just need the doctor to patch you up and you'll be fine."

I chuckled but it turned into a moan. "Fine might be a bit optimistic, but I'll make it back into the competition."

"And you'll win," Emory stated, with all the bossy attitude I'd seen her aim at others. "Dia doesn't need the win. She's just competitive whether she wants to admit it or not. Zeno …" A cocky grin stretched across her face. "Let's just say that one will be taken care of. I don't trust Maya—hell, I don't trust anybody—but she gives me bad vibes. Don't give her a chance to screw you over."

"Yes, ma'am." I smiled at her weakly, and she rolled her eyes. "You pushed Zeno off the rock columns during the training race, huh?"

"Your doctor's here," Emory said, with a twinkle in her eye as she ignored my question. She absolutely *had* done it. "Good luck, Kade. I'm rooting for you."

The doctor teleported me from the pillars over to the charred ground at the edge of the lava pit. A golden light surrounded his hands as he scanned, identifying every injury Natalie had left behind. Cadence sat beside me, biting her lip as she watched him confirm several bruised ribs. Luckily, they weren't broken. She handed me a goblet of water to take my pain medicine with when the doctor excused himself. Then fretted like a mama cow over her newborn calf as I got painfully to my feet. I assured her I was fine, but she clearly didn't believe me. I walked out the pain until the meds kicked in. Cadence hovered by my side until I sent her away to be with the other guides.

Zeno hobbled over to sit a few feet away and snarled at the doctor when he started examining him. The man I'd knocked off a forty-foot-tall pillar was bruised, cut, and burned but still able to flip me off when I stopped to apologize. I just nodded and walked toward the nearest cluster of trees, needing some space.

Jaxon had Dia pinned against a tree on the outer edge of the mini forest and was kissing her passionately. I gave them a wide berth since I wasn't in any shape to get punched right now and walked deeper into the forest. When I was out of sight, I leaned back carefully against one of the trees, my head against the bark as I looked up at the clear blue sky. Guilt and sorrow gnawed at my insides. "I'm sorry, Chris."

The rustling of leaves sounded nearby letting me know I wasn't alone. Ariana stepped out of the trees looking unsure of herself as she came toward me. The Kyrion mask slipped into place as she stopped before me, and I wanted to rip down the walls between us with my bare hands. A boy had died today, and it'd been a close call for the rest of us as well. Life was short. I'd lost too much already to gamble away the minutes that none of us were promised. Every person who had ever owned a piece of my heart had gotten all of me, and I had no regrets. Why should Ariana be any different? Yes, the Desmòs worried me. But Mama's life had fallen apart because she didn't share that connection with my biological father.

"Potential Downing, I am sorry for the loss—" Ariana

started to say, but cut off abruptly when her hand lifted to rest over my heart.

The only good thing Natalie had done was show me how to use my powers. "Don't move," I told her as I pulled my powers away. Ariana stared at her hand resting on my chest in disbelief. Only a thin layer of material separated our skin, and I wanted to remove that too, but I knew she wasn't ready. She shifted uneasily, and I came up with an excuse to keep her close. "You'll hurt my ribs if you move around too much." She stilled immediately, and I wanted to smile. "I'm not touchin' you, and I won't unless you want me to. But you can touch me anytime, anywhere.

"Look at me, Ariana," I commanded roughly, pulling her from her dazed shock. When her eyes met mine, there was a deep vulnerability in them that made me want to lay the world at her feet. *No regrets.* When I thought I was dying today, that had been the thing that haunted me. I didn't want to leave this world with regrets, and there was a major one that had been on my short list. "You saw what happened out there today. Any one of us could have died." She looked away, but not before I saw the fear there. Was that for me? I leaned toward her. "Look at me, Ari. Let me see those beautiful green eyes."

Her head whipped back around and irritation sparked in those pale green depths. I smiled down at her, loving that strength that never kept her down for long. "Don't yell at me just yet. I have somethin' to say." She stared at me warily. "I'm sorry. Peithō, or rather, Natalie has been in my head for days. She forced me to kiss Dia."

It sounded bad that I hadn't told her about the voice in my head controlling me before, especially knowing now how dangerous Natalie was. I rushed on to finish what I needed to say, and then I would face whatever the consequences were. "Thinkin' back on it, she was probably in my head since the day that she offered herself up as my prize in the first competition. She kissed me, and I was addicted. I'm sorry for keepin' everythin' from you. She took me to the jungle the night you fought the Olympians too. There might be more that I'm forgettin', but I think that's the big things. I want you to know that I'll give you any information that I have."

Ariana's eyes widened a moment, and I could see she was sorting through everything I'd said. "Natalie was responsible for all of that?"

I nodded. "She called herself Peithō when she talked to me. I thought she was some evil part of me, and I was too scared to tell anyone about it."

"I do not think there is any part of you that could be evil, Kade," Ariana stated quietly, as a blush swept across her cheeks. Then she quickly changed the subject. "You said she used the name Peithō? In Greek mythology, she was a goddess of persuasion and seduction. The mythologies were created by the Omàda to set themselves up as gods. They made up stories to cast doubt and fear amongst the humans. But that was long ago. Why would Natalie use that name? She is a descendant of Eros like Jaxon, yet very few have powers like hers. Persuasion through kiss was more Aphrodite's style."

"She talked about a lot of things that didn't make sense to me but maybe they would to you?"

"Thank you for your offer to share what knowledge you may have gained from her."

"I don't have anythin' to hide. Not anymore." I took a deep breath and plunged in. "You know my secrets now, but I don't know much about you. I'd like to change that."

She started to say something, but I held my finger up to her lips. Not touching just hovering there. I wanted to touch her skin on skin, but I wouldn't. Not until she was ready. One day she'd realize that physical touch didn't have to mean pain. Hopefully she'd tell me about her past and we could face all the leftover trauma together. I dropped my hand.

"There's a lot of reasons why we shouldn't be together. But you're my partner in these Games, and if you give me a chance maybe we can be a lot more."

I moved closer until our lips were only inches apart. "I could've died today without ever givin' this a try, and that would've been a damn shame." My finger traced the air over her bottom lip. "To never kiss your pretty pink lips until they're red and the taste of you is burned into my memory. To never map every spot on your body that smells like vanilla bloomin' in an exotic forest until I'm covered in your scent." My finger traced through the air above her neck and across her bare shoulder. Her warm breath panted against my lips. As much as I craved her kiss, I wouldn't take it from her. Whatever her past was, it had left scars, and I wanted to show her that they didn't have to define her. They didn't have to be a prison keeping her isolated from everyone. "Kiss me, Ariana."

A needful little sob escaped her parted lips and struck me like lightning. "Prove to us both that what's between us is more than just the pull of the Desmòs." Her hand trembled on my chest, and I could see she was still fighting this. "If there's even a chance that what I feel is real, I'm willin' to risk it." She tried to move away, but I refused to allow her to put distance between us. My powers wrapped around her waist gently holding her in place. My voice came out gruff when I demanded, "Kiss me now, Ariana. Show us both that you don't fear a thing."

She made an irritated little growl but rose to the challenge. Her trembling lips brushed mine like the fluttering of a moth's wings. I dared not move a muscle. I dropped my hands to fist them at my sides as I fought my need to touch her. Her lips brushed mine again. Then again. Finally, her lips locked fully with mine, and I nearly shouted with joy. She had done it!

Her lips were stiff and unsure against mine. I slowly

guided her through the kiss. It was the most innocent kiss I'd ever had, but it burned my lips like the best whiskey. Her other hand brushed against my bearded cheek, and I celebrated the first unprompted touch from her. Ariana made a soft humming noise of appreciation that went straight to my dick. Damn, I was about to embarrass myself.

A shout sounded in the distance. Ariana's hand bumped my chest, and I grunted in pain. She pulled away. "Oh my goddess, I am sorry," she said, taking a step back. Her cheeks were flushed, and her lips were shiny from our kiss. I wanted to say to hell with the rest of the world and keep her here until she agreed to give us a shot.

Her fingers pressed against her lips as she looked at me with nervous awe. "We agreed the Desmòs was a mistake. What are we doing?" That blue ring was around her eyes again, and I had to guess from the way she stared at me that my eyes were doing the same thing.

"I know what we said, but I want the chance to see where this could go." No regrets. "Forget our fears about the Desmòs and the fact the gods hand-picked us for each other. The gods didn't make my heart break a little every time you showed me your vulnerabilities. They didn't make me want to do crazy things just to see you smile. The gods didn't make me crave the feel of your touch or fill me with pride every time you refuse to back down from somethin'." I used my powers to brush a curl back over her shoulder. "I think the gods gave us the Desmòs to recognize what we might have together if we give this a try. The rest is up to us."

She stared up at me with a wistful look. "I ... I want ..."

I caught a glimpse of movement over her shoulder and Ekert stepped from the trees. "Kyrion Gaia, what a surprise you are." Ekert said with a smile on his face that reminded me of the villains from those superhero cartoons I'd loved as a kid. Ariana jumped and her face went deathly white. She tore herself away from me, putting a couple of feet between us. Was she afraid for us to be seen together?

"How was it your father described you when we signed the betrothal contract?" Ekert asked as he walked toward us. "Oh yes, a bleeding heart who would never jeopardize her people or the *brother* she cares about. Yet, here you are kissing a man who is not your betrothed."

"What betrothal?" I asked.

"Ekert, stop," Ariana begged in a shaky voice. She didn't turn to face Ekert, but her eyes darted in his direction with fear. What didn't she want him to say? I stepped forward wanting to protect her from whatever was happening here. She held up a trembling hand that stopped me in my tracks. "This was me, not Kade. There is nothing here that would change my commitments to those I care about."

Was she saying she cared about Ekert? "Ariana, please can we ju—"

"I'm willing to forgive you," Ekert replied as he stopped next to us. He placed a hand over his heart and looked at Ariana with compassion. "After all, as your bond-mate I will be promising to honor and *protect* you during our Bonding Ceremony. But if you've changed your mind, we will have to tell your father about—"

"No!" Ariana said as she stepped between me and Ekert. "Nothing has changed."

My heart stopped. My eyes found Ariana's and the misery in them confirmed my worst fear. I'd never understood how my real father could walk away from my mama, but I'd felt the pull of the Desmòs now. I understood a little better the strength of that connection. But I'd thought there was more between us. Something that we could build a future on.

"Ariana, please tell me what's happenin' here." I tried once more to reach for her, hoping this was a misunderstanding. She flinched away and my hand dropped limply to my side.

That familiar cold mask slipped over her face and she looked right through me as if I were nothing. "Potential Downing, I believe you have a competition to win. Return to the Games while I speak to my betrothed."

I walked away, leaving the woman the gods had picked to be mine with the man she had chosen to spend her life with.

Tears stung my eyes as I pressed my fingers against my lips where Kade's kiss still lingered. I should have hated Kade for hiding that Natalie had controlled him. I should have locked him away for killing another contestant even if he had been under Natalie's influence. But I couldn't. All I had cared about was making sure he was ok when I followed him into the woods. Our connection had grown strong enough that his presence had pulled me to him and left my body tingling with static electricity. All I had wanted was to fall into his arms and reassure myself that he was safe. My need for him was a weakness that had damned us both. The harsh reality of my life had intruded, and I'd had to push Kade away again. Letting him walk away had taken all of my restraint, but I would protect Kade from everyone. Especially the manipulations of my father and the man standing behind me.

Ekert had no qualms about threatening to use my brother or Kade against me as evidenced by his threats. I couldn't let Kade become another person to threaten me with, for either of our sakes. Kade made me want to see the world the way he did. He made me want to experience and feel all that life had to offer. Those were all dangerous weaknesses that Father and

Ekert would use against me. They were distractions that would pull me from where my focus was needed most: on saving my people. I prayed to the goddess that pushing Kade away had saved us both.

"Ekert." I spat his name like it was poison on my tongue. At this moment his name was synonymous with every bit of pain that lived inside of me. "Your threats were poorly concealed. It seems my father has much more to teach you."

I tried to gather my tattered defenses while my mind raced to find a way out of this mess. I mourned the loss of my protective walls that had kept me safe from this emotional torment my whole life. Maybe the burdens I carried had finally become too much, and I was too weary to keep up my defenses any longer. Maybe when Kade had found the chink in my armor he had weakened my defenses too much for me to lock away my feelings ever again. Whatever the case, I had been roused from my icy tower of numbness. But I was ill-equipped to handle the emotions that constantly shifted inside me.

"My threats were as transparent as your connection with that boy," Ekert sneered. "Come now, there's no need to hide the proof from me," he said as he walked around to face me. I looked at him with a level of contempt that nearly rivaled what I felt for my father. "I saw the light of the Desmòs in the boy's eyes. The same blue glow that surrounds your own eyes."

The man standing before me wasn't the bumbling idiot that I'd come to expect. This man stood tall and confidence radiated off of him. His eyes scanned me now with a cunning intelligence. "Are you surprised, Kyrion Gaia?" he asked. "That I'm not the simpleton I portrayed all this time."

"Actually, I am. Who knew there was an ounce of intelligence hidden in that head of yours?"

He smiled and clasped his hands behind his back like my father did sometimes. "Unfortunately for you, I'm smart enough to take advantage of what I just saw. The untouchable Kyrion Gaia has a true bond-mate."

"An unclaimed bond-mate," I informed him with a defiant tilt of my chin. "There is no need to be concerned with the Potential. We can settle this without my father—"

"Ah, there's the real reason the new Archigós stands trembling before me." Ekert's eyes raked over me with disgust. "You fear your father's reaction to your dirty secret but haven't a concern for mine. You treat me like an unwanted dog you can order around but no more. I was there when you made your pretty little speech about Kyrion not getting distracted by a bond-mate among the contestants. I was there when you made the rule to declare any identified bond-mate. Yet, you're here rubbing yourself all over your true bond-mate that no one knows about. You think you're above us all, don't you?"

"No," I said between clenched teeth. "You are right. I did break the rules. I will gladly go now and confess to the K—"

"I don't think you will," Ekert replied as he cocked his head to study me. "You never do anything without a reason. Why would you keep this from the other Kyrion?" A knowing smile stretched across his lips. "You're protecting the boy. I can help you. This can all stay between us. Your father doesn't ever have to find out about Kade."

"Syris would be proud," I replied. Ekert had fooled us all, even Father. "What is it that you want?"

"The throne." Ekert tapped his ever-present clipboard against his leg. "I want us to complete the Bonding Ceremony next month, and I want you to leave all Kyrion duties to me. I won't tell anyone your secret, and you will have nothing to do with that boy again. Are we agreed?"

My heart ached as if Ekert had reached inside me and squeezed it in his fist. How could I give up everything I had been working toward all these years? And Kade … I hadn't realized that I still held onto a small sliver of hope that I could have it all. But I was once again caught in someone's web, and this time there was nowhere else to maneuver. The Kyrion decided the punishment for breaking the rules of the Games, but I worried their displeasure with me—especially Bennett and Theia's—would see me put on trial just as Lia had been. And what would happen to Kade or my people then? The trap closed around me, and my dreams slipped through my fingers. I felt myself drowning in helplessness once more.

"I have conditions of my own," I countered, refusing to give up completely. Ekert nodded for me to continue. "You will tell me where my brother is being kept and release him into my care. And you will not let Syris dictate to you. I refuse to see our people suffer more under his influence."

Ekert frowned. "I don't know where they keep your brother, but my father does. He joins your father in visits there sometimes. I'll have him make the arrangements with your father as your bonding gift." He tapped the clipboard against his leg again, lost in thought. "Your father is a smart man in some ways, but his greed outpaces his vision. I never intended to let him live long past our Bonding Ceremony. I agree to your conditions."

A cold chill washed over me at Ekert's nonchalant mention of killing my father. Would he think me as expendable once he had the throne? I would have to make sure I studied my new opponent better. For now, at least I would have my brother back, and our people would be free of Father's influence. Why then did I feel like I had lost everything that mattered?

"Agreed," I replied. I didn't trust anything Ekert said but our agreement would buy me time to find a way out of this. Father knew

I had traded my dreams for the lives of those I loved. I just prayed to the goddess it was enough.

26

KADE

I WALKED SLOWLY BACK out of the trees; my eyes trained on the ground as I mulled over what had just happened. I refused to destroy Ariana's relationship like the Desmòs had done to my parents. But it felt like I'd ripped my chest open and pulled out my still-beating heart. That reaction surprised me. I cared for Ariana, but I hadn't realized how much. I guess there was a reason all those songs were written about not knowing what you had until it was gone. Except we'd never even gotten the chance to see where things would go. I scrubbed my hand over my short hair as if I could rub her out of my head.

I felt her, now more than ever, like the soft brush of flower petals against my skin. There was a tugging inside me whenever she was around, almost like some part of me reached for her. My back itched and burned when we got close. It would be torture feeling all of that and knowing I couldn't do a damn thing about it. After this competition I would ask to be assigned to one of the other Kyrion. Then when the Games were over, I'd never have to see her again.

Cadence hugged me gently when I reached the edge of the lava pit and handed me a pole. Either these things were indestructible, or they had come prepared with backups since mine had gotten thrown into the lava. I lined up with the other contestants and forced myself to focus on what needed to be done. Emory nodded to me, but did a double take when she noticed my eyes. I had forgotten the bright blue ring that formed around our eyes when the Desmòs activated. Emory watched as Ariana walked past with her hand shielding her eyes as if the sun were too bright. The guide shot me a knowing look, but I didn't say a thing.

The contestants were teleported from the side of the pit back onto our House pillars. The Kyrion returned to their spots inside the stone eyes on the cliff wall. I gripped the pole in my hand and picked out my path. The tan grains of my powers mingled with the white streaks of lightning that flashed dully now that my anger had faded. I cut off the flow of powers. I didn't need them to win this. At some unseen signal the pillars started to move again. I got into a rhythm: spin, leap, land, and repeat. Even with his injuries Zeno was the first across, but I was a close second. We raced up the steps to the giant red doors with me only a couple of paces behind him. Emory appeared like a ghostly version of herself beside Zeno at he reached the top step. She thrust out her pole to make him trip, but he jumped over it with a laugh. I could hear the other contestants gaining ground behind me.

Zeno slammed his body into one of the giant red metal doors making a loud clanging sound. I collapsed my pole and slammed my shoulder into the other door. Neither door budged an inch. Zeno sneered at me and rammed his door again. Ariana's words from our sparring ran through my head: *"The Games are about what is not seen as much as about what is."* I stepped back to take a look at the entrance. The doors set flush with the smooth cliff face. There were no visible doorknobs or latches. A sense of déjà vu slipped over me as I remembered the false entrance to Stone Shadow Castle during the second competition. This way was too obvious.

What was it Tartarus had said? *Truth will show you the way.*

What truth did he mean? I walked back down a couple of steps to look around the area. This House was located in a dangerous place surrounded by hot springs and volcanic features. They obviously liked things hot. Judging from the course so far, they also liked to shock people; the waterfall and the shifting pillars were great examples of that. A glare of yellow light caught my eye. My powers stirred inside me and my vision doubled. For a moment, I saw a circle of sparkling yellow gems near the center of the lava pit. Then I blinked and all I saw were the pillars. Would they ...? Nah, no one was that crazy, right?

Still, I couldn't shake the feeling that I was onto something. I glanced over my shoulder to see the other contestants had given up on trying to force the doors open and had started searching around the walls. Emory glanced my way and arched an eyebrow. Her eyes darted toward the pit as if to say "well, get on with it." Then she turned around and said loudly, "I think I found something." I owed her a beer after all of this was over.

Then I ran back toward the pit.

I tried to hold that picture in my head of the circle I'd seen. I vaulted through the areas still crusted over from our earlier trip across until I landed on a House of Truth symbol. Golden-yellow light flared, but this wasn't like before when the whole symbol on the pillars lit up. I kneeled down and brushed my fingers over the center of the hammer symbol. Rays of light beamed across my face from a yellow diamond. A feeling of rightness settled into me, and I got back up to quickly move to the next House of Truth pillar. I completed the circle just as the other contestants caught on to what I was doing. They shouted at me, but their voices were drowned out by rumbling as the pillar I was standing on started to sink. I looked around frantically trying to find a safe spot, but my feet were stuck in place. A circle of six pillars lowered.

Below, the blackened crust that had formed broke apart and the lava flowed free once more.

The pillars stopped. I waited to feel the first burning touch of that liquid death only inches below my feet, but it never came. Instead, the lava in the center of the circle of pillars hardened into black rock again. The yellow diamonds from the pillars floated into the air and formed a double-sided hammer, which drifted down to lie in the center of that black circle. I hesitantly placed one foot out on the black rock to test the surface. When that held, I took another step and then another. I picked up the hammer and a sibilant whisper filled my head: *Kade Downing, descendant. See your truth. Embrace what you are. She is waiting.*

I raised the hammer high overhead and slammed it down onto the rock at my feet. The rock beneath me cracked. I raised the hammer high again, and the whole circle of rock shattered this time as it made contact. I fell, not into agonizing hot lava, but into cold water. A bubble of air surrounded my head letting me breath easily. The hammer beamed through the dark like a headlight as it dragged me down toward the bottom of the ocean. It pulled me through a maze of under-water reef formations in white, blue, and pink. A school of fish scurried past. A swordfish darted forward aggressively nearly stabbing me in the leg. Luckily, we picked up speed and left the big fish behind.

I was pulled into a narrow crevice that seemed familiar. A memory of swimming through this crevice to get to the valley where our horses waited for us in the second competition popped into my head. Lights embedded into the rock above blinked on as I moved past. Then I dived into the inky dark-ness below. The temperature dropped, and the darkness seemed to be alive as it swirled around me, painfully lashing against my body. Lightning arced through the water narrowly missing me. The hammer pulled me into twists and turns, avoiding each strike. Finally, I pushed through a wall of bubbling water and fell to my knees in a dry cavern. I dropped the hammer like it was a branding iron. The light inside it went out, plunging the cavern into compete darkness. Shit! I didn't want to touch it again, but I needed the light.

I picked the hammer back up and stepped further into the cavern. The golden-yellow light spilled across a space that was about as wide as my ranch house back home. The ceiling was a couple of feet above my head. Every so often there were columns of gray rock with some type of ancient writing on them. Water dripped down from the ceiling to form puddles along the uneven floor. My breath misted in the freezing air. Once again, I was thankful for the jumpsuit that seemed to keep away the worst of the cold.

I moved further into the cavern wondering why I was brought here. Near the center of the cavern the normal gray stone floor gave way to pure white. The white rock formed a perfect circle around a large stalagmite of the same color, as if this area had been bleached. I stepped into the circle, drawn to the stalagmite for some reason. The moment I stepped into the circle the rock no longer looked like a stalagmite but the body of a woman. She was half sunk into the ground, her face set in fierce determination and her left hand stretched up toward the ceiling as if reaching for help. I leaned closer to get a better look at her face. "Mama?"

"*Save me*," Mama's voice said inside my head.

"Hold on, Mama!"

I grabbed her outstretched hand. White-hot lightning built inside me. I yelled as I pulled her hand with all my might. This time I would fight for her. I would save her.

Lightning surged up through me and into the rock. The stalagmite cracked. White light spilled out into the cavern from the cracks that ran down its entire length. I shielded my eyes with my free arm as it brightened and the rock crumbled. The rumble of stone crashing to the ground filled the cavern. The hard stone beneath my captured hand changed into something cold and soft. I looked down to find I was holding the hand of a beautiful woman.

Was I missing Mama so much that I was imagining her everywhere now?

The woman crouched on the floor. Long black hair framed a pale, naked body of perfection. Lightning flashed in the irises of her black eyes. Ancient words spilled from her pale lips as she used our linked hands to pull herself up. She stumbled into me, and I instinctively wrapped my arms around her. She muttered a string of words that didn't sound very friendly. Then glanced down at my chest at the House of Seasons symbol on my jumpsuit and hissed. Even as frail as she felt in my arms, the woman fought like a wildcat until we both fell in a tangle to the floor. I quickly rolled away from her and got to my knees. This had been the weirdest and most exhausting day of my life. If the stone-turned-woman wanted to be left to her comfy spot here in this damp, cold, forgotten cavern, who was I to argue?

She stepped forward, her foreign words, filled with determination, echoing around the cavern as she slowly moved across the floor on shaky legs. She stopped at the edge of the white circle and swiped aside the long black hair that fell around her hips. She hesitantly stepped across that dividing line. But as soon as her foot touched down, the gray rock turned into a black sticky substance like tar. She grunted with effort as each step formed more sticky tar that clung to her feet. Shear stubbornness got her close to the wall of bubbles that led out into the ocean. Until her legs gave out and she fell to the ground. Her fists beat against the stone and everywhere she touched the rock, black tar pulled her down. She finally stopped moving but I could tell from the strangled sounds she made that she was in pain.

Don't do it, Kade. She doesn't need you to save her. You need to figure out how to get back to the Games.

The pale woman lurched forward again, her fingers scrabbling across the stone as she tried to pull her body toward the opening of the cavern. Shit, shit, shit! I couldn't sit by and watch her suffer like this. I got to my feet and walked toward her. She lashed out at me with razor-sharp nails when I got near, but her strength was gone.

"Ma'am, I'm gonna help you but you hav'ta promise not to gouge me with those sharp claws," I said, as I inched closer to her. The disgusted look on her face said she hated that she needed my help at all. I carefully gathered her into my arms, the tar sliding away as soon as her skin no longer touched the floor. I glanced over at the wall of bubbles. "We're under the ocean. Pretty deep down too. You won't be able to swim far and neither will I. Not until we've rested."

I turned back to the area where I found her, and she struggled feebly in my arms. "Ma'am, we'll both die if we try to swim outta here right now. I'm gonna put you back down on the spot where you, uh, came to life." I sat her on her feet in the white circle. When the floor didn't turn to tar, I stepped back to put distance between us. Her frail body trembled, and I gripped her forearms to keep her from falling. I shifted my gaze to the side to give her privacy.

I started to remove my arms, but she clung to me. "Uh, I don't suppose you have any clothes? Maybe a sheet or somethin'?"

She let out a husky chuckle and responded in a familiar heavily accented voice, "Does my bare flesh make you uneasy?"

I swallowed thickly, "Well, we don't usually go around naked where I'm from."

Her strange eyes trailed over my body. "How then do you procreate?"

I nearly choked, but covered it up with a cough. "Uh, well, when a man loves a woman then the nakedness happens for … pr-procreation." The sting of embarrassment covered my cheeks as I gave a birds and bees talk to a living rock. Her hand raised to press against my cheek, but I turned away. "Uh, this isn't … You shouldn't—"

I backed up another step, but her fingers lifted my chin forcing me to meet her gaze. I stopped in my tracks. It felt like the lightning flashing in her eyes zapped my whole body because I couldn't move. A faint white glow appeared where her skin touched mine. Her grip on my other arm grew stronger, and she straightened from her slumped position. Her skin began to glow faintly with white light as her other hand gripped mine and placed it between her breasts.

"Open yourself to your goddess." She held my hand pressed against her as I struggled to get my body to work again. "Freely give me what I need, and a spark of power will remain yours to sustain your life." She traced her fingers along my arm. "For your gift, I will make this exchange pleasurable."

Her body shifted and suddenly, I was looking at Ariana. It was Ariana's voice that pleaded with me, "I am weak. Only your power can save me. Lie with me, Kade. We will complete the Desmòs and be together forever."

The illusion wavered, and the goddess stood in front of me once more. My skin crawled and my stomach sank as memories of Natalie filled me. I'd been manipulated and used by one woman already; I wouldn't go through that again. I pictured Hope, the soft innocence and trust on her face that day she'd taken my hand and pulled me back from becoming a monster like Daddy. Her face changed into Mama's, Cadence's, Chris's and a dozen others I'd stood up for throughout my life. Finally, I saw myself. That scared, helpless little boy. I took his hand and pulled him into my arms. It was time I protected me too.

"No," I stated firmly, trying to break free of her hold. "I'm sure any man would be honored to be with a pretty woman like you, but—"

"Pretty!" she scoffed and waved her hand. My lips sealed together. "In my day men fell upon their swords for the honor of looking upon my form. Yet, you who have come to the depths of my personal nightmare to free me, insult me by turning away from the gift of my touch. Then call me that"— her lips lifted into a snarl—"common word. 'Pretty' is a word used for humans. I am a goddess. My beauty once drove men to the heights of madness for the chance to lie with me."

Her body glowed brighter as my own inner light began to fade. She was draining my powers! A see-through black dress studded with bright crescent moons formed over her body. My heart galloped in my chest as my vision started to blur. My limbs grew cold as my heartbeat slowed.

"Stop! You're killing me!" I mentally shouted at her.

"What is it, little boy? Did you think that the universe would not demand payment for releasing me from my slumber?" She brushed a kiss against my lips. "I agreed to wait for the prophecy to unfold. Never to be trapped here after my awakening, surrounded by the foul stench of the Olympians who betrayed us." Her hands wrapped around my neck as she began to squeeze. "Do not worry, little boy; your sacrifice will not be in vain. Tainted though your blood may be by Demeter, your life will restore my powers that I may be free of this prison." White light swirled down her arms and she lifted me into the air. "By Chaos, I swear on your life and those of my people that were slain at the hand of the Olympian traitors that I will bring justice to you all. You should feel blessed, little boy, for the Goddess Nyx has made an oath to you."

Blinding white light filled the cavern. Nyx's presence plunged into me. Unlike Natalie's oily darkness or Emory's weightless shadow, the goddess was a storm full of thunder and lightning. My insides were scorched from the bolts of lightning. Every strike lashed away at my power—my life. My bones rattled from the pounding beat of thunder. My battered body trembled with weakness. My memories splintered apart and slipped through my fingers until only two images remained. Hope's name trembled on my lips before she too was torn away. All that was left was Ariana. I found our connection and wrapped it up in my hands as if I could protect this last piece of me—of us. But the lightning burned my hands until they turned to ash.

"Gaia ... Ariana, I love you," I whispered with my last breath as I slumped to the ground.

BELOW WHERE I sat in the carved eye above the entrance to Minos, Kafàli Harris called a restart to the competition. My fingers twisted in the tree roots that made up the skirt of my dress, my head full of a thousand thoughts. I had issued another command as Archigós before meeting with Kade in the woods. The contestants were under the protection of the Kyrion, and now Chris was dead. I had contacted Bennett's father to demand that he appear before the Order to be questioned regarding Natalie's actions. As her stepfather, he had been responsible for getting her the help she needed after the last series of attacks that she carried out against Lia. Bennett had been too soft in his handling of her punishment, but I would not make the same mistake. Natalie was a traitor and would be punished accordingly. I was worried about Bennett, though. He had looked drawn and pale when I told him of my decision. He had lost a lot recently, and now his family had brought dishonor to his House once again.

The sound of the metal doors scraping across the floor below echoed up to where I sat, and I glanced down to see Kade standing on a lit pillar for the House of Truth. He had won this competition. I should have felt elated by Kade's win, but all I felt was numb. After days of wishing my feelings away, I wanted them back. But I had made my bargain, and my future was set.

I touched my lips again wishing I could hang on to the feel of Kade's lips on mine forever. I don't know exactly when it happened, but Kade had become my weakness. That kiss earlier had proved it. Kade was the first person I had touched since I was a child, and my powers hadn't tried to hurt him. In that moment I'd longed for a life with him, full of his goodness and light. A far cry from the unpleasant life my father envisioned for me with Ekert, with my powers chained and my usefulness limited to bearing children. Then Ekert had stepped out of the trees with his passive-aggressive threats, and any hope for us shattered at my feet. Kade deserved more than a life of subterfuge surrounded by my father and his allies. I had protected Kade in the only way I could—by rejecting him.

Someone shouted, pulling me from my thoughts. I looked down at the pillars to find Kade lift a glowing hammer over his head and shatter the circle of lava rock that he stood on. Terror made my heart skip a beat as he disappeared through a dark portal. I jumped to my feet, but I could do nothing. Remy had already denied my request to intervene once when Kade attacked the other contestants. The descendants of Tartarus believed that actions revealed the truth of a person. Remy would wait to see how this played out.

The gods were at work here. There was no other explanation for how Kade had found a portal that no one else knew existed. Kade had to be a Chosen. If he was, the question now was which god would claim him and would he survive it?

A couple of the guides gathered the remaining contestants and took them back by boat to Titan Tower. Minutes turned into what felt like hours. The Kyrion teleported to the ground below to wait for Kade to return. I wanted to declare to my fellow Kyrion that here—the claiming of the Chosen and waking of the gods—was proof that we were on the right path to save our world. Surely, the other Kyrion could see that now?

I paced along the edge of the pit not caring that the Kyrion and remaining guides watched me curiously. Not when the man who I'd come to care about faced off with one of the gods. Somehow against all odds Kade had managed to claim a piece of me as his own. Just knowing he was alive and safe in the world made the endless days stretching into my bleak future without him seem brighter. He had to be ok.

Goddess Gaia, guide Kade and protect him.

I cradled my hand to my stomach still feeling Kade's hard chest beneath my palm. I'd never dared hope for a true bond-mate. My life was pain and rules. That was all that my father and instructors had trained me for. How could anyone care for me? Me, with my need for rules, my sharp tongue, and aversion to being touched? I was a creature shaped by my horrible past; it influenced everything I did. Why would anyone want to share a life with someone so stunted and afraid? Yet, Kade had wanted to give us a try, and I'd pushed him away. I'd run from the one man who was all things good and kind. I'd turned instead toward a man who was safe. Because with Ekert I felt nothing. I could barricade myself behind my defenses for the rest of my life, and he would never care.

Kade had made me question myself and my bleak existence. He kissed me and the solid ground I thought I knew was knocked out from under me. His steadfast soul hummed with an electric resiliency that had reached out to mine and shown it how to flourish again. A thousand possibilities had been birthed in that brief moment that we shared in the trees. I wanted to gather them all like a delicate bouquet of flowers and protect them from the crushing weight of my obligations. The truth was that I could envision a bonded life with Kade all too easily. It was the loss of everything I'd never dared to dream of that I couldn't stand, because that was the inevitable conclusion to all of those possibilities. Even if I never had that moment of lapse where my powers escaped my command, my obligations to my people had to come first. What kind of life could I promise him when my whole world was on the brink of war and destruction?

I tried to convince myself it was better this way. That being with Ekert would allow me to focus on helping my people. But I felt like I had betrayed not only myself but Kade too.

Kade's voice filled my mind. *"Gaia ... Ariana, I love you."*

His words pierced through the self-loathing I was wallowing in. *"Kade! What has happened?"* I mentally shouted back, but there was no reply. Fear spiked through me, and my hands shook as I stared down into the portal in the pit below. He had to be ok.

The Goddess Gaia's strength poured into me as her voice whispered, *"Dutiful daughter, the strongest tree is the one whose roots find anchor in the right soil. Too hard and the roots will never penetrate. Too soft and the tree will topple."*

What did that mean? Was she telling me that Kade was my anchor? The one person who could ground my powers and weather the seasons of life with me? I didn't have time to figure it out. Kade had called out to Gaia—to me—and I would answer. The oath he had accepted when he pledged himself as my Potential meant I would be teleported directly to his location when I answered his call. *"Cadence! Kade has initiated the oath to call on me for help. I will leave my connection to you open to follow if there is trouble."*

"But—" Cadence tried to reach me, but I wasn't waiting a moment longer.

I teleported away and darkness surrounded me as I reappeared wherever Kade was. The link between us through the oath required that I be taken to within twenty feet of his location; he was close, but I couldn't call out to him. I had no idea what had happened here or who I might be facing to save the man I was starting to think I might not be able live without. I shielded my presence and walked silently across the cold stone. A female voice spat curses in ancient Greek that echoed off the walls of what appeared to be a cavern.

I let my powers out a little at a time, searching the area. The life signatures of sea creatures reached out to me, and I used their eyes to show me views of where I was. Glimpses of the ocean beyond these walls flickered through my head. However, they all ended abruptly in the crevice that the contestants had swam through during the last competition. The darkest depths of the crevice was a dangerous place that no person or animal dared to venture. Yet, it seemed like that was exactly where I was.

My fingers brushed against a rock column, and I slid behind it just as a woman glowing white with power passed within feet of me. The cussing came again as she struggled with each step. I attempted to trace Kade through the connection the oath had opened up between us, but it had disappeared after serving its purpose. Our unclaimed Desmòs connection had faded a while ago. Careful to keep my shield intact, I inched across the floor in the opposite direction of the woman. My foot brushed against something with more give than the rock, and I crouched down. My hands traced over fabric until they encountered cold skin. A sob threatened to break from my throat, but I held it back. My fingers trembled as they traced across the familiar lines of the face that I knew better than my own. *Please be alive.*

The golden-yellow glow of the hammer Kade had used to break through the portal lay partially under his body. I grabbed it and raised it to look down on his pale face. His lively blue eyes stared vacantly at the ceiling. The lips that were always quick to smile and had kissed me so gently were locked in a grimace of pain. For a moment I was transported back to that day when I had killed the servant woman at

Tantalus. A wail of guilt and pain built in my chest. I choked off the sob that escaped and held back the emotions shredding my chest like broken glass.

"Goddess Gaia, I will gladly devote all of my time to your worship, if you grant me this one thing. I cannot deny my heart any longer. Not when it lies cold and lifeless here on this floor. I plead to you, Mother Goddess, bring Kade back to me. and I will not deny the gift of our bond any longer."

A yellow butterfly landed on my chest where my House symbol was.

"Daughter of the earth, you need not grovel before me," the Goddess Gaia said in a gentle voice. *"Like the willow, you and your Kade are both strong. You have both withstood great challenges. Through the Desmòs your combined strengths could have moved mountains. Yet, without your bond to anchor him, Kade's soul could not be reborn as Chosen."* The yellow butterfly fluttered against my wet cheek like a kiss from the goddess. Then disappeared. *"Daughter, fear chains you as surely as the gods now find themselves imprisoned. Love, whether it lasts a day or a lifetime, is a gift to be cherished. A gift that frees us all."*

"Tell me what to do. Please! I will do anything to bring him back," I pleaded, gathering Kade into my arms. For the first time in my life, I freely gave into my emotions and shattered the defenses I hid behind. Tears fell from my eyes in a torrent. Sobs wracked my chest until I could barely breath. I tilted back my head and screamed. Rocks rained down from the ceiling as the cavern quaked. Vines cracked though the rock floor and lashed the air. Ocean animals for miles went into a frenzy. Cold hands wrapped around my neck and squeezed, cutting off my scream.

"THAT WAS QUITE THE SHOW, tree lover," a woman's heavily accented voice gloated above me. "What is a descendant of Gaia doing in my chamber?" I struggled to speak around her tight grip and reached out with my powers to the vines nearby. "Pity for you my curiosity has been exhausted for this day along with much of the powers your lover provided. I will make the same oath to you that I did for the little boy in your arms. Your sacrifice will not be in va—"

"Halt!" a male voice boomed. The sound of dripping water ceased. The vines slithering toward the woman stopped moving. Droplets of water hung suspended in mid-air. The woman above me froze in place, and so did I. Someone had stopped time itself and used Voice—a power that compelled others to do what you wanted regardless of their will—to halt every living thing in the cavern. Both were powers not seen in centuries. They had been outlawed long ago by our ancestors because they were too dangerous. Suddenly a starry night sky filled the cavern. A blinding ball of light formed above, spreading out around us. The starry darkness dissolved into a tall, naked man. His long black hair swept across the rock floor as he stepped toward me and waved his hand. The woman disappeared from above me and reappeared at his side.

"Little sister, you were always quick to kill first then ask questions," the man said with a chuckle. Thick muscles flexed across his naked body as he lifted long black hair away from the woman's face. He dropped his hand and glanced at me with eyes that swirled with multiple colors.

Was I staring at a naked god? As if he heard my thoughts a long black kilt appeared around his hips. "I forget that in this day you wish to cover your bodies at all times. Yes, daughter of Gaia, you are staring at a god."

He stepped back from the woman just as she unfroze. She snarled and raised her hand. White lightning flashed in her eyes and across her skin as she prepared to unleash her powers on the man. Then she faltered. "T-Titan?"

The man smiled at her. "Hello, Nyx."

The lightning died away as Nyx stared at him in awe. "You perished beneath the Aegean, taking all of Atlantaiònia and the Olympian traitors with you. We felt our connection to you sever as your earthly form bled out and your powers faded."

"I am Chaos, little sister. My father rules the stars. Did you really think I would fall beneath the treachery of the Olympians that easily?"

"Yes," Nyx stated boldly, propping her hands on her hips. "You chose sides, and your father—the God of Chaos —turned his back on you. On us. You—the brutal lord, the great benevolent *king*—broke the balance. Not for the honor and glory of battle, but for a woman." She spat on the ground in disgust. "Tell me, brother, did the vengeance for your queen's death bring you peace? Was she worth the punishment we all suffer now because of your choice?"

Titan's fists clenched and deep groves of pain scored his face. "I am sorry that my actions have hurt you. That *all* of the descendants have suffered for my sins. But I will not apolo-

gize for loving Lyannìa. One day I hope that you too will
know a love that you will do anything to preserve."

"Hurt me? I am not *hurt*, brother." Nyx declared, her lip
curling in a sneer. "I am trapped here"—she waved her hand
to encompass the cavern—"with the screams of the dying and
destruction of our world as my only companions. Century
upon century have passed as our sacrifice to preserve the last
of our powers in slumber turned to an agonizing cage from
which we could not escape. Forgive me, brother, if I doubted
that you yet lived while we suffered this … existence."

Titan held out his hand but dropped it when she refused
him. "I cannot change what was done. Take heart that there is
hope yet for our future." His eyes swirled with regrets and
possibilities as he glanced toward me and Kade. Were we the
"hope" he spoke of?

"We must hurry, my powers grow weaker by the minute
as I hold back the time, and your Chosen's soul slips further
away." He motioned toward Kade, whose stiff body lay
across my lap.

"You must replace the power you took, Nyx. His bond-
mate does not hold his soul, but I am keeping it from leaving
this world. Move quickly, little sister. Your freedom is closer
than ever."

"The Chosen are a lie, made up by a boy we should never
have trusted to lead us," Nyx rebuffed. "My freedom is my
own to secure. I was nearly there before you stopped me. This
worthless boy is dead." She pointed to Kade. "Let his soul go
to meet the stars and be done with it."

"*Save him*," I shouted, pushing my mental message out
with all my might to reach them. "*Trust in the Chosen. I too
have doubted but will never falter in my faith again. They are here
and they will save us. Please … help him.*"

Nyx glanced at me and for a second, I could swear I saw a
deep pool of yearning in her eyes. A yellow butterfly landed
on Nyx's shoulder, and she attempted to flick it off. The

butterfly avoided her fingers and flew straight at the goddess's forehead. It thumped against her head and settled into her skin like one of our symbols. She scrubbed at the spot cussing in ancient Greek.

"As Gaia's messenger says, we must trust in the Chosen," Titan stated with a grin as the butterfly finally disappeared from Nyx's skin. "Trust in *me* once more, Nyx," Titan implored. "Without our powers fully restored, none can truly be free. The defenses set around this chamber were cleverly designed to drain you, but the layer beyond this is even more powerful. What you experienced walking from the circle"— he swept his hands out to indicate the white circle on the rock floor that we were standing on—"is nothing compared to what waits for you beyond that entrance." He pointed to the wall of bubbles at the entrance of the cavern. "If you step beyond this cavern before we restore our powers, you will return to my father as part of his essence. You will cease to exist."

Nyx stared at him for several long moments. I was afraid the sins of the past and her stubborn nature would win. I wanted to tell her not to make my mistakes, but eventually she nodded.

Kade's limp body lifted from the floor and moved to hang suspended in the air between the two gods. Titan's fist punched through Kade's back. Nyx punched her fist through his chest from the front. I wanted to go to him, to hold him close as he hung in the balance between life and death. With every fiber of my being, I prayed to the God of Chaos to let this work. Lightning leaped from Nyx's body into Kade's. Tan and white lights poured from the places where the gods' fists were buried in his body. The power that held me immobile snapped, and I slumped forward onto my hands. I pushed to my feet watching as the fate of our world was molded in this one moment. Suddenly Nyx slumped against Kade, her light nothing more than a faint glow upon her skin.

All of my life I had feared my powers, and my father
never let me forget why I was a danger to everyone around
me. I had followed very strict rules for living that I thought
kept others safe from me. I hadn't realized I'd also been
protecting myself, but I'd locked myself away so completely
that I was just going through the motions of living. Kade had
showed me the way out from behind my walls and that there
was more to this world than pain and rules. The God of
Chaos had blessed me with a bond-mate, and I would claim
him as mine, rules be damned.

I had taken so much from others in my past. I pictured the
servant woman at Tantalus that I had accidentally killed as a
child. In my mind I held her hand once more. *"I am sorry. I did
not understand my power then, but I do now. I will never let my
anger or my thirst for power hurt another."* Her kind smile lit up
her face as she patted my cheek. Then she turned into a bright
light and joined the stars in the night sky. I apologized to
every person I had ever harmed and let the guilt go.

Then I did what I had never done before and offered my
power. Still kneeling on the floor, I held my had up toward
Nyx. The green light of my powers twisted up from the
palm of my hand. She glanced at me with a sneer of disdain.
Then she glanced at Titan and down to Kade. A gentle light
of understanding appeared in her eyes for a moment. Then
she reached out and grasped my hand. The tug on my
powers felt like sandpaper scraping away at my insides. But
it was bearable compared to the black flame's insatiable
hunger.

It seemed like hours later when Titan and Nyx stepped
back. Kade floated to the floor and I gathered him into my
arms once more, placing my hand over his heart. The faint
rhythm beneath my palm was the most beautiful thing in the
world. Nyx sank onto the white rock a few feet away, looking
exhausted. Titan brushed his hand over her head, "You did
well, little sister. Rest and renew. The prophecy draws closer

to fulfillment, and we will all need to be ready." Titan glanced at Kade. "Especially the Chosen."

Those swirling multi-colored eyes landed on me. "He has been claimed, but his powers will not fully rise until the Desmòs is completed."

Then Titan vanished. Nyx looked at the place he had been with a sad aching that I knew all too well. As much as I hated to admit it, we had a lot in common. We were both stubborn and prideful creatures forged by our painful pasts, but at our core we both longed to end our lonely isolation. And we felt the hole in our lives that separation from our brothers had caused. I had found someone to pull me from my own darkness. Someone I vowed I would spend the rest of my life with no matter what I had to do to make that happen. I hoped Nyx could one day say the same.

Her dark eyes found mine and she gritted out, "Tell my Chosen that I give nothing for free. He will train here with me every day. Once I am assured that his skills are as sharp as the deadliest blade, we will cut out the hearts of the Olympians together."

Kade's hand clenched around mine, and my heart leaped in my chest. "It will be done, Goddess Nyx. May the God of Chaos bless you and restore your powers."

"*He* took my brother from me," Nyx growled. "I want nothing of the God of Chaos's blessings."

Then she turned into a white stone statue.

ARIANA

KADE'S EYES snapped open and he flipped to his feet so quickly I could barely track his movements. Lightning flashed in his baby blue eyes as he crouched in front of me. His muscles flexed as if he were ready to pounce. "Kade," I said softly. "You are safe. No one will hurt you again." I tentatively reached out my hand.

His otherworldly eyes bore into me, and for a moment, I feared that the man I had come to love had been lost in his re-birth. Then the lightning faded, and he took my hand to place it over his heart. He looked around the cavern still visible in the floating light Titan had left behind. "What happened?"

I explained everything that had happened. He listened intently, asking questions when needed.

"I thought it was a dream. Nyx really did kill me and bring me back to life?"

"Y-yes." I sobbed in relief. Now that I'd allowed myself to release the tears, they didn't seem to want to stop.

"Ariana." He breathed my name with such reverence. His fingers flexed around my hand still pressed against his heart. He caught a teardrop from my cheek on the tip of his finger. "You're crying. Because of me?"

"Yes," I whispered and took a deep breath. I didn't want to be imprisoned by my past any longer. I thought freedom meant only from the ties my father used to control me but really, I had the power to free myself from my own cage all this time. "I … I …" *Goddess, give me strength.* I swallowed thickly and blurted, "I love you, Kade Downing."

His other hand cupped my cheek. "Ariana—uh, what's your last name?"

"My name is Ariana Gian Dupree," I stated with pride. "I am Kyrion of the House of Seasons and your bond-mate … if you will have me?"

"What about Ekert?" he asked cautiously.

I shook my head. "Our bonding was arranged by my father. I want no one but you."

Kade pressed both hands to the sides of my neck and used his thumbs to nudge my chin up. "I think I've loved you since the moment I saw you standin' on that stage lookin' like a fairy-tale princess. But I knew I couldn't live without you when we trained together, and you lectured me about not bein' a gentleman." I started to apologize, but he cut me off. "No, don't be sorry for what you said. You were right. I've spent my whole life takin' care of everyone else. You don't need me to fight your battles for you, and I love that about you."

Tears slipped down my cheeks again, and he kissed them away. "I never thought too much about my future before. I'd always just kinda thought I'd inherit the ranch that's been in my family for decades and raise the next generation of Downings." His fingers lightly touched the area over my heart. "I dunno what my future looks like now, but I wanna spend every second of it with you. I want you to be mine for always. Will you marry me, Ariana?"

I smiled up at him. "You have made me break every one of my rules. And I cannot thank you enough. I do not know either how our future will unfold. But I want to find out." I pressed a kiss to his lips, craving his touch after denying it all this time. "Yes, I will marry you." I took his hand and laid it over my heart. "My heart is yours, forever."

Kade wrapped his arms around me, and I clung to him for once without fear of hurting him. He hissed in pain as my hands pressed against his back, and I quickly pulled away. "What is it?"

"My back feels all raw," he said as he carefully stood up. He flexed his pinky. "Huh. My finger's healed."

The light Titan had left behind had started to fade around the edges, but there was still plenty left for me to see the symbol on Kade's back as we carefully pulled down his jumpsuit. A giant crescent moon—Nyx's symbol—stretched from his shoulder blades to the base of his spine. The ends of the crescent shape looked like sharp sickle blades. The rest of the crescent shape had swirling lines and sections where wheat stalks grew. One day soon when we completed the Desmòs, my tree symbol would be there too, telling everyone he was mine.

"We need to get back to the House of Truth," I told Kade as he tied the sleeves of the jumpsuit around his waist leaving his upper body bare. I wanted to trace every line of muscle but instead distracted myself by scooping up the no-longer-glowing hammer from the floor. Kade gave the statue of Nyx a wide berth as he walked toward the entrance to the cavern. "The other Kyrion will be waiting for our return."

The light of Titan's powers was fading faster now. I doubted it would last much longer if the god had returned to his slumber. I handed Kade the hammer, and he placed it in the loop on the side of his jumpsuit. "Do you know the way back? I wasn't really payin' much attention on my trip here."

"I will teleport us."

"You'll have to teach me that one," he said with that winsome smile that never failed to heat my skin. He tugged on one of the curls that had escaped my pins and watched as it bounced back into place. "It sure would come in handy checkin' fences on my ranch."

I forced a smile but deep down inside worries began to nibble at me. Did Kade still intend to go back to Texas? Did he see me giving up my position as Kyrion to become a rancher's wife? How did these relationships work?

My heartbeat tripled like a frightened animal taken from its natural habitat. I had broken all of my rules, but that didn't mean I could change a lifetime of relying on them. Even now I wanted to sit down and write out all of the details that would govern this new path I'd chosen. Maybe it was a security blanket that I would eventually learn to live without; or maybe I would always feel this way. I didn't know, but I would conquer even my own idiosyncrasies to be with Kade.

I leaned forward to breathe in the comforting scents of wheatgrass and the faint hint of ozone that clung to him now. My heart calmed as I thanked Gaia again that he was alive. I tensed as Kade wrapped his arms around me. Panic tried to steal this moment from me, but I refused to let it. Being in his arms had to be the safest place in the world. I just wasn't used to being touched yet. I needed to hang on to the belief that neither of us would hurt the other. *One step at a time, Ariana. That is how you will build your future together.* I took a deep breath and let the tension go as I stepped into his embrace. I rested my head against his chest, and he kissed my curls. I never thought I would be able to enjoy the touch of another person but here I was wrapped in the arms of my bond-mate.

You were right, Aegeus. I needed to believe in myself. What neither of us realized is that I needed someone I could believe in too.

The roadmap of wounds across my body might no longer be visible, but my memories kept their pain alive. Kade's embrace quieted the memories and soothed the burning ache that seemed as real to me as those moments when the whip tore into my skin. The relief was staggering after living with it for so long. I held tightly to him for another minute before I forced myself to back away. It would be too easy to disregard the world outside of his arms and revel in the peace he brought me, but a whole society of people were now relying on us.

Still, I craved just a few more minutes together before my duties called me back. "I will tell you about teleporting," I stated, "but it is a power that takes time to perfect."

"I enjoy your lessons." He trailed his finger down the side of my neck making me shiver with arousal. How did even the smallest touch from him have my body blooming when I had never wanted any man to touch me before now?

I ignored the twinkle in his eyes as a hot blush traveled up my neck. I cleared my throat and said, "Teleporting is about concentrating on every fiber of your existence and visualizing a destination. You will likely find that your powers have gotten stronger now that you have been claimed as a Chosen. Dia also got physically stronger. When we are bonded—"

"What happens when we're bonded?" Kade asked.

"We will need to plan our Bonding Ceremony. That is how we declare an engagement in our world. Then … the intimate part is where we complete our bond. It will take at least a couple of days to arrange the ceremony since they are typically large celebrations." I realized he might think I was pushing him to complete our bonding, and I hurried to say, "But there is no rush. We can wait a few months or years—"

Kade released my fingers and cupped my face. Then he kissed me until the worries flew out of my head. When he pulled away, I had to grip his arms to steady my shaky legs. "Ariana, stop thinkin' so damn much. I don't wanna wait months or years. If there was a preacher available, I'd marry you right here."

My smile was so wide that my cheeks hurt. "I will contact my advisor to start making arrangements."

My smile faded as I thought about what he'd said. Did he

understand that our bonding wasn't like a human marriage? The Bonding Ceremony was only a declaration of intent done before the witnesses of my House in a display of power and traditional words. Only when he spilled himself inside my body as we exchanged the words of the Desmòs would we be "married" in the eyes of the gods and our people. I knew that humans did things differently, but I had never learned their mating customs. I would agree to a human ceremony if that was what he wished, provided there were no animal sacrifices. That seemed to be a tradition in the ancient Greek ceremonies I'd read about in some of our books. Did he know what else the Desmòs did?

Kade tapped my chin with his finger. "Out with it. What's that overactive mind of yours frettin' about now?"

I hesitated a moment before laying it all out. "The Desmòs is considered both a blessing and a curse. It is not a commitment to be entered into lightly. There is no way to break the connection once made. We would share thoughts, feelings, our past, and our powers. If one of us dies, so does the other. And there is a symbol that appears on our skin to mark us as bond-mates. Typically, the bonded pair would receive the symbol of the most powerful partner, and they would become members of that House. However, as with most things, the Chosen appear to be different. Jaxon and Bennett received smaller versions of their bond-mate's symbol, but their original mark did not change."

I took a deep breath after spouting all of that and waited for his reaction. He ducked down until we were eye level, those blue eyes holding me hostage with their intensity. "Do you know what I learned today?" I shook my head. "There are no dark hidden parts inside me waitin' to turn me into the devil Daddy claimed I was. My powers aren't evil. They're another tool that I can use to protect others and myself. I won't fear them or myself any longer.

"I learned that my parents' lives, and choices were their

own. I will never be them because I have my own path to carve out. Daddy beat us because he said we were evil, but that was just an excuse. He couldn't admit that he'd run our ranch into the ground and didn't know how to fix it. It was easier to fall in line with what Downing men did best— drinkin' and bettin' anything of value on a hand of cards. It was easier to blame us."

My finger traced under his left eye where I knew there would have been tears if either of us had anymore to give. But we were both through giving our parents any more pieces of us.

"Mama … I loved her like crazy, but she wasn't strong like you. The man she loved found his true bond-mate and left her. I spent my whole life thinkin' the Desmòs forced people to leave their families behind, all because some god said to." His finger trailed across the top of my dress and tapped my House symbol. "But the gods were just given' us a helpin' hand in findin' our soulmate. I learned from you that we all still have choices. Mama thought the gods stole her bond-mate and she would never find love again. She married the first human who paid attention to her and refused to admit she had made a mistake. She made every excuse there was to stay with my daddy, no matter how he treated us. I'm not sayin' it was easy, but she made choices I don't understand. But they were hers to make."

Kade gave me a teasing smile. "What I'm sayin' is, I've made my choice. I choose you. Even though you get all prickly and fierce, I love you anyway."

I scowled at him, and he laughed. His smile turned to a tender look as he took my hands in his. "Ariana, I'll never be my parents because I refuse to hide. My eyes are wide open, and I'm strong enough to face whatever happens. I want to be marked with your symbol. I want to hear your every thought. I might be a greedy bastard, but I want it all with you." He kissed my nose. Then trailed kisses across my cheek until he reached my ear. He nipped at my ear lobe, and I squeaked in surprise. His husky laugh brushed again my ear making me shiver as passion stirred to life inside me. "I gotta admit I also like the idea of you wearin' my ring in the human way, so everyone knows you're mine no matter where we go."

I swallowed thickly as he kissed my neck. Goddess! Was every touch from this man going to make my knees weak and my body react like a flower opening its arms toward the sun? "I-I cannot leave my people," I blurted out as he pulled me flush against his body.

He looked down at me with a puzzled frown. "Is that what you think? That I'd ask you to give up your world for mine?"

I stepped back and wrapped my arms around my waist being careful to avoid the bandage from my injury. "I did not mean to bring that up now. We can discuss living arrangements at a later time."

"But it's botherin' you." His calloused finger traced the edge of the white bandage on my arm. "I don't want you hurtin' in any way, especially when it's somethin' I can fix." I shot him an annoyed look. I didn't need him to fix anything for me. "Don't get all mad. You don't need me to take care of you, but I'm goin' to try anyway."

"I do not know how to do this relationship thing," I explained. "I built rules around my life to keep people safe, including myself. I no longer know how to operate without them. I need you to tell me the rules. How do we decide what is right?"

"If you need rules to help you feel safe, then we'll make 'em together. As for where we'll live ..." He scratched at his bearded chin, and I could see the wheels turning behind those amazing eyes. "To be honest with you, I think part of the reason I've fought so hard to win this money and save my ranch is to show my daddy that he couldn't take it from me. That asshole is in prison where he belongs, and I'm still lettin' him have a hold on me. I shoulda just told Hope that we'd find our own place. The Downing 'legacy' ain't worth a hill of beans, but she loves that ranch."

I knew from Jaxon's research there was a sister, but I thought Kade lived alone. A cold chill crept across my skin and it wasn't from the air in the cavern. Why had he never mentioned this woman before? Had he already bonded with a human? I tried to look calm as I asked, "Hope?"

"Yeah, it ain't always easy but we make it work," Kade said with a smile that told me how much he cared for this woman. Jealousy stung me like an angry bee. "Hope can be a brat sometimes but she's a great kid."

"Kid?" The strangled sound of my voice made me wince.

"She hates it when I call her that. I guess she's really a young lady, now that she's eighteen. Seems like only yesterday she was in diapers, which she also hates hearin' me talk about."

My heart ached as I pictured a girl with his ginger hair and blue eyes. He would be an amazing father. "She is lucky to have you. I-is her mother part of your lives?"

Kade's brow furrowed for a moment but then he smiled. "Oh, no, she's not mine. I mean, yeah, I've raised her since she was three, after Mama died. Hope is my sister."

I would have loved any child of Kade's, but I couldn't deny I was relieved. I selfishly wanted to forget he had ever been with anyone but me.

"I lost myself for a bit when the cancer took Mama. I came home one night to find Daddy had hit Hope and locked her in a closet." I shivered as I remembered all the times that had happened to me. That poor baby. "She'd looked up at me with those frightened blue eyes and my whole world changed. I was only sixteen, but I knew right then I wasn't gonna let anybody hurt her ever again. I beat my daddy so badly he never came at either of us again and moved out to the bunkhouse. I took over runnin' the ranch and raisin' my sister. Hope saved me."

"It sounds like you saved her as well," I said as I reached for his hand. "I will have to thank Hope sometime."

Kade linked his fingers with mine just as the last of Titan's light faded. "I can't wait for you to meet her. I have a feelin' you'll soon be plottin' together to find ways to keep me on my toes."

"I look forward to that," I said with a grin. Then gripped his hand tightly. "Now, we need to leave and inform the others what has happened. I have not been able to reach anyone mentally since I entered this cavern and that concerns me."

I TELEPORTED us back to Minos and we appeared at the base of
the steps before the entrance. But no one was there to greet
us. I dropped Kade's hand and walked up the steps to check
the tall red doors. They were sealed once more. I turned to
scan the area, shielding my eyes from the bright midday sun.
Where was everyone? The Kyrion never left a competition
site until all contestants were accounted for. I needed to
contact Cadence to see what had happened. But first I would
take a brief moment to contact my advisor. Kade had nearly
slipped through my fingers today because I was afraid of
opening my heart to our bond, I wouldn't make that mistake
again.

I told Kade what I was doing, and his face lit up with a
smile that made my heart flutter with happiness.

"Fayel," I called through our connection.

"Yes, my lady," she replied immediately.

*"Please see that a Bonding Ceremony is prepared for two nights
from now,"* I requested. *"Get assistance from the village if the
kitchen staff need help preparing the meal."*

*"Even with every person in the valley helping we wouldn't be
able to put the ceremony together in two days, ma fille,"* Fayel

replied, sounding amused. *"Who's in such a hurry to bond that they can't wait a few months to prepare properly?"*

"Me," I stated bluntly. *"The gods have blessed me with a true bond-mate, Fayel. I nearly lost him today, and I will not wait longer than necessary to complete the Desmòs. Even if you are the only one to bear witness to our bonding, I want to do this. Please ..."* I swallowed down my pride and said words I'd never uttered in my life. *"I need your help."*

"Bless the goddess for this gift," Fayel cried out with joy. *"Of course, I will help you. Leave it all to me. I will have the seamstresses simplify your betrothal gown design. The gifts—"*

"Seeds," I blurted. It was tradition for the people to offer gifts to bless the bonding of their Kyrion. Seeds were the perfect gift that would not add any additional work to my people since they would be readily available or easily created with their power. *"I would like seeds to be our gifts. They will represent a new future full of potential for my bonding and our people."*

"Very wise, ma fille. I will make your wishes known."

"Thank you, Fayel," I replied, truly grateful to have her by my side. *"Preparations must be done quietly for now. There is the matter of my betrothal contract with Ekert that must be dealt with. I will return to Kardia tonight to settle any issues with his father."*

"What about Syris?" she asked. *"He hasn't returned to the valley."*

"I should have known that Father would find a way around our agreement. He loses his control over me if I get Aegeus back." I wanted to track Father down myself and force my brother's location from him. But I was stuck here doing my duties, and he knew it. I would be paying a visit to Ekert tonight as well and the gods help him if I didn't get my answers. *"Please keep the Talosi on patrols, and if anyone sees my father notify me immediately."*

"It will be done. Gaia's blessings on you and your bond-mate,

my lady." Fayel said before ending our connection to get to work.

Kade watched me curiously. "Mama could do that too, but I never learned. How does it work?"

"Telepathy works much like those human speaking devices—the ah, Teflon," I replied, as I scanned the area looking for clues about what had happened. Kade laughed, and I turned to him wondering what he found funny."

"I think you mean the telephone," he said with a wide grin.

I made mental note of the word but doubted I would remember it. The human world was very confusing. "Yes, the telephone. Telepathy and telekinesis are the most common powers amongst our people and are not restricted by the god we descend from."

"Can I talk to everyone with my mind?"

Kade's sad eyes were trained on the pit area where his friend had died. Grief was etched upon his face. He had paid a heavy price today for Natalie meddling in his head. I could tell he still blamed himself and likely would for a long time to come. I wanted to comfort him, but I didn't know how. I descended the steps to join him on the cobblestone path once more and placed my hand on his arm.

"Possibly, with time and practice," I answered quietly. I didn't know how to comfort him, but I could offer him a distraction in the form of learning about our world. "Telepathy is linked in some ways to our powers; the stronger the power, the more connections that can be formed."

His gaze stayed on the pit as he struggled with his emotions, but his hand slipped over mine.

"A Kyrion is the strongest member of our society—or they were before the Chosen came along. The Kyrion can mentally connect to every person in their House. The Archigós who is the head Kyrion, can connect with any Paldimori. The Chosen, well, we have yet to see what you will be fully capable of. For most, connections form only with close family members. Bond-mates only receive the connection if they have completed the Desmòs."

These were things Kade should have been taught, but in the human world he had been forced to conceal his powers. From what he had said of his mother it was likely she had only told him the barest essentials—what a young child in our world would know. In that respect he was no different than Lia or Dia in learning their powers. His mother had likely tried to protect him in the only way she knew how, by limiting his skills to better keep them hidden from his father. I knew what it was like to live with that kind of fear. It wore away at your self-esteem, your willpower, and your soul. Until you would do anything to make the pain stop; even turn yourself into someone that you hated. Despite it all, Kade was an amazing man, and some part of that was owed to his mother.

Titan had been right: all of the descendants had suffered. I hated what members of the Olympian Omàda had done to our people and what they were still doing. But maybe there were some among them like Kade and his mother who had no interest in fighting. Both sides had suffered enough. Now more than ever, I was convinced that this war had to be stopped.

I pulled my hand from Kade and touched the rock I had molded around my torso into a corset. He glanced at me, his eyes widening as the rock and the tree embedded into it shifted beneath my hand to form a deep V between my breasts where my House symbol was revealed. Kade hissed out a breath and crossed his hands over his groin. His sadness replaced by a grimace of discomfort. "Are you tryin' to torture me? There's barely enough room in this jumpsuit as it is without havin' an unexpected arisin'."

I traced my fingers slowly down the symbol enjoying this new-found power of teasing my bond-mate. "My marking is here, positioned at the top of my torso to indicate the strongest level of power outside of those who receive the Archigós mark on their back." Kade nodded absently while watching my fingers as if mesmerized. "The Chosen marks occur on your backs as well, but we do not know yet what that means. The prophecy and the true reason behind the Games have been lost over time. But we have long awaited the arrival of the Chosen."

I left the deep V open in my corset top and smiled as his throat worked as I stepped closer. "Before the gods disappeared, they imbued this island and six gems with a portion of their powers to keep our energy flowing in their absence. The large gems were divided into smaller ones within each House. But the heart of each gem remains intact and is the most powerful. It is given to the Potentials, we thought, to draw out their true strength. You wear the emerald from my House," I gestured to the torque necklace that hung around his neck. "The gems offer protection and amplify powers."

Kade pulled the torque necklace away from his skin to look at it. "Each time I came back here my powers seemed to get a bit stronger. I could do things I'd never done before."

I touched the emerald set within the tree on his necklace. "Perhaps even the gems were designed to assist with our search for the Chosen."

Kade's hand covered mine. My powers flowed into the emerald between our hands, and it began to glow. I pulled Kade's hand away and cupped it in mine. The emerald turned into a glowing liquid that circled around our hands. It pooled into Kade's palm and reshaped itself into an emerald crown.

Kade stared at the crown speechless. I took it from his hands and placed it on his head. "I will tell you a secret of the gems that only Kyrion know. The hearts of the gems were once worn as crowns by the Primordial Gods. They will only take that shape again for a god-sanctioned Kyrion and their true bond-mate. You belong to this world, Kade. As my part-ner." I winked at him, and he laughed. "And by my side as co-ruler of the House of Seasons."

His wide eyes danced with wonder as he pulled the crown from his head, and it dissolved back into his necklace. "Whoa. That is the coolest thing I've seen yet."

I laughed, and he traced my bottom lip. "You should do that more often. In fact, I think we need to put that on the list of rules: Ariana must laugh at least ten times a day."

"I will make a note of it," I teased.

He looked up at the eyes carved out of the cliff face then back at me. Then rubbed his hand over his short hair looking worried. "I don't know anythin' about bein' a Chosen or a co-ruler. I'm not sure I'm cut out for all this."

I slowly stood on my tiptoes and pressed my lips to his. His hands gripped my waist to hold me in place. "You are everything I want and need. And my people will adore you. We do not have to have all of the answers today. Wh—"

"*Ariana!*" Jaxon's voice slammed into my mind with such force I stumbled into Kade's chest.

Kade wrapped his arms around me and asked, "Are you ok?"

"Give me a moment. Jaxon is contacting me," I told Kade, and then switched over to mentally speak with Jaxon. "*I am here.*"

"*Thank the gods. We couldn't reach you through our connec-tion.*" Jaxon sounded short of breath as if he had been running. "*We have a problem back at Titan Tower. Come to the floor where Lia is being kept.*"

I dropped back into the present with dread burning a hole in my stomach. Lia. Where she was involved, there was bound to be serious trouble. Could I face my biggest foe and not drain her life away now that my defenses were in ruins?

"Something has happened. I must go."

"I'll come with you," Kade stated, with a determined edge that told me he wouldn't be talked out of it.

I grabbed his hand and teleported us to Lia's floor. Cadence rushed across the living room toward us. She smacked into another guide, sending them both stumbling before she righted herself. Then rushed up to grab Kade in a hug. "Oh my gods, you're alive!" She turned to me and gave me a teary smile. "You're both alive!"

I looked around at the devastation of the room. The elevator off to my left was a smoking mangled mass of metal. The furniture in the sunken living room was crushed, as if a giant had stomped on it. The walls were gouged and dented. In some places pieces of glass or metal stuck into the drywall. A doctor worked frantically over two bodies on the beige and gold-swirled marble tiles just outside of the elevator. The wide hall that led to one of the bedrooms ended in a swirling mass of white light with black smudges. Three of the Kyrion stood examining it from the kitchen entrance.

"What happened here?" I asked Cadence quietly.

"The guides returned to Minos to wait with the Kyrion after delivering the other contestants back to the Tower. Kyrion Chaos shouted out Lia's name and teleported away. Kyrion Nyx fell to the ground unconscious at the same time." Cadence's freckles stood out against her pale face as she twisted her hands together. "Kyrion Eros and Devon followed Kyrion Chaos. The rest of us stayed to help Kyrion Nyx, who woke up about the time the doctor came. She had a headache and was talking about how her powers were stronger, but she was fine.

"Devon sent out a call for all guides to come to the Tower. We teleported back and there was this pressure in the air like before your ears pop. A loud blast went off that shook the whole mountain." Cadence's emerald eyes were wide with fear and her fingers never stopped moving. "The Talosi assigned here are in bad shape. We don't know what happened, but Kyrion Chaos is behind that bubble-looking thing"—she pointed down the hallway—"with Lia. No one has been able to get through."

Jaxon, Remy, and Maddox noticed my presence and walked over to join us.

"The Goddess Nyx claimed Kade as her Chosen," I explained. "His powers were fully unlocked which means that Lia has received Nyx's powers as well."

"That explains some things," Jaxon said. "But if this keeps escalating each time Lia gets a new power, I'm not sure the Tower is going to remain standing." Jaxon eyed my bond-mate until I slipped my hand into Kade's. Then he smiled at me with smug satisfaction. "Looks like someone already staked their claim on our newest Chosen."

"I have been blessed by the gods with a bond-mate," I declared with my chin held high. "Kade and I will be traveling to Kardia to complete our Bonding Ceremony once I am sure everyone is safe here."

I expected them to complain or demand punishment for breaking my own rule about declaring bond-mates, but they did neither. Maddox nodded, not seeming surprised at all. Remy snorted. "About time."

Jaxon held out his hand to Kade. "Welcome to the Paldimori, Kade. If you touch my wife again—or hurt Ariana —I'll take you to my home in Mexico and drop you into a pit of fer-de-lance vipers."

Kade shook his hand. "I'm sorry that I kissed Dia. You have my word nothin' like that will ever happen again."

"Jaxon," I admonished, "he was under your sister's influence; that was not his fault."

"Yeah, I know. That's why I didn't punch him in the face again," Jaxon said with a grin.

I glared at Jaxon, but he just shrugged. "Well, Kade, now that you've got Nyx's powers maybe you can help get my brother and Lia out of that bubble?" Jaxon hitched his thumb over his shoulder. "Theia is resting in her rooms, and the rest of us have all gotten a nasty shock from trying to get through."

"I am going to have the guides get a headcount and make sure there are no other injuries. Then we will see about repairs." I started to step away, but then looked at each of them. "It seems to me that the stronger Lia's powers grow, the more Bennett is also affected. I do not know what is happening in there, but I trust our gods. Bennett and Lia have much to work through, including their shared powers. My advice would be to leave them alone and let this resolve itself."

"Is that an order from our new leader," Theia snarled from behind me.

I turned to face her. Her skin seemed to glow with power as she walked toward me. "No, it is not an order. I do not want to take your voice or your freedom from you. My only intention was to delay going to war until we are ready. You do not have to agree with me, Theia, but you do have to respect me. I will no longer be the target you use to avoid your own insecurities. Figure yourself out and join us as a true leader with the best interests of *all* of our people in mind, or go home to daddy."

I left her standing there with her mouth propped open as Jaxon said, "Damn, Ariana's taken off her gloves, and she's coming out swinging."

ARIANA TOOK MY HAND, and my heart skipped a beat. Every time she touched me was like a gift. She still hadn't said much about her past, but hopefully today I would learn more about her since we were heading to her home deep in the Congo rainforest to get ready for our Bonding Ceremony. Tomorrow I would be a married man. The goofy smile on my face faded as I thought of Hope. I wished she could be there with us.

"Are you ready?" Ariana asked.

I pulled her into my arms. "Ready."

Then I pressed my lips to hers as we teleported away. Teleporting while kissing Ariana was one of my new of favorite things to do. Well, anything that involved kissing my bond-mate actually was. I loved it when I could make her overactive brain stop worrying for a few minutes and just enjoy life. And I loved it when she got feisty and protective of me. All she had to do was look at me with a smile on her pretty pink lips and I would do anything she asked. Yeah, I was head-over-heels for my bond-mate, and I didn't give a damn who knew.

We popped back into existence and the sweltering heat of the Congo hit me. I pulled away from Ariana's lips long before I wanted to, but I was struggling to breathe in the humid jungle air. Within seconds sweat poured down my neck and my T-shirt was soaked. September in Texas could be hot and humid, but there was usually a breeze blowing. Here, even if there was a breeze, I doubted it could reach us through the tightly packed forest. This was a lot different than the open sky and fields I was used to.

"Welcome to Kardia, the home base for the House of Seasons," Ariana said with the first real hint of excitement I'd seen from her. "This is the eastern part of our lands." The trees and plants around us seemed to lean in closer as if wanting to be near her. There was a relaxed air about her that I'd never seen before. "The jungle is my home more than any other place. That is why I brought you here instead of closer to the valley. The forest and its creatures are my family."

Ariana laced her fingers with mine, and I silently celebrated another victory. "No one can teleport directly into the valley where we live as a safety measure. We will walk from here. There are elephant paths to the river from here that I have taken many times. They help to make it easier to move through the jungle." She looked up at me with what I was now calling her Kyrion look, all cold command and confidence. "The forest is a dangerous place, Kade. The animals, plants, and even some of the local human tribes could kill you. Never leave the palace without me."

"Got it," I agreed, keeping my words short since the humidity made it feel like I was breathing underwater. I swiped the sweat from my face for the millionth time.

She pointed up to the dense tree coverage overhead. "Our Talosi use the canopy often since it is the easiest way to travel. The barrier that hides us from the humans is still being repaired and the Talosi are keeping watch. They will warn us if there is trouble."

"Ok," I said, eyeing the trees suspiciously. What else moved around up there?

She smiled and tugged me along with her. I assumed this was the way to her home but if there was a path, I couldn't make it out. My boots sank into mud puddles and tromped over soggy ground. Droplets of water fell down from the trees to thump against my cowboy hat. A big brown snake clung to a downed tree and flicked its tongue at us as we passed by too close for my comfort. But Ariana didn't even look its way. I clumsily stumbled over roots and vines that Ariana navigated with ease. In narrow sections, wet leaves smacked against my much broader shoulders. My hat was nocked askew at least a dozen times by limbs and vines that Ariana passed under with no problem.

A screech filled the air, and a colorful bird took flight. I stopped to watch as it flew so close to Ariana that its bright red and yellow wings brushed her arm. Hope would love this. The animals would be the ones running for their lives if I brought her here. She would study them all and talk my ear off listing all of the fun facts she would have researched about them.

Ariana turned to me, and it was like all of the stress she carried had melted away now that we were here. She stepped forward to straighten my hat and asked, "What has made that frown on your face?"

"It's nothin'. Just thinkin' about home."

"I am strong enough to help you shoulder your burdens as well as my own," she stated quietly.

It would be easy to brush off her help, but with Ariana it was what was behind the words that mattered the most. What she was really saying was "don't hide things from me or shut me out." I got the feeling that she hadn't had many people she could count on in her life and that left its own kinda mark. Her wariness was evident in the ruler-straight posture and the cold formality of the way she talked. All clues I'd have to be careful to pay attention to with my bond-mate.

"You're the strongest woman I know, Ariana." I took her

hand and pressed it over my heart. "And you're right, we're partners now. I don't wanna hide anythin' from you." I brushed a loose curl over her shoulder. "Back home, Hope's in school to learn how to care for sick animals. I was thinkin' 'bout how much she would love it here."

"Then one day we will bring her here," Ariana promised.

I brought her hand up to press a kiss against the back. "We'd both be really grateful."

She blushed. Then twisted her hand around to grab mine and pull me through the jungle once more. One minute we were surrounded by trees and the next, we stepped out onto the bank of a river. I stumbled into Ariana's back when I realized we weren't alone. I stared in awe at a small group of elephants across the shallow section of the stream from where we stood. "Remain calm. The forest elephants are friendly. They are used to seeing the local human tribes who fish the river. And me, since I often use this entrance to the valley."

A brightly colored bird similar to the one we'd seen earlier sat on the back of one of the biggest elephants in the group. I counted eight elephants in total: five larger ones and three smaller. The largest was about seven feet tall and watched us while the younger ones played in the water.

"The young bull there," Ariana waved her hand toward one of the adult-looking elephants hanging back from the group. "He has nearly reached maturity. He will soon be ready to leave his family to roam alone for most of his life unless he is mating. But he has been shown all he needs to survive. The next steps are up to him."

She waved her hand and several green oval-shaped fruits floated from the trees and over to the elephants. The mangoes had barely landed on the bank before the elephants scooped them up with their long trunks and shoved them into their mouths.

Ariana glanced at me quickly, then turned her gaze back to the elephants. Her hands gripped the skirt of her dress tightly. What was it she was afraid to tell me? "My life was much like the young elephant's will soon be. Alone, with only the cold comfort of my duties. My powers … they do not work as other's do, and I was kept apart until I learned to control them. I trained as a Kyrion not because I was my brother's successor but because I was to serve a purpose. My family has sat on the throne of the House of Seasons for several generations. Among other things, my father wanted to ensure the throne remained in our family."

She smiled as the smallest elephant trumpeted in our direction as if asking for more fruit. "That one I call Mango. I have been feeding her since she was a newborn. She is a greedy little tyrant now when it comes to her fruit."

Ariana waved her hand and several more mangoes landed on the bank near the elephants. Then she said, "My father has been in control of most of my life, even my choice of bond-mate. But as I informed Ekert before we left this afternoon, I am taking back my life and making it my own. I am the supreme leader now of all of my people, and I will no longer be told by anyone what is right for me."

She finally turned to face me, and there was a tentative hope written across her face. "I do not know how a family is supposed to work. My mother was never part of my life, and my father cared for little except his own agenda. My brother tried in his own ways to be close to me, but I was too closed off by then." She ran her finger over the emerald in my torque necklace. "I do not know how to be a bond-mate either. But I have made my choice, and it is you. You are what is right for me. I-I guess what I am asking for is your patience."

I had thought I would be prepared for her story when she was ready to tell me, but I hadn't been. She had glossed over the details, but I was learning how to listen for more than just her words. Ariana had been neglected and abandoned by everyone who should have been there for her. Her fierce independence had been learned as a survival skill.

I tugged her into my arms and waited until the tension eased from her body. Her eyes stared up with that guarded expression I knew all too well. "I'm sorry that you had to go through all that. I wanna say I'll protect you from ever feelin' an ounce of pain again, but you don't need me to protect you. You've done a damn fine job of that all your life, and I'm in awe of your strength." I tucked a curl behind her ear and traced a finger across her cheek. "You could have given in and wallowed in self-pity. Instead, you've fought for every ounce of freedom." I pulled her tighter against me, wanting her to know I wasn't going anywhere. "You already have my heart, anything else you need from me is yours too. I don't know how to be a bond-mate either or a Kyrion. We're gonna do this together, partner."

She moved onto her toes to brush a kiss across my lips. I deepened the kiss, sealing my promise to her. Her arms locked around my neck knocking my hat to the ground. My hands gripped her waist pulling her tighter against me, and I grunted as she made contact with the hardness pushing against my jeans. She stilled for a moment, and I gentled my kisses letting her get used to feeling me. I'd known since the first time we kissed that Ariana had no experience with men. A primitive part of me savored the idea that I would be her first ... everything. I slowly slid my hands down her arms, loving the way she shivered against me. My fingers laced with hers as I pulled her hands up and placed them on my chest. "I'm yours to touch. Anytime. Anywhere."

I released her hands as they began to tentatively explore my chest. Her physical touch was as soft as the flower-petal touch of her mind when we were near. Her fingers traced every line of muscle through my thin T-shirt, and when they slipped underneath to meet the heated skin right above my jeans, I hissed in pleasure. She hesitated a moment, checking to make sure I was fine, and I nodded for her to continue.

I pulled my T-shirt off and tossed it aside, desperate for

her to touch every bit of my skin. She laughed at my eagerness, and I pulled her into me to taste her smile. Her body pressed against mine, every soft curve sinking against my hardness. My hands grabbed her hips to rock her against my erection, and she let out a needy little whimper that drove me crazy. Her hands gripped my shoulders as she lifted herself higher to rub against me just right. I tugged up the long length of her skirts and brought her leg up to wrap around my hip. Her breath caught on a sexy little sob as she arched back against my other arm. Her eyes never left mine as she shifted her skirt higher. I watched her pink lips part on a panted breath as my hand moved up the inside of her thigh, pushing her dress aside to reveal her to me. My breath hitched. My sexy little bond-mate wasn't wearing underwear. My finger traced over the patch of dark blonde curls, heading toward that pretty pink perfection below.

My fingers brushed over her damp center just as a blast of water soaked us both. I lost my balance and fell backwards, bringing Ariana with me. I landed on my back in the shallow water with Ariana sitting across my thighs looking stunned. A long gray trunk patted her head, and I tipped my head back to find the little elephant she called Mango. Its ears flapped as it raised its trunk and let out a rumbling sound that I guess was a laugh. I looked back up at Ariana, and we both started laughing. My heart did a happy little dance in my chest at seeing her so carefree for once. She was the most beautiful thing I'd ever seen. The sun beamed down on her making her gauzy, wet dress transparent. Wet curls stuck to her face and neck. Her pale green eyes danced with happy little emerald lights.

Her laughter quieted as she reached out to pet the small elephant. "Very funny. Is this any way to treat the person who brings you fruits? Us women are supposed to stick together."

The little elephant nudged Ariana's chest and would have sent her toppling backwards if I hadn't grabbed her hips. The elephant trumpeted and splashed back across the stream to join her family. "I like your friend," I said, cupping her cheek.

"I may have created a monster. She has become quite demanding of my attention when I visit." The smile on Ariana's face said she loved giving the attention as well.

I tugged her hips forward and her pretty pink lips rounded in surprise. Yeah, even the water hadn't cooled me off. "Would it be forward of me to say that I like you in this position?"

"Yes, very," she replied in a husky voice. "But … I like it too."

I groaned as she adjusted her weight. "Ariana, it's been a while. If you keep movin' I'm gonna embarrass myself in front of the elephants."

She stilled immediately, and I almost begged her not to stop. But these wet jeans were uncomfortable and the last thing I needed was friction burn on sensitive areas. She hiked up her dress to find her footing, and I groaned again at the sight of those dark blonde curls between her legs. She blushed and hurriedly backed away.

God give me strength. She had no clue what she was doin' to me.

I carefully stood up and turned my back toward her to adjust myself. I hadn't lied about it being a while. The last person I'd had sex with was Natalie, and that had been months ago. At the thought of that evil woman my hard-on faded quickly. I scrubbed the water from my short hair and beard as I walked back out of the river. Ariana held my hat out to me, and I put it back on. "Thanks. And thank you for bringin' me here to your jungle to meet your family."

"I needed to show us both that I can share my life with you. When we are bonded there will be no barriers between us unless we create them." She picked up the wet strands of hair against her cheeks and tucked them behind her ears. Then picked up the hem of her long dress and began to wring it out. She stayed focused on her task as she said, "My memories are not pleasant. When you see them, I hope you will remember our time here."

I took her hand and waited until she looked at me. "There's nothing that I'll find here or in your past that will change the way I feel about you."

"I hope that is true," she whispered.

Only time would convince her. I was determined to spend the rest of our combined lives making sure she knew I would never abandon her.

Then she smiled wickedly as she pulled her hand from mine to raise her skirt higher and higher. Then tied the skirt over one hip displaying shapely legs that had me forgetting what I was doing. "Now let me show you how to enter the valley from here. Take my hand and hold tight."

As soon as my hand wrapped around hers my feet left the ground. I wobbled back and forth as we levitated off the ground. We moved slowly through the air until we were over the water. "Do not let go, Kade."

I looked at the amazing woman beside me and said, "Never."

A section of water lifted up to meet our feet and it was like we were standing on a surfboard. Then we zoomed away. Ariana's laugh and my curses filled the air all along the river as she took me to her home.

I COULDN'T REMEMBER the last time I had laughed this much or felt this free. The wind beat against us as we skidded around bends and hopped down rapids following the portion of the Lomami River that cut through my lands. We frightened a family of great crested grebes diving for fish. Kade almost lost his hat to a troop of red colobus monkeys swinging from the trees overhanging the river. When we entered the portion where the river flowed underground, Kade gripped my hand tightly enough to cut off circulation. I laughed again, and the happy sound echoed through the dark. Moments later we entered the valley, and I slowed us down until we came to a stop. The mid-morning sun peeked over the ridges that surrounded the valley, bathing my home in its golden rays.

Deep down inside a small kernel of hope blossomed. Kade would help me rid this valley of the darkness that still lingered here from everything my father had done.

I sat us down gently on the bank and released the water to return to the river. Then untied my nearly dry skirts. Here at the back end of the valley the forest remained mostly untouched by Father's alterations and walking to the palace would take half the day. "I will teleport us to the palace from here. Your room should be stocked with clothes more suitable to the rainforest. We will change, and then I have something to show you."

I appreciated what those wet jeans were doing to his rear, but we both needed lighter weight clothing that could breathe easily and dry quickly. As if to prove my point, rain began to fall. I could control the seasons but stopping the rain during one of the wettest times of the year would be a full-time job. Instead, I used the sudden shower as an excuse to spend a few more minutes alone with my bond-mate.

I took Kade's hand and led him under a large *Millettia laurentii* tree. The branches were loaded with green leaves and purple flowers. These trees were one of the additions my father had demanded, due to the deceptive beauty of the tree. The bark and roots contained toxins used on our people's fishing spears. The branches shifted to offer us more protection as the rain picked up, and I placed my hand against the leaves in thanks. A pair of okapi peeked their heads out from the bushes several feet away. Relatives of the giraffe but much shorter at about five feet tall, they were a favorite of the children in the hamlet. They looked like a strange mixture of a deer and zebra with black-and-white strips on their legs. They were typically shy, but as with most animals here, they knew me and sensed my soothing connection to the earth. Their deep brown coats turned almost black as they stepped from the shelter of the bushes and into the rain.

Kade stared in wonder as they crept closer. Each of them carried a fruit in their mouth and dropped the gifts into my palms. I thanked them through our connection and encouraged Kade to pet them. His large hands rubbed gently across their necks, and I was happy to be sharing this moment with him. They gave us one last playful nudge and then left as silently as they had come.

I offered Kade one of the dark blue bush pears, and he eyed it with amusement. "You're a regular Dr. Doolittle," he said with a chuckle. He must have noticed my confusion because he said, "The animals, they treat you like you're the queen of the jungle."

"Am I not?" I replied in an overly offended tone. Kade stuttered an apology, and I laughed. I picked up my skirts and settled onto the ground. "Most of my free time has been spent in the jungle. But it belongs to no one but the Goddess Gaia and her creations. She gifted her descendants the ability to talk to the plants and animals. Both are sensitive to our powers, as if they feel that we carry some part of the goddess within us."

"I wonder if I'll be able to talk to my horse, Juniper, someday," Kade mused out loud, dropping down beside me.

I nodded. "Once we are bonded and share powers, I will show you how."

"My sister would love to have the power to talk to all those animals she heals." Kade rolled the pear between his hands looking troubled.

"We will find a way for you to maintain your relationship with her," I reassured him.

Kade nodded and then cleared his throat. "So, you like being outdoors. Seems we have that in common. I spent a lot of time in the fields and canyons back home." He motioned toward the forest around us. "This is gonna take some gettin' used to, though. I hope you'll be patient with me too."

I looked around, trying to see my home through his eyes. The greenish-brown river was framed between tightly packed trees of every size fighting for their space. Sheer grayish-brown cliffs on all sides eclipsed everything else in the valley. Birds sang in the treetops, and monkeys grunted to each other. Rain pounded the ground, forming muddy puddles and increasing the humidity. This was a far cry from the flat fields of a ranch. "Of course, I am sure there will be many adjustments for the both of us."

"Speaking of adjustments ..." Kade turned to me with a

tender look on his face. "Ariana, I know you said you've been alone a lot. It'll probably take some time before you get used to sharin' things with me. But I want you to know you can tell me anythin'."

I wasn't ready. I would never be ready to talk about my past. It would be easier to leave this to our bonding when our souls connected, and we would experience each other's lives as if we lived them. But I refused to be imprisoned any longer by my father or my past.

I used my telekinesis to bring one of my short knives to me from my room and carved out pieces of the pear. Kade watched carefully and did the same when I passed the knife to him. I appreciated his confident use of the tool for a few moments while gathering my thoughts. "Every Paldimori child is born with their symbol, but their powers do not manifest until later. Children are first given primers to practice with when they are two. For the House of Seasons, it is a seed they will look after and encourage to grow. That is not what happened with me."

I placed a piece of the fruit in my mouth. The normally rich, buttery flavor was tasteless as I confessed to the sin I had committed that started it all. My birth. "My powers triggered during my birth, but they were not like the normal life-giving powers of Gaia. They were hungry and wild." I twisted my fingers in my skirts, not daring to look at Kade afraid to see fear and disgust on his face. Would he call me an abomination too? "My powers fed off of my mother's, draining her nearly to the point of death. The midwife quickly wrapped me in thick blankets to prevent anyone touching my skin, but the damage was already done. My mother's mind was damaged beyond repair."

I stared down at the fruit spread across my skirt and forced myself to select another piece. I chewed and swallowed by rote. "Aegeus was only five, but he saved my life that day by throwing a tantrum and demanding that no one hurt his baby sister. Unfortunately, he also doomed us both by showing how much he cared for me and giving my father, Syris, exactly what he wanted—leverage to use against us." I picked at the pear in my lap not having the stomach to eat one more bite or tell Kade all of the ways my father had used two small children against each other.

"Mother lives in the west tower where she is seen to by caretakers daily. I visit her as my father demands once each month." Syris liked to use my visits as a reminder of what I had done to my family and the sins I must atone for.

"Ari—" Kade started in a choked whisper, but I powered on.

"Not many know that my powers can take the energy away from any living thing. I was kept in the east tower until I turned six. Then Aegeus convinced Father to send me to Tantalus where all Kyrion are trained. I lived there until I had gained enough control to leave."

"You were a child!" Kade's shout startled birds from the trees. "How could they lock you away like an animal?"

"I was a dangerous child. One that very nearly killed my mother and others who came into contact with me before I learned control." I tossed the remains of my pear into the undergrowth and wiped my knife on the grass. "At least my training taught me discipline."

I sent my knife back to my room and focused on pressing the wrinkles from my skirt. Anything to avoid seeing my bond-mate look at me with condemnation. "Tantalus was"—*misery, pain, my destruction*—"difficult. Most of the Kyrion you know trained there together. Aegeus took the throne when he was sixteen as is our tradition. I stayed on at Tantalus for five more years before my command over my powers was good enough for me to be released to go home." Aegeus had visited me several times a year, but he was not the same boy I remembered, and my protective walls had grown too thick to let him in.

"Four years ago, Aegeus was held prisoner by the Olympian Omàda and never recovered from their torture." I swallowed down the bitter memories of seeing his pale, broken body brought back to the palace. Out of the corner of my eye I watched Kade angrily toss the remains of his pear into the forest. "Aegeus has been under my father's care since then. I see him when Father allows, but one day soon that will change."

I finally raised my eyes to meet Kade's. His lips were pressed into a hard line. Lightning crackled along the tense muscles of his arms. His chest heaved. There was a dangerous look on his face that sent my heart racing in fear. In this moment he was every bit the deadly enemy I had pictured all Olympians to be. My powers stirred. "Kade?"

A strangled growl was his only answer. Green lights poured from my fingertips as I slowly raised up onto my knees. Tan grains of light fell from Kade's clenched fists onto the ground and the grass grew several inches. Lightning flashed in his eyes as he reached for me. I scrambled to my feet to keep him from touching me when my powers saw him as a threat. I just needed a few moments to calm down.

This is Kade, Ariana. He will not hurt you. But a lifetime of pain and treachery drove me to defend myself. My skin tingled as his powers built, and I started to back away.

Kade surged to his feet faster than I could track and gripped my hands in a bruising grip. "Stop!" I yelled. "Kade, no."

The deep well of power in him called to me to take and take. The parched roots of my tree grabbed on and took the first long pull. Kade gasped as his powers flowed from him and into me. White and tan lights tangled with my green. I remembered the burning pain of having my powers taken by the black flames and that empty feeling left behind. I was killing my bond-mate, and I couldn't stop.

With every last bit of my strength, I ripped my powers

away as I teleported to the other side of the river. Kade lay face down under the tree where we had eaten. I dropped to my knees heaving in a great lungful of air as a scream of denial built in my chest. Just when I thought I would break apart from the pain and heartache filling me, Kade rolled to his back with a cough. *Thank the goddess!* I pressed my hands into the mud as the rain slowed to a gentle rhythm. The thrum of the jungle life pressed back at me through the ground, attempting to calm my racing heart.

"Ariana, are you ok?" Kade's worried voice carried across the twenty feet of river between us.

I had thought that the gods had blessed Kade to be the one person who was safe from my powers. He had touched me all day today, and I'd never felt the urge to take his powers. But I had been wrong. Everything I had gone through to save Kade would be undone if I bonded with him. I knew what I had to do, and I hated myself for it. I had been right all along; I was meant to be alone. A sob escaped before I could lock it out. My heart burned with agony as if Kade's lightning had scorched me.

"*Fayel,*" I called mentally.

The despair I felt must have translated through our connection because she answered in gentle voice, "*I am here, ma fille.*"

"*I am sending my bond-mate to his rooms within the palace. Please make sure he has everything he needs and that he is protected.*"

"*Of course, my lady.*"

"*There has been a change in plans.*" My fists squeezed the mud until it hardened and broke apart in my hands. "*You will accompany Kade to the place I intended to take him this afternoon. Give him as much as he needs and do not take no for an answer. Have the gems converted into cash for him and then send him home.*"

"*My lady, the ceremony—*"

"*Is cancelled*," I stated harshly. I would go on breathing after this, but my heart would exist in Texas. Far from my deadly powers and the war that was coming.

Fayel's voice was full of indignant anger when she replied, "*If he has done anything t—*"

"*Kade is a good man. He deserves better than what our world would do to him.*" I forced myself to look at him one last time. He was shouting something at me, but I couldn't hear over the frantic beating of my heart. "*Dia is our Chosen. We will find the others, and they will be enough.*"

Her confusion came through our connection as she said, "*But he is your bond-mate. The God of Chaos himself has said it's so.*"

"*I did not ask for your advice,*" I replied coldly. "*Obey my orders, Archai.*"

"*Yes, Kyrion Gaia,*" Fayel replied with displeasure. "*You may wish to know your father has returned to the valley.*"

I winced as she broke our connection. I hated that I continued to hurt the people I cared for. I mentally reached out to Father and requested he meet me at the thrones in an hour.

I forced the rain to stop and the sun beamed down on my wet skin. I got to my feet ignoring the mud that coated my dress and the wet locks of hair hanging in my face. I focused on the tree over Kade's head as I said, "I am teleporting you to the palace. Fayel will assist you with whatever you need."

"What I need is you. Don't push me away, Ari." The nickname said in his gentle voice nearly broke my will to see this through. "What happened was my fault. I lost my head for a minute when I heard what all you've been through. I'm sorry. Please come back to this side of the river and talk to me," Kade pleaded.

"I must meet with my father in an hour to settle a few matters," I replied coolly.

His transparent white shirt showed off every tense muscle as he said, "I'll go with you."

He thought I needed protection, but it was the other way around. I needed to protect him.

"No," I stated quickly. *Push him away, Ariana. It is for the best.* "I thought you respected my strength, yet you are trying to coddle me. I neither want nor need your protection, Kade."

"Don't go pickin' fights because you're afraid," Kade growled, his fists clenching rhythmically at his sides.

"This is not a fight," I corrected him.

It was a surrender. The gods had it wrong this time, I was meant to be alone. Because this was the only way to protect Kade from his greatest threat—me.

33

ARIANA

I TELEPORTED us both to the palace, deposited Kade in his rooms, and quickly traveled to mine before he could say a word. I mentally commanded two guides assigned to him to keep him safe while he was here. Then showered and put on a thin dress with swirls of emerald and fuchsia. It was one of the few dresses I had selected for myself and it boosted my confidence every time I wore it. I needed every bit of confidence I could gather to finally face my father and demand Aegeus's return. Now that I had broken my bond contract with Ekert our deal was off, and I was on my own, freeing myself from Father's clutches once more. Ekert had been furious about my change of heart and threatened all kinds of things. He was currently in a cage of vines in the lowest level of the palace after Fayel retrieved him from Titan Tower this morning.

I teleported to the arbor in the center of the courtyard. Twisted vines of the *Mondia whitei* plants made up the three walls and the ceiling of the arbor. Purple and white starfish-shaped flowers dotted the vines and perfumed the air with a hint of vanilla. Two stone thrones sat at the back of the arbor.

Their tall backs were inlaid with emeralds that formed the symbol for our House and were my father's addition to the previously plain slabs. Syris stood next to my throne and bowed respectfully as I approached. I didn't admonish him for entering the grove before me or for not maintaining his bowed position until I acknowledged him. His disregard for my position would no longer be a concern after tonight. I stayed standing instead of taking my seat on the throne.

"You have been away for some time, Father," I stated, trying to gauge his mood.

"I had some adjustments to make in one of my … business ventures. A client isn't happy that our product was less reliable than they expected," he replied. His voice would have convinced anyone less in tune with his body language that all was well, but I knew better. His arms were folded behind his back and his chest was puffed out in what I called his intimidation pose. "I'm sure you understand how unexpected events sometimes need to be dealt with personally. How certain actions need to be taken to prevent the destruction of everything you've worked toward."

I understood that last part all too well. That's what I was here to do today: find my brother and finally take action against my father.

But what product was he talking about? One of his gadgets from the human world? This was the first I had heard of his business venture and that worried me. An icy pool of dread settled in my stomach.

"Did you manage to salvage your business?" I asked cautiously, hoping he would give me some clue what he was up to.

"I believe the changes we agreed to will get the needed results." He stepped forward, and I wanted to back away, but I held my ground. "The problem, you see, was that we were focused on the wrong thing. We thought we needed a power source to produce power. But it seems we might need the opposite."

"Well, it appears you have found your solution. Now, it is time we discuss Aegeus—"

"There's no need to discuss your brother," Syris assured me in a tone that was far from reassuring. He walked a few steps closer and panic clawed at my chest.

"*Track me.*" I flung out the mental message not liking the hunted feeling creeping over me as Syris stepped forward once more.

"There is every reason to discuss him." I balled my fists into my skirts as my powers built. "Our agreement is fulfilled. Aegeus is to be released into my care."

Syris smiled with smug satisfaction. "It seems that several agreements are being broken today."

Ekert! He must have contacted Father. That meant … Kade!

I frantically traced our tentative connection but couldn't sense anything more than his presence still in the valley. I started to reach out to him, but Father made a tsking sound that drew my attention.

"You've come a long way from that sniveling little brat who peed herself in fright whenever I needed to punish you. You'll never replace Aegeus, but you have a bit more of my backbone than he did. It's a pity, really."

Ah, there was the man I knew. "Pity? I am surprised you know the word. You had no pity or compassion for the little girl you beat repeatedly for powers that I did not ask for." My powers pushed against my skin, begging to be released. "Who is it that you think deserves pity?"

"Your father, of course," Ekert said from behind me.

I spun around to find him and his father wearing matching triumphant grins. I turned to press my back into the wall of the arbor to keep them all in my sights.

"This could have gone differently, if the gods had only given me the powers I deserved." Syris sneered. "I could have held the throne for centuries and worked through my children to control it even longer. Yet I was denied the Kyrion powers and a male heir strong enough to hold the throne."

"But Aegeus—" I argued. What was going on here?

A warm presence brushed against the doorway in my mind, and I eased it open. I needed other witnesses to this plot and back-up in case my father had any more secrets to divulge tonight.

"Was weak." Syris sighed. "I tried to make him strong, but it only partially worked."

"Even without the powers of the Kyrion, Syris ruled us," Ekert stated with a sickening case of hero worship shining across his face. "The first male ruler of our House. Your father is a brilliant man. You women have ruled this House since the beginning, but now it's our time. What Syris did with you and your brother was groundbreaking. What he has come up with now … Syris will be a legend, and the House of Seasons will be ruled by those *we* choose for eternity."

This was madness! I couldn't let that happen.

My powers lashed out toward Ekert and his father. A loud crack sounded, and my stomach burned. The green lights of my powers shut off as if someone had severed them. My hand pressed against my stomach and came away wet with blood. My gaze met my father's, and I noticed the human device called a gun in his hand. We had learned about such weapons in Tantalus in case we needed to defend ourselves from the humans. But I had never imagined any of our people —especially my own father—using one against me.

I sagged against the vines behind me as my blood continued to seep through my fingers.

"We couldn't have you teleporting away or using your powers on us," Syris explained as he handed the gun to Ekert. "Surprisingly, the humans' weapons are quite effective in subduing our people. Our natural response is to lash out with our powers rather than shield ourselves, and these weapons do not give off any energy signatures like our powers do. They are essentially undetectable."

"Stop this madness ..." My voice trailed off as my vision went fuzzy.

"Once your father perfects the process, no one will be calling him mad," Ekert's father said and clapped Syris on the back. "No more babies marked at the whim of the God of Chaos to become Kyrion. We will control who will sit on the throne."

I gasped at what they were planning. They were tampering with the natural order of our world and the will of the gods. "You cannot stop the God of Chaos."

"Ah, but we can. There are no more successors left in the House of Seasons." Syris chuckled. "The God of Chaos thinks he's very clever to mark a baby as a Kyrion when the prior one's life is fading, or their service is nearly done. It's convenient really that those babies are brought to the palace right away. It made my work to get rid of them that much easier."

How many times had I been on the brink of death from the malnourishment and beatings that a successor had been marked? My powers surged as a silent scream of denial built inside me. Syris's cruel laughter filled the air. "I can see you're putting the pieces together. Yes, all those times you felt that calling and your powers reaching out for someone was a successor being born. I have wondered if my killing the successors prompted the God of Chaos to prolong your life. You should thank me, daughter."

"You made me believe I was killing people when my powers reached out." I said, the words coming out slurred. He only grinned in response. "The successors ... I was not born Kyrion, Aegeus was. They should have been born when he nearly died. Why?"

Father grinned. "Why indeed? I think I will let you determine that for yourself." Syris motioned Ekert and his father forward. They rolled out a woven mat of palm fronds next to me. "Poor little Ariana, your fear has made it all too easy to manipulate you."

The men started to reach for me to lift me onto the mat, but I couldn't let them take me. My powers lashed out with barb tips that tore through Father's tunic to leave bloody slashes across his chest. A vine from the arbor wall wrapped around Ekert's throat, and he made a choking sound as it lifted him off his feet. I caught an orange streak out of the corner of my eye and Ekert's father shouted as he fell to the ground. Snarls joined the sound of his screams to get the damn fox off of him.

"*Bramble, hide!*" I commanded through our link.

Father had recovered and his telekinesis shoved me across the ground. I slammed into the arbor wall with a grunt and flowers rained down around me. My hold on my powers broke, and Ekert fell to the ground as the vines released him. His father got to his feet wrapping his fingers around a bloody bite mark on his arm. I held out my blood-stained hand toward them, but weakness overtook me before I could do anything. My arm dropped, and I lay there looking up at the three men who would be my death.

"Your fight is admirable but pointless. I will always win," Syris gloated.

Ekert leaned over me and painfully yanked my head back by my hair. "You should have taken my deal, and this would have been much less painful." He raised a needle filled with glowing golden liquid. I tried to push away from the liquid I recognized as the memory serum the House of Light had created, but my body wouldn't obey. "This should keep your mind too busy to think of new ways to fight against us."

Ekert stabbed the needle into my arm. Cold liquid filled my veins, and I gasped. I turned my head away to hide the helpless tears stinging my eyes and met the pair of amber-colored eyes watching me from between the tangle of the arbor vines. I reached for the warm presence of my connection. *"Kade, I love you,"* I whispered. Then the world faded away.

34

KADE

ARIANA HAD LEFT me in this bedroom almost an hour ago. She would be meeting with her father soon, and I hated that she was going alone. I tried for the millionth time to teleport using what I'd seen from Natalie's control of me and what Ariana had said. Then slumped against the wall in defeat. I eyed the bedroom door again, wondering if I'd have a better shot this time of getting past the two guides blocking the only exit. Not even my Texas charm had worked to get information outta them. My next attempt hadn't gone any better. They had forcibly shoved me back into the room when I tried to make a run for it.

"*Ariana, can you hear me?*" I mentally called out.

There was no answer.

I pushed away from the wall and prowled around the room. Palm plants in all sizes dotted the area. Dozens of candles in glass bowls hung from the ceiling. Short tree trunks supported a wide bed that took up half of the wall off to the left. A large tub took up one corner along the right wall. A stone table with two wooden chairs stood to the left of that. The empty plate from my supper of roasted fish, rice, and mango still sat on the table, along with a now empty mug of water. I pivoted toward the only other set of doors and shoved them open. The moon peeked above the cliffs in the distance, its light falling across the balcony in front of me. I stepped out into the humid night and noticed monkeys watching me from a couple of trees whose wide branches brushed against the balcony. I leaned over the side of the balcony but could barely make out the ground a couple of stories below. And the bottom third of the tall trees didn't have any branches to allow me to climb down. So much for getting out that way.

My fist pounded down on the stone wall surrounding the balcony. Movement in the trees caught my attention, and I glanced up to see the monkeys had gotten closer. "Ya'll wouldn't happen to know a sharp-tongued female about this tall, would you?" I held my hand up to my chest. "Pretty green eyes and more stubborn than the mule my sister talked me into buyin' her when she was ten." I scrubbed a hand over my short hair with a sigh of frustration. "How 'bout a way outta this room?"

My chin dropped to my chest as I searched for that connection between us and tried to follow it to my other half. But Ariana must have blocked me somehow. My heart ached every time I remembered that tormented look on her face as she kneeled in the mud on the other side of the river. All this time I thought Ariana shied away from touch because of what others had done to her and that was part of it. But what really scared her was that she might hurt someone else. I hadn't seen it until it was too late to protect either of us. For those few seconds our hands were locked together and her powers were pulling on mine, I had felt her fear and panic.

I had caused that. Rage had filled me with every word she had painfully offered to me about what she'd endured. The craving for justice had shattered every ounce of civility in me, and my powers had spilled out of me looking to find those responsible. I heard her thoughts when her powers clashed with mine; she had seen my Olympian half fully come out and acted on instinct. Every minute Ariana put distance between us was more time for her to rebuild the icy walls of her defenses. If she succeeded in rebuilding those walls, I was afraid I'd never reach her again.

A scuffling sounded close by, and I looked up to see a tan rope dangling in front of me. I swiped the sweat from my brow onto the sleeve of the green tunic top with the House of Seasons symbol on the hems that I'd changed into after a shower earlier. Three monkeys sat on the branch closest to me. The white fur around their eyes, ears, and throats stood out against the growing darkness. Their small faces mimicked human expressions well and right now, they gave me a "what are you waiting for" look.

"Guess ya'll do know a way out. Thanks," I said as I pulled the rope from the branches to check its length.

I patted the knife tucked along the small of my back and into the waist of my pants. It had been hanging on the wall along with some other decorative items. The knife was about six inches long with a cork handle and writing on the double-sided blade. I didn't know what to expect after hearing about the way Ariana had grown up here, so I wasn't taking any chances. I tugged the rope again, putting my full weight on it. The length would get me close enough to the ground to jump and, hopefully, not break anything. I swung my leg over the balcony railing, and the monkeys screeched excitedly.

"I'm not sure if they're laughin' at me or cheerin' me on," I muttered under my breath. "Well, here goes."

The sound of a throat clearing stopped me in my tracks. I turned to find the white-haired woman I'd seen defend the hunters in the jungle when Natalie had control of me.

"Uh, hi. Nice night for a stroll, huh?" I asked with a

warble to my voice. I was nervous as a long-tailed cat in a room full of rocking chairs. It wasn't just the knives strapped across her chest but her dark green eyes that felt like they were searching my soul. The woman was several inches shorter than Ariana, but I'd seen her fight. No way was I going up against her.

"Homme fou," she replied with a shake of her head. "Tu vas te casser le cou."

"Uh, sorry I only speak English."

She huffed. "I said you're a crazy man who's going to break his neck. The monkeys would play with you like a cat with a mouse. Then screech their heads off until the Talosi come to cut you from the ropes," she explained, with a wicked little tilt of her lips. "The monkeys are a great security system."

I shot the monkeys a disappointed look "We coulda done great things together." They just grinned back at me and took off running along the branches. I brought my leg back over the railing and let the rope go. Then I faced the woman. "Who are you? And can you please take me to see Ariana?"

"I am Archai Fayel, advisor to Kyrion Gaia," she replied. "The Kyrion has asked me to escort you." She pulled a knife from her bandolier and tested the sharp end against her finger. "If you hurt Kyrion Gaia I will wring the apologies from your lips as I carve each of your sins into your skin. Am I understood?"

"Yes, ma'am," I replied with a gulp, knowing she meant every word "I'll never harm a hair on her head, and I'll try my best to protect her heart too."

She huffed again and said, "Take my hand."

I placed my hand in hers, and we teleported away. We reappeared at the opposite end of the valley from where Ariana had brought me earlier. Fayel explained as we walked that the dark tunnel under the cliff was the main entrance to the valley. We exited on the other side between the roots of a tree that were as tall as me. Fayel transported us again, and this time, we appeared at the base of a waterfall. I looked around in awe at the untouched beauty around us. The waterfall fell from a wall of green vegetation into a wide pool and flowed out into a stream split in two directions by a massive rock. The spray of the water rose into a mist around us and brought relief from the constant heat. Fayel wasted no time picking her way around the edge of the pool, and I followed along. We stopped within feet of the pounding water and Fayel waved her hand. Green lights cut upward through the falling water, and it parted to form an entrance for us.

Fayel led the way through a shallow stream until we came to a chamber where light filtered through several small openings in the rock ceiling. This seemed an odd place to meet Ariana, but I kept quiet. We trudged into the pool of aqua blue water that filled the chamber until we reached the center. The knee-deep water soaked my linen pants and was a cold shock to my heated skin. Fayel walked in a circle as she used her powers to slide the water away from us.

The water rose up in a wall around the four-foot-wide circle of dry rock where we stood. Fayel placed her hand on the rock, and a rumbling noise started beneath our feet. When the circle we stood on made a grating noise and started to sink, I couldn't help but flinch. Fayel's raspy laugh echoed through the dark as we dropped further and further from the chamber. The loud sound of rock settling again rock filled the dark space as we came to a stop.

"Only Kyrion Gaia and I can enter here," Fayel explained, with a warning in her tone. I got the unspoken message: tell no one about this. "What she has created for the future of our people is a secret that she wishes to share now with you."

"I thought you were takin' me to her," I said, my voice rising to echo off the walls. "Where's Ariana?"

"Where she needs to be," Fayel said, ignoring my panic.

Fayel kneeled on the ground, and her powers flowed out. Green light traveled down through the depths of water, and slowly, a lake started to become clear in the light as formations under the water began to glow. "My lady will not take from her people like her father did. She only gives."

The pride and affection Fayel felt for Ariana was clear in every word she said. "Most of our people live a simple life. We do not run businesses or have investments like the other Paldimori Houses. My lady found a way to take the pieces of the emeralds we were given by the goddess and grow more."

I was looking at a lake nearly the size of a stadium full of glowing emeralds. "Fayel this is …" I had no words. Ariana kept doing that to me. Every time I thought I knew how incredible this woman was, I learned new levels of respect and amazement.

"Choose," Fayel commanded.

I turned to face her. "Choose what, ma'am?"

"This is her gift to you," Fayel said watching me closely. "You can take all the emeralds you want. Enough to buy your ranch or a small country. Choose."

Even when she pushed me away Ariana tried to make sure I would be ok. I loved her even more for her big heart, but I wanted to yell at her right now. If she thought I would take this and walk away she underestimated how persistent I can be. "Then I choose Ariana," I said. "I don't want her emeralds. I want the life with her that she promised me."

"Take the gems," Fayel insisted. "My lady has called off the Bonding Ceremony. There is nothing left for you here."

"I didn't agree to callin' anythin' off," I growled. "You tell the people plannin' that shindig to keep on workin'. I died without her once. Livin' without her would be the same thing."

"Why?"

"Because I love her. I'm not scared of her past or her

powers." I stepped forward to tower over the small woman. "Take me to her so I can prove it."

Fayel laughed. "You have a lot of work with that one." She patted my cheek the way my mama used to. "I think you will be good for ma fille. I'll take you to her. But first …"

She held out her hand and a large rock studded with emeralds floated up from the water. "The Bonding Ceremony requires an exchange of gifts. One thing a bond-mate can ask for that the other can't deny as long as it's within their power to grant. Ariana asked that you take an emerald and save your ranch for your sister. A smart man could use this to his advantage."

I wasn't exactly up on the customs, but I think I got what she was saying. "If I take the emeralds …" I picked up the rock bigger than my fist and turned it over. "This would be a bonding gift from Ariana, right?"

"Ma fille has met her match in all ways," Fayel hugged me. "Use her gift to hold her to initiating the Bonding Ceremony. I'm sending this to be converted into cash for you. It'll be deposited into the bank Kyrion Eros has set up for dealing with the humans." Her power flowed over the rock encrusted with emeralds and it disappeared. "Now let us g—"

"*Track me,*" Ariana's voice whispered urgently through my head, and I felt the tension bleeding off of Fayel beside me. She must have heard it too.

I focused on Ariana's voice in my head and noticed a trail of her powers. I pictured the door in my mind like Emory had told me and walked through it. At first nothing happened, but then I heard voices. I pictured Ariana's beautiful face and the trail appeared again. I followed that trail until it came to a door. The door was made of stones and tree branches. It seemed to be sealed shut with razor-sharp briars. A red fox blocked the doorway and growled at me as I got near.

The doorway slipped open silently, and the scent of vanilla in an exotic forest hit me. Ariana!

The fox stopped growling and turned to trot through the now open doorway. I looked to my left to find Fayel there looking very worried. We joined the fox on the other side of that doorway, and I realized I had just entered Ariana's mind.

Voices surrounded us. Images played like videos around us.

I turned to Fayel. "How are we all—?"

"Ariana is sharing what she is experiencing right now. Something is wrong. Listen …"

Anger and disgust nearly choked me as we listened to Ariana's conversation with her father, Ekert, and Ekert's father.

Then I watched in horror as Ariana stumbled back in pain and lifted a bloody hand away from her stomach. I was frozen in place and had no idea what to do. I listened as her father confessed to evil acts that would haunt me forever, and my heart broke all over again for my bond-mate. I reached for her, but there was nothing here to hold on to.

From a distance I heard Fayel shouting my name, but Ariana's pain from her wound and her anguish over her father's confession was seeping into me. A ghost-like image of Ariana appeared in front of me, and I reached out only to have my hands pass right through her.

"*I love you, Kade,*" Ariana whispered before everything went dark.

Someone was calling my name, but I couldn't leave this dark place without Ariana. She couldn't be gone. I had to find her. Pain slammed into my gut knocking me out of Ariana's mind. I rubbed my stomach where Fayel had hit me. Her furious gaze raked over me.

"Good, you are unharmed. Lingering in the mind of someone who is injured is dangerous, especially with how closely you two are connected. You could get trapped in her pain, and what she experiences, so would you." She glanced away, and I saw the sheen of tears in her eyes. "Get your powers under control."

Only then did I realize Fayel was surrounded by a translucent green bubble of protection. I looked around noticing the scorch marks on the rock around me and the lightning still flashing along my body. I struggled to pull my powers back, but grief consumed me, and I fell to my knees.

35

KADE

I KNEELED before the lake of emeralds and pressed my fists into the rock floor hard enough to split my knuckles. It didn't lessen the ache in my chest, but it made me focus on something other than the empty place where my connection to Ariana had been. All I could see was the last image Ariana had seen—red drops of blood on the petals of starfish-shaped flowers and Bramble watching her from between the vines. All I could hear were her last words telling me she loved me before she slipped away. My bond-mate was gone before we'd ever had a chance to build a life together.

The muscles in my forearms bulged as I pressed my fists harder against the rock and gritted my teeth against the pain of her loss. My powers burst from me. Every lightning strike sounded like the call for justice. Stalks of wheat launched like missiles through the air as if seeking out the men responsible for taking my bond-mate away. The cavern shook as the wheat hit with such a devastating impact that the stalks buried themselves within the rock walls. Fayel shouted behind me, but anger was building alongside the pain. Her father had done this. That bastard had taken the other half of my soul from me and that meant Syris Dupree had to die.

"*Justice*" whispered that part of me that came from the
Goddess Nyx.

I pushed to my feet, and lightning skipped across the
water. It climbed up the rock walls around the lake shattering
the wheat stalks and sending debris raining down. I turned to
Fayel. On the other side of that translucent bubble, she stood
rigidly with her hand clenched tight around one of the knives
across her chest. Her eyes were dark green pools of pain and
rage that likely matched my own. We shared a silent moment
of understanding. There was no room for discussion; we were
two people aligned in bringing justice to a man who was long
past due for it.

"Bramble is on the move," Fayel said, her voice hoarse
with repressed emotions. "She lost Syris in the lower part of
the palace but has picked up the trail again."

I looked down at the lightning playing over my bloody
knuckles and closed my hands cutting off my powers. I
would save my strength, and when the time came, I would
throw everything I had at the man who had taken from this
world for the last time. "Time to hunt."

Fayel's protective bubble disappeared. She raised her
hand, and the water of the lake rushed toward us. The water
flowed beneath the circle of rock we stood on and began
lifting it toward the opening in the chamber above. The rock
circle settled into place, sealing off the cavern of emeralds
below. The circular wall of water that had hid our descent
into the cavern dropped away with a splash. We traveled
back the way we had come to reach the valley, then Fayel teleported us into the palace.

Trees grew within the gray block walls of a long hallway.
The smell of bleach and something floral filled the air. We
passed serval other hallways as we moved silently. Ariana's
advisor never slowed down, still following her connection
with Bramble. A flash of orange up ahead caught my eye but
was gone again before I could get a closer look. Voices

sounded down the hall, and we quickly ducked into a dimly lit room. We pressed against the wall beside the door as two men walked by and I recognized their voices right away—Ekert and his father. It took every ounce of my strength to keep my powers under wraps and not give us away.

"Good work, son. Ariana absorbed the powers from the test subjects and replenished her own just like you thought she would," Ekert's father stated with pride.

"She is even more powerful than we suspected. If we hadn't needed her to secure the Archigós position, we could've had her powers all along. It has been fun toying with her, though." Ekert laughed and his father joined in. The psychos laughed about hurting my bond-mate! "We'll no longer have to deal with Ariana's defiance once we find a way to transfer all of that stolen power to us."

Lightning arced across my knuckles, and Fayel shook her head. She pulled two knives from her bandolier and motioned toward the doorway. I reached behind my back and took out the knife hidden there. When Fayel stepped out into the hall, I was right beside her. She stepped up behind the father and leaped onto his back to shove the blades into either side of his neck. Ekert turned, but before he could say anything, my knife plunged into his heart and a flash of lightning lit up the blade. His wide eyes met mine and my hand trembled as I pulled the knife out of his chest. He fell to the floor across the body of his father. I'd never killed a person before, but I would have to sort out my feelings about that later. They had hurt Ariana and others for the last time.

We dragged the bodies into the empty room, and something fell from Ekert's hand. I cursed when I saw it was a long lock of Ariana's hair.

Fayel crouched down to wipe her knives off on the other man's tunic. "Thank the goddess my lady found you when she did. I never liked Syris and his men, but even I had believed Ekert harmless."

"Why would Ariana marry him?"

"It was Syris's price for giving Ariana her brother back."
Fayel glanced up at me with sad eyes. "Ariana has been
searching for the place her father hid Aegeus for years. Syris
wanted control of the throne, and he used those children
against each other to get it."

I wiped my blade off as well and tucked it into the back of
my pants again. She stood and checked the hallway. Then
whispered, "Syris is a disease that infects people with his
cruelty wherever he goes. I begged my lady to let me kill him,
but she played by the rules. I should have done it anyway;
maybe she would still be alive."

I placed my hand on her shoulder. "None of us could've
talked Ariana outta somethin' once it was set in her head.
This is all on Syris. Don't give him an out by takin' on his
blame."

Fayel's shoulders slumped, but then her head snapped up.
"Bramble!"

Knives in hand, she darted out the door, and I ran down
the hallway after her. We ran down several hallways until we
came to a dead end. I stopped as the wall rippled and then
disappeared. Beyond that, the hallway continued for another
few feet before ending in a room. "Uh, Fayel, what're you
doin'?"

She worked her hands along the walls, looking for something. She waved her hand at the hallway leading to the room
and it rippled again. "It's an illusion. I think I've cut the trap,
but be careful."

I nearly jumped outta my skin when something cold and
wet pressed against my hand. Bramble looked up at me with
a whine in her throat. Fayel walked through the illusion wall
without a problem. I pulled my knife out and followed.

We stepped into a stark white office with a single desk and
no other furniture. Bramble had backed a woman I assumed
was the owner of the desk into a corner. The fox growled at

her and the woman cried out in fear. She was similar to Fayel in looks and wore the same simple clothes. I walked over to a large metal door set into the back wall and pulled on the handle. Nothing happened. Then I noticed the keyhole.

I glanced at the woman in the corner. "Open it."

"I c-c-can't. Kyrion Syris will k-kill me if I—" She squeaked as Fayel moved so fast she must have teleported and pressed a knife against the woman's throat. "Your Kyrion is Ariana Dupree, not that coward who craves the throne. Unlock that door, or I will kill you right now."

The woman lifted a cord from her neck with a key dangling off the end. She handed it to Fayel who used her telekinesis to send it over to me. A thump sounded behind me as I unlocked the door, and I glanced over to see Fayel dragging the unconscious woman across the floor. She roughly stuffed the woman under the desk and joined me.

I eased the door open, bracing myself for whatever we would find on the other side. Bramble scrambled between my legs and squeezed through the opening. The fox growled and shouts rang out from the other side. I went through the door, knife raised and ready to fight. Fayel was right behind me. Men and women in white lab coats scrambled across a black floor with a central drainage grate. Bramble nipped at them, herding them toward the back wall where images played on a large projection screen in front of a cluster of desks. Glass rooms lined the left and right sides of the space. White beds filled with motionless bodies took up most of the area inside each one. Lines dropped from the ceiling and pumped a glowing golden liquid into each person.

"What is this place?"

"I do not know." Fayel stepped forward to stand beside me, and I saw fear on her face for the first time. "There are powers at work here that are not of the Paldimori."

An image on the far-right screen at the back of the room caught my attention, and I strode forward. The lab people scrambled to get out of my way and Fayel instructed them to move aside. All my focus was on the woman in the top-right screen. My lips formed Ariana's name. My bond-mate wore a long white dress that stood out against the dark forest all around her. None of the pictures appeared to have sound, but I could tell by the way she kept looking over her shoulder that *she* was hearing something. Was this old footage of her? Why would they be watching it? And what the hell were they doing to all those people in the beds?

Bramble let out a mournful whine, and I turned to see her scratching at one of the glass doors. Fayel stood before the group of lab people at the back of the room asking questions. Bramble continued to paw at the door as I approached, not even sparing me a look. When I saw who was lying on the bed looking pale and beautiful, I couldn't look away either. A frosted glass handprint on the upper part of the door was the only thing on the smooth glass wall that might get me in. I placed my hand over it, but nothing happened. What would the group of power-hungry men from this House use to lock up their prize possession?

I placed my hand back on the wall and pushed my powers into the glass. The glass wall dissolved. I rushed to the bed and stood there like an idiot staring down at my bond-mate's still form. Bramble jumped onto the bed and licked her hand, but Ariana didn't move. I couldn't feel our connection at all even this close. My hand trembled as I reached over to touch her cheek. She would hate being this vulnerable. Anger hit me hard as I noticed the section of hair chopped off at her right temple. Her arms were covered in bruises, the injury from days ago, and multiple IV lines. Thick padding was wrapped around her torso under her white hospital gown from where she had been shot.

I leaned down to kiss her cheek and whispered, "I love you, Ari. It's time to wake up. We've got a bonding to finish."

Bramble jumped to her feet still on top of the bed and

snarled toward the doorway. I turned toward the entrance, shifting my body to shield Ariana as much as possible. Syris's green eyes, the same shade as Ariana's, watched me from just outside the room. The color of their eyes was the only thing they shared; in his there was nothing except a greedy hunger that would never be satisfied.

"Interesting," Syris stated, his gaze locked on my hand wrapped around Ariana's. "She has drained power from everyone who has touched her skin except for you. Seems my daughter doesn't find you a threat." Syris offered his hand as if we were a couple of businessmen meeting for lunch. "Kade Downing, I presume; the would-be bond-mate Ekert told me about."

"Syris Dupree," I said in a menacing growl to match Bramble's, ignoring his outstretched hand. "My future ex-father-in-law."

"Very cl—"

Bramble launched herself off the bed straight at Syris's face. He waved his hand, and the animal went flying into the glass side wall. She shook off the fall and charged him again. I shouted at her to stop but it was too late. His powers slammed her into the wall again, and she yelped in pain before slumping to the floor. She didn't get back up. Damn him to hell for everything he'd done.

I brushed my hand over the short hairs on the side of Ariana's head and kissed her lips. "I'll be back. Just need to take out the trash."

I turned to face Syris, and my powers exploded out into the room.

36

ARIANA

I LOOKED around the desiccated landscape of my rainforest and tears traced down my cheeks only to be absorbed into the parched soil. Gone was the lush green jungle full of life. In its place was only death. Tall petrified trees stood like ghosts across the land. Blackened vines hung from their brittle broken branches. The dry ground crumbled beneath every step I took. A cold, dry wind buffeted my body making my skin feel as dry as this land. A menacing growl followed me, but every time I turned around, there was nothing there. A distant voice begged someone to make it stop. Another screamed threats. Still more moaned in pain. And one called my name over and over.

I dropped down to the ground, sending up a cloud of dust. I sat cross-legged and used the skills I learned to survive Tantalus. I shut everything out one at a time until all that was left was me. Then I searched for the voice calling my name. Once I locked onto it, I stood and continued to walk. Jagged limbs snagged at me, and trees toppled into my path to block my way, but I never stopped moving toward my goal. I came to a thicket completely covered in blackened vines.

A familiar male voice whispered from somewhere nearby. "Ariana … you came."

My hand pressed against my lips to hold back the sob as I finally recognized the voice I hadn't heard in years.

"Aegeus?"

"Yes."

He was in a coma. How could he be here?

"The truth is tangled in the past. Come in and see," my brother invited.

I reached up to the closest vine and tugged until it snapped. Then I was inside someone else's mind.

"Aegeus, it's time," Syris stood at the doorway and held out his hand to my brother. Aegeus's chubby little boy face lit up with a gap-toothed smile as he rushed over to wrap his arms around Father's leg.

"Is my baby thither here?" Aegeus asked as he looked up at Syris with all the innocent love of a five-year-old.

"Not yet, but soon your sister will be born," Syris replied as they walked hand in hand down the hall leading to the Kyrion rooms. I trailed along behind wondering how I had gotten here to see my own birth.

Large green doors opened as we neared the bedroom, and the Talosi guarding the Kyrion chambers bowed low. We stepped into the room that looked much different than it did now that this room was mine. Gold and emerald accents decorated the walls, ceiling, and floor. Steam rose into the air from a wide bathing pool on one side of the room. On the other, three women stood around a wide bed. The terrace doors directly across from us were open, and the humid night air brought with it the sounds of the jungle.

We moved closer to the bed, and I barely recognized my mother as the panting, groaning woman lying there. Her swollen belly rippled as I fought to come into the world. My head spun at the realization that I was both still there in my mother's womb and here inside someone else's head watching.

The oldest of the women patted the bed, and my father lifted Aegeus up to sit beside Mother. The old woman had long gray hair in a braid down her back and strange periwinkle eyes that matched her dress. Her wrinkled skin made me think of the elephants in the jungle. She snapped at the other two women to leave. Then pushed my mother's skirts up, and the person's mind I was in quickly looked away.

The old woman tutted to herself and mumbled words I didn't understand. The person I was with walked over to stand beside my father. Mother turned her head toward Aegeus and gave him a weak smile. Then her back bowed and she cried out.

Father paid her no attention as he pulled off Aegeus's sleep shirt revealing our House symbol about midway up the right side of his torso. *That can't be right*, I thought. Aegeus's symbol was in the same place as mine, only bigger.

"What're you doing, Father?" Aegeus asked as he played with the sleeve of Mother's nightdress.

"Securing the future," Syris replied as he pushed Aegeus down to lay flat on the bed next to Mother.

"Do I havta thare my toyth with my new thither?" Aegeus asked as he wiggled on the bed and snuggled against Mother.

I couldn't help but smile. My brother had never liked to share.

"You won't have to share a thing, Aegeus, my boy," Father said as he ruffled my brother's hair.

The old woman came around the side of the bed with a bowl. She dipped her bony fingers in the bowl of glittery purple goo and drew shapes across my brother's chest.

The little boy giggled. "That tickles."

"Be still, son." Syris grabbed my brother's arms, pushing them down against the bed. "She'll be finished in a minute."

Mother gasped and gripped the covers as the old woman

started mumbling again. After a few moments of panting, Mother asked, "Syris, what are you doing?"

"What you should have been able to do, you useless weakling," Father yelled, and smacked Mother across the face. She cried out in pain. I tried to shout at him to stop, but I was only a silent observer. Aegeus had gone suspiciously quiet, still lying there on the bed with his small chest rising with rapid breaths. What was wrong with him? What had the woman done?

Father's hand wrapped around Mother's neck as he leaned over her. "You were supposed to give me powerful sons to rule this damn world. Instead, you give me a son too weak to ever claim the Kyrion throne and a daughter strong enough to take the highest position of all as Archigós. The watchers have seen the future, but I refuse to live under anyone else's thumb. If I can't become Archigós myself, then I will control the child that will. Your daughter"— he spat the word out as if it were poison—"will be strong of power and of will. Too strong to be controlled unless she is broken."

"The baby is crowning," the old woman said with a heavy accent I didn't recognize. The old woman's skin began to smooth out as she drew symbols across my mother's belly. Her gray hair melted away to reveal a honey-brown color. A woman in her late twenties now stood in the old woman's place. The periwinkle eyes and dress were the only things that remained the same. She finished drawing on my mother and snapped her fingers at my brother. "Stay awake, you're about to receive a gift to change the winds of our future."

Mother screamed just as a baby cried. The young woman cut the umbilical cord and held the baby up in the air. There on the squirming infant's back was the tree symbol of our House. I had been born with an Archigós mark! Shock rocked me to my foundations as purple lights that matched the midwife's eyes traveled over her hands and into the tiny body that she held.

Mother began to shout and crawled across the bed. The baby's cries joined in as the large tree symbol lit up and a ripple of power rushed across the room. Green light brighter than the sun rose from the Archigós mark up into the air and then crashed into my brother. Mother wrapped her hands around the baby to tug her away but screams ripped from her throat as her powers were pulled from her. Aegeus's screams joined the other two, and his House symbol lit up. It moved from his ribs up to the location I knew it to be in today between his pectoral muscles. The sinister smile on my father's face knocked me from my shocked stupor, and I lashed out with my powers trying to break free of whoever's mind I was trapped in.

Father was killing us all, and I was helpless to stop him, just as I had been all my life. My own screams joined those of my family as I watched the powers move from my mother into me as a baby, as mine drained into my brother. The baby's pink skin turned blue as her life slipped away. Mother trembled upon the bed in her bloody nightdress as she struggled to pull the baby away.

Mother's screams turned to pleas, "Not my baby! Do not take my baby!"

Mother gathered the last of her strength and kicked the other woman in the chest. The woman stumbled away. Aegeus curled into a ball upon the bed, sobbing. Blood soaked the sheets as my mother sat on her knees and gathered the baby to her. Green lights of power flowed from my mother into the baby until that little body turned pink again. My mother's crazed eyes looked over to my father as she became weaker. "You will not … kill her … kill her," she mumbled repeatedly until her eyes rolled back into her head and she slumped to the mattress. The baby rolled across the bed toward Aegeus, making hiccupping cries. My brother's tear-stained face peeked out from the nest of his arms to look at the baby now with the symbol on her chest exactly like mine. He gently placed a hand on the baby's cheek, and she went quiet.

Aegeus looked back at Father and all that innocent love was gone. In its place was fear and a small spark of determination as he said, "You will not kill her."

The images faded, and I was back at the edge of the blackened vine-tangled thicket in my own body. I curled onto my side on the dry and dusty ground. I had been shown someone's memories of my birth. Successors had never been born when Aegeus nearly died because he *wasn't* born the Kyrion —I was. And Syris had taken that from me. Syris's thirst for power had destroyed our family. *He* had been the one who tried to drain my mother's powers. And Aegeus—poor sweet Aegeus—had watched it all. No wonder my brother had spent his whole life fearful of our father after what he had been through. Aegeus also knew that he wasn't the real Kyrion and would never have the full powers unless he killed me to take them. My brother had protected me since the day I was born.

Violent sobs wracked my body, my tears wetting the parched ground beneath me. I cried for the family that could have been if not for the monster that manipulated us all. I cried for the mother that I had blamed my whole life for what had happened to us only to realize she had given part of her life for mine. I cried for the little boy who had witnessed the man he worshipped turn on him and using him as a tool to build his own legacy of power.

"Shhhh, Ariana, do not cry." That voice poured over me like a warm blanket. "You were always stronger than all of us. We need your strength now. Tear down the lies."

Even though part of me felt too broken to carry on, I fed every ounce of heartache into defying the limits anyone would place on me—even the ones I placed on myself. I climbed to my feet and ripped at the remaining blackened vines with a snarl. Memories hit me of the cruel manipulations my father had carefully covered up over the years. Natalie being sent to seduce my brother and use her persuasion powers to keep him obedient. People from my House that I had thought had become outcasts but were tortured in experimental labs. Father using his spies to lure children like Fayel through the barrier around Kardia and into the hands of mercenaries all to fund his luxuries. The woman with the periwinkle eyes that shared my father's bed and plotted with him. Secret meetings with the Omàda that led to the destruction of outcast villages.

There was so much pain and destruction it nearly crippled me. I gathered my strength and tore away the last of the vines.

Aegeus sat on the ground in a circle of green grass staring up at me with a wide smile. The green jungle I knew and loved crowded in behind him. I stood there staring. It had been so long since I had seen those vivid green eyes open. He no longer looked like that frail body lying in the bed, never moving and never speaking. His chestnut-colored skin was no longer pale. His thin body had filled out some. And his curly brown hair no longer hung limp around his shoulders. This was the Aegeus I remembered before he was captured.

"You did it, sister," he said. "You found me."

I DROPPED to my knees and cupped Aegeus's face. "Aegeus? How are you here?"

"Y-you are touching me," Aegeus said in shock.

"Thank my bond-mate for showing me how to believe in myself," I replied, ignoring the ache of what could have been if I hadn't sent Kade away.

Aegeus pulled me into his arms, and a sob escaped me. I never thought I'd hear my brother's voice or feel his arms around me again. He kissed my hair and said, "I am so very proud of you. And happy you have found your bond-mate."

Tears poured down my cheeks as I gripped him tighter. "My goddess, all this time—"

He pushed me back and wiped the tears from my cheeks. "No, little sister, none of this was your fault. You cannot control the hands of the gods." He chuckled. "Although, if anyone could sway them, it would be you. The first time I looked at you I knew you were destined for great things."

"Thank you, brother." I looked around at the green jungle surrounding Aegeus and the dead forest beyond. "How are you here, Aegeus? Where are we?"

"Do you remember the serum the House of Light developed to let them see the memories of others?"

I jolted as I realized what he was trying to tell me. "Now I remember ... Ekert pressed a needle of the serum into my arm. That is why I am here with you now. This is a dreamscape."

"Yes, the serum can be administered many different ways and is very effective," Aegeus rubbed the bend of his arm as if remembering the needle himself. "Most people walk their own memories over and over unless they are given a certain memory to relive. Few can enter the dreamscape like this to connect with others and interact. Luckily, they have not yet penetrated this deeply into my mind."

He pushed to his feet and walked toward the jungle. "I have hidden in this place since the day the Omàda began their experiments on me. Much has been taken from me, but they could not take this. Although, Father has tried." Aegeus gestured toward the dead forest that I had walked through earlier. "Father comes to talk to me sometimes, and I hear the people talking who work in the labs. There are others resisting like I have here. I knew if I could hold out long enough that you would find me."

"I am sorry. I tried to find you ..." My throat closed up around the words that meant very little compared to all that he had gone through.

"Little sister, you never gave up, and that is enough." He brushed a curl over my shoulder.

I grabbed his arm remembering everything else I had been shown. "I saw—"

"Yes," he said with a sad smile. "All that you needed to right the wrongs of the past. You are the future of our people, Ariana. You were always meant to be Kyrion, just as you were meant to become Archigós. So much was stolen from you, but you never became corrupt like Father. What you did become is what Father calls a power-drinker." He looked off into the dark forest with a troubled frown. "Your powers were always seeking those pieces stolen from you; trying to make you whole once more. Father wants to create more like you but with the ability to transfer the powers taken to those he chooses."

"He has conspired with the Omàda." Fury quaked through me at all Father had hidden right beneath my nose.

"Yes, Father's thirst for power aligns well with the Omàda's," Aegeus agreed. "He wants the Archigós position for the power but also to expand his experiments."

"The labs?" I asked, remembering the experiments from the images I'd been shown.

Aegeus nodded. "With the aid of that witch from the House of Watchers, he has gotten very close to achieving his goal of creating more power-drinkers."

"You mean the woman who helped birth me in your memories." If I ever saw her again, she would not live to hurt another child. "With that eye color I should have known she was a descendant of Hera." I remembered the image I had been shown of her whispering with my father as they planned attacks on the outcast villages. "She has been using farseeing to aid Father."

Farseeing was the ability to see snippets of time minutes, hours, or a few days before they happened. It was a power from the God Erebus's line passed on to his daughter, Hera. Visions also came from Erebus, but the descendants with that power were thought to have been lost. At least until Lia's visions started.

A thought occurred to me. "The Omàda have always been one step ahead of us. Now we know why. With the serum, farseeing, and our father's help, how have they not located our House bases before now? Maybe Father was only giving them select information. If so, what has changed that he would now allow them to attack Kardia?"

Father's strange mention of the unhappy client came back

to me. "What if Father has been giving his experimental power-drinkers to the Omàda? They would be displeased if their 'product' did not live up to any promises Father made. Maybe the Omàda has known all along how to find Kardia, if not all of the Houses, but had never attacked before now because of Father's experiments."

"Yes," Aegeus sighed, "that does sound like something Father would do."

He took my hand, his familiar face filled with a lifetime of sadness. "I wish I had been able to tell you everything before now, but many of my memories were repressed until I came here. There was a time that I was not as obedient, but Father found a way to correct that. He sent one of Aphrodite's descendants to me, and I fell under her persuasion—"

"Natalie," I growled, hating her more than ever knowing now what that she had done to my brother.

Aegeus laughed. "You always disliked her." His smile faded away. "Apparently, for good reason. Trapped here I have lived through every one of my memories a thousand times. I did things … It is right that this should be my punishment." He looked at where the blackened vines once surrounded his jungle. "It is fitting that I used Father's own web of lies as the walls that kept me safe from him."

"The things Natalie and Syris forced you to do are not your fault."

He nodded, but I could tell he didn't believe me.

"If Father is successful in creating these power-drinkers the Omàda would have an unstoppable army. No one, not even the Chosen, would be able to survive having all of their powers taken away." I jumped to my feet, determination filling me. My legs went weak and I nearly fell. "Aegeus, we have to leave here and stop Father."

"Yes, you must leave here," Aegeus stood and took my hands. "Father thinks you are the missing piece he needs. He weakened you with the gunshot wound, but you have been drawing powers from those around you. Your powers will be strong but your body will be weak when you wake. No matter what, you must get free." He pressed my hands against his heart. "You were the best part of my life, Ariana. I wish I could have protected you better from our father and the instructors at Tantalus. I did not know until later what was happening and by then I was under Natalie's persuasion."

"If not for you, I would have died soon after my birth. I never blamed you for any of what happened, and I still do not." I wrapped my arms around him, thanking Kade for giving me back the confidence to hug someone. "You have always been the sun that kept me from drowning in darkness. We will return together. Once Father is locked away, we will release Mother from the tower. Finally, we will be the family we should have been without Syris."

Aegeus pressed a kiss to my temple. "I would love that … but I cannot return."

My breath stalled. "What do you mean?"

"My own powers were depleted the day I was taken prisoner," he whispered against my hair. "I should have died that day, but the powers I stole from you remained. They are all that has kept me alive and now I need you to take them back."

I tried to pull away, but he only squeezed me tighter. "No! I will not do it."

"Ariana, the powers are yours. You must take them back to truly become all you were meant to be and fight against our enemies."

I struggled to free myself, but my parched tree reached out with those partially withered roots seeking power. Why now? Aegeus wasn't a threat, and he wasn't extremely powerful. Was this happening because my powers recognized their missing piece in my brother? "Let me go, Aegeus! Please, you must let me go." I managed to wedge my arm between our chests enough to put a few inches between us. "I cannot lose you again. Please … Please."

Goddess Gaia, please do not take him!

Light flared beneath my palm where it rested on his chest. A yellow butterfly landed on my hand and the goddess's voice filled my head, "*I am sorry, daughter. This is your path, your destiny. All great warriors are forged in fire, and you will be among the greatest.*"

My powers speared into Aegeus's chest and he gasped. The first strong pull from his powers and a soothing energy filled me. The bark of my parched tree turned a healthy looking brown while Aegeus's skin grew pale. Panic and hatred for my powers filled me. A scream lodged in my throat as my brother's fingers dug into my back and his arms began to shake. I tried and tried to lift my hand from his chest, but it would not budge. His muscles turned gaunt. His breaths labored with a raspy noise in his chest. All the life was draining from him and into me. The branches of my parched tree mended, and leaves unfurled from the tips. That constant thirst that had been with me all my life faded. My powers filled every inch of my body until it felt like I would burst. My back burned, and my symbol slowly disappeared from my chest. The gods had blessed me with the Archigós mark on my back like Bennett's but it wasn't worth this price.

I felt more whole and alive than I ever had, while my brother withered away in front of my eyes.

Aegeus's bony hand brushed against my cheek like he had done in that memory of my birth. "I love you, little sister. I should have tried harder to be a part of your life instead of letting you push me away. My regrets in this life are many, but that I was not there to see you grow into the beautiful woman you are today is my biggest regret. In spite of all we went through, you became a force to be reckoned with, and I am proud to be your brother."

The only things that hadn't faded were his vibrant green

eyes, and in their depths was relief. He wrapped me in his fragile embrace one last time and whispered, "Thank you for freeing me."

Sobs tore from my chest and tears poured from my eyes. My brother faded into a gentle mist upon my skin and was gone.

"Aegeus!" I screamed, but only the echo of my screams answered me.

38

Syris chuckled as I rounded the bed where Ariana lay. "You are no more than a fledgling trying to fly when you haven't even walked. Do you even know how to access your powers yet, Chosen? What is it that you want? Walk away from my daughter, and I will see you get it."

Lightning arced across my knuckles as I punched him in the face. "I've already heard your evil-villain speech to Ariana, and I'm not interested in hearin' more."

He staggered back a step and laughed. "I like you, Kade. I could use someone like you when I replace the rest of those idiot Kyrion in the other Houses. What do you say? Want to run a House of your own?"

"No." My lightning slammed into his chest. Syris flew out the open door of the glass cube and skidded several feet across the floor.

I pulled the knife from the back of my pants and stalked toward him.

He laughed and then disappeared.

The glass door of Ariana's cube reformed, and I slammed right into it. Then a heavy weight crashed into my back and I dropped my knife. The hard object pressed mercilessly against me, pushing me into the glass door like a bug on a windshield. I pulled on my powers as I struggled to breathe with my chest getting smashed against the glass. White light flashed along my body. The glass heated and then exploded outward in a shower of shards. I stumbled forward, my boots crunching over the glass. I turned toward Ariana's room to find a large boulder where I'd been standing. Syris stepped from the room with a grin. His hand shot out and thorns as long as a football launched at me. I tried to teleport, focusing on every piece of me but it wasn't working. I braced myself for impact. A streak of green was all I saw as a body knocked me on my ass.

Fayel stood over me. Her shield surrounding us like a bubble. Swirls of transparent green shifted around us before the shield popped. Fayel dropped to her knees in front of me, and I grabbed her before she hit the ground. One of the thorns was buried nearly all the way through her thigh. "P-poison," she whispered through trembling lips. "A favorite of h-his."

"Don't you die, Fayel," I demanded. "Ariana needs you."

Syris straightened the circlet of gold around his head. He glanced to the right cube beside Ariana's where the frail body of a man filled the bed. With a wave of his hand the boulder flashed out of Ariana's cube and smashed down onto the man. The bed broke into pieces and blood ran along the floor toward the central drainage grate. Syris's bare feet lifted off of the floor, and he floated above the broken glass coming toward us. "Clearly you have some power. And look, we have an opening. I think I'll make you my own personal project."

Syris raised his hand again, and I braced myself for the final blow. It never came.

"I think not," Ariana said from the broken doorway of her room. She looked beautiful in her white hospital gown with anger flushing her cheeks. My knife flew from her hand to bury into her father's shoulder.

Syris' mouth rounded in a shout of pain as blood seeped through his tunic. Ariana staggered forward and waved her hand. The water cooler at the end of the row of cubes crashed onto the floor. Ariana lifted the water into the air and used it like a broom to sweep the broken glass into the grate. I snapped threats at the lab people to get help for Fayel and two of them hurried over. I promised to make them suffer if they didn't fix Ariana's advisor as I got to my feet. Tan light pulsed between my palms as I grew a long, thick piece of grass and tied the end into a lasso.

Syris's body blurred like he was trying to teleport away. A silver cuff of leaves appeared in Ariana's hand and shot toward Syris, wrapping around his bicep. I roped him around the waist at the same time as her powers spread over him. Her green light was so bright it nearly blinded me, but I wanted that asshole away from my bond-mate. I reeled him toward me like the ugliest big-mouth bass I'd ever seen. My knife was still sticking out of his right shoulder, but he continued to fight me. He suddenly glanced up at me, and I knew he'd just thought of a way out.

Not gonna happen.

My powers wrapped around the hilt of the knife in his shoulder and pushed it forward. Lightning and the blade punched through the other side of his shoulder as he screamed. He groaned as I hit him with another bolt to his stomach. Wheat stalks broke through the floor, growing twelve feet high as they hugged him tight making thousands of cuts along his body. "I may be new to this world and still learnin' about my powers, but I'm a Chosen. You come at the people we love and we'll kick your ass."

His lips curled back as he snarled, "The only Chosen that matter are with the Omàda. They know the real prophecy. You—"

"No more!" I shouted. Lightning flashed across the room. Grains of wheat fell from the ceiling. My hand raised, but slender fingers wrapped around my wrist. The scent of vanilla in an exotic forest wrapped around me, the feel of soft petals brushed against my mind.

"Not like this, Kade," Ariana said. "He will answer for his crimes, but not like this. No more death."

I looked at Ariana and was surprised to find a tan-handled sickle blade in my grip. "How? I ..."

"A new part of your powers, it seems," Ariana said with an admiring eye for the blade. "We have a lot of training to do."

She wrapped her arms around my waist, and everything inside me settled. My powers retreated and the sickle disappeared. I wrapped my arms around her not giving a shit that I'd tugged on the lasso still around Syris making him smack into the wheat stalks surrounding him. He shouted threats, but we ignored him. I kissed the short section of hair at Ariana's temple and breathed her in for a minute. A whimper had us turning as Bramble limped from Ariana's cube. She walked up to Syris and peed on his bare foot. We chuckled, and Ariana reached down to pet the fox as she lay down next to us.

A throat cleared, and I looked over to find a nervous-looking woman in a lab coat. "M-my lady, the ... Fayel has been treated with the antidote for the poison. They're stitching the wound in her leg now. She's expected to make a full recovery. I-I thought you'd want to know."

Ariana straightened as best she could, still holding her stomach. "See that Fayel is given the best care. And stop the serum you have been giving these people. You will care for each of them as if your lives depend on their survival."

The woman bowed deeply and rushed away to tell the other lab people.

A group of about ten men and women in the dark green

tunics of the Talosi barged through the metal door at the end
to the room. Ariana swung into Kyrion mode with all of her
normal confidence even though she was weak, bruised, and
wearing nothing but a thin hospital gown. "Make sure the
people in the lab coats take care of these people," she pointed
toward the glass cubes. "When they are finished, place them
all into holding cells to be questioned and sentenced for their
crimes."

All but two Talosi jogged off to do as they were told.

"Here," Ariana said taking the rope I still held onto and
giving it to the two remaining Talosi. She waved her hand
and the wheat stalks Syris had been trapped behind disappeared. Syris tried to wiggle away but the Talosi held him in
place. "Syris Dupree is a traitor to all Paldimori. Lock him up
and make sure he remains under constant guard."

"Yes, my lady," they answered and hauled Syris away.

I pulled her against me and cupped her cheek. "I thought
I'd lost you."

"No more close brushes with death for either of us," she
said as I leaned down to kiss her.

"No more pushin' each other away either," I said and
nipped her bottom lip. "We were meant to be together.
Besides you gave me a rock full of emeralds that I'm claimin'
as my bonding gift. No refunds. That means you're stuck
with me."

She chuckled. "I sense Fayel's influence. Is that how it is
going to be? You two conspiring against me?"

"I'm gonna need all the help I can get with you," I said
with a wink. "Since you chose my gift, I'm tellin' you what
you'll get. You, my bond-mate, get my heart, my love, and my
promise to be by your side for as long as we live." I pulled the
small circle from my pocket and held it up between my
fingers. I'd braided the ring from strips of palm leaves from
the bedroom I'd been locked in earlier with the intention of
tying Ariana down every way possible. "Humans have their

own symbol for the lifelong joinin' of two people. The weddin' ring is a never-ending circle of devotion. This is just some leaves, but I'll get you a real ring when I can get to a jewelry store." I looked down at the woman I loved. "Ari, will you wear my ring?"

"Yes, absolutely," she beamed at me with teary eyes. "I love you, Kade. I only want you and I am happy to wear your symbol. That you made this is all the more special. I accept your gift and will cherish it always."

I took her hand and slid the makeshift ring around her finger. "I love you too, Ariana."

She admired the ring around her finger for a moment, and then held out her hand to me. "There is someone I would like for you to meet."

She led me to a room separated from the others in the far back corner. She waved her hand and the black door ripped from the wall. She looked at the door hanging suspended in the air like it had offended her. Then she propped it gently against the wall. "My powers have grown; I will need to train as well."

Inside was a much larger room with a single large monitor on the side wall. The harsh lights outlined every angle of the sunken body on the bed. At one time I'm sure the man had been handsome, but it was hard to tell with the lines of strain carved into his hollow cheeks. Patches of brown hair were still visible amongst the white. But it was the symbol for the House of Seasons over the right side of his protruding ribs that caught my attention.

"Kade, meet my brother, Aegeus." Ariana brushed her hand over his hair tenderly.

"Ari, I think ... Sweetheart, he's ..." I couldn't say it. She'd lost so much already. I wanted to take her from this room and keep on pretending that we'd never discovered this truth.

"He died to give me back my life," she whispered. Her

eyes were pools of pain as tears slipped down her cheeks. "S-so that I could live and love without fear."

"Then he gave us both the greatest gift of all, and I'll be grateful for eternity," I said as I took her other hand looking down on the man who I'd never get to know but who I owed so much to.

39

ARIANA

My FATHER and his supporters had been locked up in holding cells down the hall from the lab. Most of the previous occupants from the lab had recovered enough to be moved to a regular room, but some hadn't made it. My heart ached for the families who had learned what really happened to their loved ones. The last three days had been filled with unraveling Father's network and discussions with the other Kyrion. I realized now that as long as there were people like Father in the world there would never be peace. War was coming. Theia had been right about that, and I had apologized to her. Surprisingly, we had a very civilized conversation working out the details of Lia's upcoming stay in the House of Night as the first part of her punishment. Maybe one day Theia and I could eliminate the animosity that had existed between our Houses for so long.

Kade and I had dropped into bed each night too exhausted to do anything more than hold each other. And when I roused in the night to go searching for my brother, Kade would hold me in his arms as I relived Aegeus's death and cried myself back to sleep. We'd buried Aegeus and the others who had died the day after the confrontation in the lab. The other House leaders had all made a brief appearance to honor a former Kyrion. My people had gathered to mourn the lives taken by my father and his allies. I had stood surrounded by my people for once, instead of keeping myself apart out of fear of my powers. As if they sensed the change in me, my people had welcomed me with pats on the arm or hugs. And I thanked Aegeus for every touch that came without fear.

Today we planned to celebrate life. Kade and Fayel had insisted we not postpone the Bonding Ceremony any longer. Any worries I'd had about completing the ceremony so soon after such tragedy was alleviated by my people's response to the announcement. They had thrown themselves wholeheartedly into the preparations. The whole valley had buzzed with conversations and laughter as my people, no matter their power level, worked side-by-side. Now after these past days of constant bustle and noise, the valley seemed too quiet.

I looked down at Bramble. "Everyone is waiting for us. Are you ready, girl?"

Bramble trotted across the meadow behind the palace, the splint on her leg barely slowing her down. I placed a hand over the bandage covering the bullet wound in my stomach. The scars from our ordeal would linger but for once I had hope for our future. Bramble looked back at me and let out a yip as if to say "hurry up." I laughed, and lifted the long skirt of my dress to follow her. The bright sunshine dimmed as we stepped into the valley's forest. Someone had rearranged the forest to form an open pathway dusted with the purple flowers from the *Millettia laurentii* trees on either side. Animals of all kinds stood amongst the trees as I passed along the path. I stopped as I neared the clearing where all ceremonies were held. My favorite shrub, the *Mondia whitei*, covered the entire clearing like a vanilla-scented blanket. My people bowed on either side of me as I walked toward the man who waited for me near the statue of the Goddess Gaia in the center of the area.

I stopped as I reached the front of the crowd of people and bent to kiss the cheek of the lady that sat beside Fayel. I brushed a hand over Mother's gray-streaked dark blond hair as she smiled up at me. When we had freed her from the tower, she had rushed to me and wrapped me in her arms. She'd whispered in a broken voice, "Not … killed." One of her caretakers had confessed that my father often visited Mother to torment her with his plans. All those times she had screamed "kill her" into the night she had been begging my father not to kill me. Mother's mind might never recover, but deep in those vivid green eyes so like Aegeus's, there was a small spark of recognition and determination. That gave me hope because Mother was a fighter, and like her, I would never give up on those I loved.

Bramble sat down beside Mother and laid her head in the frail woman's lap. Mother cooed to the fox as she stroked Bramble's soft fur. I smiled at the pair of them, then looked to the girl on the other side of Fayel. Hope's eyes were wide with wonder as she scanned every inch of the clearing. I wasn't sure how we were going to handle this going forward, but I was surprisingly ok with not having all of the rules laid out. For now it was enough that I was able to give Kade what he had really wanted as his bonding gift: his sister to be here sharing this day with him. I gave her a smile, and then turned to face my future.

Kade swallowed thickly as his eyes scanned me from head to toe. I had sold the fancy dress my father had requested made for my betrothal and instead gone with something more my style. The light green chiffon dress matched my eyes and had a slit over each leg up to the tops of my thighs. A row of emeralds circled the dress just under my breasts and another around my waistline. It had been worth every second of sitting with the dressmakers to see Kade's reaction. He looked handsome in the simple green tunic with a hem that had been altered to reflect the joining of our two lines with crescent moons, wheat spikes, and the tree symbol from my House. I joined him beside the statue of Gaia and took his hand. Looking into those baby blue eyes I said, "Kade Downing, I claim you as my eternal bond-mate."

Kade brushed my loose curls back over my shoulder. "Ariana Gian Dupree, I claim you as my eternal bond-mate."

Together we said loudly, "We are born from the earth."

Kade's powers brushed against me through our connection. Our linked hands thrust into the air and raindrops fell down around us. "We are nourished from her waters."

We stacked our hands together. Kade's eyes sparkled with happiness as he smiled down at me, and my heart soared. Our powers dug down into the soil. Grass sprouted from the ground and twisted up toward our joined hands forming a rope. My powers added dozens of *Mondia whitei* flowers along the grass rope. The rope and the flowers grew together as one as did our connection. The rope wrapped around our clasped hands binding us together for life, and our connection strengthened into the brightest pathway I could form with any other person. We smiled at each other and said, "From here on we grow together as one. We will honor and protect each other until we return to Gaia's arms. We are bonded through her blessing."

The rope disappeared from around our hands. People and animal sounds raised in cheer as we turned to face our people. Bramble walked over to sit in front of Kade and tilted her head up at him. He hesitantly held out his hand, and she butted against his palm. I scratched her under her chin. *Thank you, my friend, for giving us your blessing.* She gave me one last nudge, then followed the servants who were bringing in the food. We spent the next few hours receiving the gifts of seeds from our people, eating, and dancing.

The sun was sinking lower in the sky when we walked back to the palace hand in hand. I tugged Kade along until we reached the tall trees near the west tower. I held up my hand, and the ropes in the tree tied themselves together. Then lowered a looped end down to each of us. We grabbed the ropes and slipped our feet into the loops. The ropes pulled us up until we reached the wide branches closest to my balcony. Monkeys chittered around us seeming to take an interest in teasing Kade. I laughed as he tried to dodge their little hands and crawled onto the branch I stood on. I pressed my hand against the trunk of the tree and asked it to assist us to the balcony. The branch moved, taking us closer. Kade hugged the limb tightly refusing to stand up until we had stopped moving.

I walked along the branch and jumped down onto the balcony. "You faced my father with only a knife and newly formed powers. Yet, you cower at a moving tree and some monkeys?"

I watched with a huge smile as Kade inched along the branch, batting away furry little hands. He hopped onto the balcony barely escaping the monkeys. If he'd been wearing his hat it would have been long gone by now. "In my defense," he said, backing toward the door to my rooms, "I'm a cowboy. The furthest I usually am from the ground is on the back of a horse, and the horse doesn't try to steal my stuff. Those monkeys have stolen my backpack, my hat, and my clothes. Not once but multiple times since we've been here."

I pressed a kiss to his cheek. The monkeys were fascinated by Kade, and I couldn't blame them. "They are only playing," I said as I walked into my bedroom trying not to laugh as Kade closed and locked the balcony doors behind us. I picked a banana from the bowl on the table and turned to face my bond-mate.

Kade growled as he lunged for me. I laughed as I dodge him and skirted around the table. I tossed my banana on the table, knocking over the whole bowl of fruit. I tried to keep the fruit from falling while Kade stalked me. He reached for me, and I leaped up on the table. My foot caught in the strap of his backpack laying on the table and Kade scooped me up. His backpack went flying but Kade was already halfway across the room when it landed with a thump. He laid me on the bed and leaned over me. His blue eyes were full of love and a white-hot desire that made me squirm.

"My turn to play," he said in a husky voice as his finger traced the side of my neck. His lips pressed against the pulse beating heavily there. Then trailed his lips up to press a soft kiss against mine. "I love you, Ari."

"I love you, Kade," I placed my hand over his heart. "I thought giving my heart, mind, and body to another would imprison me. But you showed me that love is not a cage but the wings to set me free. Love is a promise that I will never be alone again" I brushed my hand over his bearded cheek. "I choose to be tied to you in all ways. Make love to me, my bond-mate"

Kade's fingers trailed over the shorn section of my hair, and I tensed for a moment before making myself relax. It was foolish to feel nervous. Kade had seen me at my worst and still looked at me like I was his everything, He pressed his lips to the short section of hair. Then kissed the bruises still covering my arms. He pressed gentle kisses against my still healing stomach. Then trailed kisses back up my body until he looked down into my eyes once more. The blue ring around his eyes glowed, signifying our connection. "Every part of you, Ari, is beautiful."

Then he took my lips, drinking from them until my nerves were drowned out by my need to get closer to him. Kade pressed kisses along the shell of my ear and down my throat.

My skin tingled with anticipation as his lips followed the strap of my dress as it slid down my arm. A startled moan left me as his lips landed on the side of my breast. My hands scrambled across his back, needing to feel his skin on mine. Finally, I found the hem of his shirt and pulled until he sat up to take it off.

My hands greedily touched every inch of his toned chest. His calloused fingers wrapped around my left ankle and he lifted my leg to kiss the side of my calf. Arousal bloomed between my thighs as his lips trailed higher. My panted breaths got stuck on a strangled cry when his tongue traced across my thigh at the top of the slit in my dress. A warm breath touched between my thighs, and I writhed in need. "Kade!"

He chuckled as he moved back up to press kisses down the other side of my neck and slip my other strap down. Slowly he tugged at my dress revealing my breasts. His other hand pressed my hips down into the bed preventing me from hurrying him along. Cool air hit my nipple, and then it was enveloped in heat. Kade pressed his pelvis forward at the same time. "Yes! Please … please, Kade …"

He pressed himself against me, the outline of his erection hitting parts of me that I didn't know could feel so much. His mouth worked over my other nipple as his fingers traced up the inside of both of my legs and pushed them wide apart. His thumbs met beneath my underwear and traced along the lips of my sex. His thumbs never stopped teasing over me as Kade nibbled his way up to my ear. "Just like I thought, you smell like vanilla in an exotic forest all over. Before the night is done, I'll have that scent all over my skin."

He nipped my ear just as his finger slipped inside me, and my body erupted in pleasure. "Beautiful," Kade said in a husky voice. Then his hands were everywhere pulling off clothes until we were both naked. Seeing his tanned skin against mine was a beautiful sight. Kade kissed every single inch of my body. Then he brought me to the heavens and started all over again. By the time he nudged against my opening I was too relaxed to feel nervous. There was a slight pinch of discomfort as he seated himself inside me, but then all I felt was full.

Our bond would be sealed for life after this day. We reached for each other at the same time. Our lips met as Kade moved slowly within me. The passion unfurled inside me once more and my hips moved against his.

I broke our kiss and placed my hand over his heart. "Kade Downing you have my mind, body, and soul. All of who I am is yours forever."

"I love you, Ari," Kade panted, his muscles flexing as he brought us closer to the brink. "Ariana Gian Dupree—my wife—I am yours for always."

Tan and white lights swirled across Kade's skin. The light of my own powers danced across my skin in rhythm with his. Deep inside me, the tree that had been restored with the return of my powers burst into bloom as I slipped over the edge into bliss. Kade's arms wrapped around me and his forehead pressed to mine as he found his release. We whispered the words to each other to complete the Desmòs, "Body of my body. Soul of my soul. We are one."

Kade hissed and his back heated beneath my hands as my symbol formed to join his others. My own back burned, and I gasped. Above the tree symbol that covered from the bottom of my shoulder blades down to the small of my back, Kade's symbol formed.

Kade's eyes widened as the glowing blue ring of light around them erupted into a thousand colors. His smell of wheatgrass and ozone filled my nose. Kade's powers, his thoughts, his feelings, his past merged with mine. I lived his memories with him all over again seeing first-hand the trials he'd gone through to become the man I loved and respected. I felt the bottomless well of love and goodness in him. When the memories cleared away, I felt him there inside me. Strong, resilient, kind, and very much in love with me no matter that he'd seen all of my past too. I reached out to him with my mind and felt our powers intertwine. "*Hello, my love.*"

EPILOGUE
KADE

ARIANA SLEPT PEACEFULLY BESIDE ME, and I couldn't help but stare at her. Birds sang in the branches of the four large trees that surrounded her bed and made up the roof of her room. I tugged the blanket up around her bare shoulders feeling extremely protective after living through her past alongside her when we bonded. I had no idea how she'd survived it all and still remained so pure. She was a miracle. My gift from the gods, and I would do anything to keep her safe. It was gonna take a while before I ever let her outta my sight again. My stubborn wife would probably kick my ass for it to prove again how much she didn't need me to protect her. And I looked forward to it.

I slipped from the bed, passing Ariana's alcove of dresses hanging from large red spikes of flowers. Then took care of business in the bathroom, smiling to myself the whole time as I smelled Ariana on my skin. At the mirror I turned to admire the symbols on my back. Nyx's large crescent moon intertwined with features of the symbols from Demeter stretched across my back. There cradled by the moon was Ariana's mark: the tree of Gaia.

I had pressed kisses all along the new symbols on my

bond-mate's back as we had made love again last night. I loved seeing my braided palm ring on her finger and the symbol of my moon above Gaia's tree. I padded back to the bed ready to spend the day holed up in this room with my wife. Until I noticed the mess on the other side of the room. My clothes, hat, knife, and toiletries were scattered across the floor around the sitting area. But it was the sight of the scattered pages of my mama's journal that froze me in place. Then my stomach burned with regret as I remembered us knocking my backpack off the table last night. I rushed around the room, picking up all of the pages and gently stacking them on top of the table.

The journal lay open, face up near the bathing pool, the leather cord and binding broken. I breathed a sigh of relief that none of the pages had fallen into the water. Bending to pick up the journal, I noticed something sticking out of the broken bindings. I gently lifted the book and carried it to the table. About half of the pages still clung to the bindings. The back side of the cover showed the eighteen symbols of the Paldimori and Olympians Houses all together. I carefully wiggled my fingers into the gap in the binding and grabbed the piece of paper.

I carefully unfolded the yellowed page and read the two lines:

> Six to burn them all to ash
> Six to save them all at last

"Kade, are you ok?"

Ariana sat up in our bed, looking rumpled and gorgeous. "Yeah," I replied as I turned the page over but there was nothing more. "I found this page in Mama's journal that I've never seen before. It was hidden in the binding."

Ariana waved her hand and a robe appeared suspended in the air next to the bed. She slipped into it, nearly distracting me from my finding. "Would your mother have hidden something there knowing your father would not look for it?"

"Daddy read some of the journal and threatened to burn it. Mama hid it out in the woods after that." I hooked my thumb in the belt loop of my jeans as I thought about it. "I don't think this was Mama's doin'. Look at the paper. It's pretty old and the bindin' on the journal hasn't been replaced recently."

I handed Ariana the page and watched her brow furrow in confusion. Then her mouth dropped open in shock, and I felt her excitement through our bond. "Do you know what this means?"

Ariana turned the note over, examining every edge. "This is a part of the prophecy."

I used our connection to listen in on her thoughts. She glanced up at me with a smile and reached for my hand. Her mind compared pieces of information, weighed angles, examined and discarded conclusions in a rapid pace. I didn't understand the significance of most of it, but I did get that this was about the Chosen.

"This is a missing piece of the puzzle," she said breathlessly. "I think I know why both the Paldimori and the Omàda have pieces of the prophecy."

She rushed across the room to the giant closet and pulled out clothes. She tossed a tunic top toward me. Then stepped into a simple greenish-blue dress. "I need to speak with Lia. I want Jaxon to look at this as well. I want to know what he thinks before I voice my thoughts. If I am right, our search for the Chosen just got more dire and complicated." She hesitated a moment. Then she grabbed her staff and she headed toward the balcony. "And Jaxon … we need to restore his memories. My brother said something about Natalie that—"

I pulled on my shirt and grabbed my bond-mate by the shoulders. "Whoa, slow down. Where're we goin'?"

Ariana pressed her hand to my cheek and said, "We must return to Sotirìa. You must finish the Games. And I ... I have put off this confrontation for too long. I must face Lia and uncover her true role in the prophecy." She glanced nervously toward the balcony and the early morning sun rising above the cliffs. "It may already be too late."

"Too late for what?"

"To stop Lia's punishment from being carried out. If she has already been taken to the House of Night to begin the terms of her sentencing, not even the Archigós can call her back. Not without a fight with Theia, and we cannot afford that right now." Ariana handed me the page from Mama's journal back. "Keep it safe. I will teleport us to Lia's floor at Titan Tower."

I gently re-folded the paper and placed it between the pages of the journal. I grabbed my backpack and the other pages packing it all inside. Then took Ariana's hand. It felt like we burst apart into millions of pieces and got sucked up in a giant vacuum cleaner. Then we were standing outside Lia's bedroom door.

Ariana straightened her shoulders like she was preparing for battle. The cold mask of the Kyrion was in place as she knocked briskly on the door. It opened soundlessly but no one greeted us. We walked into the room but stopped abruptly. Black scorch marks scored the floor, ceiling, and walls. A hole in the shape of a body was cut out of the round mattress in the center of the room and black sand littered the floor. Bennett sat on the edge of the bed with a handful of that black sand in one hand and a golden ink pen laying in the other.

He looked up at us with the face of a man who had lost everything and said, "She is gone."

ACKNOWLEDGMENTS

This book was one of the hardest to write but has given me a sense of peace that I was struggling to find with the recent passing of my younger sister. There were a lot of tears shed along the way but in the end I'm glad I was able to say goodbye even if it was through a story. No regrets!

Thanks sooo much to my editor, Bernadette, who never fails to take my messy first drafts and polish them into something far greater than I could have ever accomplished alone. I learn something new each and every time we work together.

To my superstars on the Dragon's Hoard street team: You give your precious time to provide me with support, feedback, and spread the word about my books. I'm amazed by your dedication and can't say enough how much I appreciate you.

Thanks to my family who remind me that I need to sleep and shower every now and then, lol. An extra gigantic thanks to my husband who holds down the fort when I'm writing.

Finally, to my readers … I'm speechless. The reviews and emails I've gotten from fans amaze me each and every time. I couldn't be living this dream without you. THANK YOU!

ABOUT THE AUTHOR

T.L. Callahan is the author of the fantasy/paranormal romance adventure series Paldimori Gods Rising. She has always been a book lover; devouring romance, fantasy, and poetry since she was a young girl growing up in Kentucky. Her love for the outdoors inspired hours of wandering the woods pretending to be on adventures discovering magical creatures and being the heroine of her own stories. That hasn't changed much these days. Never knowing what you can find around the next corner keeps her seeking out new adventures from backpacking in the Wind River Range of Wyoming to piloting a sailboat down the Tagus River in Portugal. T.L. lives in Ohio with her husband, son, and a cat that thinks he's a dog.

Connect with me by signing up for my newsletter or joining my street team:

www.tlcallahanauthor.com

www.facebook.com/tlcallahanauthor/